"Feltman's final novel in a speculative trilogy tells a tense, intimate postapocalyptic story of familial conflict, set in the subway tunnels of what used to be New York City. The Colony of New York, built underneath the ruins of the city following the great hurricane of 2085, faces mounting challenges as the 24th century draws to a close ... **Feltman's postapocalyptic setting is well developed** and filled with the just the right amount of detail to make it feel lived in, without inundating the reader with minutiae. **However, much to the novel's credit, the setting mostly serves as a backdrop to a taut, unflinching portrayal of a difficult father-child relationship with high stakes that extend well beyond their home. Feltman excels at ratcheting up tension,** but she also finds hope in unexpected places, leading to some hard-earned, authentically joyous and optimistic moments. Manny, in particular, is a memorable protagonist, often difficult to like but ultimately deserving of the reader's admiration." - from Kirkus Reviews

"This author has a grand imagination ... **Susan Greenberg Feltman's world-building is exceptional,** seamlessly blending the remnants of a once-thriving massive city with the challenges of life underground. The pacing of the story balances well with the action ... **What a captivating story and unpredictable, with twists all the way to the end. As the Waters Rise** is a definite recommendation." – from Amy's Bookshelf Reviews

"The story is **extremely well written, psychologically sound** ... the pacing is excellent, starting slowly but gradually accelerating into a spellbinding drama, keeping the reader on the edge of their seat. The characters are very well drawn, familiar, and credible ... the descriptions are vivid, easily followed by the reader, and the futuristic, dystopian environment of a community living underground is depicted with convincing details. **It is one of those rare novels** that successfully combine riveting storytelling with relevant social commentary that easily applies to our era. I very highly recommend **As the Waters Rise** ..." - from Readers' Favorite

As the Waters

Rise

Susan Greenberg Feltman

ANJ Press, Leonia, NJ

This book is dedicated to

Amy,

beloved daughter and friend.

"The words of the prophets are written on the subway walls ..." - Simon and Garfunkel, Sound of Silence

"If you really think that the environment is less important than the economy, try holding your breath while you count your money." - Guy McPherson

"We do not inherit the earth from our ancestors. We borrow it from our children." - Native American Proverb

"If you don't act against climate change, then no matter how much money you leave for your children, it'll not even cover their healthcare bills, due to living in an unhealthy planet." - Abhijit Naskar

"Nobody made a greater mistake than he who did nothing because he could do only a little." - Edmund Burke

"We don't have to engage in grand, heroic actions to participate in change. Small acts, when multiplied by millions of people, can transform the world." - Howard Zinn

"Never doubt that a small group of thoughtful, committed citizens can change the world. Indeed, it is the only thing that ever has." - Margaret Mead

"Global warming threatens us with nothing less than extinction. It is happening now, in slow motion, right in front of us. How sad that by the time we took climate change seriously, it was already too late." - Susan Greenberg Feltman

PRELUDE

As the Waters Rise, published in 2025, is a work of speculative fiction. It is the third book in the Starlight and Ashes Trilogy. The first book, Never See the Sun Again, was published in 2021. The second book, Starlight, Shadows and Tears, was published in 2023.

In the year 2085 AD, a massive hurricane swept across New York City. The East River on one side and the Hudson River on the other side rose up and flooded across downtown Manhattan. The ocean, whipped to a frenzy by the howling wind, added its mighty power to the storm, causing widespread damage. When the storm abated, the retreating ocean pulled damaged skyscrapers back out to sea, indiscriminately drowning thousands of people.

In the end, only about 7,000 people survived, mostly by hiding in the subway during the storm.

Weeks turned into months. Despite pleas for help, no government agencies responded. FEMA was bankrupt, and the administration, strongly conservative, was in no hurry to rebuild a Democratic stronghold.

Soon there were temporary lean-to shelters set up, to give families some semblance of privacy. Later, more permanent structures appeared. With each generation, the Colony became more and more permanent. After several generations, it was widely accepted that humans should stay underground. The outside world was considered to be too dangerous, and hostile to human life.

Malcolm "Manny" Stewart, now in his mid-thirties, has reached the pinnacle of his career. As Police Commissioner for the Colony of New York, he is a powerful man whose word is law. Manny knows from the geologists' reports that a large earthquake could be coming soon, but no one seems concerned. He continues to push City Council for an emergency evacuation plan in case of an earthquake or flood, but meets with stubborn resistance at every turn.

At home, things are not going smoothly. His second marriage has proven to be something of a disappoint-men, and his adolescent son, Zach, is difficult and defiant.

Although Manny's father Patrick Stewart has been dead for many years, he continues to cast a long shadow. As Manny struggles with his rebellious son, the memories of his own childhood rise up to haunt him. While trying to juggle problems at home with the business of running the Colony and keeping everyone safe, Manny is horrified to discover that a long-resolved issue is about to come undone, in a very public way.

Chapter 1.

T he principal settled himself uneasily into his desk chair, dreading the conversation he was about to have. He glanced one last time at the troublesome youngster staring out the window in his office, thirteen-year-old Zachary Stewart. Clearing his throat as he opened up his padlet, he hologrammed Zach's father, Malcolm "Manny" Stewart, the Commissioner of Police for the Colony of New York.

"Commissioner, it's Principal Pham, from the middle school," he began. "I apologize, but I need you to come down to the school. There has been an incident."

"An incident?" Manny replied, not bothering to hide his impatience. "I'm a busy man, Principal Pham. Why don't you text my wife, she'll come."

"Mrs. Stewart is already on her way, Commissioner," the principal replied respectfully. "This is a delicate matter, one that I will only discuss in person. We are careful to preserve our students' privacy."

Manny paused a moment to convey his displeasure, then replied coldly, "I'll be there in an hour. That's the best I can do."

"Very well then," replied the principal reluctantly. "We will wait here for you."

Manny hung up and quickly hologrammed Tyler Watkins, his lawyer. Tyler was Manny's personal attorney, and had been his late father's attorney during his tenure as Chief of Police. At Manny's request, Tyler's firm also did work for the Colony.

Tyler's secretary, a stout, elderly purple-haired woman in her mid-fifties, answered the hologram. Her ghostly six-inch-tall figure stood on Manny's desktop.

"Can I help you, Commissioner?" she asked politely, patting her upswept hairdo into place. "Mr. Watkins is in a meeting."

"Then get him out of his meeting!" Manny growled. "Tell him I need him *now!* There's an emergency."

A heartbeat later, Tyler's miniature hologram image stood on his desk. "What's going on?" he asked. At that moment,

Manny greatly appreciated his lawyer's awkward inability to make small talk.

"Zach's principal called and asked me to come down to the middle school. He called Marya, too; she's already on her way," Manny explained. "I don't know what happened, but it can't be good if he needs both parents. I want you to come with me, you or one of your senior people."

"I'll meet you there, Manny," Tyler said, and hung up.

Manny walked quickly, careful of his sciatica. His son's school was located underneath the old Rockefeller Center, at the 50th Street stop, in what had once been a promenade filled with little shops and restaurants. There was no other way to get to the school; walking was the only option for getting around, for himself and everyone else in the Colony. He arrived at the school just in time to see Tyler coming from the opposite direction.

"Manny!" Tyler said, out of breath. "A word, before we go in."

The two men paused by the school entrance. "Whatever Zach's done, it must be fairly serious," said Tyler. "I suggest you let me do the talking. I'll take my cues from you, of course, but I think I can best protect Zach if -"

"Fine," said Manny curtly. He pressed the palm scanner by the door, and the two men were allowed in. The principal's office was at the end of the corridor.

"Well? What's he done this time?" demanded Manny, eyeing Zach, who was skulking by the window, avoiding looking at his father.

"Commissioner, thank you for coming," the principal said politely, bowing low to Manny, right hand on his left shoulder. He turned to Tyler. "And this is?"

"My lawyer, Tyler Watkins," Manny said brusquely. He nodded to Marya, already seated in front of the desk. The principal rose and pulled an extra chair around for Tyler.

"Now that we're all here," the principal said, "I can tell you what happened this morning. It was most unfortunate, most unfortunate!" Principal Pham closed his office door before returning to his desk.

"A young lady, a classmate, barely thirteen years old. She was in the hall when classes were changing, on the stairs. Zach pushed her up against the wall and kissed her! He *kissed* her, on the mouth! A thirteen-year-old girl!"

The principal stopped to catch his breath. When he spoke, it was in a near-whisper. "Not only that, Commissioner, Mrs.

Stewart, he had his hands *beneath her shirt.*" Such demonstrative behavior was shockingly indecent. It was utterly unacceptable for two adolescents to engage in any kind of sexual activity, let alone in public.

"Did you see this happen?" asked Tyler.

The principal replied, "No, but I have hall monitors who -"

"Is there surveillance footage of the stairwell?" asked Tyler.

"Usually, but the camera is being replaced in that stairwell. It should have been done weeks ago, but -"

"Are there witnesses?" pursued Tyler. Marya looked questioningly at Manny, who pressed his lips together.

"Yes, but you will need their parents' consent to question them," said the principal reluctantly, frowning at the notion.

Tyler glanced at Manny, who nodded almost imperceptibly. "Then I suggest that you speak to this girl's family, Principal Pham, and make it very clear to them that their daughter has sexually assaulted a minor child, and that such behavior is not only abhorrent; it is illegal. We trust our schools to keep our children safe. The Stewarts have every right to sue this girl, her family, the school, and you personally, Principal Pham. Look what my young client has had to endure! A public spectacle! His reputation is ruined, his innocence has been taken from him! That cannot be reversed."

"It wasn't like that," protested Zach. "She didn't attack me or anything."

"Shut up, Zach," Manny snapped, glaring at him.

"Zach will be back in school tomorrow morning," Tyler continued firmly, "and the Commissioner expects the girl to be expelled by then. We will have a restraining order against the girl by the end of today. If the Stewarts hear even an iota of grumbling about the incident, if Zach is made to feel uncomfortable in any way, then we will see you in court."

The principal, clearly taken aback, took a moment to gather his thoughts.

"As you know, this isn't the first time Zach has been sent to my office," he said, perspiration appearing across his forehead. "He doesn't pay attention in class, doesn't do his homework. His behavior has only grown more and more disruptive, and there have been several incidents of bullying. We've tried working with Zach, not only myself, but also his teacher and the guidance counselor. As you can see, he shows no remorse at all."

Manny waited a moment before he prompted, "And?"

"I believe we've done everything we can for your son. Perhaps Zach would be more comfortable elsewhere," the principal suggested hopefully. "There are boarding schools that have a higher ratio of teachers to students, where the environment is more conducive to discipline and proper behavior."

Manny stood up, glaring angrily at him. He placed his palms on the principal's desk and leaned over closer towards him. "What did you say to me?" he asked slowly, his tone unmistakably menacing.

The principal swallowed hard. He had known this meeting wasn't going to be easy, but with the Police Commissioner glowering down at him, he found it hard to think of what to say.

Without turning his head, Manny barked, "Tyler. Take Marya and Zach and wait for me in the hall." Principal Pham frowned as he watched Zach leave his office, uncomfortably aware that he had lost control of the situation.

"Principal," Manny said, as soon as Zach was out of hearing, "my son is perfectly happy here. Next year will be his last year in middle school. If you're unable to handle a mere boy, then perhaps *you* might be more comfortable elsewhere."

"I am responsible for the safety of all of our young people, not just your son," the principal protested, folding trembling hands firmly across his stomach.

"Then I suggest that you learn to manage this situation," Manny snapped, his face dark with rage. Without bowing or saying goodbye, he turned and walked out of the office, leaving the spluttering principal with much to say, but no one to say it to.

Once they had left the school building, Manny took Zach's arm and asked angrily, "What's gotten into you, Zach? What were you thinking?!"

"Dad, it wasn't my fault!" Zach protested. "I was just minding my own business, walking to class, and she was there walking down the stairs! She grabbed me!"

"Grabbed you?" asked Tyler, taking notes on his padlet. A padlet, the ubiquitous electronic device which every citizen of the Colony was required to carry at all times, was both cellphone and tablet.

"Yeah, and started kissing me!" explained Zach. "I hardly know her!"

"Did you put your hands under her shirt?" asked Tyler, still taking notes.

"NO!" responded Zach, his face reddening. "She sort of put them there."

"Under her shirt," repeated Manny flatly, his disbelief showing. "In a crowded stairwell. As classes were changing."

Tyler said, "Manny, I think now I've got everything I need. If they give Zach any trouble, let me know." He bowed to him and Marya, then turned to walk back to his office.

Manny let go of Zach's arm. "You and I need to have a talk, young man," he said, his mouth set in a grim line. "It's time you learn how the world works."

"Dad!" protested Zach, turning beet red. "I already know all about that."

"No, not *that!*" Manny said. "Did it occur to you that this young lady may have been trying to entrap you?"

"Entrap him?" repeated Marya. "Manny, they're children!"

"They're not that young any more, Marya, look at him! He's got hair on his lip and his voice is changing," replied Manny, gesturing at his son, whose utter embarrassment might have been comical, in other circumstances.

"Zach comes from a rich family," explained Manny. "I'm guessing this girl doesn't. Most likely her parents encouraged her to stage this little encounter, get him to touch her, so they could make it into something it wasn't, and claim that Zach molested her."

Zach was so surprised that he actually stopped walking. "She was trying to frame me?" he asked. "I thought she was just glad to see me."

"You really need to listen to me on this one, Zach," Manny said. "She's trying to take advantage of you. Unfortunately, this is something you'll have to guard against."

The edges of Manny's padlet lit up scarlet, pulsing to show an incoming urgent personal text. He opened it and laughed humorlessly. "That didn't take long," he said. "Listen to this, it's from the girl's father," he said, reading the text out loud:

Commissioner, we need to talk in person about an urgent matter that happened today at the middle school. Please let me know when we can meet. J. Perez

Manny texted back:

Talk to my lawyer, Tyler Watkins, at Watkins, Obama & Kinziger. M. Stewart, Police Commissioner for the Colony of New York

5

Manny snapped his padlet shut and rolled it up, stuffing it into his pocket.

"Would we really sue the girl for attacking Zach?" asked Marya.

"We will, if her family goes after us saying Zach attacked the girl," replied Manny. "I've seen this kind of thing before. A minor can be prosecuted for attacking another minor."

"So it's over?" Zach asked hopefully.

"Let's hope so," Manny replied sternly. "I'm not entirely convinced that you didn't have some role in this, young man. Did you kiss her back?"

Zach looked confused. It had all happened so fast.

Marya placed her hand on Manny's arm. "Manny. Please. I'm sure that Zach didn't mean to do anything wrong. He was just so surprised, he didn't know what to do," she said. "After all, what would you have done at his age?"

I'd have kissed her back and asked questions later, he thought. Aloud, he said, "He knows better, we raised him better than this."

They walked the rest of the way home in silence.

Manny and Zach, walking side by side, made an unlikely pair. Zach was already as tall as his father, but there the resemblance ended. With his mother's bright red curly hair and alabaster white skin, he was a stark contrast to his father, who had unremarkable brown eyes and straight dark brown hair.

Home at last, Manny waved his palm over the Scentsor at the front door, which swung open. He turned to Zach and said, "Go to your room, young man! And try and behave yourself from now on, OK? That could just as easily have been you, expelled and disgraced, instead of her."

Zach disappeared up the stairs and into his room, slamming the door with a bang.

"Why do you always have to be so stern with him?" demanded Marya. "It's entirely possible that he didn't do anything wrong." She turned to go upstairs.

Manny grabbed her wrist, forcing her around to face him. "Don't you *ever* question my authority in front of my son like that," he said angrily. "We need to present a united front, the two of us."

"*Your* son? You mean *our* son, don't you?" she retorted, green eyes blazing. Marya, who was Manny's second wife, was actually Zach's aunt. Her older sister Naztazya had been

Manny's first wife. Naztazya was Zach's biological mother, dying tragically in a fire when Zach was five years old.

"Let go of my arm!" Marya exclaimed. She struggled and pulled, but he only tightened his grip, his angry face inches from hers. "Owww, Manny, you're hurting me!" she protested.

"I'm sorry," he replied, abruptly letting go of her arm. "I don't mean to hurt you. But you have to listen to me on this. He'll just try and play one of us against the other, if we disagree."

"Isn't that what kids do?" she countered. "Play one parent against the other?"

"I wouldn't know," he retorted pointedly. Manny had lost his mother when he was seven years old; he had no brothers or sisters. *She should have remembered that about me,* he thought resentfully. *Naztazya would never have said that.*

Chapter 2.

After dinner, Manny and Marya went into the study to finish their conversation about Zach. "Somehow, we have to find a way to get through to him," Manny said, closing the study door.

"I agree, we can't just let this go," Marya said. "But please, let's not crush his spirit, either. He's still only a child."

I know what my old man would have done, Manny thought grimly. Patrick Stewart, Chief of Police, had never been reticent about punishing his little boy. He had only gotten more physically abusive as Manny got older, until one day, Patrick dislocated Manny's shoulder when he was "disciplining" him. Manny had fallen down the stairs and landed unconscious at the bottom, where his best friend Julio found him and took him to the infirmary. Manny had gone afterwards to live with Julio.

"He's grounded for two weeks, and no padlet when he's home," Manny said firmly. "I'll talk to him."

"No, Manny, that's too much!" protested Marya. "One week is plenty. And let me talk to him."

"I said I'll do it!" Manny snapped. "It's time he realizes that he has to behave."

"You're so hard on him, Manny! Please, let me. I know I can get through to him," Marya pleaded.

"All you do is coddle him!" he retorted. "You'll talk and talk, and he'll agree to whatever you say, and nothing will change."

"You'll never change his behavior by being so strict," she warned, shaking her head. "We need to show him that we love him, but that we don't approve of the way he's acting."

"How's that working so far?" Manny asked sardonically.

Marya sighed. They'd had this conversation before, too many times. "At least promise me you'll spend more time with him, not just punish him and then disappear until the next time he acts up."

"OK, I promise," he conceded. It was an easy promise, one he had little intention of keeping.

At the office, Manny's word was law. But he had learned to give in to Marya whenever possible, when it came to raising Zach. It wasn't that he thought she was right; it just made Marya easier to deal with. If he didn't make at least some kind of concession to her, he knew there would be another argument coming soon.

Manny went upstairs to Zach's bedroom. He opened the door to find Zach sitting on the bed, padlet in hand. The room was transformed into an ancient smoke-filled battlefield complete with warriors dressed in armor, shields up and swords swinging. "Turn it off, Zach," he said sternly.

Zach barely acknowledged him. "Not now," he said shortly, fingers moving across his gamer board.

Manny moved forward and grabbed the gamer board out of Zach's hands, turning off the game.

Zach howled with outrage. "Dad! I'll lose my points! Give it back!!" The room slowly dissolved back into a bedroom, warriors fading away.

"You're grounded for one week. No going out, no screen time except for homework. Do you understand?" Manny said. "And no video games."

"No video games! Dad!!" Zach protested.

"Do your homework," Manny warned. "If I find you playing video games or watching SuperFlix, you'll be sorry."

~ ~ ~ ~ ~ ~

The Stewart mansion was quiet and dark. Julio and Anna Suarez, Manny's foster brother and his wife, had gone to sleep; a single light shone at the far end of the long hallway from their daughter Julie's room as she finished writing a paper for grad school. Julio, Anna, and Julie lived in the spacious Stewart mansion along with Manny, Marya and Zach. Extended families often shared a home in the Colony, as much from custom as from necessity.

Down the hall in the master bedroom, Manny and Marya were getting ready for bed. Manny dropped his sweatpants and teeshirt on the floor by the bed, pulling down the quilt and settling in against the headboard. Marya came out of the bathroom, the fragrance of her mother-in-law's homemade hand cream drifting into the room.

"Marya, I'm so sorry I grabbed your arm," Manny began. As he knew from conversations with his Deputy Commissioner and best friend David Wu, women like an apology. Manny and Dave, friends from their earliest days at the Police Academy, used to pass the time on nighttime stakeouts by having long conversations about women. *If there's a fight, tell her you're sorry,* Dave had advised. *Tell her you can't live without her, and you don't know what came over you. Whatever you do, don't rehash what happened. No, stick to emotions. They love it when you talk about emotions.*

"I don't know what came over me, Marya," he added smoothly. "You're everything to me, you and Zach. I would never hurt you."

Marya brightened visibly, sitting down on the bed next to Manny. "You scared me, Manny," she said simply, her eyes beseeching him.

He took her hand in his and turned it to kiss her palm. "I'm so sorry," he repeated. He was surprised to see that there were bruises encircling her wrist. He pushed back her sleeve. Her forearm also was bruised, five little dark blue splotches, one for each of his fingers.

"Marya, please forgive me," he said, making a mental note that he must remember how easily she bruised. Slowly he tried to draw her closer, hoping to gauge her mood. She turned towards him, her hand brushing the hair back from her face.

The smallest of sounds from across the hall interrupted them. "Did you hear that?" he asked Marya.

"What?" she replied. "I didn't hear anything."

Manny was already up and across the room, pulling open the door very quietly. Sure enough, there was a light coming from beneath the door to Zach's room. Moving silently across the hall in his bare feet, Manny yanked open Zach's door to find him intently playing his video game with the sound turned off, the bedroom a smoldering scene filled with silent, gory wounded.

Grabbing the padlet out of Zach's hands, he said, "Did I not say 'no video games,' young man?!"

"Give that back!" protested Zach. He added quickly, "I need it for my homework."

"You should have finished your homework hours ago. You can have your padlet back in the morning," Manny said. "I'll leave it for you in the kitchen." He sat down on the bed holding the padlet, searching for the video game. Ignoring Zach's desperate attempts to persuade him otherwise, Manny deleted the game.

"What are you doing?! I'll lose all my points! Dad, that's not fair!" Zach implored.

"I warned you, Zach! You're now grounded for *two weeks,* not one," Manny said angrily. He knew, as all parents know, that he had to win this battle. "And if I catch you trying to cheat, you'll be sorry."

Manny left Zach's bedroom, closing the door behind him. Then, instead of returning to his bedroom, he stole quietly down the stairs.

Manny had grown up in the Stewart mansion. Even now, as a middle-aged man of thirty-five, he knew every creaky floorboard and could still move silently up and down the stairs. He sat down in the dark kitchen at the end of the long table, placing Zach's padlet squarely in front of him, and waited.

With the patience and discipline of a veteran detective, Manny sat without moving or making a sound for nearly twenty minutes. Then Zach's bedroom door swung open, and he came tiptoeing down the stairs and into the kitchen, snapping on the light.

"Dad! I-I thought you went to bed!" he exclaimed with dismay.

"What are you doing downstairs at this hour?" Manny demanded.

Zach hung his head. For once, he had nothing to say. His eyes went to his padlet, lying on the table.

"Don't even think about it, Zach," Manny said, shaking his head. "Go back to bed!" He watched as his defeated youngster returned to his bedroom.

"What did you say to him?" asked Marya, as Manny slid into bed next to her.

"I told him to go back to bed," said Manny. "He'll behave now, I'm sure."

Marya chuckled. "We'll see about that," she said. "Anna says he's very smart. Apparently, he's a natural with computers, just understands programming intuitively. I bet he's got backups somewhere."

"He may have backups," said Manny, "but I've blocked him from downloading the game, so a backup of his account isn't going to do him any good."

"If only we could get Zach to apply himself," Marya said. "The hard part is to find something that engages his interest.

Remember when he played that trick on Julie, when he was ten? Anna told me all about it."

"Yeah, I remember," Manny said. The two were silent, thinking about the "trick" that Zach had played on his cousin. At ten years old, Zach had locked Julie out of her school, banking and SoshMedia accounts, all because she had taken his notebook to school by mistake.

Julio and Anna had been livid. *Why didn't you just ask her to return the notebook?* Manny had asked Zach at the time. *I wanted to show her what happens if she messes with me,* Zach had explained.

"It's hard to find something that really motivates him. Nobody can get Zach to do anything except Zach," remarked Manny dismissively. He yawned.

Silence filled the bedroom as the night settled around them. Marya's fingers tentatively began to play with the little hairs on Manny's bare chest.

Manny smiled to himself. His wife only did that when she wanted something. He waited.

"Manny," Marya said hesitantly, "I've been thinking. I want to go see Madame Elayna. You know, the Seer."

"Madame Elayna!" he repeated, surprised. "I didn't know you believed in fortune tellers. Are you serious?"

"Yes, and I want you to come with me," she replied.

Madame Elayna was the Colony's most successful fortune teller. In an age where scientific research was largely stalled, people often turned to whatever was available to give them a sense of control over their lives. Many prominent citizens and celebrities swore by Madame Elayna's predictions.

But not everyone was a fan. As Commissioner, Manny had access to the Colony's police records. He knew that Madame Elayna had been born Elaine Rebecca Holmes. She had a rap sheet filled with petty crimes like shoplifting and forgery.

After a stint in jail, she had turned to acting to make a living, renaming herself Elayne Patricia Brazille. Ms. Brazille's acting career was cut short when she was arrested for stealing and reselling costumes, and was sentenced to six months in prison. When she was released, she reinvented herself once again, this time as a fortune teller named Madame Elayna, adding the title "Seer" to her resume.

"You mean you want her to tell you whether you'll have another baby?" Manny said softly.

"Yes," she answered, falling silent.

"OK," he said reluctantly to his wife, "although I seriously doubt whether she knows anything." When Marya did not reply, he added, "But, yeah. Go ahead and make an appointment."

"Thank you, Manny!" She gave him a grateful kiss. "You'll go in too, right? So she can tell your fortune?"

"We'll see," he said vaguely, wondering what he had gotten himself into.

Chapter 3.

Madame Elayna's establishment was a tiny little cubbyhole above a Latin takeout restaurant, up two flights of an ancient metal spiral staircase. There were two rooms, a waiting area in the front, and a private room in the back where Madame would bring her clients, one at a time.

The dimly lit waiting area was too warm, filled with cloying incense. Fringed scarves were draped over the two Zolar lamps, casting a lurid reddish glow. The private room, partitioned from the waiting room by a hanging curtain of beads, was shrouded in darkness.

Madame Elayna was an elderly woman in her mid-fifties, an age when many people had already retired. Her face was caked with makeup. *She certainly plays the part well,* Manny thought, as she came forward to greet them. A long, full skirt swirled around her ankles as she pulled her sequined shawl close. Tiny bells tinkled from her bracelets as she bowed first to Manny, and then to Marya.

"Greetings! Good health and prosperity to you, Commissioner, Madame!" she said softly, bowing low with her right hand on her left shoulder, in the Colony's traditional greeting. Manny murmured something in response, offering the briefest possible polite bow.

"I'll go first," he offered. He followed Madame Elayna into the back room, as she pulled aside the curtain of hanging beads with a dramatic flourish.

The back room was quite dark, lit only by a single candle, an item that was illegal in the Colony due to the risk of fire. Manny recognized the brand; it was his family's trading company that imported it from the Colony of Philadelphia.

Decades earlier, Manny's father Patrick Stewart had been intrigued by a teenager's prize-winning science project, a battery that could be recharged with artificial light and that could run her father's bakery mixer for many hours. If it could run an industrial mixer, mused Patrick, what else could it do?

After much trial and error, Patrick found a single rusted out, ancient train that would run, albeit very slowly, using the battery. One day he boldly took the train all the way to the end of the tracks, discovering the flourishing Colony of Philadelphia at the other end, and the black market was born. The illegal venture had grown exponentially each year, making the family fabulously wealthy. Many of the black market's biggest investors came from within the police community and the Mayor's office.

Dutifully, Manny sat down at the tiny table across from Madame Elayna, trying not to react as she took his hand. While physical contact with anyone except medical personnel or a family member was forbidden, as much from cultural norms as from concerns about infection, there were exceptions, distasteful though they might be.

"I see many obstacles, Commissioner," she intoned, long black hair keeping her face in shadow as she bent over his outstretched hand. "What is dear to your heart will never be." Madame Elayna frowned. "Your wife, your children," she said, her voice trailing off.

Neither of them spoke. Manny suspected that she was waiting for him to offer some information that would give her a clue as to what to say next. He kept silent.

Madame moved closer to his hand. "A single candle lights a thousand flames, Commissioner, and yet you will not live to see it," she warned, her finger tracing a delicate line down his palm. Her breath was warm and moist against his skin.

"That's enough," he exclaimed in disgust, pulling his hand free from her grasp, wiping it against his pants. Her words were conveniently vague and general. Besides, if she had bothered to research her clients before today's appointment, she would have known that they only had one child. He stood up.

"I'll send my wife in," he said abruptly. He returned to the outer room, where Marya was waiting.

Marya entered the inner room and sat down across the tiny table, extending her hand. Madame Elayna searched Marya's palm closely for a long time. Finally, she said quietly, "You have troubles, Matrushka."

"Yes," replied Marya, barely daring to breathe.

"You seek assurance," continued Madame, her voice guarded.

"I need to know – I mean, is it permitted to ask ..." She swallowed hard, her voice trailing off uncertainly. Marya began to tremble.

"Hush," said Madame Elayna, the way a mother would comfort a child. "Let me see." There was another long pause as she studied both of Marya's palms.

Suddenly, she looked up, hooded eyes intent on Marya's face. She said excitedly, "I see for you, in time, a great blessing." Marya burst into tears.

"She will *know*," Madame intoned, her voice rising. Abruptly, she stood. "In the blackness of the tomb, it will be. When others hide and weep, she will be strong." And with that, Madame Elayna abruptly let go of Marya's hands and collapsed into her chair, breathing unevenly, her face gaunt and exhausted.

Manny had heard enough. He'd gone along with the visit because Marya wanted it, but he wasn't going to condone any more of this superstitious nonsense. He strode into the private room and took Marya firmly by the elbow.

"We're leaving," he said, pulling her up from her seat. Madame Elayna said nothing, as her two prominent clients left her establishment.

"Manny, you won't believe what she said to me," Marya said in a hushed voice, as they slowly navigated their way down the metal spiral staircase.

"I heard it all, Sweetheart. She knew what you wanted to hear," he cautioned. "Think about what she said."

"I am thinking about it, Manny," Marya responded. "She was confident that I'll have another child."

Manny sighed. "Marya, please," he said. "You need to be realistic. Psychics are right about half the time."

"She's not a psychic, Manny! She's a Seer," Marya protested indignantly.

And a much better actress than I gave her credit for, Manny thought ruefully.

Marya had been twenty years old when Manny married her eight years earlier. One of five sisters, she dearly wanted a large family. But months turned into years, and she did not conceive. It was a problem throughout the Colony. The birth rate was falling, the rate of miscarriages steadily climbing. Doctors and scientists had theories, but no proof as to why it was happening.

A year ago, after they had all but given up, suddenly Marya was pregnant. She was twenty-seven years old, an age when most women had already finished having babies. Usually, women married after graduating from high school or grad school and had their children in their early twenties. Women went through menopause in their mid-thirties.

The household held its collective breath until the first months had passed, and breathed a sigh of relief when her belly began to show. She glowed, her happiness a lovely thing to behold.

Manny often would come home from work to find her in the nursery across the hall from their bedroom, sitting in the rocking chair by the window, hands folded tenderly across her belly, singing softly to her unborn child. Marya had a lovely singing voice, clear as a flute.

"That's nice, Marya. What is that?" Manny asked one evening, standing in the doorway. "It sounds familiar."

"It's just an old nursery rhyme that my mother used to sing to us when we were little," Marya replied dreamily. "It's The Song the Flowers Sing."

"I thought I recognized it! Naz used to sing it to Zach, when he was little," Manny said.

Marya was in her sixth month of pregnancy when something went horribly wrong. Manny woke up to find her standing next to the bed, gripping the back of the velvet chair that had been his mother's, eyes squeezed shut, breathing hard through her teeth. Manny hologrammed the midwife, who arrived very quickly. Leaving the two women alone in the bedroom, Manny fled downstairs, sitting in the front parlor with Julio, his foster brother.

Hours dragged past, dread twisting tendrils around his heart. What if something was wrong with the baby? What if something happened to *Marya?* He couldn't bear to lose another wife.

The midwife appeared in the front parlor doorway, wiping blood from her bare forearms onto a white linen towel. "Commissioner. I'm so sorry," she said. "I did everything I could. The baby was stillborn."

The baby was ... what? Manny tried to arrange his thoughts, which seemed to have stopped working.

"And Marya?" asked Julio. "How is she?"

"Physically, she's fine," the midwife said. "You can see her now."

Marya was lying in bed, staring up at the ceiling. Her face was whiter than the white pillowcase as she turned towards Manny, her glassy green eyes blank and empty. He knelt by the

17

bed and held her hand, but she seemed to be in some kind of shock. After a moment, he slid into bed next to her and held her close, stroking her hair, speaking softly to her. Moments passed. Finally, she buried her face against his shoulder and burst into tears, long, shuddering sobs that echoed throughout the house.

For several months afterwards, Marya had shown little interest in anything, moving around the house like an exhausted wraith, rarely going out. It was only lately that her spirits had begun to lift.

"How about something to eat?" Manny asked. "There's a good Chinese place, Chung's, not far from here." Then he stopped.

"Wait, I forgot to pay her. Stay here, I'll be right back." Manny climbed back up the spiral staircase, impatiently ignoring the warning ache in his left leg where his sciatica lurked, and knocked on the door, entering Madame Elayna's waiting room.

"I forgot to pay you, I'm sorry," he said. There was no response. "Madame?" he said, pushing aside the curtain of beads to the inner room.

Madame Elayna was kneeling on the floor, hands clasped together on the chair seat in front of her, eyes closed, lips moving, tears streaming down her uplifted face. She seemed completely unaware of Manny's presence. Hairs rising on the back of his neck, Manny backed out of the room, swiping the implanted bank chip in his wrist over the processor by the door as he quickly exited the waiting room. *She's just a crazy old bat, she doesn't know anything,* he reassured himself. Still, it was unnerving.

"Everything OK?" asked Marya, as Manny came slowly down the stairs, denying the gathering pain shooting down his left leg.

"Fine," he said brusquely, ignoring Marya's inquisitive look. He decided not to mention what he had just seen in Madame Elayna's establishment. "I took the stairs too quickly, that's all." They walked together in silence, Manny trying not to limp, each alone with his or her thoughts.

The restaurant was nearly empty. Manny eased himself carefully into his chair. A few moments passed.

"You seem more like yourself lately," he ventured cautiously.

"I've been feeling better," she said. "It's good to get out and do things."

18

"That's good," he replied. They ordered food and settled in to wait. Marya shifted her gaze to the doorway, watching the passersby. Manny studied his hands.

"What's Zach up to, now that he's grounded?" Manny asked, for something to say.

"I've got him cleaning out all the closets and trimming the bushes out front," Marya replied.

"I hope he makes some friends when school starts in the fall," Manny remarked. Zach didn't have any friends. No one came over after school, and he was always at home alone upstairs in his room, playing his video games. Manny remembered his own childhood, after he met Julio. They had been inseparable, as close as brothers.

"I agree, we need to encourage that," Marya said. *She makes a wonderful stepmother,* Manny thought for the thousandth time. Marya truly loved Zach, and wanted what was best for him. "He spends too much time alone in his room. I'm not even sure what he does in there. He always seems to be working on something."

"Just as long as he's not playing video games on his padlet, after I doubled his punishment," Manny said.

"He wouldn't outright defy you like that, Manny," said Marya, looking up as the waiter bot rolled towards the table with their food. "He's only thirteen."

Chapter 4.

Early the next morning, Manny opened his eyes to see Marya already awake, sitting up and watching him. "Hey, Sleepyhead," she greeted him, bending over to kiss him. She stretched her arms above her head, long red hair rippling over her shoulders. "I've been thinking. Maybe I should go shopping, get some new clothes."

"Good idea," he agreed. "Take Zach with you. He can help carry things."

This was a welcome development. It had been ages since Marya had proposed a shopping trip. Shopping would keep Zach busy, too, while he was grounded. Manny smiled to himself, imagining his son's dismay. Clothes shopping with his mother on a Saturday morning was the last thing Zach would want to do.

Downstairs in the kitchen, the family was eating breakfast. Zach's cousin Julie was standing at the counter holding two slices of toast folded together. Her waist-length hair was bundled up inside a prim "modesta," a simple white cotton pleated cap with a shoulder-length ribbon, pink to match her dress, hanging down on either side. It was all the rage with the younger women. She looked very pretty in it, and Manny told her so.

"Thanks, Uncle Manny!" she replied, surprised. *She looks just like her Aunt Naz when she smiles,* he thought with a sudden pang. Naztazya, Manny's first wife and childhood sweetheart, had been a little younger than Julie when Manny fell in love with her.

Naztazya had been a year younger than Anna, Julie's mother; the two sisters had been very close, living together in the Stewart mansion, sharing household and childrearing responsibilities. Naz had been like a second mother to Julie.

"Where's Zach?" Anna asked. "Is he up yet?"

"I haven't seen him," Manny replied. "You're right, he should be up by now." He sipped his coffee. "I'll check on him as soon as I finish this."

Julie sang out, "Bye, Mom, Uncle Manny," pushing her padlet into her purse as she strode through the front door, on her way to a friend's house.

"I'd better go, too," said Anna. "I've got lots to catch up on before Monday. See you tonight, Manny." She picked up her coffee cup and shuffled down the hall in her bathrobe and fuzzy slippers to her at-home office. Originally a maid's room off the kitchen, the space was small, but very convenient. Anna, a gifted computer analyst, was a senior supervisor at the Jonathan King Institute for Computer Sciences. Like most professionals, she worked from home to conserve office space, going in to the office only when she was needed.

Alone in the kitchen, Manny finished his coffee and glanced at the time. Somehow, he was already running late. He went upstairs to find Zach.

With his hand on Zach's bedroom doorknob, he paused. He could hear the unmistakable sound of music, the volume turned down very low.

Now that he was grounded, Zach had been handing over his padlet to his parents each night before bed. It was still safely stored in Manny's bedroom closet; he'd checked on it earlier, as he got dressed. So where was this music coming from?

Manny pulled open the door.

There was Zach, sitting on his bed in his pajamas, holding a padlet in his hand, intently watching a music video projected onto his wall.

"Dad! I thought you left!" Zach exclaimed as he shoved the padlet beneath the blankets.

"Give me that!" Manny demanded, reaching over and retrieving the padlet. "Where did you get this??"

"It's mine! Give it back!" Zach exclaimed indignantly.

"It is *not* yours, it should have been turned in when you got your new padlet!" Manny replied, shocked at this flagrant disregard for the rules. "I warned you, Zach. I said if you didn't behave, you'd be sorry," Manny said sternly.

He eyed his son with distaste. "No more screen time for another week, except for homework! And no allowance, either. Have I made myself clear?"

"Yes, sir," said Zach, regretfully eyeing the padlet.

Manny also was eyeing the padlet. "How'd you do it, Zach? I blocked your account so you couldn't play this game!"

"You mean the parental dashboard?" asked Zach scornfully. "I just disabled it, it wasn't even hard. A child could do it!"

"Get dressed and go downstairs," Manny snapped. "You can have breakfast with your mother and help her with her shopping. Then I want you to clean up your room, sort all of this ... stuff," he said, motioning to the pile of things on the floor by the window. "And for goodness' sake, Zach, behave yourself!"

Zach mumbled something which Manny charitably took to be acquiescence.

Manny made an effort to control his impatience. *Be a good father,* he admonished himself. *Teach him, don't just punish him.* "Zach, what did you think was going to happen, when you started using that padlet?"

"I didn't think. I just ... it's pretty boring, that's all," Zach said dejectedly, his defiance gone. Somehow, he looked smaller, sitting there in his pajamas, a reminder of the little boy he had been.

"There are consequences to things, Zach. Think ahead next time," Manny said gruffly. He reached over and touched Zach's shoulder. "I'll see you tonight."

~ ~ ~ ~ ~ ~

"Good morning, Commissioner," said Agnes Delgado, his secretary. When Edith, the unit's secretary, retired a few years earlier, Manny had promoted his previous unit's secretary to work for himself and the Deputy Commissioner. "Tea?"

"Yes, thanks, Agnes," Manny replied gratefully, hanging up his coat on a hook in the ceiling-high and extremely narrow coat closet in his office. He used Mr. Grabby, the ubiquitous long-handled tool with a grabbing mechanism on the end, to place his hat on the "hat shelf," the narrow little shelf at the very top, up near the ceiling.

The Commissioner's office was one of only a few offices with its own private closet. The office was simply enormous, with a table and six chairs for impromptu meetings, a visitor's chair, and a huge, ancient wooden desk with many drawers. The desk was a one-person desk, unlike every other desk in the police complex. All other desks had two places for people to work, placed diagonally for easy sharing.

David Wu, Manny's Deputy Commissioner and closest friend, had the office across from his. Manny and Dave had known each other since the Academy, and had come up together, first as street cops, then as detectives, and eventually, in their present jobs.

"Morning, Dave," Manny called out, looking into his friend's office. Teacup in hand, Manny stopped in the doorway to gauge whether Dave was too busy for their usual early morning chat. Dave waved to Manny, but continued talking to three miniature ghostly figures standing on his desktop, holograming from the Mayor's office about the budget.

Once settled behind his desk, Manny began to sift through the day's mail. A neat stack of correspondence awaited his attention. Sipping his tea, he reached for the first item.

The report detailed a proposed redesign of the Colony's padlets. Manny skimmed the text, barely glancing at the sketch of the new prototype. *Interesting, but why do they need me?* he thought impatiently. Too much of his time was taken up with issues that had nothing to do with police work; he'd have to speak to Nigel, his aide, about prioritizing his inbox.

The next memorandum concerned the long-abandoned subway cars, located at the northern-most end of the Colony.

When the Colony was first formed, all of the subway cars had been driven as far north as they could go, where they were chained together permanently. After the power to the third rail was turned off, the subway tracks were filled in using crushed concrete and stones gleaned from the ruined buildings above ground, to create more living space.

It didn't take long before the Colony's homeless population (nicknamed "Baggers" because in the earliest days of the Colony, they slept in sleeping bags on the hard concrete platforms) realized that the empty subway cars made wonderful free housing. Subway cars became cherished family "possessions," passed down by squatters from one generation to the next. Eventually, though, the subway cars had become rusted out and unsafe. Many of the chains holding them in place had broken apart with age.

"I don't see what difference it really makes," Manny said to Dave later that morning, seated comfortably in Dave's office at the diagonal end of his desk. Manny and Dave had worked together at a diagonal desk for years, when they were detectives working in the same unit. It amused them both to continue that habit now.

"Seems like old times," Dave had said, the first time Manny came into his office and sat down at the opposite corner of his desk, to which Manny had replied, "Yeah, but our offices are so much nicer."

23

"If the tracks are filled in right up to the last car, then what's the difference if the chains are broken or missing?" Manny said pragmatically. "There's no point in repairing them. The cars can't move. There's nowhere for them to go."

"I agree," replied Dave. "What about repairing the inside of the cars, though? You know, where the floors have broken through?"

"I don't think we need to worry about that either," Manny replied. "Technically, no one should be living in the subway cars anyway. They don't own them, and the Colony doesn't maintain them. Once the floors have rusted out and the cars become unlivable, the homeless population will have to find someplace else to live. But that's a problem for another day." He yawned.

"With your leave, Boss, I have a unit meeting to supervise," Dave said. "Wanna come?"

"Yeah, I'd like that," replied Manny, and the two walked down the hall to the conference room where the special task force for cold cases was having its weekly meeting.

Manny looked forward to listening to the unit's meetings. As much as Manny enjoyed being Commissioner, at heart he was still a detective. He often read the unit's cold case files at night, when he was alone in his study.

Naomi Chandler, the unit's lieutenant, was just beginning the briefing. She nodded to Manny and Dave as they took seats in the back of the room, continuing with her presentation.

Today's cold case was a child's murder which had never been solved. The child, a teenage boy, had died from a gunshot wound. Shootings were rare in the Colony, mostly because guns were so strictly controlled. Only police officers and security personnel were licensed to carry a gun.

Thousands of guns had been smuggled into the subway during the great hurricane in 2085 AD, inside backpacks and duffel bags, coat pockets and ladies' purses, most of them illegal. Even now, with natural attrition over the years, there were still more guns than people. The guns were stored in a carefully guarded armory, cleaned and kept in good working condition by a devoted team of specially trained police technicians.

Manny listened to the presentation, but his mind began to wander. The boy who had been murdered was only thirteen years old, the same age as Zach. He'd had few friends until he got involved with a gang, the Raptors, several months before his death. He'd gone quickly from being the lookout to shoplifting and purse snatching. And then one day, the boy was dead.

Manny's padlet buzzed; a hologram was trying to connect. Manny excused himself and left the conference room.

"Tyler?" he said, closing the door to his office. Tyler Watkins's hologrammed image appeared on the desk.

"Manny, I have news for you," Tyler said. "Shall we talk in person?"

"Yes. Can you come to the house tonight around 6:30?" Manny asked. "All of us will be there."

Tyler nodded, his hologrammed figure fading away.

Chapter 5.

"Let's all go into the library," Manny suggested as Anna and Julie finished clearing the dinner plates from the table. "I've asked Tyler to come over. He's been looking into something for me. Remember when we talked about buying land in the Central Park?"

"Aren't you waiting until Mr. Jha retires, so you can get Council approval?" asked Luis. Luis and Lucinda Suarez were Julio's parents, and Manny's foster parents. They lived in a townhouse not far from the Stewart mansion and were frequent visitors.

"Yeah, I've been hoping the old buzzard would retire, but he's still going strong," replied Manny, referring to his rival on the Council. "I'm tired of his delays, skipping meetings so there's no quorum for a vote, postponing and canceling meetings. We're going to try a different route."

"You sure you want to do this, Manny? Having the business pay for the shelters?" Luis asked dubiously. This had been a frequent topic of conversation. Luis and his son Julio were equal partners with Manny in the family business, Suarez & Sons, although Manny's enormous wealth inherited from his father far exceeded his partners' holdings.

"I'm committed to paying for a large portion of it myself," Manny replied. "I believe strongly in this. It could save lives, potentially hundreds of lives. We don't need to wait for Council approval."

"What does Tyler say? Was it good news for us, could you tell?" asked Luis.

"I couldn't tell. You know Tyler," replied Manny, shaking his head. "He's better at saying nothing than anyone I know."

They settled more comfortably into the chairs in the library, sipping the last of their blooming herbal tea, admiring it as the colors swirled in the glasses, slowly changing from deep pink to light purple to pale blue and back again.

"How's Zach doing?" asked Lucinda, concerned. "I hear he's been grounded again?"

"I've added another week to his sentence," replied Manny. "After I took away his padlet, he pulled out a 'spare' padlet and kept right on playing his video games. After I told him not to!"

"I thought you blocked him from downloading that game," said Marya, frowning.

"I did," replied Manny, exasperated. "He said parental controls are for children." Julio burst out laughing, then stopped abruptly after a glance from his wife.

"I'm not surprised," replied Anna. "He's a natural with computers."

"Great. Now my teenage son knows more about parental controls than I do," replied Manny indignantly. "Besides, he was hiding that spare padlet all along, when it should have been turned in."

"I seem to remember someone else who once had a 'spare' padlet," Lucinda reminded him gently.

"And it's a good thing you did!" added Luis.

When Manny and Julio were teenagers still living in the Suarez family home at the 14th Street stop, Luis had been stranded outside, far from the Colony's entrance. Wounded and unconscious, Luis was unable to call for help. Manny's unregistered padlet had been instrumental in finding Luis, while eluding his father's police surveillance.

Tyler arrived, interrupting their reverie. He stopped at the library entrance to admire the magnificent oil paintings on the walls between floor-to-ceiling shelves of antique paper books, carefully stored behind glass. The end tables and coffee table were all antiques, beautifully carved from oak and mahogany, with white marble tops. Even the tiny figurines on the tables had been chosen for their beauty and value.

"I have good news for you," Tyler announced, sitting down gingerly on one end of the dark brown velvet antique sofa with gold fringe around the bottom. "My firm has opined that no one owns the land in the Central Park. It once belonged to the City of New York, but there is no City any longer. The Colony of New York has never addressed this issue. If you want to buy that land, you can."

"Are there restrictions on its use?" asked Luis.

"No, no restrictions," Tyler explained. "If it's your land, then no one can tell you what to do with it."

"How do we go about it?" asked Manny. "I want to make sure no one can question its validity," he added, thinking of Mr. Jha, who was a retired trial lawyer.

"We suggest that you buy small parcels, one or two at a time. Put a public notice in SoshMedia or one of the other public platforms two weeks before the purchase. Bury it in the middle of a long article about something else. Once notice is properly given according to our laws, assuming there are no objections, we'll take care of the rest for you."

"And the price?" asked Luis. "What will this land cost?"

"That's anybody's guess," responded Tyler. "I'd suggest ten Krowns per acre."

This was met with laughter. Ten Krowns was the equivalent of five American dollars, referring to the old-fashioned system of paper money which had been in use before the great hurricane of 2085 AD.

The use of paper money was now frowned upon, and was used mostly by drug dealers and their hapless customers. Everyone else had an implanted chip in their forearms which contained banking information, as well as medical history, school and local affiliations, and home address. It was a proud moment for children when they reached their tenth birthday, old enough to have their own chips implanted.

"There are 843 acres of land in the Central Park," said Anna, reading from her padlet. She looked up at Tyler. "How much land should we buy?"

"Let's start off slow, so we don't attract attention," said Marya, surprising everyone. Marya, so much younger than Manny, Julio and Anna, rarely offered an opinion in family business meetings. "We should probably put the land in each of our names. The children, too. Who knows what this land might be worth in the future?"

"That's right, Marya," agreed Tyler. "You should purchase land for each family member."

"How do we pay for it?" asked Anna. "Who gets the money, if nobody owns the land?"

"That's a good question," responded Tyler, nodding appreciatively. "I've set up an escrow account which will hold the money indefinitely. I seriously doubt that anyone is going to come looking for it, but if they do, this is above-board. You'll transfer the money to me, and I'll place it in the firm's escrow account."

"I'll post the first notice tomorrow, and take it slow. By the end of the summer, we'll have eight acres of land," said Manny.

"No, wait, let's make that ten acres. I'd like to give Dave and Jenny two acres as a gift. Can I do that?" he asked, turning to Tyler.

"I don't see any reason why not," responded Tyler.

"You're gifting land to Dave and Jenny?" asked Anna.

"Yeah, I'd like to. Dave's been my friend since we were kids, back at the Academy. And as Marya says, we don't know what this land may be worth in the future," replied Manny. *Maybe someday, our great-grandchildren can play together outside in the sunshine,* he thought.

"Why don't you transfer the money into the escrow account now for the first purchase?" said Manny. "I'll post the notice tomorrow, and after two weeks, move on to the next notice."

"Sure, I can do that," said Tyler, pulling out his padlet.

"And send me the Deed to Dave and Jenny's land as soon as it's ready, OK?" Manny said.

Tyler nodded. "Of course," he said. He opened up the family's investment and household accounts spreadsheet. "Which of the accounts do you want me to use?"

Manny pointed to the bottom of the list. "Use that one at the bottom, there. The joint account, the one we use for personal expenses."

Tyler issued a few commands and the transfer was complete.

"It's going to take years, you know, to build these shelters," Tyler cautioned them. "And lots of money."

"Our money," Luis reminded them, "since I don't think the Colony is ever going to pay us back for them."

"You're probably right," agreed Manny. "That's one of Mr. Jha's favorite talking points, how there's no money in the budget for this. If we own the shelters outright, though, we can always rent them to the Colony if they are needed."

"What if the shelters are never needed?" asked Anna. "We'll have spent all that money on nothing."

"Not on nothing, Anna. We'll have the peace of mind of knowing that we've done everything we can to prepare. Imagine thousands of people streaming up out of the subway, not knowing where to go, families with children milling about," Manny responded. "We'll be able to point them in the direction of a shelter, where there's food and water, beds and a roof over their heads. They'd be safe."

There was more to it than that, but as Commissioner, Manny understood the value of keeping his darkest thoughts to himself. He seriously doubted that the shelters would never be used.

After an earthquake had shaken the Colony eight years earlier, he had met with the Colony's top geologists. They warned him that climate change takes place underground, too, not just above ground. The earth surrounding the tunnels was warming, shifting and changing. More tremors were likely, hopefully very mild ones, and were likely to continue for some time.

During the earthquake, several major water pipes had broken, causing panic among the population. The Mayor's office was flooded, along with many other buildings, ruining everything on the first and second floors. Houses were condemned and torn down as water poured from the ceilings and streamed down the walkways. Waterproof/fire doors were slammed shut to contain the damage. Families moved in with relatives, disrupting work and school schedules. Engineers and plumbers were kept busy round the clock.

In the days following the earthquake, there had been some talk in City Council about establishing evacuation plans. But humans, with their remarkable penchant for doing nothing, soon forgot about the emergency, once the pipes had been repaired. Displaced families eased into their new living quarters, schedules were adjusted, new jobs were found. For most people, the earthquake was now a one-off, already forgotten – but not to Manny, who understood that another one was more likely, rather than less likely.

"Nobody has built anything outside in a long time. Do we even know how to dig a foundation?" asked Julio.

"Hasan will know," Manny reassured them. Hasan Blumberg was Sara Blumberg's husband, an experienced contractor with connections to all sorts of workmen. Sara, a retired teacher, had once been Manny's tutor after his father's death during his senior year in high school, and now served as his eyes and ears on the Council.

Manny knew that Hasan would do a fine job on any project he accepted. Manny also knew that he had never been outside. If he accepted the job, Hasan and his workers were going to have to work outside daily. *I'll take Hasan outside, just the two of us,* thought Manny. *That will be more tactful, in case he needs time to get acclimated. I don't want to embarrass him in front of his crew.*

Despite a loosening of the restrictions on leaving the Colony, only a handful of adventurous souls had opted to go outside. Most people were more than reluctant to leave the safety and familiarity of their underground homes. They had been successfully indoctrinated as children to believe that storms or wild temperature swings would harm them, if the night air didn't kill them outright.

Manny unrolled his padlet and texted Hasan.

Chapter 6.

I t's right through here," said Manny. He and Hasan were at the 59th Street stop near Columbus Circle, across the street from the Central Park. Manny walked quickly up the stairs to street level, pushing open the double glass doors.

"Take a look at this old padlock, Hasan!" exclaimed Manny, pointing to the ancient padlock and rusted length of chain hanging from one of the doors. "Hasan?"

He turned and looked back. Hasan was standing at the bottom of the stairs, one hand gripping the railing, his face white.

"It's fine, don't worry," Manny said reassuringly. "I wouldn't ask you to do this if I thought it could hurt you."

"I don't know, Manny," Hasan said nervously. He wiped his mouth with the back of his hand.

"Here, climb up the stairs and stand next to me," Manny said. "We'll still be inside, at the top of the stairs."

Hasan reluctantly climbed the stairs and stopped next to Manny, embarrassed but no less afraid. Manny pushed open the doors and stepped outside into the sunshine, waving his arms and smiling reassuringly at his friend, who was watching warily from inside the door.

"Look! I'm outside!" Manny exclaimed. "Nothing bad is happening to me. I'm fine!"

Hasan took a deep breath. He bravely stepped through the doorway and took several steps onto what was once the roadway called Central Park South, now completely reclaimed by weeds and grasses. He looked all around, nodding cautiously to himself, taking a few steps toward Manny. Then Hasan turned his face up to the sky. He gasped, his breath becoming ragged and unsteady.

"It's OK, I was just like you, the first time," Manny said reassuringly, as he rushed to stand by Hasan, his hand hovering inches from Hasan's elbow. Hasan looked like he was about to pass out, and Manny needed this outing to end well. "Here, Hasan, let's sit down."

The two men sat together on the ground. "It's interesting, isn't it?" Manny said conversationally, giving Hasan time to pull himself together. "Look at the horizon. The ground looks like it actually meets the sky."

Hasan glanced up at the horizon and then hastily back down at the ground. "It takes some getting used to," Manny added.

Hasan moved his hand wonderingly over the grass. He pushed his fingers down past a tuft of dead grass to the solid, hard asphalt which had once covered Central Park South. "Is this the blacktop that made up their roads?"

"Yeah, that's the theory. It's called ass-fault. They covered the ground with it, so their gasoline-powered cars could have a smooth surface," Manny replied.

"It's not water-permeable, though," Hasan remarked thoughtfully. "No wonder they had floods all the time. You'd think someone would have created a roadway that rainwater could pass through, so the soil could soak it up."

"I guess nobody cared about that," Manny replied. The two men were silent for a moment.

Hasan waved his hand in front of his face. "What's that?" he asked curiously.

"That? You mean the breeze?" Manny asked. "It's wind. Some days it blows hard, other days hardly at all."

"Why is that?" Hasan asked curiously. "Wouldn't you think it would be the same each day?"

"I don't know," Manny responded. "It just is." The two men continued to sit on the ground, talking about their surroundings. The color returned to Hasan's face.

"I feel better," Hasan said, "as long as I don't look up at the sky."

"Then don't look at it," Manny advised. "Eventually, you'll get used to it."

"What are those, Manny?" asked Hasan, pointing to two large black birds some distance away which were busily tearing with their claws and beaks at something lying on the ground.

"Those are birds," explained Manny. "They're afraid of people. I doubt they'll come any closer to us."

"But what are they doing?" persisted Hasan.

"It looks like they're eating," Manny replied hesitantly. To his detective's mind, the next logical question would be to ask what they were eating, and why it was dead. Manny didn't want to unsettle his friend even more by getting into a conversation about the food chain out in the wild.

Hasan considered for a moment. "I guess everything has to eat," he observed. "I'm not sure I want to know what they're eating, though."

To change the subject, Manny said, "The first time I went outside, it was such a surprise to me! Julio and I got to see the sun come up. That was pure magic."

Hasan had many questions about Manny's first venture outside, including why Julio had been there, but didn't want to appear nosy. Manny was his most important customer. Instead, he said, "Let's have a look at the site for the first shelter."

Together, the two men stood up, brushed themselves off and started across what had once been a busy street in midtown Manhattan. "If you feel light-headed," Manny said, "look down at your feet."

Once in the park, Manny looked around. "Would over here be OK?" he asked tentatively. "How do we know if this is a good spot?"

Hasan looked all around, shading his eyes with his hands against the fathomless blue sky. "This will do nicely," he said. "It's good and flat. These bushes and things, they won't be hard to clear out. And there are lots of cinderblocks from ruined buildings; we can use them for the foundations. We could build the first row of shelters right along here."

"Sounds good," Manny agreed. "We're close enough to the Colony that we could run out the doors and across to where we are standing in no time, in case we had to evacuate."

Hasan said curiously, "You really think we'll need to evacuate the Colony, Manny? We've never needed to do that before."

"Just because something has never happened before, doesn't mean that it won't happen," cautioned Manny. "Have you noticed how the homes inside the Colony all have cracks in the walls, little things here and there? And the broken water pipes – will that ever end? I've had reports this past week of another dozen flooded areas that will require resettling the occupants until the buildings can be repaired."

"Broken pipes and cracked walls are good for business, Manny," Hasan replied, laughing.

"It's not a laughing matter, though," Manny admonished.

"You're right, I shouldn't be laughing about it," responded Hasan. "There was another report just this morning. There's a whole row of houses with leaks, right down the line, including one that we repaired not that long ago. We'll have a crew over there to patch them up soon."

Manny blinked in surprise, but quickly recovered. Hasan could be referring to any row of houses. There was no reason to suspect that it might be in Aviva Johnson's neighborhood.

The two men headed across the street and were soon safely back inside, doors pulled firmly shut behind them. They clambered down the steps, Hasan's patched leather work boots echoing loudly.

"Stop by my office tomorrow, I'll have your contract drawn up by then," Manny said. "This will mean years of work for your company."

"Thank you, Manny! You know I appreciate you," Hasan said, bowing respectfully. "We'll start right away."

Manny bowed briefly. "Sounds good," he replied.

Manny's padlet buzzed once, lighting up cobalt blue around the edges, denoting a personal text from Zach of the lowest level of urgency. He turned the volume off and shoved the padlet back into his pocket. Zach would have to wait.

"What do you plan to do about the exit doors, Manny?" asked Hasan. "Aren't the outer doors chained shut, all over the Colony?"

"That's my next project," replied Manny. "It's a safety issue. I'll write up the orders to have the chains cut on all of the outside doors. Can your men take care of that?"

"Yeah, we can do that," replied Hasan. "I'll get right on it."

"Do you think you can get it done in the next few weeks?" asked Manny hopefully. "Before the next Council meeting?"

"That should work," replied Hasan. "You mean, before they can tell you not to do it?"

"Exactly," said Manny.

~ ~ ~ ~ ~ ~

"You did *what?!*" asked Mr. Jha incredulously. "Commissioner, are you trying to entice people into going outside? Where they may be injured or worse?"

"No, I am trying to keep people safe," Manny retorted. The other Council members were listening attentively. "Chaining them inside the Colony could turn a simple emergency into a full-on disaster."

"And what are these *'simple emergencies'* you keep referring to?" asked Mr. Jha rhetorically. "We have not had any emergencies in years!"

"It's been eight years since the earthquake, to be precise. There is no guarantee that there won't be any future emergencies," replied Manny. "Suppose we have another water main break? People could rush up the nearest stairwell to safety, rather than try to find the nearest fireproof-waterproof door." It was true, if there was a fire or flood, people often died of trampling injuries or smoke inhalation, as they searched frantically for a way out.

"Commissioner," Mr. Jha explained in the tone of voice he reserved for the profoundly stupid, "if you unlock all of the doors, people will go outside."

"You can't keep people locked inside forever," Manny warned. "They should be free to go outside if they want to."

"To become ill from the night air?" Ponderously, Mr. Jha stood, pointing his finger at Manny, one of his most cherished tricks from his long career as a prosecutor. "You, Commissioner! *You* will unleash havoc upon our children! Who knows what the long-term effects might be, or if they would even recover!"

"Long-terms effects of what?" retorted Manny. "You and your fear mongering are keeping this Colony on lock-down, when the need for that ended a long time ago."

"Perhaps we should have a committee set up to study the environment, see if it has changed in any way," suggested Mr. Jha.

"Are you kidding?" replied Manny incredulously. "I suggested that years ago! You re-interviewed every one of the scientists I chose, then brought on some new people, then dismissed the whole lot and started interviewing all over again. As I recall, this Council voted to table the study after two years of your *studying*. No! We're not wasting our time and taxpayers' money on another so-called 'study.' I've had about enough of your delays!"

Mr. Jha drew himself up to his full height. "*You've* had enough?" he said icily. "*You* are not in charge! This Council will govern our Colony, not the Police Commissioner!"

Mr. Jha looked around at his supporters, their faces uplifted towards him. "This meeting is adjourned!" he declared triumphantly. One of his cronies seconded the motion before Mr. Jha had finished speaking.

Manny gathered up his papers, swept them into his briefcase and stormed out of the meeting.

Walking towards home, Manny reflected on the meeting and his confrontation with Mr. Jha. It had gone well. There had been no need to orchestrate a confrontation; their argument had been both spontaneous and convincing.

The next time I see Mr. Jha, I'll tell him that I'm done trying to get the Council to approve building the shelters. Let him think he's convinced me. By the time we start building, it will be too late for him to stop me.

School let out for the summer. Children in the Colony attended school from early September through the end of June. Long ago, children had been needed on the family farm during the growing and harvest seasons, but centuries had passed since this was necessary. Even so, the custom was stubbornly popular; every time someone proposed a change in the law, it was voted down.

As promised, Manny crafted a series of very long and detailed articles describing the various municipal bonds offered by the Colony. Buried in mid-sentence in the last paragraph of each article was this: "purch 2 acres c park m stewart," and then the sentence continued on as if there had been no interruption.

True to Tyler's prediction, no one noticed, and over the course of the summer, the family amassed ten acres of land in the Central Park, close to the 59th Street subway entrance. Manny and Marya, Julio and Anna, Luis and Lucinda, Julie and Zach each owned an acre of land, as well as Dave and Jenny Wu.

Manny intended to give Dave and Jenny their deed as a surprise, in honor of their friendship and long history together. No one, least of all Manny, could have foreseen that this generous act would eventually lead to the most serious of consequences.

Chapter 7.

Did you hear** that Madame Elayna retired?" asked Anna, as the family sat down to Sunday dinner. "There was a segment on Catching Up Tonight," she added, referring to one of Lucinda's favorite evening talk shows.

"Retired!" exclaimed Marya. "That's too bad."

"She said in the interview that she was retiring because she'd accomplished her goals," Anna added. "What was it she said to you, Marya?"

"She said, 'I see for you, in time, a great blessing,'" Marya responded without hesitation. "She said, 'She will *know*. In the blackness of the tomb, it will be. When others hide and weep, she will be strong." Marya's voice was a flat singsong, as if she had repeated the words over and over many times.

"She had quite a flare for the dramatic," Manny said, uncomfortable with the direction the conversation had taken. Marya had never mentioned Madame Elayna again after their visit, although when he was looking for a paper clip a few weeks later in her desk drawer, Manny had come across a piece of paper on which Marya had written down exactly what Madame had said to her.

"Did you know that she was an actress, before becoming a fortune teller?" Manny added casually, addressing the table as a whole.

"I guess those skills came in handy," observed Julio.

"Before that, she was a thief, serving time in jail for shoplifting," Manny added conversationally, ignoring Marya's obvious dismay.

"How did she get to be so popular?" asked Anna.

"She had rich clients who paid her well to tell them what they wanted to hear," said Manny dismissively. "With us, though, she didn't do her homework. She thought we had more than one child."

"Maybe we will," retorted Marya stubbornly.

"What did she say to you, Manny, anything?" Anna asked.

"Not much," Manny replied with a twinge of discomfort. "I don't recall her exact words."

"She told him, 'A single candle lights a thousand flames, Commissioner, and yet you will not live to see it,'" Marya responded without hesitation.

"That's conveniently vague. It could mean anything," replied Manny. He shrugged, his eyes on his dinner plate as he busied himself with his fork and knife.

~ ~ ~ ~ ~ ~

Manny got up from his desk chair and stretched, arms high over his head, as Dr. Patel had advised. "Don't just sit behind your desk all day," she warned, "get up and stretch, walk around. Sciatica only gets worse, if you don't keep moving."

He decided to walk around the office for a few minutes, following Dr. Patel's advice. Going down the hall past the task force, he was surprised to see that PriscillaJain Miller's desk was empty. PJ was a talented detective who worked on cold cases. She had been out for three days the preceding week as well. Detectives are a hard-working and competitive bunch; it was rare for a detective to take any time off at all. The official reason given for her absence was "personal matters," which generally referred to problems like childcare or marital issues, rather than actual illness.

"Good morning, Agnes. What's going on with PJ?" Manny asked his secretary when she came in with his morning cup of tea.

"I don't know," she replied, avoiding his eyes as she put down the cup of tea.

"Off the record?" he suggested softly, leaning forward in a conspiratorial way.

"Well," she said in a half-whisper, "rumor has it that she miscarried. So sad," she added, shaking her head.

Having seen firsthand how a miscarriage could affect a woman, he nodded. "That's a tough one," he agreed.

After Agnes left his office, he found that he was unable to concentrate on the stack of memos and emails waiting for him. Too many of their women experienced this terrible loss. It was not only devastating for the would-be mothers, as he knew first-hand from watching his own wife deal with her grief and postpartum depression; it was also very bad from an economic point of view, causing hours of lost time in the workplace.

He texted the Mayor.

Manny: *I've been looking into the growing number of absences in the workplace among women of childbearing age. The rate of miscarriages has risen dramatically in the past decade. Is there anyone in your office looking into this?*

Mayor: *No, that's not a problem for this office. Check with the Department of Health.*

Manny reflected for a moment. A request from the Police Commissioner to the Department of Health concerning miscarriages was not likely to get results. He decided to hologram Dr. Patel.

"Monica, it's Manny." They were on a first-name basis, not just because she was his personal physician, but also because they had known each other for most of their lives, having gone to school together as children.

"How would you like to be a special liaison to the Commissioner's Office?" he asked. "There's a growing problem with the high rate of miscarriages in our women. I want to make sure the Office of Public Health is aware of this and is looking into the matter."

"Well, I do have my practice, you know. But if it's a part-time position, sure, I'd like that," she replied.

"Good!" he said. "Nigel, my aide, he'll be in touch with you to complete the paperwork and introduce you to our people over there. You can let me know what you find out."

~ ~ ~ ~ ~ ~

It was evening, after the family had eaten dinner. Luis and Lucinda had gone home early; Lucinda was exhausted and wanted to lie down. Marya had kept a plate of food warm for Manny in the oven. The Stewart family had in their home one of the few private ovens in the Colony. Most people rented space in bakers' ovens at the end of the day, when the bakers were finished with the days' baking, hurrying home to their families before their roasted casseroles could cool off.

Marya sat down with Manny while he ate. "I have such exciting news," she announced. "Manny, you'll never guess! Zach has two friends over! They're upstairs in his room with him now, playing video games."

40

Manny's eyebrows went up. "Seriously?" he asked. "Wow, that is wonderful news. Who are they, do you know?"

"No, I don't know anything else about them," she replied. "We'll have to wait until they leave to ask Zach."

A few minutes later, two young men clambered unsteadily down the stairs. The large, gracefully curved wooden staircase in the center of the foyer often puzzled people who had never seen anything other than a metal spiral staircase with triangular shaped steps, the kind employed by builders throughout the Colony because a spiral staircase uses very little floor space. The two boys clomped clumsily down the wide steps, holding tightly to the carved, highly polished oak banister.

Manny looked closely at the boys, but couldn't see much of their faces. They both were wearing the new style of hooded sweatshirt called "Scuba," so popular now among the young people, which zipped up the front into a high collar that covered the mouth, ending right beneath the nose.

The hood of the sweatshirt was close-fitting and came down low in front, nearly covering the eyebrows. In effect, the Scuba, when zipped up, covered all of the face except for the nose and eyes.

Obviously, law enforcement objected strongly to this new fashion, as the security cameras all over the communal spaces in the Colony often could not triangulate identifications with so little to go on.

The boys were large, which surprised Manny. Zach was tall for his age, although whipcord slender. Most boys Zach's age weren't as tall. *I wonder if they're older than Zach,* Manny thought.

He started to get up, but Marya put her hand on his and said, "Wait, let's let Zach tell us about them. We don't want to scare them away." Reluctantly, he stayed in the kitchen with Marya as the boys, who had not noticed the two curious parents peering at them from the kitchen, walked through the foyer on their way out.

"Zach! Come downstairs!" called Marya. His door opened, music blasting as he closed it behind him.

"Tell us!" said Marya, smiling warmly. "Who are these two boys?"

"They're just some guys I met at the school yard. Playing ball. Their names are Prithviraj Gopalaswami and Edward Oh," replied Zach.

"What grade are they in?" asked Manny casually.

"They're both a year ahead of me. Eddie is repeating a grade," replied Zach. "They're cousins. Can I go now? I have homework to do."

"Just a minute," said Manny. "How exactly did you meet them, these two older boys?"

"Why?" asked Zach. "You think because they want to be my friends, there must be something wrong?" He scowled, turning to Marya. "Can I go upstairs?"

Marya nodded, and Zach fled to the sanctity of his bedroom, music blaring briefly as he opened the door.

"Just be happy he has friends," Marya admonished. "This is a good thing."

"Maybe," Manny said. "But I want to know more about them."

"Manny, not everything requires an investigation," Marya scolded. "They're just kids."

"OK, maybe you're right," Manny conceded, but only to silence her. He had a bad feeling about Zach's new friends.

Manny had been raised by a detective. His father had risen through the ranks and made a reputation for himself as a detective before attaining the role of Chief of Police. Patrick Stewart was an alcoholic, professionally a hard man with an iron fist, and an abusive, sometimes sadistic father. In the evenings, he would come home and drink while talking to Manny about his job, the criminals he and his men caught, how they would interrogate them for hours to wear them down, how they would trick them into confessing.

From about the age of nine, Manny had listened very carefully to these tales, storing away all the little details about various crimes and how people had gotten caught. By the time he was Zach's age, Manny was an accomplished thief. Although he later learned to think like a detective, he still could think like a thief, a skill which continued to serve him well in his career.

Manny lay awake long after Marya had fallen asleep. She wasn't worried about Zach's new friends, but Manny knew from experience that any kid could get caught up in a bad crowd and wind up in a lot of trouble.

Gopalaswami, Manny repeated to himself with a growing sense of unease. He turned over, careful not to wake Marya, trying to find a more comfortable position. There was a gang called the Skulls which was a very small, highly organized criminal organization run by the Gopalaswami family. The members were all related to one another. They were involved in theft, drug trafficking and other unsavory pursuits.

Still, it was a fairly common Indian last name, and most of them were not criminals at all. They were upstanding citizens, paying their taxes and not causing any trouble.

Over the next few weeks, Zach saw his new friends Raj and Eddie almost every day, often playing ball with them in the school yard or going over to their houses to play video games.

"They were over again this afternoon. I heard them in the kitchen, eating lunch," Marya said, referring to Raj and Eddie as she and Manny were out running together. "Then they left to play ball at the school yard."

"At least he's not in his room all day," Manny remarked. "It's not healthy to spend the summer holed up in his bedroom."

"These boys just might be a good influence on him," said Marya over her shoulder. She tried not to outrun Manny, who ran more slowly these days. "Zach's very smart, but he lacks motivation. Maybe you could talk to him about it."

Manny groaned inwardly. "He lacks discipline, Marya," he said. "We need to teach him to apply himself."

"Maybe he just needs a little fatherly encouragement! You know, Manny, you could spend a little more time with him," she scolded.

"The job doesn't leave me a lot of free time," he replied smoothly. "I've got a lot on my mind."

"He'll be grown soon, it goes by so fast," she replied. "We have so little time left to teach him everything he needs to know."

Manny also was calculating how long it would be before his son was seventeen, a full adult in the Colony, but for different reasons than his wife. He was more than glad to see their home emerge as they rounded a curve in the passageway, effectively ending their conversation.

Manny's heart swelled with pride as the mansion came into view, windows shining in the late afternoon light. The Stewart mansion had been created from two separate townhouses purchased by Patrick decades earlier and renovated into one house. It was one of the largest homes in the Colony, an astonishing thirty feet wide, not including the tiny yard on either side of the building. Inside, there was a front parlor, a library, a study, a large kitchen with a huge table that could seat ten people, and Anna's office. Upstairs, there were many bedrooms, including the master suite, which had its own private bathroom.

There were 840 miles of subway tunnels, including 472 platforms, in the Colony of New York. In the nicer neighborhoods, like Manny's, the subway tunnels were spacious and wide, as much as 50 feet wide with ceilings as high as 18 feet. In the less desirable neighborhoods, passageways could be so narrow that two people could not walk side by side.

"I've got a Council meeting later," Manny reminded his wife as they stopped outside of the house to catch their breath. Manny, hands on his knees, was bent over, winded. He'd put on a little weight around his middle, since he'd been dealing with sciatica.

"Do you want dinner first?" Marya asked.

"I'm not hungry, I'll eat when I get home," Manny replied smoothly. There was something he wanted to take care of, and just enough time before the meeting to do it.

Chapter 8.

Manny closed the study door and sat down at the ancient oak desk which had been his father's. Opening up his padlet, he navigated to the police AI system and said quietly, "Find background on Prithviraj Gopalaswami and Edward Oh." A moment later, the results were projected onto the study wall.

There was almost nothing on Edward Oh besides his name, age, address, etc. He had no arrest record. His father's sister, though, had married into the Gopalaswami family, and not long after that, his father and two uncles joined the Skulls and started having trouble with the law. They had long rap sheets filled with petty theft, forgery and other lesser crimes.

Prithviraj Gopalaswami, on the other hand, came from a tight-knit and rather industrious criminal family. Raj's uncles, along with his father Deepak, were gang members with long arrest records. Raj's grandfather Amir and his brothers had also been members of the Skulls, all four of them dead before the age of forty.

Manny read the information about Raj's family with concern. *At least Raj doesn't have a record,* Manny thought. *Not yet, anyway.*

"Go back," Manny said to AI. "Show me the family tree."

Raj's grandfather, Amir Gopalaswami, had married Edith Perez, of Venezuelan descent. Amir's new father-in-law took Amir under his wing, teaching him how to run the family business, a loosely organized gang of petty criminals who called themselves Tocoron.

After his father-in-law's death, it was Amir Gopalaswami who seized control. He took the gang to the next level, turning the unruly group of Venezuelan brothers and cousins into a highly organized and efficient gang with lieutenants and captains, with himself at the helm. He renamed the gang the Skulls.

Manny was about to close up his padlet when the last name of Amir Gopalaswami's wife, Edith Perez, caught his attention. *I've seen that family name somewhere,* Manny thought. He sat back in his chair, hand rubbing his chin. *Isn't that the name of the classmate who kissed Zach at school?*

"Show me the family tree for Edith Perez Gopalaswami," he said. "Going back how far?" AI prompted him. "Five generations," Manny replied, picking a number at random.

Manny saw from the Perez family tree that Edith Perez Gopalaswami and Azura Perez, the girl who had kissed Zach, were related. Azura was actually a distant cousin of Raj and his siblings.

That might mean something, Manny mused. Then again, if you went back far enough, everyone was related to just about everyone else. There were close to 6,500 citizens in the Colony, living and intermarrying for generations since the great hurricane three hundred years earlier. Still, Manny felt uneasy. There was something wrong here, he could feel it.

Manny texted his aide, Nigel:

Manny: *Set up lunch with the Chief for me, would you please? Today, or tomorrow.*
Nigel: *I'll do it right away.*

Chief Joseph O'Reilly, now in his early 60's and retired, had been Manny's boss when he first joined the police force after graduating from the Academy. He had been hard on Manny at first, but gradually, the two came to respect each other as Manny gained experience and became a detective. Chief O'Reilly had been instrumental in picking Manny to be the next Deputy Commissioner. Manny and the Chief often got together over lunch to discuss issues involving the Colony. Maybe the Chief would know something about these two families.

Nigel: *The Chief's not feeling well. I scheduled lunch for next Monday.*
Manny: *Thanks, that's fine.*

Disappointed, Manny sat for a moment lost in thought. Then he glanced at the clock. He had a Council meeting, and it was growing late. In a hurry, he closed up his padlet and left.

When Manny arrived at the Council meeting at exactly 6:30 pm, it was already in session. Not an actual Council member since becoming Commissioner, he nonetheless attended many of the meetings as a guest. He wondered if they had started early as a subtle snub.

The Council was made up of thirteen people: the Council President, eight Elders, and four junior members. Mr. Jha had a cozy relationship with four of the Council members. They regularly voted with him, giving him a 5-4 majority. Junior members were not permitted to vote.

The meeting droned on and on. Manny waited patiently until the last topic had been discussed and voted upon. He stood, politely waiting to be recognized.

Mr. Jha and his cronies immediately began shuffling papers, putting them into briefcases, talking among themselves and generally pretending not to notice the Commissioner, who was standing in their midst.

Finally, the President of the Council said, "Commissioner, you have the floor."

Mr. Jha grimaced knowingly. "*Again*," he muttered loudly enough for all to hear. His cronies smirked, shifting restlessly in their chairs.

"I'd like to bring an important issue to the attention of the Council," Manny began.

"Let me guess. The need for an emergency evacuation plan?" asked Mr. Jha sarcastically in an undertone.

"No, actually, I'd like to table that discussion for the time being," Manny replied mildly, enjoying the surprised look on Mr. Jha's face. "This has to do with the falling birth rate in the Colony."

Manny went on to explain how he had appointed Dr. Patel to be his Special Liaison to the Office of Public Health. Dr. Patel would be talking to the scientists there about a number of issues, especially about the rising number of miscarriages.

"For the past three years, we have seen an average of 1.1 children born per family, a rate that cannot be sustained," Manny explained. "In a generation or two, there will be far too few people of working age to support our economy. Dr. Patel, whom I appointed to act as Special Liaison, will discuss this with the scientists at the Office of Public Health and report back to this Council. In the meantime, maybe we can come up with some practical solutions."

There was a pause, as people considered this new topic. "Any suggestions?" Manny asked. "How do we encourage couples to have more children? We can't pretend this will fix itself."

"We could start a public service campaign, praising women who have more children," suggested one member.

"Good, that's good," said Manny, nodding. "Anybody else?"

"Make abortion illegal?" suggested a man sitting in the back row.

"Absolutely not!" replied a woman, as several Council members looked up in alarm. "That's not to be considered."

"We could encourage giving up an unwanted baby for adoption, you know, making it heroic, an act of compassion for families that can't have another child," suggested another.

"We could reward women who have more than one child," suggested another. "Reduce their taxes, add a stipend for their living expenses, that sort of thing."

"How about a four-day work week?" suggested one woman. "You know, more time at home, less stress ... maybe it would help."

"We could require married women to have children," suggested a man, who was stunned by the speedy reaction of the women around him. "You're going to start a war, with that one," warned a Councilwoman.

"That's OK, we are all able to speak freely here," said Manny blandly, keeping them all on track. "Obviously, some ideas are more palatable than others. We're going to continue to discuss this issue over the coming months."

The meeting adjourned. Mr. Jha approached Manny as he was getting ready to leave. "Commissioner, a word, please?" he said.

The two men walked out of the building. "I'm curious," said Mr. Jha. "Why did you table the discussion of your little evacuation plan?"

Smiling inwardly, Manny replied, "I think it can wait. Maybe indefinitely. The Council has other, more pressing issues right now."

"You're serious, you're letting it go?" he asked in disbelief.

"I'm putting it aside," Manny said, struggling not to laugh at the look on Mr. Jha's face. For the past several years, Manny had broached the subject of his evacuation plan whenever he attended a meeting. Now, it seemed all that was over. Mr. Jha's look of disappointment was comical; he'd wanted so badly to see Manny defeated.

Mr. Jha looked shrewdly at Manny. "You're up to something, Commissioner, aren't you?" asked the old lawyer. "I can see it in your face."

Manny turned to him, his expression utterly blank. It was a skill he had learned as a child, so his face could not be read by his father, the canny Chief of Police.

"Good evening to you, Councilman," said Manny, turning to go. He did not bow, an omission that was not lost on Mr. Jha.

~ ~ ~ ~ ~ ~

"Thanks for joining me, Chief," Manny said. He stood as the Chief walked towards their table, a sign of respect for the older man. The two men bowed to each other.

"It's been awhile, Manny!" said Chief Joseph O'Reilly, sitting down at the table.

"How are you, Joe? My aide said you were feeling a little under the weather the other day," Manny asked politely.

"Oh, it was nothing," replied the Chief, "just a little dizziness. What's good here?" he asked, eyeing the restaurant menu which was scrolling across the table top.

"Try the fish casserole, it's delicious," Manny said.

"Fish? You eat that stuff?" asked the Chief dubiously. "They're real fish, right?"

"Yeah, they're actual fish," Manny confirmed. "The fish farm is doing great. You should try it, you'd like it."

The Chief made a noncommittal noise, scanning the rest of the menu. The two men placed their orders from the table app, and settled back in their chairs.

"So. What brings us together today?" asked the Chief. "Something on your mind, Commissioner?"

"Actually, yes. I'm a little concerned about my boy," Manny replied.

"Zach?" asked the Chief, surprised. "How old is he now?"

"He's just turned fourteen, and will be starting ninth grade this fall," Manny replied. "He's kind of a loner, always has been, at least until this summer."

The Chief nodded. In his sixties, the Chief was still sharp as ever, listening closely to Manny.

"He made two friends this summer, Edward Oh and Prithviraj Gopalaswami. They're going to the high school this fall. They're cousins, one of them is repeating tenth grade. There's something off about them, Joe," Manny explained.

"Let me guess. Nothing you can put your finger on, just a hunch," the Chief said. All good detectives had this sixth sense.

"Yeah," Manny agreed. "Maybe they're just kids who like playing ball together, but I don't think so. They're both older than Zach, and yet they defer to him as if he's the guy in charge. It seems phony to me. I'm worried that they're playing him, building him up to think he's a big shot, so they can draw him into the Skulls."

"And their motive for doing that?" asked the Chief quietly.

"That's the thing. I can only think of one reason, to humiliate me. If my son joins the Skulls, the person who brings him in will gain credibility and prestige in the gang," Manny replied. "But what would happen to Zach, if he joined them?"

"I can see why you're worried," the Chief replied. "Once he's in the Skulls, they would pass him around like a trophy. How impressionable is Zach?"

"He's pretty smart, but he's also at the age where he's angry at me most of the time," Manny replied. "Embarrassing me looks good to him."

The Chief looked at him shrewdly for a moment, remembering another teenage boy who had been angry enough with his father to set out to embarrass him. Not only was Joseph O'Reilly Manny's friend and mentor, he had known his father Patrick Stewart for many years. They had been close friends. Teenage Manny had done his best to embarrass his father, as the Chief well knew. Patrick had once locked Manny in a jail cell overnight, when he was caught stealing. *Like father, like son,* Manny thought, surprised by a twinge of guilt.

"What do you think, Joe? Am I seeing motive where there's nothing but shadows?" Manny asked, to turn the conversation back to Zach.

"That depends," the Chief said. "Tell me more about your relationship with the Skulls. Do any of them hold a grudge against you?"

"There's no relationship; I don't even know any of them. I researched them, and didn't see anything obvious," Manny replied. "The Skulls are run by the Gopalaswami family, going back to my dad's generation. Amir Gopalaswami married Edith Perez, and when her father died, Amir assumed control."

"The Perez family?" repeated the Chief, carefully controlling his voice. "The Venezuelans?"

Chapter 9.

"Yeah, that's the name AI came up with," confirmed Manny. "The family is Venezuelan. Why, do you know something?"

The Chief sat silently for a moment. "Maybe," he said hesitantly. "Amir Perez, along with his brothers, his wife's brothers and her cousins, ran a thriving little enterprise before they had a run-in with your old man. You know your dad wasn't always a straight-shooter, right, Manny?"

Manny nodded. He had known from childhood that some of Patrick's dealings were illegal, although he didn't know any of the details.

"These guys, they called themselves the Skulls. They went from shoplifting a few items here and there, nothing very noteworthy, to hijacking entire deliveries. We tried to crack down on them, but it was really your old man who brought them down. Patrick arrested a bunch of them, and then let them go on condition that they pay a kickback to him every time they pulled a job," the Chief explained.

"Uh-huh," Manny said, wondering where this was leading.

"Finally, Amir Perez got tired of paying off Patrick. After Patrick stopped by to pick up his money for the month, Amir sent two men after him. They beat him up pretty bad, grabbed the money, and ran. You were just a baby then, Manny, you wouldn't remember. Patrick arrested both of them, and interrogated them for days until they turned on their boss. Patrick had Amir arrested for organizing the attempted murder of a police officer. He did twenty years in prison, and your dad was promoted to detective. So yeah, you could say there's a history."

Manny sat silently, appalled.

"The gang is mostly Indian now, right? They're not big on vendettas," said the Chief kindly.

"There's something else," Manny said slowly. "Before school let out this spring, there was an incident. A girl grabbed Zach in the stairwell when classes were changing and kissed him, right there in front of everyone. The principal wanted to suspend him."

"How'd that go?" asked the Chief.

"Tyler made short work of it," Manny replied grimly, referring to his lawyer Tyler Watkins. "He turned it around so the girl was expelled and warned to keep away from Zach, or we would prosecute her."

Joe snorted appreciatively. "He's a good lawyer, that one."

"The girl's father texted me not long after it happened, saying he wanted to meet," Manny continued. "I told him to contact Tyler. At the time, I thought it was a simple attempt to extort money from my family. Now, I'm not so sure."

"And the girl's name?" asked Joe.

"Azura Perez," Manny replied.

~ ~ ~ ~ ~ ~

"Sorry I'm late. Have you eaten yet?" Manny asked Marya, as he came home several nights later. He took off his jacket in the foyer, dropping his briefcase on the marble-topped table.

"No, we're waiting for Zach," answered Marya. "He's on his way now. He was playing ball with his friends."

Manny chuckled. "That's a first," he noted.

The door opened and Zach, flushed and sweaty, came into the foyer. "Hey," he said, his mouth covered by the Scuba hood.

"Zach, if you're going to be late, please let your mother know, OK?" Manny said. Zach mumbled something unintelligible.

Lucinda and Luis, who had been in the study with Julio and Anna, joined them as the family assembled for dinner.

"Please take off your sweatshirt," Manny said to Zach as they slid into their seats, Manny at the head of the table, Zach on one side and Marya on the other.

"Nah, I want it on," he replied easily.

"At least unzip it," Manny insisted. "How are you going to eat with that hood covering your face?" The Scuba hood, designed to leave only the nose and eyes uncovered, made eating impossible.

Zach did not answer. He reached for the plate of sliced bread next to him. Manny exchanged glances with Marya, who frowned. Her eyes said, *Let it go.*

52

Manny turned to Julio and asked, "How was work today?" Julio had assumed more and more of the responsibilities for the family business, as Luis grew closer to retirement. Manny was a silent partner, and less involved than Julio and Luis.

"Yeah, you know, not bad," Julio replied, ladling potato and purple leek soup into a mug. "Did you make this, Mama?"

Lucinda nodded. "Yes, Anna and I made it this afternoon," she said.

"It smells really good," Julio said, sniffing appreciatively.

Zach also ladled some soup into his mug. Manny watched from the corner of his eye as Zach tried to spoon the soup into his mouth, which was completely covered by the Scuba. As anticipated, he soon made a mess of things.

"Zach! Unzip that sweatshirt before you get soup all over it," he admonished.

"No," said Zach calmly, putting down his spoon.

"What did you say to me?" asked Manny. He had not raised his voice, but everyone heard the implied menace in it. Around the table, conversation ceased.

Zach cleared his throat. "I believe I said no," he repeated insolently. He picked up a slice of bread and tore off a piece, pushing it into his mouth and chewing industriously.

"Is there a reason why you refuse to do this simple thing?" Manny said. His voice was still soft, but beneath the table, his hands were two iron fists.

Zach ignored him. Infuriated, Manny stood up. "Either you take off that ridiculous sweatshirt this instant, or you will be grounded for a week, young man," he exclaimed.

Zach also stood up, facing his father. Zach was growing as only a teenage boy can grow, at least an inch taller than at the beginning of the summer, forcing Manny to look up into Zach's face. Manny was surprised not only by his defiance, but also his composure. When had this young pup grown confident enough to challenge him?

Manny's face turned a dark shade of red. "Take it off, or I'll take it off for you!" he threatened. His hand gripped Zach's forearm.

Zach tried to pull his arm out of his father's grip, but Manny, a veteran of many street fights in his early days as a cop, only pulled him closer. He leaned over and said softly, so no one else could hear, "You can't win this, Zach. Take it off."

When Zach did not respond, Manny reached with both hands for the zipper and unzipped the sweatshirt, yanking it down past Zach's shoulders.

There was a collective gasp from everyone seated at the dinner table.

Zach had shaved the front half of his head from ear to ear. His shoulder length bright red curls still covered the back of his head. Beneath the kitchen lights, his round semi-bald pate glistened, flushed bright pink with embarrassment.

"Who did this to you?" demanded Manny, thinking that perhaps Zach had been bullied.

"Nobody! I mean, I wanted to do it," answered Zach.

Lucinda gently cleared her throat. When she spoke, her voice was carefully modulated. "Zach, why don't you tell us what you were thinking, when you shaved off your hair. And Manny. Please. Both of you. Sit down."

Reluctantly, Manny and Zach sat down, to the relief of the rest of the family. All eyes were on Zach.

"It was sort of a loyalty test. You know, like in the old-time Mafia," explained Zach. "It was Raj's older brother's idea. He said that if we're really gonna be blood brothers, then we'd have to share a sign, like shaving off our hair."

"Wait. Raj and Eddie did this, too?" asked Manny.

"Yeah," replied Zach. "Actually, it was Raj's sister who shaved off our hair. She has these clipper things."

"Well. It's just hair, and hair grows back," said Lucinda dismissively. "Pass me the bread, would you please, Zach?"

But Manny wasn't about to let this go.

"Tell me more about this loyalty test," he said. He'd heard plenty about loyalty tests among gang members, but these boys were children. Zach was going into ninth grade; Raj and Eddie were going into tenth grade. Gangs usually recruited boys who were at least a year or two older. Besides, he'd never seen a haircut like this one, and Manny, as Commissioner, knew all of the gangs' identifiers.

"Not much to tell," said Zach gruffly. "Raj said either you're with me or you're not."

"So it's a club? A brotherhood?" asked Manny.

"Yeah, we're like a family," Zach responded, a note of defiance creeping into his voice. "They're always glad to see me."

The hair on the back of Manny's neck stood up. Without using the word "gang," his son had described perfectly why most young people choose to join a gang. Still, he cautioned himself, there was no point in making assumptions. *Assumptions can get you killed,* he thought, something he'd learned at the Police Academy.

When dinner was over, Lucinda followed Manny into the study.

"I'm concerned about Zach," she said, settling herself in one of the two leather club chairs. "He's growing up, Manny. He's going to test you, push your buttons. It's all part of maturing. You're going to need a longer fuse! Remember, you're the father. It's your job to guide him into becoming a good man. Don't let him get under your skin like that."

Lucinda had been a loving presence in Manny's life since he was eleven years old. He always listened to her advice, even when he didn't like what he heard.

"Are you aware that when you were speaking to Zach, your hands were clenched into two tight fists?" she asked him.

He shook his head wonderingly. He'd have to do a better job of hiding his anger.

"Did you see how he stood up to confront me? He's taller than me now, and he wants to be sure I know it," Manny replied. "It's a challenge to my authority."

Lucinda nodded. "And you'd be wise to ignore that. Suppose instead of reacting the way you did, you hadn't said much of anything. He probably would have been disappointed at your lack of reaction."

Manny sighed. "I want to be a good father," he said heavily. "Somehow, I never get it right."

"When was the last time you two did something together, for fun?" she asked. Manny tried to remember, but nothing came to mind. "Why not spend some time with him when there's no crisis?" she suggested.

Upstairs later that night, Marya also had much to say about the confrontation at dinner. "I don't understand," she said. "Why was it such a big deal? After all, it's his hair, not yours."

"It's not just the hair. Didn't you hear the way he talked to me?" Manny replied. "He defied me! I can't let that go."

"Why not?" she countered. "What's so horrible? There's lots more like this coming, as he gets older. You can't blow up at him over every little thing."

"Every little thing!" he repeated, surprised. "Marya, look at him, he's half bald! What would you have done?"

"I'd have let it go. You don't want our son to be a little wimp, do you?" Marya continued. "Tonight I saw a young man who is making choices on his own instead of asking his parents if it's OK. We want to nurture that independence, not squash it."

Manny sighed with frustration. He had it all wrong, as usual. It was on the tip of his tongue to tell her about his lunch with the Chief and the research he had done on Raj and Eddie, but as much as he wanted to convince her that he was right, he also didn't want to worry her unnecessarily. She'd just pester him with her questions and her fears, and he'd have to calm her down, reassure her that nothing bad would happen. Just thinking about it was exhausting.

For a fleeting moment, he dearly missed Naz, who had always known what to do. He carefully squelched the thought as disloyal. Besides, maybe Marya was right. Maybe he had over-reacted.

"OK, I'll try it your way," Manny said reluctantly. "I'll spend more time with him."

"What do you think you'd like to do with Zach, just the two of you?" she asked.

"Oh, uh, I'll ask him if he wants to go out for a run with me. He runs, right?" Manny asked. Actually, he wasn't sure if his son liked to run or not.

Marya chuckled. "Yes, he runs. That's a good idea, Manny, the two of you running together."

It was a simple decision. Yet, sometimes even the simplest of decisions can have all sorts of consequences.

Chapter 10.

Zach, **get your** shoes and your padlet. We're going for a run," said Manny after his morning cup of coffee. Julio, sitting at the kitchen table across from Anna, snorted with laughter. Unfortunately, his mouth was full of coffee at the time, which spurted alarmingly out of his nose.

Manny turned to Julio, handing him a large silver maple leaf, used everywhere in the colony in place of cloth napkins, from the basket on the table. "What's so funny?"

"You'll see," said Julio, mopping coffee off his shirt. Anna pressed her lips together firmly to keep from laughing.

Zach went into the foyer to find his cap and running shoes, while Manny sat down on a sofa in the front parlor to put his shoes on.

"You boys have fun," Julio called from the kitchen. Manny could hear Julio and Anna in the kitchen, whispering and laughing.

It didn't take long for Manny to see what was so funny. His young son was not only taller than he was, he was also quite a bit faster. Manny, always mindful not to wake up his sciatica, ran slowly in a kind of plodding, methodical stride. Zach, on the other hand, ran like a marathon runner, easily and very fast.

"Zach, wait up," Manny said, breathing hard. Zach looked over his shoulder and stopped, waiting for his father to catch up. Manny saw that Zach wasn't even out of breath. "Do you run in gym class?"

"Yeah, we all do. It's required," Zach replied. "Here, I'll slow down." He did a good job of it for several minutes, but then returned to his natural pace. To amuse himself, he began to run long circles around Manny, doubling back and taking off again.

"Let's stop here, we can pick up some sandwiches for lunch," Manny said, glad that there was a place to sit down. He stopped, hands on his knees, bent over and breathing hard. His left leg streaked a warning pain down to his heel, but he ignored it.

They went into the sandwich shop. It was mostly a takeout restaurant, but there were a few booths for customers. Zach sat down while Manny ordered lunch at the counter, then came to join Zach at the table while they waited.

Seated in a booth directly across from them, a man in his forties was sitting next to a young girl with very long blond hair and large hoop earrings. The girl was wearing a skimpy denim dress and boots, sitting too close to the man. *Lovebirds,* Manny thought idly, glancing at Zach. He had noticed them, too.

The girl began to stand up, saying, "I need to use the bathroom."

The man reached up, hooking his finger through one of her hoop earrings and pulling down firmly. "You'll wait 'til I say so," he said.

"Quit it!" cried the girl, scratching his hand with her long fingernails. She shook him off and stood up. "I'll be right back, I swear!"

The man grabbed a handful of her long blond hair and yanked, forcing her back down to the seat next to him. With one fist twisted firmly in her hair, he calmly finished his sandwich.

Manny judged the girl to be somewhere between fifteen and twenty years old, and that was a problem. It wasn't only that the relationship between the two of them looked to be abusive, although that was bad enough. There were strict laws in the Colony protecting minors. If the girl was underage, not yet seventeen years old, then he might have stumbled upon a situation.

Manny was not in uniform and had no badge with him. He could pull out his padlet and call for backup, but by the time it arrived, the couple would be gone. Still, he couldn't just ignore what was happening.

Zach had noticed, too. "Dad! Did you see?" he asked urgently in an undertone. Manny thought fast. His boy was young, but tall for his age. He was strong, too. It just might work.

"Zach, how would you like to be my deputy?" he asked. Zach, surprised, nodded. "OK, I hereby deputize you to be a police officer for the next hour, to follow my instructions and do what I say. Do you understand?" Zach nodded.

"You're to stand in the doorway and make sure that those two don't leave, got it?" he said to Zach.

"You mean grab them, if they try and run?" Zach asked.

"Don't touch them unless you have to, the girl especially." Manny didn't want anyone getting hurt, and the girl looked very thin and fragile. "Just engage them in conversation, block their way if you have to."

Manny was to reflect later that the look in his son's eyes as he took his place in the doorway was exactly the look he wanted to see in his young police officers' eyes: alert, excited, unafraid.

Manny stood up and walked over to the booth. "I suggest that you remove your fist from her hair," he said pleasantly.

"Oh, yeah?" responded the man. "And who are *you*?"

"Manny Stewart," he replied. "I live not far from here."

"Well, Manny Stewart, I suggest you mind your own damn business and run along home," he replied with a nasty sneer. He twisted his hand more firmly in the girl's long hair, prompting her to grab with both hands at his fist, struggling against him.

Manny sat down across from them, pulling out his padlet. "How old are you, young lady?" he asked calmly.

"That ain't none of your business," replied the man belligerently. He started to get up.

Manny said, "I wouldn't do that, if I were you." He pressed a button on his padlet, which connected instantly to the precinct front desk.

"Commissioner, what is your request?" responded Gilda, the precinct's AI.

"Desk Sergeant," declared Manny.

Instantly, the desk sergeant picked up. "Commissioner? Everything OK there, Sir?"

"I've got a situation here, a domestic dispute," said Manny, eyeing the two people across from him. The man had let go of the girl's hair and now both of them were standing, uncertainly eyeing the doorway where Zach was stationed, arms akimbo, cap pulled down low over his eyebrows. "Send a couple of street cops here right away."

"On their way," replied the sergeant, as Gilda instantly pinpointed Manny's location.

"You're some kinda police?" asked the man suspiciously, eyes narrowing.

"Something like that," responded Manny. He stood up, reaching across the table for the man's forearm. The girl slipped past him like an eel, running straight for the door. Manny, busy subduing the man by twisting his arm up behind his back, heard a crash, followed by a high-pitched scream.

"Zach?" he called without turning around.

"We're good," replied his son.

"Young lady, come over here," Manny said to the girl. She seemed fascinated by Zach, who acted with such authority, but seemed quite young, not unlike herself. She returned to the table.

"Now," said Manny. "Tell me how old you are."

"Sixteen," she whispered to him, eyes round and wide. Through the doorway, Manny could see two street cops rapidly making their way towards the restaurant.

"Are you with this man because you want to be, or because he won't let you leave?" asked Manny.

"Both, sorta," she whispered, glancing at her tormentor.

"Shut up, will ya!" he said angrily to her, trying to take a step towards her. Manny held on firmly.

The two officers strode into the restaurant. "Commissioner," they said, saluting.

"You're the *Police Commissioner*?" asked the man, the realization dawning too late in his eyes.

"That's right, today's your lucky day," replied Manny. He turned to the two street cops. "Put cuffs on this one, then take them both down to the station. I'll testify. I saw him pulling her hair and preventing her from leaving."

The two were led away, the man in handcuffs and the woman clinging to his arm, weeping. *Why do they always do that?* wondered Manny. It was a sad truth that battered women often clung to and defended their abusive partners. She would have no choice but to press charges, though; the law was clear on that.

Manny turned to Zach, whose face was flushed with excitement. "Did you see, Dad? I wouldn't let her leave!"

"Did you touch her, Zach?" Manny asked. "I heard a scream."

"Nah, I just got in her face a little, that's all. I didn't touch her," Zach replied.

"Good job!" he replied. He awkwardly patted his son's shoulder. "You kept her here until the officers arrived! That was all you, Zach. I was busy with her boyfriend."

Now that the excitement of the moment had passed, Manny became aware of a dull throbbing in his back, and down his left leg. He turned to the front counter, retrieving their sandwiches, gingerly testing the leg.

"We're going to have to walk home, Zach, my leg's bothering me a little," he said.

"That's OK," Zach said, still bubbling with excitement. "Dad! How did you learn how to do that? You know, crank his arm up behind his back like that?"

Manny didn't want to tell him that he'd first learned about that from his father, who had dislocated Manny's shoulder by sharply twisting his arm up high between his shoulder blades. Willing the thought away, he said, "You learn all about those things at the Academy."

Maybe Zach might like the Academy, he thought. He was strong, clear-headed and had that certain streak of aggression which was such a positive attribute in a police officer. Manny had seen a number of recruits in his day that looked fine on paper, but just didn't have the temperament needed to catch and subdue a suspect.

"You know, maybe you might want to be a cop someday. You could go to the Academy, maybe become an undercover cop and catch all sorts of bad actors," Manny said.

Zach's eyes filled with excitement. "Me, at the Academy?"

"Why not?" replied Manny. It was a good idea. They hadn't really talked much about what his son might want to do for a career. "You'd be the third generation of our family to be police."

Zach and Manny were walking home, Manny trying hard not to limp. He badly wanted his cane, but it was at home.

"There's a club, a police youth group for teenagers who are interested in law enforcement as a career. I'll find out more about it for you. You know, if you're interested," Manny said, limping along.

"Thanks, Dad," said Zach. Manny had never seen him so excited. It made him feel hopeful that this could be a good thing for the two of them. *You see, Naz, look how happy he is!* he thought.

On the day Zach was born, Manny had promised Naz that he would be a good father, that his son would not suffer as he had. He had meant every word of it; he just had not realized how hard it would be.

When the house came into sight, Zach left Manny's side to run up the walk and into the house. "Mom! Mom!" he called excitedly. "You'll never guess what happened!"

Marya, Anna and Julio were all in the foyer, listening to Zach's animated retelling of his adventure, by the time Manny walked up to the door. He leaned against the door frame, listening as Zach gave a somewhat embellished account of his role in subduing the girl.

61

"Is that so?" asked Julio, playfully punching Zach in the arm. "You really did all that?" Eyebrows raised, he looked at Manny.

"Yeah, he really did," he said. "Zach was right there where I needed him to be. The girl would have bolted, if he hadn't blocked her way."

"You put our son in danger?" asked Marya. "I thought you two were just going out for a run!"

"No, not in danger," replied Manny. "The dangerous one was the man, and he never came near Zach."

"Dad's going to find out if I can join the police youth group. It's for kids who want to go to the Academy," Zach continued, his face alight with excitement.

"That's wonderful, Zach," said Anna.

Marya gave Zach a hug, and a big kiss on the cheek. Embarrassed, he mumbled something and took off, up the stairs and into his room. A moment later, music blasted, then the door closed.

"Sounds like you two had a good day," said Marya.

"It was good, actually," replied Manny. "It would have been even better, if somebody had warned me that he runs like a rabbit!"

Chapter 11.

Manny was in his study, participating in a virtual meeting with the Mayor's office. Thanks to the powerful VirchMeeting software, tiny hologram figures of the Mayor, her aide and several other people, including Manny, were seated around a long oval mahogany table in a virtual conference room with pearl gray carpet, soft pink overhead lighting and long, dark gray silk curtains.

Each of them was dressed in proper business attire. Manny knew that to them, he appeared to be wearing his uniform, sitting at the conference table, while in reality, he was wearing running shorts and a teeshirt while seated behind his desk. They had each created avatars of themselves, professionally dressed, when they first began using VirchMeeting. He wondered idly what the Mayor was really wearing. *It's like one of Zach's video games,* thought Manny, *only without the gory warriors and the smoke.* He stifled a yawn. Someone from the Parts Department was speaking.

"As you know," the man said, "we are running out of plastic to make new padlets. There are limitations on how many times plastic can be melted down and reshaped. We don't have any other suitable replacement materials. So what we have here is something completely different."

He reached into his briefcase and with a flourish, retrieved a metal cuff, shiny silver with five color-coded buttons on its surface. There was a button for projecting a virtual screen onto the wall; a button to project a keyboard onto a desk or table; a button to send a text; another to send a hologram; and a button to connect to Millicent, the Colony's AI assistant.

"Each of you should have received by now a prototype of the new padlet," he continued smoothly. "We are especially interested in your feedback."

"How do you make a phone call on this thing?" asked Manny, interrupting. The man's smarmy, salesman-like presentation was grating on Manny's nerves, making him impatient.

"When was the last time you actually made a phone call?" the man responded. "We all use texts, emails, and holograms far more often. To save materials, we've eliminated phone calls."

"But what if there's an emergency?" persisted Manny. Every police officer knew that in an emergency, the first choice was always a phone call.

"There are actually very few phone calls made each year," countered the representative confidently.

Zach knocked softly on the door to the study and opened it.

"Not now," Manny said softly, motioning him to back out and close the door behind him.

"Dad, did you see my text asking you about the police youth program?" Zach asked.

Damn, Manny thought, *I forgot.* After trying unsuccessfully to talk to Manny about it a couple of times, Zach had taken to texting him during the day, when he was in the office. Manny muted the sound in the VirchMeeting app.

"Zach, I forgot all about your text, I'm sorry," Manny said.

"When will you have a chance to look into it?" Zach asked impatiently.

"I don't know, but I will, I promise! I haven't forgotten, I've just been busy," Manny replied. "Now's not a good time to talk, Zach. As you can see, I'm in a meeting."

Zach, disappointed, nodded and left, closing the door behind him.

Manny left the meeting early, not bothering to explain. He watched as the VirchMeeting conference room dissolved around him, leaving him sitting alone in his study in his teeshirt and shorts. He glanced at the clock; it was well past lunchtime.

On his way into the kitchen, Manny nearly collided with Zach and his friends, as the three boys headed down the stairs.

"Hold on there, boys!" he said, hoping to strike a friendly tone. "Where are you going in such a hurry?"

"We're going to Raj's house," replied Zach. Looking over his shoulder, Zach said to his friends, "Come on, we're going to be late!" They nodded and all three hustled out the door, Zach first, followed by the other two, leaving Manny staring thoughtfully after them. The hair on the back of his neck was standing up straight, a bad sign.

There's something going on here, I'm sure of it, he thought. *Maybe I missed something in my research. Better try again.*

"What are you looking at?" asked Marya, passing through the foyer on her way to the kitchen. She peered out the front door, where the boys were fast disappearing from view. "Did something happen?"

"No, everything's fine," he said quickly.

Manny returned to his study and closed the door. Pulling out his padlet, with the help of AI, he searched once again for the names Oh and Gopalaswami, the boys' school records, team memberships, health records, any SoshMedia clips that were relevant. Nothing came up which Manny had not seen before.

Manny was about to close his padlet, when something interesting appeared. It seemed that Raj had an older half-brother named Kiaan Patel. Kiaan lived for the first ten years of his life with his unmarried mother, who eventually married and had other children. When she died, the stepfather didn't want Kiaan, who then went to live with his biological father, Deepak Gopalaswami. Kiaan, finally acknowledged by his biological father, began using Gopalaswami as his last name.

Manny researched Kiaan, who had an impressive rap sheet. He read the information twice. Then he rolled up his padlet and sat, lost in thought, for a long time.

Later that evening, when the family was seated around the kitchen table for dinner, Manny asked Zach if he'd met Raj's or Eddie's parents.

"Nah, they work, they're not around much," Zach replied dismissively. He was lounging in his chair, one arm draped over the back of the chair, knees spread wide.

"Zach, sit up in your chair," Manny admonished. "That's just disrespectful, sitting like that after your Abuela and Aunt Anna worked so hard on this meal."

Zach shrugged. He shifted in his chair, straightening up just enough to escape further scrutiny.

"But you've met their siblings?" Manny persisted. "Raj has brothers and a sister, right?"

"Yeah," Zach mumbled.

"Have you met his older brother, Kiaan?" Manny asked.

Zach blinked, surprised; then he looked warily at Manny. "Yeah, I've met Kiaan," he replied.

"How exactly did you do that? I mean, given that he is nineteen and a convicted felon, currently in jail serving a five-year sentence for gang violence?" asked Manny. Conversation around the dinner table ceased.

"He gets to have visitors, you know," replied Zach defensively, ambushed by his father's interrogation.

"Who gave you permission to visit a jail?" demanded Manny. "You're a minor! You don't just go waltzing into a jail for a social visit with a convicted criminal!"

Marya turned to Zach. "You visited his brother in jail?! Whatever for, Zach?"

"He deserves to see his family, doesn't he? Besides, he's really cool!" Zach responded. "He didn't do half the things they say he did."

"If you want to get into the police youth program, you can't go around associating with convicts," admonished Manny. "They won't accept you."

That did make him pause. "I didn't think of that," Zach replied.

"That's why you have parents," Lucinda said gently. "You should listen to them, Zach."

"You've been shaving your head again, I see," Manny observed, looking closely at his son's hair, which was shoulder length in the back and shaved completely bald in front, from one ear to the other. His half-bald pate reflected bright and shiny in the spill of the light fixture hanging above the kitchen table.

"Yeah," replied Zach defiantly. "So what?"

"I thought we agreed that it was a bad idea," said Manny.

"No, you agreed it was a bad idea," retorted Zach. "I like it."

"Now you listen to me, young man," Manny said sternly. "You're to stop shaving your head. And I want you to wear a hat when you go out, until the hair grows back. Do you understand me?"

"But I like my hair this way," protested Zach. "It's my hair, not yours!"

"As long as you're living under my roof, you'll follow my rules," insisted Manny. "You're going to let your hair grow, starting now."

Zach looked to his mother. Along with everyone else, she had been listening to the exchange with dismay. "Zach, you've made your point," she said persuasively. "You don't need to keep on making it. Is shaving your head really that important to you?"

"If it's not that important," countered Zach, "then why can't I do it?"

"You can't shave your head because you are a child," Manny retorted. "And that's the end of this conversation."

Zach stood up, pushing his chair back so hard that it screeched along the floor. He glared at Manny, then left the kitchen. A moment later, the sound of loud music came from upstairs, followed by the door banging shut.

"Teenagers," said Marya with a sigh, hoping to defuse the atmosphere in the room.

"He's barely a teenager," retorted Manny.

"You and Zach are really going at it," said Lucinda. "Are you sure you want to proceed down this road?"

Manny pushed his chair back and stood. "Excuse me, I've lost my appetite," he said. He left the kitchen.

Lucinda followed him out into the foyer. "Manny, please. We need to talk. Come with me into the study."

Once inside, she pulled the door closed for privacy. They sat down in the leather chairs, facing each other.

"I'm concerned about your relationship with Zach," Lucinda said. "Defiance, resentment, ultimatums – it doesn't have to be like this, you know. Why is Zach's hair so important to you?"

"He's making a statement, for the world to see," Manny said. "He's defying me. I don't like it."

"Manny, you don't own him. You can't micro-manage every little thing he says and does," she replied mildly. "He's old enough now that he's testing the boundaries of your authority, and that's perfectly normal. Your job is to be consistent, kind, and loving."

"I've been pretty consistent on this," Manny replied grimly.

"Keep your eye on the ball, Manny," she said gently. "The goal is to raise a mature, confident young man. You can't do that if all you do is punish him."

"I don't just punish him!" Manny protested. There was a brief silence, Lucinda waiting patiently.

"You know what they say, Manny – if something isn't working, try something different," Lucinda said encouragingly.

"OK, maybe I could spend more time with him when I'm not angry," Manny conceded. "But there's more to it than you know. It's complicated."

"Tell me," she said. He loved that about her, how she was always willing to listen to him.

There was a discreet tap at the door. "May I join in?" asked Marya.

"Of course! Come in, come in," said Lucinda, waving her to a chair. "Manny was just about to explain to me why he is so concerned about Zach."

"Raj's older brother Kiaan is a gang member, one of the Skulls," Manny explained. "He was convicted of knifing a store clerk in the commission of a robbery. Every gang is different, but you can tell them apart by the way they dress or wear their hair. The Skulls shave the heads of their new recruits as the first step of their initiation. Zach and his friends have shaved part of their heads in a pattern I've never seen before, and I'm guessing that the idea came from Kiaan."

"Manny, that's very scary," Lucinda said. "Do you think Zach and his friends will want to join this gang, when they are old enough?"

"They're too young now to join a gang, but soon they won't be. The Skulls take teenagers. And the boys already have a sponsor in Kiaan. For Raj and Eddie, it's a natural fit, with so many of their relatives already in the gang."

"And Zach? You don't think Zach would want to join them, do you?" she asked, dismayed.

"That's exactly what I'm afraid of," Manny replied. "Once they get into a gang, there's no way to get out. They're in for life." He stopped just short of telling them the rest of it, that gang members either die in jail or on the streets, but never of old age.

Chapter 12.

Manny stared at the confidential report that Dave had left for him. He closed it and pushed it across his desk. Then a moment later, he changed his mind and reached for it again.

Dave knocked discreetly on his door and then entered Manny's office, sitting down in the visitor's chair. "I see you've seen the report," he said.

"I'm not surprised," Manny said grimly. "Let's just keep this between you and me, for the time being."

Dave nodded. "Sure thing, Boss," he replied. "Nobody got hurt, nothing valuable was taken. When they realized who he was, the cops returned the items to the store owners and gave all three of them a warning before letting them go home."

Manny grimaced. "I don't want Zach thinking he can do whatever he wants because he's the Commissioner's son," he said.

"I'm sure you can handle this privately," Dave said. "Like I said, no harm was done."

"I'm worried about him, Dave," Manny confided to his friend. He described Zach's burgeoning friendship with Raj and Eddie, his research into their families and the possible connection with the Perez family. "Zach never had any friends before. Now he has two friends, both older than him and both related to the Skulls."

There was a silence, as the two men remembered their years as street cops. The Colony's gangs were well organized and ruthless. Violence was encouraged, especially among the newer recruits, who were given knives and brass knuckles at their initiation. In at least two of the gangs, the younger members were expected to cull the weakest newbies from their ranks.

"I'm sorry, man," Dave said. "Let me know if there's anything I can do to help."

"How old are your kids now?" Manny asked.

"Jonathan Henry is eight, and Alessandra is six," Dave replied.

"Just wait," Manny warned grimly. "It sneaks up on you so fast."

Manny folded the report and put it in his pocket. "Oh, I almost forgot. I've got a little something for you."

Manny reached for an ornate brown envelope lying on his desk. He held it out to Dave. "Open it," he said encouragingly. "It's for you and Jenny."

"What's this?" asked Dave, surprised. "It says it's a Deed. It's a real Deed, for land? Outside?"

"Yeah, and who knows? The land out there could be valuable someday," Manny explained. "At least, we're gambling that it will. I've bought land for all my family members, and for you and Jenny, too."

"Manny, thank you!" Dave said, blushing. "That's very generous of you!" He stood up and bowed deeply to his friend, right hand on his left shoulder.

"It's nothing, really," Manny said. "We're buying the land dirt cheap. So far nobody has challenged us. By the time they realize what we're doing, we'll have half the park in our control."

As Dave was leaving, a text came in for Manny, pulsing scarlet around the edges of the padlet to denote a personal text requiring an immediate response. He unrolled his padlet and opened the text.

Mr. Jha: *Commissioner, are you available for lunch tomorrow?*

Manny stared at the text, wondering if he was being pranked. Why would his arch-nemesis be inviting him to lunch? Still, he couldn't very well ignore it.

Manny: *Yes, I'm free. Do you like Chinese? Chung's is good, I've eaten there many times.*
Mr. Jha: *Sounds good. 12:30?*
Manny: *12:30 is fine. See you there.*

Manny re-read the text, looking for clues. He had no idea what Mr. Jha might want from him that couldn't wait until the next Council meeting.

70

A soft knock on Manny's door interrupted his thoughts. "Come in, Nigel," said Manny, waving him in. "What's up?"

Nigel settled himself in the visitor's chair. "I need your response concerning the proposed padlet design," he said carefully. A few days earlier, when a messenger had dropped off the new prototype, Manny had shoved it impatiently across his desk, asking Nigel to get rid of it.

Manny laughed tonelessly. "Where is the damned thing?" he asked. "I might as well drop it off at the Parts Department, on my way to the Mayor's office. I can let them know in person exactly what I think of their new design."

Prototype in his pocket, Manny donned jacket and hat, and left his office. It was good to get out of the office at lunchtime, he'd discovered. After years of working long hours, sometimes eating both lunch and dinner at his desk, Manny appreciated being able to relax a bit. He'd found that as Commissioner, he often had an hour or two during the day when he didn't have anything planned. As he'd told Marya, it wasn't that the job was less stressful; it was just stressful differently.

The Parts Department was not far from the Mayor's office. It didn't take him long to walk there. The Parts Department was home to anything and everything that could be repurposed.

The building was a sprawling warehouse lined inside with ceiling-high rows of shelves. Worn out clothing, old shoes, broken pottery, ancient pillows, bed linens and towels, eyeglasses, sofas and backpacks all found their way eventually to the Parts Department, where they were stored until they could be made into something new. A lady's dress could be made into children's clothing. A child's overalls, too small to be reimagined, could be used for patches. A pillow could often be repaired or made into a smaller pillow. A jacket, worn out at the elbows, could be made into a vest. The Colony depended on recycling and repurposing.

Manny pulled open the door and walked inside.

He stopped, astonished. Behind the front counter, Manny could see row after row of mostly empty shelves. Rather than the usual hustle and bustle of a busy workplace, it was eerily quiet. Normally, there was a staff of three or four greeters at the front counter, directing customers where to go. Today, there was only one young man, who was leaning his chair backwards on two legs, one finger industriously picking his nose as he watched a music video on his padlet, ear-kernels in.

Manny reached over and shoved the back of the chair so all four legs landed with a thud on the floor. The young man jumped up, pulling out his ear-kernels. His expression changed from outrage to shock as he recognized the uniformed Commissioner of Police standing at his counter. He stared, open-mouthed.

"I don't think they pay you to watch music videos, do they?" Manny demanded.

The young man swallowed, Adam's apple bobbing. "No, Sir!" he said. "I apologize. I didn't see you there."

"Yes, I can see that," Manny replied drily, disgusted by this total lack of discipline. "Where is everyone?"

"A bunch of people were laid off a few months ago," he replied. "There's not much work lately." He gestured to the empty shelves. "We're running low on just about everything."

Manny took the padlet prototype out of his pocket. "Here, I'm returning this," he said, handing it to the young man. "Tell your supervisor to stop wasting my time." He turned on his heel and walked out of the building, leaving the young man staring after him, prototype in hand.

Manny left the sprawling complex, a cloud of dread settling over him. He came to a nearby "rest-up," one of many such areas commonly found throughout the Colony, especially in the nicer neighborhoods. There was a stone bench and a few flowering bushes around a tiny Zolar-powered fountain; two long-haired young women were just getting up to leave.

Manny nodded absently to them and sat down on the stone bench to think, idly watching the fountain gurgle and splash. *What happens when we run out of things to recycle?* he thought.

The meeting at the Mayor's office ran well into the evening hours, something that often happened when he visited the Mayor. She was a powerhouse of a public official, popular among the citizens, a woman who got things done. Manny admired her greatly.

She opened the meeting by telling Manny not to give up on his evacuation plan. *I see I'm not the only one with spies at the Council meetings,* Manny thought. He had Sara Blumberg, his friend and former tutor, to keep him up to date on Council developments. He wondered who the Mayor's informant might be.

"Actually, I've stopped trying to get the Council to approve it, but I haven't given up on it entirely," he said.

"I think it could be a good thing, going forward," she said encouragingly.

"There are so many problems," Manny began. "Sometimes I don't know where to start."

"What's your biggest problem?" asked the Mayor.

"The worst problem, the one that keeps me up at night, is giving access to everyone to the shelters, not just people who live in midtown," Manny said. "We've unchained all of the doors, all up and down the Colony, but someone living way uptown isn't going to walk to midtown to the shelters."

"That's a tough one, I agree," said the Mayor, considering. "Maybe you could reassure them that eventually, more shelters will be built, so all citizens will have access."

"It's going to be a long time before even one shelter is built," Manny said. "We have to see how the first one goes, before we invest more."

"It's a great humanitarian gift, what you and your family are doing," the Mayor said, "a gift to our citizens. It will be a fine legacy, Manny."

"We'll have to see about that," Manny said wryly. "Right now, all we have is a plan on paper and a public service campaign that has fallen flat, thanks to the competition. They've run a good counter-campaign, appealing to parents to keep their children safe by keeping them inside."

"You know who's behind that, don't you?" asked the Mayor. "It's your friend Mr. Jha."

"I thought so," said Manny. "You know, it's the strangest thing, but he texted me yesterday and invited me to lunch. I haven't had a civil conversation with him in years. And now he wants to have lunch."

"It might have something to do with a certain purchase of land out there, hmm?" asked the Mayor, one eyebrow raised delicately.

"Oh, that," replied Manny. "We wondered how long it would be before someone noticed."

"My staff noticed," the Mayor said, laughing. "You've been outed. Maybe that's why Mr. Jha wants to talk to you privately."

Manny turned toward home, thinking over what they'd covered during the meeting. The Mayor had shared a report from the Earth Sciences Institute explaining that the enormous weight of the collapsed skyscrapers above ground was weighing on the ground, sinking into it a little more each year. "One of these days, the ceiling is going to cave in and land on our heads," the Mayor joked.

It was not good news. Taken with what they already knew about underground global warming and how it affects the

73

stability of the ground surrounding the subway tunnels and the surface, it was more than worrisome.

Water pipe breaks were growing increasingly common now, as the ground shifted in tiny little increments, with plumbers and construction crews working full time to keep up.

Manny walked home slowly, deep in thought. *It's a wonder we're able to live here at all,* he thought. *At least the water supply is safe.* Water for New York City continued to flow through ancient pipes from the Croton water system, as it had since the mid-1800's, almost entirely by force of gravity.

Manny was startled out of his reverie as he got closer to the Stewart mansion. Someone was sitting on the step by the front door. Growing closer, he was surprised to see who it was: Loosey, an acquaintance of his and Julio's from their teenage years.

What's he doing here of all places, out in the open? he thought. "Loosey! Hello, come on in," he said, ushering his erstwhile friend into the house, safe from the prying eyes of SoshMedia drones, always looking for a good story for the evening news or the talk shows.

"Manny! C-Commissioner! I need to talk to you," he said. Loosey, whose real name was Ajay, was industriously twisting his hat into a crumpled wad.

"Here, let's go into the front parlor," Manny said. The two sat down. "What brings you here?" he asked.

Loosey, a few years older than Manny and Julio, had been their fence when they were in high school, buying the stolen items from their burglaries. Loosey had come to the house once before, to warn Manny of a dangerous situation. It was uncomfortable for both of them, as Loosey was still a well-known petty criminal dealing in stolen goods, while Manny was police.

"I come to tell you. I mean, I owe you that much," Loosey began. "It's about your boy."

"Zach?" Manny replied, surprised. "What about him?"

"He's running with a couple of bad guys, Manny. These two friends of his, one of them's brother's in the Skulls. He's in *jail,* Manny," Loosey emphasized. "The brother, rumor has it that he's done some very bad stuff. He's talking about sponsoring the boys to be new recruits for the Skulls. The initiation's supposed to be this summer, before school starts back up."

"You know this to be true?" Manny asked with dismay.

"I wouldn't be here if I wasn't sure about it," Loosey insisted.

"Do you know anything about the initiation?" Manny asked. Maybe if he knew when and where, he could stop it.

"No, but if I hear anything, I'll let you know," Loosey said.

"Thanks, man, I appreciate you," Manny said. He walked him to the door. "Stay in touch, OK? Nothing written. Just come over, like you did today."

The two men bowed to each other, right hands on their left shoulders, Loosey taking care to bow more slowly and deeply than Manny, as befitted their social positions. "Health and prosperity to you," they murmured to each other, and then Loosey was gone, hat pulled down low over his forehead, hands in his pockets, walking quickly.

Marya came down the stairs and into the foyer. "I thought I heard you talking to someone," she said.

"Just a work thing, Sweetheart, nothing to worry about," he said dismissively. He'd find a way to put a stop to this initiation, if in fact it was even true, and would tell Marya about it afterwards.

Chapter 13.

Mr. Jha," said Manny by way of greeting, rising from the little table to bow politely to him. "Health and prosperity to you." Mr. Jha returned the bow, murmuring the same greeting, perfectly copying Manny's bow in a subtle but unmistakable message that they were equals.

They sat down. Chung's, Manny's favorite Chinese take-out restaurant, had only four tables for dine-in customers. Two tables were filled, both by women with young children, who were unlikely to eavesdrop on their conversation. He noted that Mr. Jha also scanned the restaurant, much the same as he had done.

"What do you like to eat here?" asked Mr. Jha, reading the central display that was scrolling the menu across their tabletop.

"Try the vegetable lo mein, it's very good," replied Manny.

"Sounds fine," said Mr. Jha. The two men used the touch screen to order their food. A man behind the counter waved to Manny, acknowledging the order.

"So. To what do I owe this pleasure?" Manny asked Mr. Jha.

"You and I, we're not the best of friends," Mr. Jha began. "Colleagues, certainly, but not always on the same side." He cleared his throat, taking his time. "There are certain people in the Colony who are growing concerned about your purchase of land out there in the Central Park."

"Oh, that," responded Manny easily. *First the Mayor, and now him,* he thought. *The news is getting around.*

Manny knew how important it was to show confidence. "It's perfectly legal, you know," he said. "We had Tyler Watkins's firm opine regarding who actually owns the land out there. It turns out that no one does."

"Yes, I've spoken to Tyler," replied Mr. Jha. As lawyers, of course, they would know each other, but it still surprised

Manny. "You're right, it appears that there is nothing the Council can do to stop you."

"Why would the Council want to stop me?" asked Manny, his expression the picture of innocence. "If it's not illegal, then what's it have to do with the Council?"

"Because first, you've made it plain to everyone on the planet that you want to build emergency shelters outside, and second, you've got the funds to do it on your own, without help from the Colony," retorted Mr. Jha.

"Well, now, what I do on my own land is my own business," responded Manny.

"I understand," said Mr. Jha, pausing as the server bot rolled towards their table, balancing two juice glasses on its round tray. The glasses slid forward precariously on the wet tray as the bot came rolling to a stop. They reached forward to rescue their glasses before they landed on the floor.

"You were saying?" prompted Manny, as the bot reversed direction, retreating back into the kitchen.

"Commissioner, there are several businesspersons in the Colony, wealthy landlords not unlike yourself, who own multiple apartment buildings," explained Mr. Jha. "These people have come to me in confidence, to ask if I know what you might be planning. For instance, if you might be planning on building permanent housing, rather than shelters."

"To live above ground? Permanently?" asked Manny, genuinely surprised. "Are you making a joke?"

"No, I'm deadly serious, Commissioner," Mr. Jha replied. "We're afraid that if you lure people outside, offering them the opportunity to buy a brand new home, then they may move out of their homes here inside the Colony. It could wreck our housing market, which isn't good for any of us." He eyed Manny meaningfully; everyone knew that Manny owned the largest portion of real estate in the Colony.

Manny shook his head. "Maybe someday, people will be able to live above ground again, but we're nowhere near to that now, not even close. I'm more concerned with being able to shelter our citizens for a few days, if they need to run from a natural disaster."

"So you're building temporary shelters? That's it?" Mr. Jha pressed him.

"Right now, it seems that all I'm building is a hole in the ground, which as of yesterday morning was filled with rainwater," Manny said wryly. The server bot returned with two plates filled with food. Manny took the plates and handed one to Mr. Jha.

Hasan had reported to him the previous morning that of the sixteen men in his crew that came with him outside to work on the foundation, two of the men had panicked at their first sight of the outside world, and had opted out. The other fourteen men had toiled diligently, but so far had only succeeded in digging and removing ten inches of rocky soil from the ground, a far cry from the three-foot depth required for a foundation.

"Commissioner, do I have your word that you will not be putting up apartment buildings out there?" Mr. Jha persisted.

"You can tell your friends that I have no interest in crashing the housing market. It would hurt me as well as them," replied Manny, putting down his chopsticks and pushing back his chair. "And now if you'll excuse me, I'm late getting back to the office."

Mr. Jha rose, too. He bowed politely to Manny, thanking him for lunch with what seemed like genuine sincerity. Manny bowed as well, murmuring something polite about colleagues taking time to get to know each other, etc.

Manny left Chung's, paying the bill by swiping the implanted bank chip in his wrist over the processor by the door as he passed by it. Lost in thought, he was turning to walk back to the office, when he heard a familiar voice saying, "Make sure that door's closed, OK?"

Looking around, he could see three young men standing outside the door to Madame Elayna's place of business, which was up two flights of stairs from street level, not far from Chung's restaurant. Two of the boys turned and pulled the door closed more firmly, testing to see if it was locked. Then all three clambered down the spiral metal staircase. Even with the Scuba sweatshirts that they wore, Manny recognized Zach and his friends Raj and Eddie.

He got up and walked over to the staircase, waiting for the boys at the bottom. As Zach descended, he reached out and grabbed him by the arm, shaking him angrily. "What do you think you're doing, young man?" he demanded.

Zach glanced at his two friends, who were watching, eyes narrowed. Raj and Eddie exchanged glances, then Raj moved quickly to one side of Manny, while Eddie moved behind Manny. Their manner was shockingly menacing. *What do they think they're doing?* Manny thought incredulously. *They've encircled me like a pack of rats.*

"Get out of here. GO!" ordered Zach, snapping his fingers at his two friends. "I'll catch up with you later." Raj and Eddie disappeared in a flash.

"What were you doing up there?" demanded Manny. He moved closer to Zach, sniffing suspiciously. "Zachary Stewart, have you been *DRINKING?*"

"I had a beer. It's lunchtime, we shared a few while we ate. What's the big deal?" said Zach brazenly.

"You broke in there to drink beer and eat lunch?" Manny asked. "What if you were seen? You could get arrested for underage drinking."

"But I didn't, did I?" Zach pointed out. "You just can't spend your life worrying about every little thing that might go wrong."

"How much did you have to drink, Zach?" Manny asked. He certainly didn't look drunk, but his breath smelled of beer.

"I had one, that's all, I swear," Zach insisted. "It's not a big deal, Dad, it's just a beer."

"Zach, we need to talk," said Manny heavily. "Do you know that I'm an alcoholic?"

"Yeah, but so what?" Zach replied. "What's that got to do with me?"

"It has everything to do with you, I'm afraid," Manny replied. "Alcoholism runs in families, and you're my son. Your mother, you know, Naztazya. She didn't have any problems with alcohol, but it's possible that you could have the same tendencies that I have."

"Nah, I'm fine," scoffed Zach. "It doesn't bother me."

"It never does, at first," replied Manny. "Listen to me on this, Zach, it's important. If you drink regularly, even a little at a time, you might find that you begin to crave it, want to have it every day, can't live without it. It's a slippery slope. Trust me, you don't want to do that to yourself. Once you get started down that road, no amount is ever enough."

Zach eyed Manny intently, thoughtfully. "Now that you mention it, I remember seeing you drunk. I was little. There was a fight, right? You and Uncle Julio?"

Manny, dismayed at the direction in which the conversation was headed, responded, "You can't possibly remember that! You were so young!"

"Don't you remember things from when you were five?" Zach replied disdainfully. "Yeah, I remember it alright. I remember you hanging onto the railing, falling all over yourself! You punched Uncle Julio in the face. There was blood on the floor in the foyer."

Manny's mind was whirling. *But it was so long ago,* he thought. No real harm had been done; he'd put it all behind him. True, the children had been there when the fight happened, but they were just kids.

It had been a terrible year, Naztazya dying in the fire along with their unborn twins. His drinking had spiraled out of control. Now Zach was grown up, standing here in front of him, judging him, reminding him that he'd seen it all, reminding him of his failures.

"Let's get you home, young man," he said sternly, hoping to steer the conversation away from his own shortcomings and back to the current problem.

"You don't need to walk me home," Zach said. "I'll go, I promise."

"OK. I have to get back to the office anyway," said Manny. "Make sure you go home and no place else. I'm going to check later."

Zach took off at a run to look for his friends, disappearing down the walkway at an amazing speed.

"All kids drink, Manny," replied Marya later that evening, when he told her about Zach having a beer at lunch. "Didn't you try out your father's liquor cabinet, when you were a kid?"

"Are you kidding me?" Manny replied. "My dad would have killed me if I touched his precious bourbon. Did you and your sisters sample your parents' liquor cabinet when you were kids?"

"Did we ever! We never took too much at a time, and always topped off the bottles with water whenever we had a drink," she replied. "Now that I think of it, they must have known."

"Somehow, I can't picture Naz drinking as a teenager," Manny mused.

Marya laughed. "She was pretty funny. But Anna was the worst," she confided. "Once, she took one of Mom's highball glasses and filled it with apple juice. When Mom saw it, Anna laughed and said, 'Fooled you, it's only apple juice!' And then the next night, Anna filled one of the glasses with scotch, and Mom just laughed, thinking it was apple juice."

"She did that? Anna?" Manny said, laughing. "I can't picture our Anna doing anything like that."

"Oh, she was a terror, when she was younger," Marya replied.

"It's not just the drinking," Manny said. "That would have been bad enough. But they were inside, the three of them, hanging out in the abandoned space where Madame Elayna used to have her business."

"That space isn't abandoned! I just read the other day about Madame's two assistants who want to continue with her business. They were like her apprentices. Anyway, it may look empty right now, but it won't for long. I read that they plan on reopening in another few weeks."

"Geez. That would change everything, if he was caught breaking into someone's place of business, not just squatting for an hour or two in an abandoned space," said Manny.

"What about the drinking? Do you want me to talk to him?" Marya said.

"No, I think I covered it," Manny said. The last thing he wanted was to rehash his year of utter humiliation, when everyone, including five-year-old Zach, had moved into Luis and Lucinda's townhouse across the street, leaving Manny to live alone in his beautiful mansion, with his precious bottles of brandy.

Chapter 14.

Summer flew by, turning into September in the blink of an eye. Another school year was about to start. *How is it that children grow up so fast?* thought Manny, looking at Zach across the table as they ate dinner. *I don't feel older at all, but look at him.* Zach, about to enter ninth grade, was no longer a gangly adolescent, all arms and legs. He had put on weight, started to shave every day. His voice was as deep as a man's voice.

"Pass the pasta, please," Luis said from the other end of the table. "Manny, how's the building going?"

"It's hit a kind of a snag, actually," Manny replied. "Hasan now says that we should have looked for an underground source of water first, before we started. We're going to need a well nearby. There will be too many people inside the shelter, if it's ever used, without a convenient source of water."

"He couldn't have thought of that earlier?" asked Luis.

"The problem is that nobody has built anything in ages," Manny explained. "I didn't think of it, either. Now he says that we may have to start over at another spot. He knows how to raise the walls and put on the roof, but this is different because it's outside, away from electricity and running water. I told him he should consult an engineer."

"You're likely to run into the same problem with an engineer," Luis replied. "They don't have any experience building outside, either." He took another bite of bread, chewing thoughtfully.

"You know, I've always wondered," Luis said, "how did they get their water to the top of those tall buildings? They had so many floors, sometimes twenty or more."

"Nobody knows," Manny replied. "We'll be doing it the old fashioned way, carrying it up the stairs."

"Did you hear about Joe O'Reilly?" asked Anna. "He's in the infirmary. He fell down the stairs in his house. When his wife found him, he was unconscious, lying on the floor. It was on the news before dinner."

"The Chief?" asked Manny. "Wow, that's terrible! Did they give any other details?"

"No, just what I told you," Anna replied.

"Maybe I'll hologram his wife after dinner," Manny said.

"I have an announcement," Zach said. Conversation stopped, as all faces turned towards him. "It's about my name," Zach continued. "I want to be called Heinrich from now on, not Zach."

"You're changing your name, Zach?" asked Lucinda.

"Yeah, from now on, I'd like to be called Heinrich," Zach replied.

Manny snorted derisively. "Don't be ridiculous. Nobody's calling you Heinrich, Zach," he exclaimed. "Stop this nonsense and eat your dinner."

Zach's face turned bright red. "I'm not responding to anything addressed to Zach from now on," he said steadily. He put on a good show of nonchalance, taking another forkful of his casserole, avoiding eye contact with his father.

Manny slapped his open-palmed hand down onto the table, making his plate and glass jump. "Your name is Zach, young man. I know this because I gave you your name. End of conversation. And no one," he said emphatically, eyeing each one of them in turn, "in this house is going to call you Heinrich."

Lucinda put down her fork and leaned forward, elbows on the table. "I seem to recall someone else who wanted a different name when he was young," she said gently. "Zach, did you know your father's given name is Malcolm?"

"*Malcolm??* Dad's real name is *Malcolm?*" Zach cried delightedly. "I didn't know that!"

"No, I didn't know that either," said Julie, looking wonderingly from Manny to Zach. "You changed your name?"

Manny, feeling distinctly ambushed, looked down at his plate in confusion. Lucinda answered instead. "He was about ten years old, I think. Isn't that right, Manny?"

"Yeah, I think so. I mean, yeah. I was ten. It was the year I met Julio," Manny replied. *Why did she have to bring this up?* he thought resentfully.

"What did your father say to you?" asked Julie. "When you asked to be called Manny, I mean."

"He said no," Manny replied. He cleared his throat. *This story is going to be told one way or another,* he thought, *so I might as well own it.* "My dad wouldn't hear of it. He knew that I hated the name Malcolm, so it was just another way to show me that I was powerless against him. He was the only person who called me Malcolm. Things are a little different between you and me, Zach."

"How so?" asked Zach, emboldened by the unexpected support from around the table.

"The relationship I had with my old man," Manny began, "you can't imagine what it was like." He stopped, his thoughts colliding in his mind, echoes of his anger, the impotent rage of an abused child, choking him speechless. It was simply impossible to distill down into a few words what it had been like to live with an abusive and physically violent parent, a man so filled with malice that he looked forward to baiting Manny, provoking him so he could have a pretext to punish him. Perhaps this wasn't the time or place for this conversation.

"Well," said Lucinda. "Patrick Stewart was a hard man, and I'm sure that living with him wasn't easy. Would you pass the giggling pickles, please?" She pointed to a large oval dish containing marinated baby pickles with tiny pink "gigglers" on their skins. When swallowed, they tickled one's throat, causing giggling.

Lucinda took a serving of baby pickles, followed by Julianna and Luis. Julie took a bite and swallowed, then burst out laughing. Luis took a tentative bite and grinned. He picked up the serving dish and passed it to Manny.

"You've got to try these," he said. Manny declined, still wounded from Lucinda's comments. Anna helped herself to a single pickle, which she carefully chewed for a long time, with everyone watching. She swallowed, and burst out laughing. "Seriously, Manny, try one!" she said.

Manny maintained his dignified silence. He picked up his plate and carried it to the kitchen sink. "I'll be in my study, I've got some things to catch up on," he said.

It was late when a tap came on the study door. Manny, deeply engrossed in reading through cold cases, was startled to see that the whole evening had gone by. "Come in," he called.

It was Lucinda. "Manny, we're going home now," she said. "I just wanted to say goodnight, and to apologize. I didn't mean to ambush you like that."

"Oh, that's alright," he replied lamely, still smarting from her remarks. "Why did you bring that up? You know, about my name being Malcolm?"

"I was trying to get you to lighten up a little. There's no need to be so stern, you know! You can be kind and patient, and still get your point across," she explained. "Promise me you'll work on that, Manny."

"OK, I promise," he replied. "But Lucinda, you undermined me, plain and simple, in front of everyone while I was dealing with Zach."

"You're right, and I shouldn't have done that. I'm sorry," she said. "I'll try harder, too." She kissed him on the cheek and left. Manny could hear her and Luis in the foyer, the door opening, then closing.

A moment later, Marya tapped on the study door. Sighing, Manny closed up his cold case file and rolled up his padlet. "Come in," he said, getting up from behind his desk.

"You've been in here all night," Marya said. "Everything OK at the office?"

"Just work," he said dismissively. "Nothing out of the ordinary."

"Then I've been wanting to ask you something," she began. "Have you had a chance to look into the police youth program for Zach?"

"No, Marya, I've been busy!" he replied. "I'll get to it, I just haven't had time."

"Honestly, Manny, how long could it take?" Marya scolded. "It's been weeks!"

"I said I'll get to it!" Manny snapped. They glared at each other.

"I think it could be really good for him," she said. "He's counting on you, Manny. Don't let him down!"

"I'm not going to let anybody down," Manny retorted, frowning at her.

"If you dangle this in front of him and then don't follow through, what's he supposed to think?" she said, her voice rising. "It'll make him mad, and then he'll start acting out again, like at dinner tonight. I don't think he really wants to be called Heinrich. I think he wants to needle you, so you'll pay attention to him. It's what kids do."

"So now it's my fault that he wants to change his name!" Manny said, exasperated.

"Why are you always angry, Manny?" she replied. "Either you're mad at Zach, or you ignore him. How about instead of

85

yelling, maybe you could talk to him calmly, have a conversation?"

"Why do you always take his side?" countered Manny. "Honestly, sometimes I feel like you're his sister, not his mother. It's almost like I'm dealing with siblings." It was true. Marya was only fifteen years older than Zach, not quite old enough to be his biological mother. Naztazya, Manny's first wife, had been seven years older than Marya.

"I'm sorry, Manny, I don't mean to do that," Marya replied. There was truth in it; they both knew it.

"I feel like we're losing him, Marya, and you're not helping! Look at him!" Manny insisted. "Instead of indulging him, pretending like we don't care if he shaves his hair or changes his name, we need to prevent him from doing it! And stop hounding me about the police youth program! Tell me, Marya, does he look like he'd fit in?"

"So you *have* changed your mind, Manny!" she exclaimed, eyes flashing angrily.

"Let's just say I'm having second thoughts," Manny replied. His hands had balled into tight fists; he made a conscious effort to unclench them. "Right now, he doesn't look like Academy material."

"All I see is a teenage boy with a funny haircut," Marya replied.

Manny grabbed her arms, giving her a little shake. "How can I make you see this isn't a joke?" he asked. "He's running with a bad couple of kids, and they're a terrible influence on him. I've heard that there may be a gang initiation before school starts."

"Manny, stop it, you're hurting me!" Marya exclaimed, wriggling out from under his hands. "A gang initiation? What do they want with him? He's too young to join a gang! Isn't he?"

"Apparently not, at least according to my informant. I know someone," Manny replied. "He's the one who told me about it." Manny started to explain to Marya the possible connection between his father and the gang, but then thought better of it. Marya would only get hysterical, and Manny had enough on his hands without having to deal with Marya.

"Can't we stop him?" she asked, appalled.

"We can try, but you see how he listens to us," Manny replied. "Now maybe you understand why it's so important that you and I present a united front when we talk to him. If he sees us disagreeing, he's sure to ignore us."

Street gangs were an intrinsic part of the fabric of the Colony, powerful and violent. There were parts of the City where it just wasn't safe, ever since a few years back, when an elderly couple had been stripped naked at knifepoint, robbed of their clothing, jewelry and electronics, and left to fend for themselves walking home.

"Street gangs," Marya said thoughtfully. "Don't the members take new names?" Absentmindedly, her hand rose to her arm, rubbing the spots where Manny's hands had gripped her.

Manny reached for her, drawing her closer, pushing her hands out of the way. Five bruises, dark blue and round, were beginning to show beneath her porcelain skin, one for each of his fingertips.

"Marya!" he exclaimed. "Are you OK? Can I get you some ice or something?"

"It's OK, Manny, I'm fine," she replied. "It's nothing."

Ashamed that he had injured his wife, Manny put his arms around her. His mind filled with memories of Patrick chasing Lila Rose, Manny's mother, through the house, grabbing her as she desperately tried to outrun him, punching her over and over while little Manny hid in the closet in the study. Lila always had bruises, blackish blue, red and purple, green fading to yellow.

He kissed Marya on the forehead. "I'm sorry, Marya. I love you. You're the last person I'd want to hurt."

"I'm fine, Manny, I know you didn't mean it," she said. "You just get carried away, that's all." She rested her head against his shoulder.

"About these gangs," she repeated thoughtfully. "Don't the younger members take another name for themselves when they join?"

"Yeah, most of them do," Manny replied, "and usually, the names are taken from white nationalists or other ultra-right wing groups. Sometimes, the names have Nazi influence."

"You mean like Heinrich," she said faintly.

"Yes," he said.

Chapter 15.

Manny was having a very bad day. He was sitting at his desk, drinking his morning tea and sifting through his emails. There was the usual weekly report regarding broken water pipes in various locations; leaks were so common now. Police patrols were adjusted every Monday to keep an eye on buildings which were temporarily empty for repairs.

Skimming through the list of locations, Manny stopped, his stomach lurching. One of the addresses was Aviva Johnson's old house, which had sprung a large, barely controlled leak several years ago. *This could be bad,* he thought grimly.

Years earlier, before Manny and Marya were married, Manny had accidentally discovered his late father's hiding place for a bottle of liquor, in his bedroom beneath the floorboards underneath Lila's velvet chair. The hiding place at first had appeared empty, but tucked away in the corner, Manny discovered a little leather pouch containing two diamond rings.

Thunderstruck by the discovery of these rings, Manny had considered carefully what to do with them. They had a long history.

As a teenager, Manny had broken into the home of an elderly woman, Mrs. Al-Sayed, and had stolen these two rings. He was leaving her house with the rings when he realized that there was surveillance watching him in real time.

Caught red-handed, sixteen-year-old Manny was arrested. He surrendered the rings to the desk sergeant at the precinct. His father, the Chief of Police, had been absolutely livid, locking him in a cell in the precinct overnight. Afterwards, Patrick told him that he had returned the rings to Mrs. Al-Sayed, in exchange for her promise not to press charges.

Years later, after Manny's appointment as Police Commissioner, the issue of the rings came up again. A group within the police department, disgruntled by Manny's appointment as Commissioner when there were older, more experienced men on the force, tried to oust Manny from his position by proving that he was a thief. The rings had never been logged into evidence, they insisted, so that must mean that Manny still had them.

Manny insisted, as he always had, that he didn't have the rings, that his father had returned them to their owner. Mrs. Al-Sayed's daughter, contacted by Manny's enemies, insisted that her mother had never gotten them back from Chief Stewart. Manny was telling the truth as he knew it – that is, it was the truth until Manny discovered the rings in his house.

As a detective, Manny knew that if his house were searched, the rings would be found; there was no safe place in the house to hide them. It would have to be somewhere outside of the house.

Miraculously, it was right around this time that Aviva Johnson's pipes sprang a leak. Her wall was torn open and exposed for repairs. The house, not far from Manny's, was deserted every night, after the workmen went home.

Manny had dinner with Marya, whom he was dating at the time. After dinner, they went for a walk to see the house. As they were leaving, Manny asked Marya to wait while he went back inside to look for his hair ribbon, which had "accidentally" fallen out of his hair.

Once inside, Manny quickly pulled the rings out of his jacket pocket and dropped them down into the bottom of the exposed wall, where the crushed concrete and other debris completely hid them. The following day, the workmen finished closing up the wall. How relieved he had been!

But now, the house was slated for more repairs. Manny sat behind his desk, his face ashen. *Stay calm,* he cautioned himself firmly, wiping his sweating palms along his pants. *Nothing says they will need to rip open that specific wall again. But even if they do, and someone found the rings, how would they know who they belonged to?*

Manny took a long sip of tea. As a seasoned police officer, he knew that criminals often give themselves away. They get flustered, they imagine that the police already know, they panic and blurt out the truth. No one would ever guess that Manny had found the rings and then discarded them outside of his house, not unless he lost his nerve and told them. He needed to keep his head on straight.

Dave chose that moment to walk into Manny's office. Manny straightened up in his chair and tried to appear normal. Dave was one of the best detectives Manny had ever known, and he didn't want his friend getting suspicious.

"Did you hear?" Dave asked, settling himself into the visitor's chair across from Manny.

"No, hear what?" Manny asked.

"The Chief. He's dead," replied Dave. "Died this morning. Can you believe it?"

"What?! I was going to hologram his wife this morning and ask how he was doing," Manny spluttered.

"You OK, Manny?" Dave asked with concern. "Your face is all white."

"I'm fine, just surprised, that's all. Go on, tell me what happened," Manny replied.

"His wife found him unconscious at the bottom of the stairs. She got him right over to the infirmary, but he never regained consciousness," Dave said, shaking his head. "So sad."

Manny, bewildered, said, "I had lunch with him, not long ago. He was fine." Then he remembered that the Chief had mentioned feeling dizzy.

I wonder if he got dizzy and fell down the stairs, Manny thought. It was a common accident in the Colony. The triangular shaped steps became treacherous as people aged.

Both in their late thirties, Dave and Manny were solidly middle aged, at the peak of their careers. The Chief had been in his sixties, an old man. Still, he'd been as sharp as ever. And now he was gone.

"I'm going to miss him," Manny said, shaking his head. "I can't believe it." The two sat silently for a moment, reflecting on their loss.

"Well. What do you have there?" Manny asked, motioning at the paper Dave was holding. "Is it bad?"

Dave was holding a confidential report on Zach's activities, produced on a single sheet of paper with no digital copies.

"I'm afraid there's been some escalation," Dave said carefully. "Zach and his buddies have been shoplifting again, but this time, Raj and Eddie went into the store and each filled up a large shopping bag, right out in the open. Security got them and called us." He handed the report to Manny.

"Was there a lookout?" Manny asked, scanning the paper.

"Yeah, it was Zach," Dave replied. "I'm sorry, Manny."

This was a serious step up from the garden variety shoplifting, which is so common among kids, taking an expensive little item which is easily concealed in a pocket or pouch, to a more brazen out-in-the-open approach, filling up a large shopping bag and walking out of the store with no pretense of hiding what they were doing. Their haul would be sold to a fence by the end of the day. It was not unheard of for the fence to sell the merchandise back to the store.

"The detectives nabbed all three of them, dragged them back into the store and made them return the merchandise, mostly clothing. And they made them take off those ridiculous Scuba sweatshirts, so store security could photograph them. They're banned from entering the store again," explained Dave.

"Serves them right," replied Manny. "Thanks, Dave. I'll speak to Zach when I get home."

"Does he know he's being followed?" asked Dave, referring to the two detectives who had been detailed to follow him and report back to Dave.

"Not yet, but he'll figure it out eventually," replied Manny grimly.

"No one's crazy enough to harm the son of the Commissioner," replied Dave, trying to reassure his friend. "There's some safety in that. You know, maybe there is no actual plan to use Zach to get to you. Maybe it's just a couple of low-level captains, trying to stick a finger in your eye, bait you into reacting."

"Yeah, but who would do that?" asked Manny.

"Maybe someone with time on his hands, like somebody in jail?" Dave suggested. "There's that half-brother, right, Kiaan Patel? Isn't he still locked up?"

Manny's heart sank. He knew that Zach looked up to Kiaan. "That's a possibility. He's Kiaan Gopalaswami now. He took his father's name after he went to live with him."

"Maybe he's pulling the strings," Dave said.

"You remember Loosey?" asked Manny. Dave nodded; everyone at the precinct knew Loosey. "He told me he's heard there's going to be an initiation this summer. He's fairly certain it's Zach, Raj and Eddie."

"It's almost the end of the summer," Dave pointed out. "He could be wrong."

"Maybe. I sure hope so," Manny replied with a sigh. He stood up. "You know what? I could use a walk to clear my head. Want to have lunch?"

"Now? Isn't it a little early?" replied Dave, laughing. "It's barely 11:00 am."

"Sounds like lunchtime to me," said Manny.

"OK, why not?" replied Dave, following his boss out of the office.

At Oodles, a favorite Asian noodle restaurant of Dave's, the two men sat down for lunch. They ordered two dishes to share, Japchae and lo mein, and two glasses of sweet and sour lemonade, made with blue and yellow striped lemons that tasted first sweet, then sour, then sweet again.

The two men settled into their lunch, enjoying being out of the office.

"Did you see that Aviva Johnson's house is on the latest list of houses with water pipe leaks?" asked Dave conversationally. "That neighborhood seems to get hit again and again."

"Yeah, I saw that," answered Manny, taking a sip of his lemonade. He carefully examined his red, white and blue striped glass straw, avoiding Dave's eyes.

"We've got leaks all over the Colony," Dave continued. "I guess it's good for the economy, right? All those plumbers and engineers are working overtime."

Manny made a noncommittal noise and took another bite of his lunch, hoping Dave would change the subject.

"Have you noticed something going on with the air quality lately?" asked Dave. "Everyone in the task force has commented on it. We're half asleep by mid-afternoon."

"Yeah, it could be better. Most days I don't notice anything, other days I feel like I can't breathe," Manny said. "Absences are up across the board, all over the Colony. Dr. Patel says that the most common complaint now is fatigue."

"There's nothing that can be done about that?" asked Dave.

"No one knows why the air quality is degrading. There's no quick fix. We could plant more trees and bushes, but that takes time," replied Manny. "Maybe we should open up all of the doors, all over the Colony, and let in some fresh air."

"You know, that's not a bad idea," replied Dave. "Would the Council approve that?"

"Are you kidding?" responded Manny.

Lunch over, the two men rose and left, Manny waving his forearm over the sensor at the doorway to pay for lunch. As they were leaving, someone came up behind him and leaning close to Manny's ear, said four words, "Friday. At the school." When Manny turned around, there was no one there.

"Look!" said Dave, pointing in front of them. It was Loosey, hat pulled down low, walking quickly. Obviously, he didn't want to be seen with them in public. "What was that?"

"He said, 'Friday. At the school.' That's all he said," replied Manny. "I guess the initiation is on."

The afternoon dragged on. At 4:00 pm, Manny gave up and left for home. He needed to have a serious conversation with Zach about what it meant to be a gang member, what it would mean for his future.

Marya was waiting outside for him, standing by the front door. She was wearing an ankle-length pale green skirt and a ruffled ivory silk blouse, her russet hair loose and rippling down her back, showing a strand of silver here and there in the late afternoon light. *Even at twenty-eight, she is still so beautiful,* thought Manny. He kissed her and said, "Everything OK?"

Marya shook her head. "I saw you coming, I've been waiting for you to come home," she explained breathlessly. "Now, don't explode, promise me, Manny."

"Let's see first what's wrong, then I'll decide how I'll deal with it," he replied guardedly.

"It's Zach," she said carefully.

Of course it is, he thought. "OK, what? Just tell me, Marya."

"He's upstairs with Raj and Eddie. They're drinking," she replied.

Chapter 16.

H ere in the house?" Manny asked incredulously.
"Marya, what are you saying? They brought liquor
into my house?"

"Now Manny, please try and keep it a civil conversation, not
a shouting match, OK?" she asked, but Manny had already
pushed past her and was on his way up to Zach's room, taking
the stairs two at a time, bad leg be damned.

"Zach! Zach!" he shouted, pounding with his clenched fist
on the closed bedroom door. Music was blasting loudly from
the other side. "Open this door!"

The door opened, releasing a cloud of beery smell. "Yeah?"
replied Zach insolently. His friends Raj and Eddie were seated
on the bed, snickering. All three of them seemed mildly drunk.

"Your friends were just leaving," Manny said with a
meaningful look at both of them. Raj and Eddie did not move.
Instead, they turned as one to look at Zach.

Zach glanced at the two of them, nodding once. They rose
and left, clambering loudly down the stairs, giggling.

"What is the meaning of this, young man?" Manny
demanded. "Turn down that damn music!" Zach reached over
and clicked his padlet, turning it off.

"What is the meaning of what?" Zach asked, a picture of
inebriated innocence.

Manny reached to the floor and gathered up six empty
bottles. "Take these downstairs to the kitchen, pour out what's
left and put the glass into recycling. Then you and I are going
to have a little talk."

"OK, *Malcolm,*" replied Zach, snickering.

"What did you call me?" Manny replied, his face darkening
dangerously.

"It's your name, isn't it?" Zach said with a smirk.

"Get those bottles out of here! And don't you ever bring liquor into this house again," Manny exclaimed. He badly needed Zach to go downstairs so he could have a moment to think clearly. He needed to be calm, be a good father, not yell so much. Marya was right. He must handle this properly.

Marya came to stand beside him. "Where's Zach going?" she asked worriedly.

"Around back, to put the empty bottles into recycling," replied Manny. "He'll be right back."

"Manny, promise me you won't make a big deal out of this," Marya pleaded.

"But it is a big deal, Marya! It is for me!" Manny said. How could she not understand what it meant for a recovering alcoholic to have liquor in the house? Naz would have understood. Naz had understood everything. Resentment, burning heavy and hot, settled like a stone in his chest.

Zach walked slowly up the stairs, finally arriving at the top. "You are not to leave this house, not for any reason, until I say so," Manny thundered. "Do you understand me?"

"Let's see. I *understand* you, Malcolm," Zach said, unsuccessfully trying to hide a hiccup, "but I don't *agree* with you. And I don't agree to staying imprisoned here." He was looking straight at Manny in a manner which was distinctly unchildlike.

"Imprisoned here!? You've got every luxury you could want, good food, your own room, intranet, books, music, games, what else do you want?" demanded Manny.

"Yeah, but it's sort of like being locked in a golden cage, isn't it?" asked Zach, sounding almost philosophical. "If I can't leave, I mean."

Manny felt the strangest echo of a memory from his early childhood, when he would come home from school to an empty house. Sometimes, his father would return from the office after he was asleep and then leave very early the next morning, missing him entirely. True, he lived in a beautiful mansion envied by most of the Colony, but children don't care about fine furnishings and valuable paintings. He had felt so isolated and alone.

But Zach wasn't little Manny. The circumstances were very different. He took a deep breath to compose himself. He might be able to keep Zach safe if only he could keep him at home. Raj and Eddie could have their damn initiation; his son was not going to join a gang.

"Zach, I want to talk to you," Manny began, trying to adopt a more moderate tone. "I wonder if you really understand what it means to belong to a gang."

"I know that they're like a family, that they always stick up for each other," replied Zach. "We're blood brothers. It's an unbreakable bond."

"Zach, *we* are family, a real family. And our physical bond truly is unbreakable," Marya said.

"My name isn't Zach anymore, Marya," replied Zach. "Please remember to call me by my name Heinrich." Manny was surprised when Marya did not react.

"Do you understand that when you join a gang, you can't change your mind? There is no un-joining a gang. They won't let you out," Manny warned.

"Why would I want out? I like them," Zach said. "They're my friends, they're always glad to see me."

"What about this initiation?" demanded Manny, gratified to see his son look startled. "Are you planning on going ahead with it?"

"How do you know about that?" Zach demanded. "Are you having me followed? I have rights, you know. You can't keep me under surveillance."

"You are a minor, young man! Don't talk to me about your rights. I'm trying to keep you from making a huge mistake. You idiot! Can't you see that I'm trying to help you?" Manny said desperately.

"I don't want your help!" replied Zach. "I'm doing just fine without it."

"Your father loves you, Zach!" said Marya, grasping his arm. "Please! Try and see that we only want to keep you safe!"

"Stop trying to save me!" shouted Zach, yanking his arm away from his mother, who had begun to cry. "Leave me alone!" Turning away from his mother, he headed for the door.

Manny tried to catch him, but like greased lightning, Zach turned sideways and ducked under his arm. He threw one leg over the banister and slid down the staircase at dizzying speed, then opened the front door before Manny was half-way down the stairs. Then he was gone, his rapid-fire footsteps staccato in the fading light.

"Where are you going?" Manny called to Marya as she ran wildly down the stairs and into the front parlor.

"I've got to catch him!! Where are my shoes?" She frantically searched the room for her shoes, finally finding them beneath the sofa.

"Marya, stop. You'll never catch him," warned Manny. "He runs like the wind, he's already gone."

Pulling his padlet out of his pocket, Manny placed a phone call.

A voice answered, "Detective Jantzen." She was breathing heavily, running hard.

"Do you and your partner have eyes on my son, Detective?" asked Manny.

"Yes, Sir," she replied.

"Apprehend him and bring him home. Cuff him if necessary," Manny said.

"Cuff him? Isn't he fourteen?" she asked, panting.

"Don't make me repeat myself, Detective," Manny said coldly.

"Yes, Sir!" she said. Manny hung up. He sat down heavily on the sofa next to Marya, who was still holding one shoe in her hand.

"What now?" Marya asked.

"We wait," Manny replied. "They'll find him and bring him home."

"And after that? How do we keep him here?" asked Marya.

Manny shook his head, taking the shoe from her hand and putting it next to the other shoe, side by side. "If he doesn't want to stay here, we can't force him."

"Maybe he should go stay with Luis and Lucinda for awhile. What do you think of that idea?" Marya asked.

Manny was about to reply when a call came in. "Yes?" he answered.

"Commissioner, your son has gone into Raj Gopalaswami's house. We rang the bell and identified ourselves, and asked permission to enter the house. The homeowner refused entry. What would you like us to do?"

Ordinarily, Manny would simply approve a search warrant so his people could enter the house, but that would create an open case. Manny wanted to ensure that there was no record of this incident.

"Text me the address, and wait for me there," Manny said. "Whatever you do, don't let my son leave."

"Understood," replied the detective.

Manny picked up his hat from the table in the foyer. Then he turned to Marya. Ignoring her hand wringing and shrill questions, he said firmly, "You're to stay here until I get back." He shut the door behind him, cutting her off in mid-sentence.

A police officer who is running attracts attention. Manny strolled, nodding pleasantly to passersby who waved to him. He recognized some of them, like those two young women he'd seen at the rest-up outside of the Parts Department. He forced himself to walk, resisting the urge to break into a run.

The Gopalaswamis' house was run down and dilapidated, part of a row of smaller, older homes in one of the tunnels, where the least desirable real estate was located. Manny walked up to the front door, where the two female detectives were waiting.

"Thank you, Detectives, I'll take it from here," he said.

He rang the bell, which didn't work. He knocked politely, resisting the urge to pound on the door with his fist. To his utter surprise, the door was opened by Azura Perez, the girl who had kissed Zach in middle school.

Manny stared at her, dumbfounded. "You?" he spluttered. "What are you doing here?"

"What's it to you?" asked a man's voice, distinctly unfriendly. Mr. Gopalaswami came forward, pushing the girl behind him. "If Azura wants to visit with family, that ain't any of your business, now, is it?"

"She's not to be within fifty feet of my son! She knows that!" Manny said angrily.

"Then maybe your boy ought to leave. Azura has every right to stay with her cousins for a few weeks," Mr. Gopalaswami said. "She didn't come here to see Zach."

Manny considered that he might actually be telling the truth, and decided to drop it. *Stay focused,* he warned himself.

"I'm sorry," he said more calmly. "Let me introduce myself. I'm Manny Stewart."

"Yeah, I know who you are," Mr. Gopalaswami replied. He leaned against the door frame as if he were too weary to stand up by himself. He looked like Raj, only older and more tired, and was badly in need of a shave. One hand was lazily scratching his crotch.

"I'd like to talk to Zach, please," Manny continued.

"But does he want to talk to you?" the man countered insolently, looking Manny up and down, taking his time.

"You are Deepak Gopalaswami?" Manny asked. "I know your son, Kiaan. I wonder if Kiaan might like a job working in the prison kitchen, instead of scrubbing toilets."

Mr. Gopalaswami looked at him warily. "I don't want no trouble," he said.

98

"I understand," Manny said, taking a single tentative step closer to the entrance. "I'll be just a minute, and then I'll leave." He took another step forward, this time putting his foot across the threshold. Finally, Mr. Gopalaswami stepped aside, and Manny moved past him into the house.

"Zach!" he shouted. There was loud music coming from upstairs, which stopped abruptly. In the silence, there were poorly stifled giggles coming from behind a closed door upstairs.

Manny climbed the stairs, and knocked on the closed door. "Zach! Open up this door right now!"

"There's nobody named Zach in here!" said one of the boys, followed by young voices joined in raucous laughter.

Manny tried the door handle, which was locked. He turned to Mr. Gopalaswami, who had come upstairs behind him. "Please," he said to him. "I must see my son."

Mr. Gopalaswami seemed embarrassed that Raj and Eddie would not open the door. He knocked on it a few times and said something stern to Raj in rapid fire Hindi. They waited, but the door remained closed.

Just as Manny was considering kicking in the door, something which he had not done in years, he was surprised by Mr. Gopalaswami angrily kicking it in himself. He exploded into a torrent of Hindi, alternately shouting and hitting his son and nephew on the shoulders and arms with his hands. There was a girl in the room with them. Mr. Gopalaswami shouted at her, too.

Manny could see at a glance what they had been doing. The girl, who must be Raj's sister, was holding a razor in her hand. Zach's head was splotched with shaving cream. He ignored his father, wiping away the shaving cream with a towel.

All three boys were now completely bald. It was a common first ask, the first step in a gang initiation. It says, "If you're serious about joining our gang, show us by shaving your head."

Manny, beyond dismayed, simply didn't trust himself to speak. He grabbed Zach's arm, twisted it up behind him and then pushed his shoulders down until he was bent over at the waist, parallel to the floor. It's difficult to walk in that position, which is why the police routinely use it to move dangerous or incalcitrant perps from point A to point B in detention. Zach struggled and squirmed, but soon realized that he could not get out of his father's iron grip. Together, they maneuvered slowly down the stairs and out the front door.

99

Chapter 17.

With a firm grip on Zach's arm, Manny slowly walked Zach home. Neither spoke for several minutes. It was slow going, though, and finally Zach began to complain.

"Dad! Come on, Dad! My back's gonna break in half, let go of me!" he protested. Manny grimly kept silent and continued walking. He knew that Zach was uncomfortable. *Serves him right,* Manny thought, *and besides, if he ever gets arrested, they're going to be a lot harder on him than this.*

As they approached the walkway leading up to the house, Manny released his grip on Zach's arm and back. Zach straightened up with a groan and turned to face his tormentor.

"Was that really necessary?" he demanded angrily.

"You tell me, Zach," replied Manny, as they entered the house. "Would you have come with me voluntarily?"

Marya was waiting anxiously in the front parlor. She rose quickly from the sofa, took one look at Zach's bald head and abruptly sat back down, speechless with dismay.

"Go upstairs to your room," Manny said. "And stay there."

"How long until dinner?" asked Zach hopefully, as if nothing unusual had happened during the day. No one answered.

"Zach," said Marya, her voice shaking. "What have you done to your hair?"

"Raj's sister shaved it for me," he replied. "Now Raj, Eddie and me, we all have shaved heads." He said it proudly, although he seemed a bit taken aback by his mother's reaction.

"What was Azura doing at Raj's house?" Manny asked. "There's a restraining order keeping her away from you, you know."

"She didn't come to see me! She was there when I got there," Zach explained. "I think she's sweet on Kiaan or something."

"Kiaan? She's a cousin, right?" Manny asked. "They're related?"

"Yeah, their grandparents were second cousins, or something," Zach said. "She's been living at Raj's house for the past month. Trouble at home, she said."

"Keep away from her, Zach," Manny warned. "She's trouble, plain and simple." Zach crossed his arms over his chest and looked away; he did not reply.

"When's the initiation?" asked Manny.

"Initiation?" repeated Zach.

"Yes, the initiation," repeated Manny. "When is it?"

"When is what?" asked Zach, smirking.

It was a practice commonly used by criminals during police interrogations; they would repeat the question back to the detective, forcing the detective to ask the question again. It could draw out an interrogation for hours. Manny had no doubt where Zach had learned this technique.

"When is it, Zach?" Manny repeated.

"You don't know, do you?" Zach replied smugly.

"I can find out, you know," Manny replied.

"Then why are you asking me?" Zach taunted. Manny's fists clenched at his sides, but he controlled his temper.

"Why should I ever tell you anything?" Zach asked mockingly. "You're nothing to me! You have no authority over me, not unless I agree that you do!"

"Is that what they taught you, your new friends?" Manny said bitterly. "I'm your father."

"Big deal! It's still my life, not yours!" Zach exclaimed angrily.

"As long as you're living in my house, you'll respect my authority and do as I say!" Manny exclaimed, his face dark with rage. "You don't like it? You can leave any time you want."

"Manny, now wait a minute," cried Marya. "Zach's not going anywhere."

"Maybe I'll go live with Raj or Eddie!" Zach shouted. "They'd be happy to have me!"

"Go ahead! But don't expect me to pay for your food and clothing, if you no longer live here," Manny threatened. "I'll cut you off without a Krown, freeze your accounts, no allowance, nothing. Don't think I won't!"

"What's going on in here?" demanded Lucinda, appearing suddenly in the doorway of the front parlor, an empty basket in her arms. "I was putting away the laundry when I heard you all shouting!" Looking at her grandson, she said, "Zach, why don't you put this basket away for me upstairs?"

You have to give her credit, Manny thought, *she didn't even blink when she saw his bald head.*

Zach gratefully took the empty basket and flew up the stairs. As soon as he was out of hearing, Lucinda looked at Manny and said softly, "What on earth has happened?"

"As you see, Lucinda," Manny replied. "He's become uncontrollable. I practically had to drag him home from his friend's house after he defied me and went out. The three of them, they've shaved their heads. It's the first step in their initiation."

Lucinda's face showed her concern and sorrow. "Manny, you deal with gangs all the time!" she pleaded. "Don't you know how to stop him?"

"I wish I did," he said wearily. Conversation ceased as Zach came bounding back down the stairs.

"Dad perp-walked me home from Raj's house," he complained, hoping his grandmother would chastise his father. He bent over at the waist, one hand behind his back, to illustrate. "Like I'm some kind of common criminal!"

"There's plenty more of that in your future, young man, if you don't start behaving yourself!" Manny retorted.

"I'm sure your father had a good reason for doing that," Lucinda replied crisply. "Young man, your actions are causing a great deal of pain in this family."

She looked at him steadily, her gaze holding his, reminding him of the relationship the two of them shared. After Naztazya's death when Zach was five years old, it was Lucinda who held him, comforted him, read to him, talked to him. She was always there for him. His defiance wavered as he looked at her. Defeated, his eyes focused on the floor, he sat down on the sofa.

"Ok, then," Lucinda said. "Dinner will be in twenty minutes. Manny, can you give me a hand, please?"

The last thing Manny wanted to do was go into the kitchen and chop vegetables. But at the moment, Lucinda was the only one in the house who could defuse these confrontations, and he didn't want to refuse her in front of Zach.

"I'll be right there," he promised. Lucinda smiled at him and made her way to the kitchen, taking her time.

"Why don't we all just take a breath. It's been a tough afternoon. Zach, go wash up for dinner," Manny said.

After he had left the room, Manny turned to Marya. "There's something I don't understand. Why didn't you stop them from bringing beer into the house?"

"At first I didn't know! The beer must have been in their backpacks. I thought they were just upstairs playing video games. When I realized that they were drinking, I told them to stop, but they just ignored me," she replied.

"Marya, you have to make them listen to you," Manny admonished her.

"What should I have done? Tell me!" she demanded. "I did my best, but Manny, there are three of them. They're big, and loud, and defiant. They just laughed at me."

"You should have marched in there and taken the beer bottles out of their hands!" Manny said in exasperation. "You're the adult! You don't ask if it's OK. If you act like you're intimidated, then you're done." He glared at her. "Suppose I'd been another hour getting home? What would you have done then? Waited for me outside the whole time, while they sat up there drinking?"

Marya stood up to face him, eyes flashing. "He's not easy to deal with, Manny, you know that! We obeyed our parents, growing up. We did it because we were supposed to, because we loved and respected them. I don't have any experience with this, this ... defiance!" Whether it was her intention or not, it came out sounding like her childhood had been perfect, so all of this must be Manny's fault, not hers.

Speechless, Manny stepped aside as Marya sailed out of the room. He watched her go upstairs, his heart filled with resentment. Naz would never have spoken to him like that. Naz was a soothing, concliliatory influence in their marriage, while Marya was more abrasive, quicker with a sharp retort or angry remark. As a middle child, she had learned to speak up loudly to defend herself. Manny marveled for the thousandth time that his second wife could be so different from his first.

With a sigh, he followed Lucinda into the kitchen.

Dinner was quiet and subdued. Afterwards, Manny and Marya went out for a walk, at Manny's request. "I'm sorry," he said, as soon as the front door closed behind them. "I've been under a lot of pressure at work, and now this thing with Zach. It's really got me on edge."

"I'm sorry, too, Manny," Marya responded. "I don't mean to lose my temper with you like that! I hate it when we fight."

Remembering Dave's advice, Manny steered clear of revisiting their earlier angry words. "I hate it too, Sweetheart," he said.

Later, upstairs in the privacy of their bedroom, Manny put his arms around her and kissed her forehead. "You mean everything to me, you know that, don't you?" Manny murmured.

"Promise me something, Manny," she said softly, her hands resting on his shoulders. "Promise me that you won't let us lose him."

"I promise," Manny replied. The words came easily. The hard part would be living up to them.

Marya fell asleep quickly, but Manny tossed and turned. Finally, at 3:00 am, he gave up and stopped trying to sleep. It wasn't only the initiation that was on his mind.

Every week, the report came out detailing which neighborhoods were scheduled to have repairs on their leaking pipes. Since he first saw Aviva Johnson's house on the list, Manny had checked carefully each week to see if repairs on the house were scheduled to move forward. The schedule kept changing, though, according to the severity of other ongoing plumbing issues, pushing the address further down the list as more urgent repairs were made.

Of course, Manny simply could ask Hasan when the repairs would be done, but he didn't want to arouse any suspicions. It was not common for the Commissioner to take an interest in these types of repairs, beyond making sure that there were adequate police patrols in the area. *No,* he told himself firmly, *just sit tight and wait. When in doubt, do nothing.* He was hopeful that the repairs would be minor, or in a different spot than the last time. In any event, there was nothing he could do about that now.

His sleepless mind then turned to the other, more urgent issue of Zach's initiation. Staring up at the ceiling, his detective's mind formed a plan to keep Zach safe, step by step.

It seemed so unlikely that there was any connection between Eddie and Raj befriending Zach and the bad blood between Patrick Stewart and Amir Gopalaswami so many years earlier, and yet the facts were there, logical and compelling. Facts, as every detective knows, are stubborn things. Manny wished he could talk to the Chief again about it, but the Chief was dead.

Dead, he repeated to himself. What's it like to suddenly have the lights go out with no warning, no chance to say goodbye to the people you've spent your life with, no chance to wrap up the things you've been working on, no time to reflect? He shivered, thinking of Naz, who had burned to death in a fire with barely any warning, and of his father, who was euthanized, with full knowledge of what was about to happen. *Hopefully, my time's a long way off,* he thought.

Sleep was a long time coming.

Chapter 18.

Manny sat at his desk, staring at the wall across his office, concentrating intensely. It was Thursday morning, the day before Loosey had warned there would be gang activity at the school.

While school was not officially back in session until the following Monday, the buildings were filled with teachers and supervisors, holding meetings and getting ready for the school year. Members of sports teams, the school orchestra and other groups showed up to pick up uniforms and schedules, etc.

"Nigel!" Manny shouted abruptly.

"Here, Sir." Nigel appeared in the doorway.

"I want you to do two things for me," Manny said. "First, have a dozen detectives meet with me in the conference room in an hour. Pull them from different units so we don't lean too much on any one unit. Also, please see to it that Kiaan Gopalaswami, you know, the gangbanger, gets a permanent job in the prison kitchen."

Nigel's eyebrows went up, but he knew better than to ask questions. "Yes, Sir," he replied.

"That will be all," Manny said, staring down at his hands.

After Nigel left, Manny went over the details in his mind one last time. There would be four undercover detectives stationed around his house, and a dozen more stationed at the middle school. Two detectives would be stationed at the high school, just in case there was activity there, too.

They needed to keep Zach safe until Friday was over and the plans for the initiation were called off. *Or,* thought Manny, *maybe they'll want to go ahead with just Raj and Eddie. I don't care, as long as Zach isn't involved.* He rather doubted that they would do that, though. He knew that whoever brought the Commissioner's son into the fold would gain street credibility in the eyes of the gang, raising his stature. Even from his jail cell, Kiaan would be a hero.

The meeting went smoothly. He explained the threat to the public and the undercover work involved, adding that his son was expected to be one of the three boys initiated that day. There was an audible murmur as that news was digested. If any of the officers wondered why Manny couldn't keep his own son at home without police assistance, no one said anything, at least not in front of him.

The meeting over, Manny breathed a sigh of relief. Surveillance was scheduled, officers had been assigned, he'd done all he could do today. Time to move on to other things.

A tap at the door caught his attention.

"Morning," said Dave, coming into Manny's office. "How's everything?"

"OK, I just finished assigning the detail for tomorrow. I decided to do both schools. And I'm going to have four undercover detectives at the house to keep Zach under wraps until Friday has come and gone," Manny replied.

"That's good, glad to hear it," replied Dave distractedly. Manny knew his former partner well. It was obvious that Dave had something he needed to tell him.

"And?" Manny asked, leaning back in his ancient, squeaky desk chair.

"There's something I need to tell you," Dave said. "The case against you, you know, with Raimone and the two rings. It's been reopened."

"What do you mean, reopened?" asked Manny, suddenly feeling as though he was standing on a trap door. Abruptly, he sat up straight. What had changed since the case was closed? The insurance company had settled with the family years ago.

"It seems that a relative found photos of the old lady wearing the rings, and is pushing for their return to the family," Dave replied reluctantly. "Enlarged, the photos are good enough for identification purposes. She says she'll be willing to return the insurance reimbursement for them, that they are family heirlooms. She's demanding ... well. "

"She's demanding what?" asked Manny, realizing as he asked the question that his good friend had just warned him that his house would be searched. "Unbelievable!" exclaimed Manny, distractedly running his fingers through his hair.

"I'm sorry, Manny, I know you've got enough on your plate right now without this," Dave said sympathetically.

"It's like it never ends," Manny remarked, more to himself than to Dave. *Shut up, shut up!* he cautioned himself sternly. *Don't give Dave any reason to wonder if I know more than I'm saying.*

"Now that there's this new evidence, they'll probably send another Internal Affairs Department low-life here to sniff around and sift through our evidence room," Dave continued. "Don't worry, they'll get soon get tired of looking."

"Who's behind this, Raimone?" asked Manny. Raimone, an overzealous IAD detective, had tried everything to find the two rings and prove that Manny was a thief, in order to derail Manny's career. When Manny continued to deny that he had the rings, Raimone became so enraged that he shot Manny in the leg.

"I doubt it, he'll be locked up for another three years," replied Dave.

After Dave left his office, Manny closed his door and sat down behind his desk. Those rings, those horrible rings! Why had he ever stolen them? Julio had warned him, back when they were teenagers, that it's dangerous to take anything too valuable. Take inexpensive, small items, Julio insisted, things that can't be traced and that the homeowner may think are misplaced, not stolen.

Even though Manny's juvenile record was sealed, that had not stopped Raimone and the people who backed him, including the judge who issued a search warrant, from trying to use it against him to remove him as Commissioner.

Looks like they still want me out, Manny thought ruefully. What was it that his predecessor, Deputy Commissioner James O'Brian, had told him, right before he died? "There are going to be many older officers who will resent your promotion. They'll be jealous; just ignore them."

James was right, as far as the advice went; but these officers who wanted Manny removed weren't just jealous; they were determined, and patient. They wanted him gone. As Raimone had said to him, right before he shot him in the leg, "Gone, by any means necessary."

Manny carefully laid out the facts in his mind. The rings were deeply buried inside a wall in Aviva Johnson's house. At the time he placed them there, he knew that even if found, no one could identify them as belonging to Aviva Johnson. But now, with a photo … yes, they might be identified.

Still, no one could prove that Manny had put them there, or had ever had possession of them at all. It was his father, Patrick

Stewart, the Chief of Police, who had kept them, despite telling Manny that he had returned them to the homeowner.

Thanks a lot, Dad, Manny thought with a spark of resentment. *You've left me quite a mess to clean up.*

And now, the Johnson house once again had a leak, and was on the list for plumbing repairs to be made. *That doesn't mean that the leak is big enough to warrant opening up the wall,* Manny reminded himself. *Maybe it's a small leak. Maybe it's in a different location. Maybe they're being proactive, since there was a serious leak there years ago.* He cautioned himself to be patient. *Don't look for trouble,* he said to himself. *Do nothing. Say nothing. Ride it out.*

Manny's hands were shaking. He clasped them tightly together, his thoughts returning to Zach. He took a deep breath, then another. Loosening his shirt collar, he forced himself to concentrate, opening up his padlet.

Manny: *Where is Zach now?*

Marya: *He's here, I've got him cleaning out the rest of the closets in the house.*

Manny: *Good, keep him in the house. I've got detectives coming tonight to make a perimeter around the house. If he tries to leave, they'll catch him, but I'd like to avoid that if we can.*

Marya: *What time will you be home?*

Manny: *I don't know. Not late.*

Manny clicked shut the padlet, rolling it up and putting it in his pocket. It was past lunchtime; he could use a sandwich. He stopped by Dave's office on his way out.

"Lunch?" he asked.

"Nah, too busy with the budget stuff from the Mayor's office," Dave said, making a face.

"I'll bring you back a sandwich," Manny offered.

It's good to get out of the office, Manny thought, inhaling deeply. It was stuffy inside the old building. It wasn't only today, either. The stuffiness was much better, once he left the building. On impulse, he texted Dr. Monica Patel, his personal physician and liaison with the Department of Public Health:

Manny: *Monica, is there something going on with the air quality lately? It seems especially stuffy inside the precinct today.*

Monica: *Yes, we've had worrisome oxygen levels all week, the worst it's been since we've been watching it. Are you feeling OK?*

Manny: *I'm fine, just tired.*

Monica: *You and most of the Colony! Nine out of ten absences now are due to fatigue.*

Manny: *What would happen if we opened up the doors and let in some fresh air?*

Monica: *Are you serious? Not joking?*

Manny: *Serious. Would it help?*

Monica: *If the air outside is more balanced, then yes, it would help. There's no way to tell, though. The only way to find out is to try it. Maybe try opening up one door as a first step.*

Manny: *Would you be willing to address the next Council meeting and tell them that fresh air might be a solution?*

Monica: *That could be career-ending for me, Manny! We don't have the ability to study the issue properly. Sorry, I respectfully decline.*

Manny: *Thanks anyway for your input, Monica. I appreciate you.*

Monica: *You're welcome!*

Manny picked up two sandwiches and a couple of melon-ades, and was on his way back to the office, when he noticed the same two women who had been at the rest-up outside the Parts Department, sitting on a bench eating their lunch. They were both looking solemnly right at him. When he waved, they waved back. *That's odd,* he thought, *I wonder who they are.* But with so much on his mind, he quickly forgot about them as he made his way back to the office.

"Dave," he said, as the two men sat diagonally across from each other at Dave's desk, lunch spread out in front of them. "I've got an idea." He explained about his conversation with Monica Patel. "The air in here makes me feel tired. It's been especially noticeable this week." Dave nodded, his mouth full.

"What if we open up the outer doors, you know, at street level, and let in some fresh air? We could do it as an experiment here in our neighborhood, maybe open only a couple of doors. If the air quality is worse, we can close them again."

Dave laughed. "Didn't I suggest that the last time we had lunch?"

Manny nodded. "Yeah, and it was a good idea. I asked Monica about it just now, and she's not willing to go out on a limb to address the Council about it, but she does think fresh air could be the solution."

"OK, let's try it," Dave said. "You're not going to ask for approval first, are you?"

"That's the plan," said Manny with a grin. "Instead of waiting for Council approval, which could take, oh, I don't know, a year or more. Yeah, let's just do it."

"Sounds good to me," said Dave. "What's the point in being Commissioner and Deputy Commissioner if you have to ask for permission to do stuff?"

"Nigel!" Manny shouted. Like magic, their aide appeared. "Nigel, please have the street level doors at the 50th Street stop opened. I want them left open all day and night until further notice."

"But Sir," Nigel began, his concern clearly showing. "Isn't that dangerous?"

"We're about to find out," Manny said.

The rest of the afternoon dragged endlessly. Manny was sure at one point that his clock was actually moving backwards. He rose and stretched, careful of his sciatica, and paced around his office a few times. Finally, at 4:15 pm, he couldn't wait any longer. He picked up his jacket and hat and headed for home.

Chapter 19.

G ood morning," Manny said to Zach early on Friday, opening up his son's bedroom door. "Did you sleep well?"

"Hey! You're supposed to knock!" said Zach, startled by his father's unusual early morning visit.

"Just wanted to say good morning," Manny said, retreating back into the hallway and closing Zach's door. He went downstairs into the kitchen, where Marya was making coffee.

"Smells good," he said, resting his hand briefly on her shoulder as he passed by on his way to the table. "I saw Zach. I opened the door to his bedroom and made sure I had eyes on him."

"He's there, I've been watching," confirmed Marya. "I was up at 6:00 am and peeked into his room. He's been in there all night."

"Good," replied Manny. "Now if we can just get through this day," he said, thinking of the hours ahead. "Don't let him out of the house for anything."

"Got it," she replied shortly. "You don't have to keep telling me."

"I'll be in touch during the day, OK? Don't go anywhere, just stay in the house with Zach," Manny said.

"Got it," she repeated. He was annoying her, he could see that.

"I'm sorry, Marya, I'm a little keyed up," he said apologetically, reaching over and taking her hand. "I know you'll do a good job."

"I want to keep him safe just as much as you do, Manny," she replied. "He's not leaving this house."

As Manny entered his floor of the precinct that morning, he could feel an undercurrent of heightened awareness, almost excitement, in the office. Everyone knew about the undercover operation at the schools involving the Commissioner's son; word travels fast within the police community.

Inside his office, Manny used his police apps to project a multi-screen collage onto the wall across from his desk, so he could monitor the activities in real time. One of the CCTV monitors showed his house from the front yard. He was gratified to see that there was nothing moving. Two plain clothes detectives were at a nearby rest-up, having coffee and a morning chat, looking like two ordinary citizens enjoying the morning. He couldn't see the other two undercover detectives, but he could hear them as one by one, everyone checked in with the Police Commissioner, who was handling today's operation personally.

Dave stopped by, knocking once on the door before walking in. "How's it going?" he asked, coffee cup in hand, looking at the neatly arranged CCTV screens on the wall, each showing a different portion of the two schools.

"So far, so good," Manny replied, pointing to the middle school's entrance. "They've identified every student as they walked in. Raj and Eddie go to the high school now, so if they try to enter the middle school, they should be stopped at the door," Manny said.

"Reporting every hour?" asked Dave, sipping his coffee.

"Every hour on the hour," replied Manny. "Otherwise, you know, it's just another Friday." He laughed. His hands were sweating; he wiped them on his pants.

"Well. It's not going to be easy to work on anything else today," Dave said, watching the monitors projected on the wall. "But there is this one thing."

"There's always one thing," laughed Manny. "What is it?"

"There's a rumor going around that the doors at street level were left open deliberately last night, to let in fresh air. Did you see this?" Dave flipped open his padlet and found the news article he wanted. "It was on NewYorkOne last night, the right-wing talk show."

"I know the show; my foster mom watches it sometimes while she cooks." Dave's eyebrows went up in surprise.

"She watches all kinds of shows," Manny explained, "mostly for amusement. It's not like she agrees with them."

"Here, let me show you this," Dave said, tapping "play" and handing the padlet to Manny.

"What on earth is this all about?" a voice was asking, as the camera showed the street level doors at the 50th Street stop, wide open to the night air, fresh air flowing freely into the

Colony. "Is it possible that someone did this deliberately? And who could that be?"

The camera went from one entrance to the other, all with wide open doors. "Is this some kind of a joke?" asked the voice-over. "Or is it a deliberate attempt to experiment on the citizens of this Colony by letting in the night air? No one has been exposed to night air in hundreds of years! Who did this, and on whose authority? NewYorkOne aims to find out." The video clip ended.

"It's not going to take them long to figure out it was me," said Manny. "I just hope it works. Why should air become dangerous, just because the sun went down?"

At that moment, the detectives started checking in on the hour one by one, as had been pre-arranged. Each one reported that there was nothing going on. Manny looked closely at the footage of his house; nothing was moving. There were still two people at the rest-up near his house, but on closer examination, he could see that they weren't detectives at all; they were the same two women that he kept seeing when he was out.

"Dave, look here. Do you see those two young women?" Manny asked.

"Yeah, I see them," Dave replied, coming to stand closer to Manny as they examined the video feed. "What about them?"

"I see them often when I go out, in different places. They're always together, and I have the eerie feeling that they're not exactly following me, but they want something from me, or for me ... I don't know. They keep popping up, and they were both looking right at me last time, when I noticed them. It seemed purposeful. Weird, huh?"

"Do you want me to find out who they are?" asked Dave. "We could have Nigel do a search. We've got perfect footage of their faces, thanks to today's surveillance."

"Yeah, let's do that," replied Manny. "Nigel!" he shouted.

Nigel appeared in the doorway. "Sir?"

"Look at these two women, here near my house. Can you find out who they are?" Manny asked.

"No need, I know who they are," replied Nigel. "They're taking over Madame Elayna's business. They were her apprentices, or colleagues, or something."

Madame Elayna. Funny how her name kept popping up. Marya hadn't mentioned their visit to see her in a long time. She hadn't mentioned wanting to have another baby in a long time either, he realized. *Today is not the day to be thinking about this!* he told himself sternly. *Prioritize. Zach first.*

~ ~ ~ ~ ~ ~

At mid-day, Manny texted Marya.

Manny: *Everything good?*
Marya: *Yes, we're fine. Zach is finishing up cleaning out the closets. I am in the same room with him, he's not going out.*
Manny: *Good job. I'll check in again later.*

Lunch, reports, staff meeting, more reports. The day dragged dismally. Each hour, the detectives checked in. Everything was calm and peaceful. At 4:30 pm, most of the staff and visitors had left the middle school, and by 5:00 pm, both schools were empty and silent. Manny, rather than breathing a sigh of relief, knew that trouble could still be coming.

"Going home?" asked Dave.

"Yeah, I think I'll keep an eye on things from there," Manny replied. "If I need help, I'll text you."

"Thanks, I hope everything stays quiet," Dave said. "Maybe they'll go ahead with the initiation without Zach."

"Maybe," said Manny. He rather doubted it, though.

Marya and Zach were downstairs in the front parlor when Manny came home. Zach was cleaning out the closet. Apparently, that involved throwing everything that had been in the closet onto the floor, but at least Zach was usefully occupied and safely inside the house.

"Hi, Zach," he said.

Zach reddened to the top of his bald skull. "My name is Heinrich," he replied angrily, averting his gaze.

"How are you today?" Manny asked, keeping his tone civil.

"How the hell do you think I am?" Zach said resentfully, turning to face his father. "You've got me locked up here like I'm in jail!"

"We're keeping you safe, Zach, not imprisoning you," Manny said. "You don't understand what you're getting into with these people, they will never let you go, once you join them."

"That's the idea," Zach replied disdainfully. "It's what we want."

Worried that another argument was about to erupt, Marya asked, "Manny, here, look at these. Do you want to keep them?" She pointed to a pile of sports equipment that had been stored in the closet, a collection of balls and gloves, knee pads and helmets. "Let's see what's here."

It was a clumsy attempt to distract, but Manny went along with it. They sorted, they talked, they even managed to laugh a little as a few stories came to mind of Zach's early days playing Mets-n-Yankees and b-ball with Julio and Julie.

Manny excused himself and went into his study, where he set up the same collage of CCTV footage he'd had in the office, neatly arranged so he could monitor the operation. The schools were quiet, nothing moving in their cameras. One by one, he heard the detectives checking in. All safe.

Dinner was a very quiet affair. Lucinda and Luis were at their house tonight; Lucinda was tired and was lying down. Julie and Anna did most of the talking. Julie, who was a senior in high school, was interviewing at different colleges; Anna would be accompanying her on the tours. Mostly, though, everyone was on edge, especially Zach, who fidgeted dismally in his chair.

Finally, Zach said, "Can I be excused?" Marya nodded. They all watched as Zach went upstairs to his room and slammed shut his door.

"He's angry," said Marya, stating the obvious. "He thinks we are treating him like a prisoner."

"Marya, he's just going to have to deal with it," Manny said. "I want him to live past twenty-five."

Marya turned pale. "Are you serious? Is that how long gang members live?" she asked.

"Have you ever seen an old gang member?" Manny asked rhetorically. "There aren't any."

After dinner, Manny took a chair out of the dining room and carried it outside. "What are you doing?" asked Marya.

Manny held his finger to his lips. "Not a word, please," he said to her. "You can come with me, but you'll have to be quiet."

Marya watched as Manny carried the chair out onto the lawn, placing it very close to the house, behind the potted bushes and underneath the overhang of the roof. From the second floor of the house, if you looked out the window, you wouldn't be able to see the chair, hidden beneath the overhang.

Manny sat down on the chair facing the lawn, and waited. Marya whispered, "What are you doing?"

"I'm keeping an eye on things out here," he said. "You're going to keep watch in the house. If Zach leaves his room, I want you to be there. The threat isn't over because it's nighttime, Marya. The threat is greater now, not less."

116

Manny settled in for a long night. It was a very long time since he'd been on a stakeout. He and Dave, back when they were newly minted street cops, had been on many a stakeout together, drinking coffee and staying up all night. He was ready for the long hours of tedious waiting. He sat motionless and alert, listening.

Hours passed. Sometime around 10:45 pm, Dave arrived, walking up the path to the front door. Before he rang the bell, Manny said, "Ssst!" to get his attention.

Dave looked around and when he saw Manny behind the bushes, he laughed softly. "Got another chair?" he whispered with a grin.

"In the house," Manny whispered. "Stay here, I'll get you one. Glad to see you! What made you decide to come?"

"I figured you need me to stay awake," Dave replied. "Can't have you falling asleep out here, you know."

"Hey, I know how to stay awake," protested Manny, laughing. "Thanks, though, seriously. It's always easier with two people than one."

"No problem! I got you, man, I got you," replied Dave.

Chapter 20.

Manny went into the house and got another chair from the dining room. Marya brought two cups of coffee out to them and returned to the house, leaving the two friends to keep watch outside. Manny and Dave sat side by side in companionable silence, listening and waiting, padlets out.

Finally, at midnight, one of the detectives texted, "Movement middle school."

They watched as the detective began to run, her forehead camera bouncing as it captured what she was seeing. In the far corner of the school yard, in the shadows beyond the spill of the lights, several figures had suddenly materialized. A fight had broken out among them. Two men were being savagely punched and kicked. Both fell to the ground and stayed there, as the vicious, brutal assault took place.

"There they are!" Dave whispered excitedly.

"Thank goodness they don't have Zach," Manny whispered back.

Running towards the altercation, the detectives identified themselves and the group immediately scattered. "Cops!" yelled someone, as the group melted away into the shadows. One man reached down to lend a hand to the two victims, who were lying motionless on the ground.

"Raj, Eddie! Come on, get up!" he urged, but Raj and Eddie were slow to rise. Limping badly, Eddie leaned on Raj as they straggled after the rest of the group, Raj wiping the blood from his mouth on the back of his hand.

"That's it, that's the initiation," whispered Manny. "First, they beat the crap out of the idiots who want to join. Then they tell them how brave they are for surviving the beating, and after that, they're in."

A tiny scraping sound caught their attention. Simultaneously, the two seasoned detectives turned their eyes to the roof, listening intently as the upstairs window slid open. A moment later, there was the sound of something heavy sliding across the roof. The trellis at the side of the house shook once, twice, followed by a loud thud as something heavy landed on the ground.

"Just where do you think you're going?" demanded Manny, materializing out of the bushes and grabbing his stupefied son by the arm.

"What the hell! Dad! Are you everywhere??" Zach demanded. "You're watching every move I make! Let me go!" He struggled mightily, which only made Manny angrier. He tightened his grip.

"Get back inside the house this instant or I swear, Zach, I will handcuff you to your bed!" Manny threatened.

"I didn't hear that," murmured Dave, who was studying his padlet. "Manny. Look, it's over now. They're gone."

Manny released his grip on Zach and pushed the padlet towards him. "Want to see what you missed tonight?" Manny asked angrily. He rolled back the footage and replayed the fight, showing Raj and Eddie being beaten, lying on the ground as they were kicked and punched. "That could have been you right now, seriously hurt, lying on the ground."

"You made me miss it! You've ruined everything!" Zach cried, reaching up to run his hands through his hair, before remembering that he had none. "Now Raj and Eddie are in, and I'm not! You bastard, I hate you! Why can't you just leave us alone?"

"That's fine, you go right ahead and hate me," Manny replied bitterly. "Someday, you'll realize what I did for you tonight."

The two stared at each other. This time, Zach did not look away.

"You think you can keep me away from them?" Zach asked defiantly. "You and all your cop friends? You can't stop me. I'll wait. I'm a patient man."

Manny suppressed a desire to laugh at his fourteen-year-old son's characterization of himself as a patient man. *Somebody's been feeding him this garbage,* Manny thought, *probably Kiaan.*

Manny's voice was menacingly quiet when he said, "I thought I told you to go inside."

Instead of obeying his father, Zach surprised Manny by suddenly bolting, running swiftly down the walk towards the

119

street. Manny and Dave did not move, confident in their detectives' abilities.

Zach headed towards Raj and Eddie's house, surprised that his father and Dave were not following him. He was shocked beyond words when four detectives suddenly materialized out of the shadows. One of them tripped him, unceremoniously pushing him down onto the ground, while another handcuffed his hands behind his back. They returned him to his father in short order, ignoring his protests as he twisted and struggled.

"I hate you!" Zach shouted, straightening up as the detectives uncuffed him in front of Dave and Manny.

"You're welcome," said Manny. "Now get in the house."

Manny and Dave picked up their chairs and headed back inside, too. "How did you know he'd climb out through the window?" Dave asked.

"I grew up in this house," Manny replied with a grin. "My old man once pushed a dresser in front of my bedroom door so I couldn't leave my bedroom, so I climbed out through the window, slid down the roof and went to Julio's house." He laughed. "It seemed like a reasonable choice at the time."

"Why is it funny when you do it, and a crime when I do it?" asked Zach resentfully.

Serious again, Manny turned to his son. "Zach, go find your mother and let her know you're safe. She's been worried sick."

"Zach, Zach!" cried Marya, hurrying down the stairs. "Are you OK? Come here, let me look at you!"

"I'm fine, nothing happened to me!" Zach protested. "Can I please just go to bed now?" Pushing quickly past Marya, Zach took the stairs two at a time and went into his room, door slamming.

Marya turned to Manny. "What happened?" she asked.

"I'll tell you all about it in a minute," he said. "For now, though, I have to talk to Zach."

"Can't it wait, Manny? Let the boy simmer down," she pleaded.

"I'll get going now," Dave said with a friendly bow. Marya opened the front door as they both thanked Dave for his help.

"We've got a problem," Manny explained to Marya as soon as Dave was gone. "Zach's friends were initiated tonight, so now they're Skulls. The Skulls are thieves. I don't want Raj and Eddie here in the house anymore. I need to explain that to Zach."

"I'll come with you," Marya offered, climbing the stairs next to Manny.

"No, actually, I thought maybe I'd try to talk to him alone," Manny replied. "If that's OK with you," he added. Marya nodded uncertainly.

In his room, Zach was sitting on the bed looking angry and defeated. "Your friends are both in the infirmary being treated right now," Manny said to him. "Raj has two broken teeth and a broken arm. Eddie has black eyes and a sprained ankle. Both of them have multiple bruises and lacerations requiring stitches. Either one of them could easily have had a more serious injury like a fractured skull or a punctured lung."

"Nah, that was never going to happen," replied Zach confidently. "Some of the Skulls are Raj's uncles. They were there. They're not going to let anybody hurt Raj or Eddie."

"I don't think you realize how easy it is to unintentionally cause a great deal of harm," replied Manny. "A smashed eye, for instance, or a fractured skull."

Zach looked at him wearily. "You just don't get it, do you?"

"What is it I don't get, Zach?" Manny replied. *This is good,* he thought, *we're talking, we're not yelling, maybe I can persuade him to stop this nonsense.*

"You can't talk me out of it. I'm joining the Skulls whether you like it or not," Zach stated flatly. "You are no longer relevant."

"No longer relevant?" repeated Manny. "Who told you that, Kiaan? He's full of wisdom, isn't he? But he's in jail, Zach. Think about that."

Zach's stubborn, defiant expression did not change.

"Why do you think they want you, Zach?" asked Manny. "You're young for a new recruit; usually they're a little older than you. What's so special about Zachary Stewart?"

Surprise flickered over Zach's face.

"Do you think it could be related in any way to you being the Police Commissioner's son?" Manny continued. "You'd be quite a prize for whoever brings you in."

"They want me for *myself*, Dad, not because I'm your son!!" protested Zach. "Raj and Eddie are my friends! Besides, Kiaan says I have potential."

"Potential for what, Zach?" asked Manny. "Does Kiaan think he's got an inside man now, in the Commissioner's house?"

Zach looked at his father in consternation. *He's a child,* Manny reminded himself. *He doesn't have the maturity, experience or judgment to see it.*

Manny stood up. "It's late, Zach, we all need to get some sleep," he said. "We'll talk again about this. But from now on,

Raj and Eddie are not allowed in our house. They're gangbangers now, and I won't have them here."

"They're my friends!" objected Zach. "How am I supposed to tell them that my old man won't let them in the house?"

"If they have any sense, and I think they do, then they already expect it, Zach," Manny explained. "They're older than you, and with coaching by Kiaan, they've done a great job of grooming you. You need to think about that, Zach, how you're being manipulated. They're two steps ahead of you on a bad day."

Zach scowled. "Nobody's manipulating anybody! They're my friends," he insisted staunchly.

"And you're to keep away from Kiaan, too," Manny added, "no more visits to the jail to see him. If I hear of you going to the jail again, you'll be grounded for a very long time. I'll have his visitor's log sent to me every day. Do we understand each other?"

Zach's face was a thundercloud of resentment. "You go to hell," he said defiantly.

"Good night, Zach," Manny said, wishing this was over, and knowing that it wasn't.

"Everything OK?" asked Marya as Manny came into their bedroom. She was sitting up in bed with her back against the pillows, her long hair reflecting in the spill of the lamp.

"Yeah. We talked, and I didn't shout," Manny replied proudly. "I may actually have made him think about why the Skulls want him. I don't think he ever considered why Raj and Eddie befriended him."

"Do you think they chose him because he's your son?" asked Marya, her eyes round with surprise. *She hadn't thought of it either,* realized Manny. To him, it seemed obvious, but then again, she wasn't police.

"Actually, I do," Manny replied. "I'm guessing that Kiaan and his buddies thought up this scheme to befriend Zach and bring him into their gang, and had Raj and Eddie reach out to Zach. The two boys obey Zach like he's their leader, but I'm pretty sure that's designed to make Zach feel powerful, like he's already one of them."

"I've noticed that," Marya said, "the way Zach snaps his fingers and Raj and Eddie do whatever he says. You think that's just an act?"

"I think it's more manipulation on their part. He's young, Marya, he really believes that Raj and Eddie are his friends, but I have my doubts." Manny pushed back the covers on the bed and climbed in with a sigh. He put his arm around Marya's shoulders.

"I've had a lot on my mind," he said. "I'm sorry if I was a little overbearing today."

"It's OK, I understand," she replied. "I'm just glad all this is over."

Chapter 21.

Manny pushed his desk chair back and stood, stretching. It had been a busy and very productive day. He glanced at the clock, an old-fashioned analog clock projected onto the wall by his padlet. It was 5:30 pm. In his early years, Manny had considered 5:30 to be mid-afternoon, often eating dinner at his desk and getting home well past dinnertime. Now that he was the Commissioner, he could leave the office earlier.

He decided to text Marya.

Manny: *Want to go for a run this afternoon?*
Marya: *Sure! Your leg feeling OK?*
Manny: *Pretty good, actually. I'm about to leave now. Be home soon.*
Marya: *See you soon!*

When Manny got home, Marya was in the kitchen slicing the ends off a bunch of howling potato-beans. He watched as she stacked the long, narrow dappled brown and tan beans neatly into a Mason jar and then poured a pungent pickling liquid over them, listening to their sudden high-pitched exhalation, a "howl" surprisingly loud for a vegetable.

"I'll just go upstairs and change," Manny said, kissing his wife. "Be right back." Manny went to his room, noticing as he passed by that Zach's room was empty and quiet. Kicking off his shoes, he tossed his uniform pants and shirt onto the floor, changing into shorts and teeshirt.

He was on his way down the stairs when he suddenly stumbled sideways, grabbing the railing to catch his balance. He stood quite still, the steps trembling beneath his feet. *Another tremor,* he thought with dismay. He waited, but it faded away. These little tremors were nothing to worry about, according to the scientists, but even minor tremors were unnerving. He decided to say nothing, and see if anyone else had noticed it.

"Where's Zach?" he asked Marya, as he came down the stairs.

"He's over at your parents' house," Marya replied. She seemed fine, calm and composed as usual. *She probably didn't even notice it,* he realized. Still, everything seemed OK now, so he dismissed it as inconsequential.

Zach often visited Luis and Lucinda in their townhouse across the street, occasionally staying for dinner. When he was a child, Zach had enjoyed sleepovers at his grandparents' house, along with Julie.

"At least he can't cause any trouble when he's over there," Manny said. "I think it's nice that he visits them so often."

Manny and Marya stood on the front steps, stretching. "Are you sure you're up to this? Your leg, I mean?" asked Marya.

Instead of answering, Manny took off running ahead of her, looking at her over his shoulder. "How's this?" he called with a grin.

Marya easily caught up to him, and the two began to run side by side. "You know, we should do this more often," Marya said to him.

"I was just thinking the same thing," he said breathlessly. "I need to get into shape again. I run like an old man."

"I was thinking more along the lines of companionship, you know, spending time together," Marya said. "It's fun."

"That, too," Manny said, panting. "Come on, then!" The two of them sprinted for as long as Manny could keep it up. He stopped, bent over with his hands on his knees, breathing hard.

"OK, Manny?" asked Marya, hovering nearby.

"Fine, I'm fine. Just need a minute," he replied, panting. "Maybe we can sit down somewhere."

"There's a rest-up not far ahead, look over there," she said, pointing to a small stone bench and fountain surrounded by potted bushes and a flowering vine of some sort. The two headed towards the rest-up.

Walking towards them from the opposite direction were two women in ankle-length skirts and shortie boots, bracelets jingling, the same two women whom Manny often saw when he was out of the office. They were not looking directly at Manny and Marya, although it seemed to him as if they were avoiding looking at them, their gaze carefully elsewhere.

"Marya, do you know these two women?" he asked as the pair drew closer. "I see them everywhere. Sometimes I think they want something from me, the way they look at me."

"Those two? I don't know them personally, but I've seen them around," Marya said, lowering her voice as the two passed them. The two women nodded politely as they passed; Manny and Marya nodded back.

"They're Madame Elayna's apprentices, the ones that are going to reopen her business," Marya continued. "Once when I was out shopping, I dropped one of the shopping bags and the tall one, the blond, she picked it up and came running after me to return it. She was very polite."

"There's something off about the two of them," Manny said thoughtfully. "I can't quite put my finger on it."

"Now that you mention it, she was acting a little odd, almost awe-struck," Marya said. "She sort of curtsied to me, when she handed me the shopping bag, holding it out to me with both hands and not looking directly at me."

"That really is strange," Manny said, laughing. "We're not royalty." A curtsy was a quaint and old-fashioned gesture that had no place in their society. Manny had actually never seen a woman curtsy, although he knew what it was.

"Shall we start back? How's your leg?" asked Marya.

"Better than yours!" Manny said, taking off ahead of her. She caught up with him easily, the pair running side by side in silence for several minutes.

"Manny," she said hesitantly, "I've been thinking."

"Oh, yeah?" he replied in a neutral voice.

"You know, the two of us don't always get along as well as we might," she said.

"The only thing we ever fight about is Zach," said Manny quickly. "Everything else is OK." He said the last part as a way to put some parameters around the conversation. His relationship with Marya could be better, although that was not a conversation he wanted to have, certainly not right now.

"It's true, raising Zach has been more than a challenge," she conceded. "But with love and kindness, I think he's going to be just fine."

"And you think I fall short in the love and kindness department?" Manny prompted.

"Well. I know that you didn't have the best role model growing up," she replied. "But you could be more loving, more kind, less of a tyrant when you talk to him."

Manny was so surprised that he stopped running. "You think I'm a tyrant?"

"Manny, now don't get mad. But yeah, you know, sometimes you are pretty hard on Zach. You get so angry over each and every little thing he does," she replied, coming to stand next to him. She placed her hand on his arm, looking into his face. "He needs your love, Manny," she said beseechingly. "He may not show it, but he's still just a boy. He needs his father."

"I just busted my butt saving him from joining a gang!" Manny protested. "Was that not enough love and kindness?"

"That was wonderful, the way you saved Zach from being initiated! That's not what I meant, though. You could spend more time with him, talk to him about school and things, just be his dad," she replied. "As things are now, every conversation is an argument. That's not going to change unless you change it," she added. "It's up to you; you're the adult."

Manny started to respond with his usual tired promise to spend more time with Zach, but then didn't. Marya sounded genuinely concerned. Besides, what they had been doing up until now obviously wasn't working. And if something isn't working, as Lucinda often said, try something different.

"You're right, Marya," he replied. "I'll try harder, I promise."

The two continued running together in companionable silence until the house swung into view. Manny stopped and turned to Marya, taking her hand in his. "Thank you," he said sincerely, kissing her gently despite being out in public. Still holding hands, the two went into the house and upstairs into their bedroom to change before dinner.

"Why do we fight?" she asked rhetorically, sitting down on the bed with a sigh. She patted the spot on the bed next to her.

"I don't know," he replied, sitting down next to her. He reached over and pulled the ribbon out of her ponytail, releasing her long russet hair. "You are so beautiful, Marya," he added. "Not to mention so much faster than me."

She smiled invitingly, leaning back against the pillows. Manny stood up and pulled his teeshirt over his head in one smooth motion, tossing it onto the floor. He kicked off his shoes, and then froze.

"The chair. Marya, where is my mother's chair?" he asked, puzzled.

The master bedroom had once belonged to his mother and father, when Manny was a child. The velvet chair had been Lila Rose's favorite place to sit when she read stories to little Manny, seated on her lap. Lila Rose had died when Manny was seven. Manny loved the velvet chair, which always reminded him of his mother.

"Oh, that! I've been meaning to tell you. I've ordered a new chair and ottoman, something more modern. That old chair was so old-fashioned and worn out, I got rid of it," Marya replied. "It just didn't look right in here. I gave it to the decorator to dispose of."

"You *got rid of it?!*" he repeated incredulously. "That chair has been in this room since before I was born. It's a family heirloom. How could you get rid of it without asking me?"

"I wanted to surprise you," she protested. "I was trying to do something nice for you, for us."

"Get it back," Manny snapped. "Maybe it hasn't been sold yet, and the designer can return it to us."

"Return it?!" she exclaimed, her voice rising. "I can't do that, Manny! It would be humiliating to ask to have that old wreck of a chair returned to us. Besides, he's probably already recycled it."

"What were you thinking, Marya?" he demanded. "You know how much that chair meant to me!"

Surprised by his reaction, Marya replied, "It's a chair, Manny! You never once mentioned it to me. How was I supposed to know it was so important to you!"

Furious, his anger spilled over before he could stop it. "That chair was my mother's! How could you give it away without asking me? Naztazya would never have done such a thing!"

"Naztazya!" Marya exclaimed, stunned. "Oh, so that's it! Precious Naz, perfect in every way! I'm sorry if I fall short of your expectations!" She looked daggers at him, her emerald eyes glittering. "You still love her, don't you?"

"Of course, I still love her," he blurted out furiously. "Don't you?" As soon as the words left his mouth, he realized his mistake.

Marya's face was marble-white, a mask of jealous fury, her eyes flashing with rage. They looked at each other for a long moment.

"I'm sorry, Marya, I shouldn't have said that," he began contritely.

"Get out!" Marya said angrily, turning her back on her husband.

"*Me*, get out?!" Manny said, astonished. "I'm not going anywhere!" He had lived in this house all his life, and this had been his bedroom long before it was hers. "I'm sure you'll be comfortable in one of the guest rooms," Manny added sarcastically.

Marya picked up her nightgown and without looking at Manny, sailed out the door with her head held high, all the way down the hall to the last of the empty guest rooms, closing the door with a resounding bang.

A few moments later, Manny heard Anna's bedroom door open, and the sound of footsteps going down the hall towards the guest rooms. *Anna's going to talk to her,* Manny thought. *Maybe she can talk some sense into her.*

A discreet knock on Manny's door surprised him. "Yes?" he asked guardedly.

"Hey, it's me," said Julio.

"Come on in," Manny said.

Julio took a step into the bedroom. "What's going on? We heard shouting."

"You're not going to believe this," Manny declared. "She got rid of my mother's chair! I'm going to reach out to the decorator and ask him if he can give it back."

Julio's eyebrows went up. "She gave away Lila's chair? Didn't she ask you first?"

"No, she did not." He sighed, his anger ebbing. "Maybe I shouldn't have been so hard on her. I said some stuff I shouldn't have."

"Oh?" asked Julio encouragingly, sitting down on the bed.

"Yeah. I said that Naz would never have gotten rid of my mother's chair," Manny said.

"I bet that went over well," Julio said. He chuckled, imagining Marya's reaction. Manny did not laugh.

"Well," said Julio, getting up. "I'll leave you to fix things with Marya. I wish you luck. Looks like you're going to need it!"

"Very funny," said Manny, as Julio left, leaving Manny sitting by himself on his bed.

Chapter 22.

Manny reached for his padlet, sending a hologram request to his wife's decorator, despite the lateness of the hour.

"Mr. Tomaino," Manny said to the ghostly figure on his night table, "there's been something of a mixup here. My wife inadvertently gave away our bedroom chair. It's actually an important family heirloom. I hope you still have it?"

"The velvet chair?" asked the decorator. "Your wife instructed that it should be discarded. I've already stripped it down and sold the frame for the wood. She's ordered a new chair and ottoman."

"Can you get it back?" asked Manny.

"Not easily, no," the man said reluctantly. "Wouldn't you rather have the new chair?"

"No," insisted Manny. "I want the old chair. It belonged to my mother, and I'd like it back. Please cancel the order for the new chair."

There was a silence, while the designer weighed his options. On the one hand, he'd been paid a tidy sum for the wooden frame of the old chair. Solid wood was hard to come by. On the other hand, he dared not antagonize such a powerful client. He hesitated.

"What's the other party paying you for the frame?" asked Manny sourly. "I'll double it."

"I'll do my best to get it back in one piece, Commissioner," the decorator responded smoothly. "But please understand that the buyer may have already taken it apart. I'll see what I can do."

"You do that," Manny said coldly. "I expect the chair to be reupholstered in something as similar as possible to the original, and returned to my home by the end of the week." He hung up, not bothering to listen to Mr. Tomaino's response.

Manny went downstairs to the kitchen, where he filled a dinner plate for himself. He took the plate and a glass of juice back up to his bedroom. If Marya was going downstairs for dinner, he didn't want to see her.

Manny spent a miserable evening alone in his bedroom. Marya did not go down to the kitchen for dinner. In fact, she never left the guestroom all evening, as far as Manny could tell. Around 10:00 pm, Anna knocked on her door, bringing her a plate of food.

Alone in his bed, eventually Manny slept, and dreamed. *Marya was lying next to him, speaking to him, laughing about something funny that little Zach had done. He pulled her close, his arms around her, but then it wasn't Marya at all. It was his father, Patrick, shoving him away. "What about Marya? Are you going to kill this one, too?!" Patrick demanded scathingly.*

He woke up exhausted, and alone.

Dressed, he went downstairs to have breakfast. Anna and Zach were sitting at the kitchen table; Julie was in the foyer looking for one of her shoes. Manny sat down across from Anna.

"You talked to Marya last night?" he asked tentatively.

"Yeah," she said. "She was pretty angry."

"I know. I said some things I shouldn't have," he said, looking down at his coffee cup.

"You compared her to Naz, Manny," Anna said flatly. "She hates that." Anna took another bite of her toast, chewing reflectively.

"Naz and I were so close. I'm eight years older than Marya, Naz was seven years older. We were more like parents to her than sisters, growing up. She always wanted to play with us, follow us around, just be with us." Anna stopped to finish her toast and take a sip of coffee. "Naz and I could have been nicer to her, I guess. Kids can be mean."

Manny, who was an only child, wasn't privy to the subtle niceties of sibling relationships. "I thought you all got along so well," he replied.

"We did, except when we didn't," Anna said ruefully. "It got better as we got older."

"I'll apologize to her," Manny said. "Any tips for me?"

"No, I think I'll keep out of this one," Anna said with a laugh. "I'll see you tonight."

~ ~ ~ ~ ~ ~

"Geez, you look awful this morning," Dave said, waving Manny into his office. He leaned back and put his feet up. "What's going on?"

"A little fight with the wife, that's all," Manny said, yawning. "We slept in different bedrooms. I was up half the night."

"That does sound bad," Dave commiserated. "Whenever I have a fight with Jenny, I start by apologizing. Then I listen to her until she's done talking, and then I say that I love her and can't live without her. Avoid the particulars and concentrate on the emotions. Works every time."

"I think I'll send her flowers, soften her up a little, so when I get home tonight, she's not on the war path," Manny said. "Nigel!" he shouted.

Nigel, aide to both men, appeared in the doorway. "Nigel, send Marya some flowers, OK?" Manny asked. "A big bouquet. She likes bluebells. The card should say, 'I could not be more sorry' and it should be delivered early today, hopefully before lunch."

"On it," replied Nigel, writing busily in his padlet.

"Let me know what happens!" Dave said with a laugh, as Manny got up to return to his office.

Later that morning, Nigel knocked on Manny's door. "Commissioner," he said formally, pushing the door open wide, "Mrs. Stewart."

"Marya! What a nice surprise," Manny said. Nigel tactfully closed the door, leaving them alone. "Sweetheart, before you say anything. I'm sorry for those things I said. I didn't mean to hurt you."

"I'm sorry too, Manny," she said, sitting down opposite him. She opened up her bag. "I'm sorry I lost my temper. I missed you last night! Thank you for the flowers this morning, they were lovely. Look, I've brought lunch with me. Do you have time?"

"For you? Of course," he said.

Marya removed a red and white checked tablecloth out of her bag, which she shook out with a flourish, spreading it over Manny's desk. There followed a loaf of bread, a jar of frog butter, a terrine made of oats, tofu, and blueberries, a plate of cookies, and a bottle of mollyberry juice. She handed him a plate, and the two of them fixed sandwiches in self-conscious silence.

132

"I missed you too, last night," said Manny, thickly spreading frog butter on two slices of bread.

"I've been thinking," she began. He braced himself. "I really want to apologize about the chair, Manny," Marya said. "I didn't realize how much it meant to you."

Manny nodded. *Avoid the particulars,* he reminded himself, *no need to get mired down.*

"I want you to understand why I got so upset," Marya said. "I've been compared to Naz and Anna more times than I can count. For years, growing up, it was always 'why can't you be more like your sisters,' and no matter how hard I tried, I never quite measured up."

Manny took another bite of his sandwich, saying only "Mmm-hmm."

"They were so close, Anna and Naz, almost like twins. They did everything together," Marya continued. "I always felt excluded."

She clasped her hands tightly together in her lap before saying, "I need to ask you something, Manny. You said you still love her. Did you mean it?"

Manny proceeded very carefully, tiptoeing around the trap he had inadvertently laid for himself. "I met Naz when she was fourteen," he replied. "We were kids. I loved your sister with all my heart, and it nearly killed me when she died."

Marya bowed her head. Manny hurried on. "But after she died, there you were, Marya. I never really noticed you before, you know, since you were so much younger, but ..." his voice trailed away as he realized that she was crying.

"Tell me honestly," she said, her voice quavering. "Did you marry me just because you wanted someone to help you care for Zach, someone to run your household and leave you free to work?"

It was the question he dreaded most. Did he marry Marya so she could take care of five-year-old Zach, make sure his meals were prepared, generally run the household so he could concentrate on his career? Yes, of course he had. What else could he have done? She had been young, single, attractive and his sister-in-law, already part of the family.

By marrying her, he gave her security, wealth and position in society. *Not a bad trade,* he reassured himself. Still, in his heart of hearts, he recognized guiltily that he had taken advantage of her. He knew that he would never love her as she deserved to be loved.

Manny recognized a minefield when one presented itself. "Marya, you are my life," he said. Marya looked up, tears rolling down her cheeks. "I can't imagine my life without you. I love you. Please forgive me for hurting you."

"But ... what you said, that you still love her," Marya said miserably, her hands twisting together in her lap. "I have to know." She looked tired, dark circles underneath her eyes, her face pale and drawn.

"I will always have a place in my heart for Naz," Manny said solemnly, putting on his most sincere facial expression. "I know that you will, too."

"Yes, but she was my sister," Marya pointed out. "Not my wife."

"And now you are my wife," Manny side-stepped smoothly, "and there is no one but you."

"You haven't answered me," Marya insisted, surprisingly resolute. "Did you marry me out of convenience?"

"No," said Manny flatly. It was time to put forth the most convincing of his painstakingly crafted arguments. "Marya, I could pay a woman to take care of my son and make sure dinner was waiting for me when I get home. I wouldn't need to marry her!"

She regarded him gravely for a moment, then laughed. "I never thought of it that way," she said, picking up her sandwich and beginning to eat. Inwardly, Manny breathed a sigh of relief.

A few minutes later, Manny's knee found the special "discretionary lever" hidden beneath his desk and pressed against it. A heartbeat later, Nigel opened the door and said, "Commissioner, your 12:30 hologram with the Mayor is in a few minutes."

"Nigel, not now! I am speaking with Mrs. Stewart," exclaimed Manny haughtily, frowning. "The Mayor will have to wait." Nigel bowed his head briefly and withdrew, closing the door behind him.

"Manny, you're busy, I'll go," said Marya.

"The Mayor can call back," Manny said with a gentle smile. He picked up his sandwich. "This frog butter is delicious."

When lunch was over, Manny walked Marya to the door. "Thanks for lunch, for doing all this," he said. "I'm glad you came." She smiled gratefully at him and squeezed his hand.

After she left, Nigel came to stand beside Manny in his doorway. Manny, eyebrows raised, exclaimed, "A 'hologram from the Mayor?' That was positively inspired!"

"Thanks, Boss," Nigel said, with a conspiratorial smile.

~ ~ ~ ~ ~ ~

After dinner that night, when Luis and Julio were busy with the dishes and Zach had returned to his room, Lucinda came to stand next to Manny. "Can we talk, son?" she said in an undertone.

"Of course," he said, taking her elbow and steering her out into the foyer. "Library or study?" he asked.

"Let's go into the library," she said. "Just as long as we're not interrupted."

Seated side by side in front of a wall of antique books preserved on glass-enclosed shelves, Manny and Lucinda settled in.

"I've been talking with Zach," Lucinda said haltingly. "You know he was just at our house." Manny nodded encouragingly. "He comes to see me often, to talk. I've always kept his confidences, but he said something that has me worried, Manny."

"What did he say?" Manny asked, bracing himself.

"He said now that you've ruined his chances to be initiated along with his friends Raj and Eddie, he has no choice but to do something big to prove himself worthy so he can join the gang," Lucinda said.

"Did Zach say if he has a plan? I mean, is this more than just talk?" Manny asked with concern.

"I'm not sure, Manny," she responded. "But he does seem fixated on joining this group."

"Thanks for telling me, Lucinda," Manny said. It was worrisome news, but it might be nothing.

Lucinda looked at Manny appraisingly. "Would it surprise you to know that your son comes to see me regularly? And that we talk about things the way you and I talked when you were a boy, struggling with your own father?"

"No, I didn't know that," Manny said. "What do you mean, the way you and I talked about Patrick? My dad was a sadistic bastard, you know that, Lucinda! I'm nothing like him."

"He asks my advice, Manny, for how to interact with you," she said gently. "He's asked me more than once why you don't love him."

"Why I don't ... what?" asked Manny in consternation. "I love him! I just don't get along with him very well." He felt distinctly uncomfortable at the idea of Zach and Lucinda discussing his shortcomings.

135

"Zach's found a foolproof way to get you to interact with him," Lucinda said. "It's destructive, but it works. If the two of you are fighting, then at least you're paying attention to him."

"I don't get it, Lucinda," Manny said in exasperation, distractedly running his fingers through his hair. "I can't make him obey me! I've given him everything he could ever want; he's got a roof over his head, food to eat, clothes on his back, a generous allowance. What on earth does the boy want?!"

"What did you want from your father, Manny? When you were growing up?" she asked, her eyes sorrowful.

"I wanted him to stop hitting me, for one thing!" Manny replied. "What do you mean, what did I want from him? I didn't want anything from that bastard!"

"Manny. Answer me," Lucinda insisted. "What did you want from your father, when you were a child? You had food, clothes, an allowance, all of those things, just like Zach."

There was a long, uncomfortable silence, during which Lucinda's gaze never wavered.

Finally, Manny admitted hoarsely, "I wanted him to love me."

"That's right," Lucinda said. "Unfortunately, Patrick was incapable of loving anyone, including you, but how could you understand that, when you were so young? All you knew was that you were entitled to his love, and he wouldn't give it to you."

In a heartbeat, it all came flooding back, the anger and resentment, the frustration, the sheer despair he'd felt as a little boy after Lila Rose died, four long years before he'd met Julio. He had been deeply ashamed that his father didn't love him, sure that it was his fault and not his father's. He had tried hard to win his approval. Sadly, his father alternated between ignoring him and tormenting him. It had been the luckiest day of Manny's life, the day that Julio took him home to meet the Suarez family.

Manny shook his head. It had all happened a long time ago, and Zach wasn't anything like Manny. It wasn't a fair comparison. *I'm a much better father than my father was to me,* he reassured himself. *I hardly ever hit him.*

"Thank you for letting me know about Zach," he said formally, getting up from his chair. He helped Lucinda up from her armchair, walking with her into the foyer.

"Please don't let him know I spoke to you," she warned in a soft voice.

"Of course not. I'll be very discreet," replied Manny.

Chapter 23.

You decided to do this *unilaterally?* Throw caution to the winds and open up the doors in one of the neighborhoods, to see what might happen?" Mr. Jha was in fine form, thumbs hooked beneath his suspenders, pacing back and forth, using his courtroom voice.

"Yes, in my neighborhood, where I live with my family," responded Manny. "No one was harmed, no one even felt sick. There were zero reports of any problems, no sudden surge of visits to the infirmary, no uptick in doctors' visits. Personally, I think the fresh air was a good thing."

"A good thing, Commissioner, or a narrow escape?" countered Mr. Jha. "Do you have any scientific information to prove that the night air was not harmful?"

"No, I do not," responded Manny. "What I do have is Dr. Patel, my Liaison to the Office of Public Health. Let's listen to what she has to say."

Manny rose and opened the door, ushering in Monica Patel, who had been waiting nervously in the hallway outside.

"Originally, I had tasked Dr. Patel with looking into the falling birth rate in our Colony, to see what our public health experts have to say about the issue," Manny said as he introduced Monica. "What she found was surprising: there seems to be a correlation between our declining air quality and the falling birth rate. But I will let Dr. Patel speak for herself."

"Thank you, Commissioner," Dr. Patel replied. She chose her words very carefully. "The department has found that the oxygen levels in the Colony are falling, resulting in subtle but far-reaching effects on our bodies. You may have noticed some of this yourselves. Fatigue, headaches and exhaustion are common now; absenteeism is up in all of our schools and workplaces. Most importantly, the department feels sure that there is a correlation between the lower levels of oxygen and the fertility rate among our women."

"Do they have any recommendations on how we could adjust the oxygen level in our air?" Manny asked.

"They advise that we should plant more bushes," Dr. Patel replied. "This will clean the air. It will take some time, though, maybe a couple of years, before the bushes are large enough to really make a difference."

"Dr. Patel," Manny continued, "was anyone harmed by the fresh air that we let into the Colony in mid-town recently?"

"As far as anyone can tell, no. It may actually have helped. The people we interviewed reported feeling more energetic and motivated, with better quality sleep," Dr. Patel responded.

"Commissioner," Mr. Jha stated flatly, "I shouldn't have to remind you that the fire-and-water-doors to the outside are to remain closed. It is the law. If you leave the doors wide open, then you have broken the law."

"It's time to change that law," Manny retorted. "People should be free to go outside, if they want to."

"Don't try and change the subject!" insisted Mr. Jha. "You can't prove that no one was injured by your foolish actions."

"Show me someone who was injured," countered Manny. The two men glared at each other.

"I've half a mind to bring you up on charges, Commissioner," threatened Mr. Jha. "Clearly, you've broken the law."

"As a matter of fact," Manny replied, "I may have overstepped my authority when I left the doors open. I've had a chance to think it over, and I believe I was wrong to do that. It was foolish, and I'm sorry. It won't happen again."

Mr. Jha stared at him open-mouthed, his anger checked. Manny had played his part well. He had admitted his fault, shown remorse, promised it would not happen again. Abruptly, the former prosecutor sat down, with nothing left to say.

After the meeting, Manny walked out with Monica Patel and Sarah Blumberg.

"How'd I do, Manny?" Monica asked. "I felt like I was walking a tightrope."

"I think it was clear that you're a spokesperson for the department, not a scientist," said Manny. "Thanks again for agreeing to speak to them today."

"You're welcome," she replied. "You know, just between us, I think it was a wonderful thing, letting in some fresh air. I went over to the open doors and stood in the doorway for several minutes. The feeling of cold fresh air on my face was amazing. It left me feeling energized for some time, even afterwards. It seems to me that it was only beneficial."

"I think so, too," Manny replied. The three colleagues walked together in amicable silence. Sarah, who had once been Manny's school teacher and tutor, was an old and trusted friend; Monica, whom Manny had known since grade school, was his trusted personal physician.

"I'm curious," Manny said. "When you were standing near the open doorway, enjoying the fresh air, why didn't you walk through the doorway and go outside?"

"You mean, *outside?*" replied Monica. "No, that's forbidden, isn't it? We were all taught as children that we have to stay underground, that the environment outside will kill us."

"Things are changing, though," Manny replied. "I don't know of anyone who's been outside who was injured by it. It's true, technically it is illegal to go outside, unless you are performing some kind of maintenance work, like repairing a door. The law states that you must have a work permit in order to go outside, but we've relaxed our criteria so that anyone can get a permit. You can apply online, and it will be approved immediately."

"Why would anyone ever want to go outside?" asked Sarah curiously. "We've got everything we need right here."

"Don't you want to see it for yourself?" asked Manny. Sarah and Monica glanced at each other.

"Maybe not just yet, Manny," Monica said politely.

They continued to walk in silence. In this wealthy neighborhood, the three of them could walk side by side, a luxury which they actively enjoyed.

"What did you think of my apology to Mr. Jha?" asked Manny, chuckling.

"It certainly took the air out of his sails," replied Sarah. "But did you mean it?"

Their laughter echoed off the subway walls.

~ ~ ~ ~ ~ ~

"That's him, sitting over there?" Manny asked Dave in an undertone, pointing with his chin. The two men were standing in the back of the conference room, listening to a weekly briefing of the Commissioner's Task Force for Cold Cases.

"Yeah, that's him. You can always tell; those guys all look the same," whispered Dave.

The man in question was dressed like the other detectives, and was seated in the middle row, near the center. He was bland vanilla in appearance, with a forgettable face and average height, middle-aged and non-descript. He was definitely undercover from IAD.

"He got here yesterday," Dave offered. "We had a little talk. He identified himself to me, as your second in command, and confirmed that Internal Affairs is looking into you."

"Well, they can look all they want," replied Manny. "They're not going to find anything."

Dave snorted appreciatively. "He'll be gone in a couple of weeks. Do you think they'll really search your house?"

"If they do," Manny replied, "they'll be greatly disappointed." Both men remembered the previous attempt by Raimone, who was also an IAD agent, to search Manny's home. Raimone had become so enraged when Manny did not confess to having the rings, that he shot Manny in the leg. Dave had been there when Raimone was arrested and led away in handcuffs.

"They're going to bug your office," Dave warned. "Probably tonight after you leave. But you didn't hear it from me."

"I figured they would," Manny replied. "How hard are they leaning on you?"

"Not too hard," Dave replied. "I don't have anything to give them, not a shred of evidence, not an overheard conversation or anything else. They can lean on me all they want."

"Let me know when they start dangling my job in front of you," Manny laughed.

They're not going to find those rings, not in my office or in my house, Manny reassured himself. For the thousandth time, he was grateful that he had told absolutely no one that he had found the rings in his bedroom, hidden beneath the floorboards, after years of insisting that he didn't have them. They were now deeply buried inside the rear wall of the Johnson house.

The house had been slated for repairs, then pushed far down the list as other, more urgent, repairs were made. Manny had been preoccupied with Zach, but he continued to check the reports each week.

Scrolling through the most recent report, Manny located Aviva Johnson's home. He was surprised to see that repairs were already well under way. The crew had filmed their demolition of the back wall. Watching the footage, Manny was dismayed to see them tearing it down to the foundation so they could reach the subway wall behind it. They had removed several of the subway wall tiles, searching for the leak, which had now been soldered shut. The wall was wide open, right down to the foundation. Another crew was not scheduled to close up the wall for at least ten days.

Manny, his heart in his throat, replayed the footage in its entirety. Finally, at the very end, the camera scanned the floor. Water had rushed out over the floor as repairs progressed, flushing out some of the bits of crushed concrete and brick that made up the material used to fill the foundation. There were a few spots on the floor that reflected light back at the camera. They were most likely shiny bits of metal or glass.

Or diamonds.

Manny broke out in a cold sweat. He wiped his forehead with a shaking hand, his detective's mind racing.

It could be anything, those reflecting spots of light, he scolded himself sternly. *What are the chances that the rings are lying there on the floor, in full view?*

There was only one way to find out. He was going to have to go there himself and look.

He could trust no one to do it for him. It would have to be fairly soon, too, as according to the schedule, the second crew would be back within ten days, to close up the wall, paint it, and clean up any remaining debris.

He could enter the house, take a good look at what was on the floor near the demolished wall, and be out of there in short order. If the rings were there, lying on the floor out in the open, he dared not allow anyone else to pick them up. Now that good photos of the rings were on file, it would be easy to identify whose rings they were.

From there, it would be a small step to questioning him to see if he knew why these two rings, which Manny had admitted to stealing when he was sixteen, had been buried in the foundation of this particular house. He'd have to involve Tyler, his lawyer; there would be a scandal, maybe even a trial. Even if he was not found guilty, he could still lose his job if the Council lost confidence in his ability to lead. *Wouldn't that make Mr. Jha happy,* he thought sourly.

It was quite risky. If he got caught breaking into the house, he had no excuse for being there. He could lose his job just for that. Again, Manny wiped his forehead with a shaking hand.

Maybe, he considered, it might be better to do nothing at all. He felt the beginnings of a severe headache pounding behind his eyes. No, he simply could not wait it out.

At least check for surveillance, he reminded himself. Going back to the report for the work done on the premises, he saw that the workers had not been required to get a security system passcode from the homeowners. *That's good news,* he thought. *The last thing I need is to be caught on camera breaking into a house.*

Manny sat quite still, concentrating hard on his plan. Fortunately, he still had his old set of tools for breaking and entering, stashed away in the back of his bedroom closet years ago. His plan was to break in through the ground floor kitchen window, the way he and Julio had done so many times. He'd go at night, when no workmen would be around, and be back at home before anyone noticed he was gone.

It was a good plan. *I hope I can get myself in through the window,* he thought ruefully. *I'm not as young as I used to be.*

Chapter 24.

For the next several days, Manny went out for a walk each night after dinner, strolling casually into the neighborhood where the Johnson house was located, sitting on a bench in a rest-up across from the house. He sipped from his water bottle as he took mental note of the police patrols. The shortest interval between patrols was an hour, and most intervals were closer to two hours. He'd have plenty of time.

A week came and went. Manny began to prepare for his "adventure," as he thought of it. He found the hand crafted leather case containing his set of lock-picking tools. As a teenager, he had carried these with him regularly. The tools needed to be cleaned and oiled, but they were in remarkably good condition, considering that they had not been used for nearly twenty years.

As it got closer to the day Manny had chosen, he started going out later in the evening, carefully watching to make sure the patrol schedules were dependable. Then he skipped going out for two nights, saying he was too tired to go for a walk.

Manny picked out clothes to wear, a black pair of pants, black teeshirt, black shoes and socks, black hat. *Good for breaking in,* he mused, *but would solid black look suspicious if someone happens to see me as I walk there and back?* At the last minute, he decided to wear a light gray teeshirt over the black teeshirt, taking it off once he was there. The hat could be kept in his knapsack, pulled on at the last minute.

Today's the day, he thought, nervous and excited. The knapsack was filled with his clothes and tools. He hung it on a hook in his closet, and went downstairs to dinner.

Luis and Lucinda were already seated at the kitchen table. Marya and Anna were putting the finishing touches on their meal.

"Zach, dinner!" Julie shouted loudly. When his door didn't open, she pulled out her padlet and texted him to come downstairs. A few minutes passed. Manny was about to go upstairs to knock on his door when Zach appeared, seating himself across from Julie.

"Hey, Zach, how are you today?" Manny asked pleasantly.

Zach mumbled something in reply, looking down at his plate. His face, surrounded by a halo of wiry bright red peach fuzz, was pale and tired.

"Are you feeling OK?" Manny asked.

"Like you care," Zach replied sullenly, grabbing his juice glass and taking a long drink.

Marya looked at Manny, concerned. "Zach, what's wrong?" she asked gently.

"Can I eat in my room, please?" Zach asked in exasperation, looking at Marya.

"Of course you can," Marya replied, "but wouldn't you rather sit here with us, tell us about your day?"

Scowling, Zach stood up, took a couple of slices of bread from the bread basket and left the room, going back upstairs.

Julie cleared her throat. "He's been sleeping a lot lately," she said, looking at her uncle. "Now that Raj and Eddie go to the high school, he doesn't have any friends to hang out with."

After dinner, when Julie had gone upstairs, Manny sat with Marya and the rest of the family.

"I'm so glad you didn't make a big deal out of Zach wanting to eat in his room," Lucinda said. "That was well done."

Manny murmured a rueful "thank you;" actually, he'd been too distracted to make a big deal out of it.

"It's bound to be hard on him for awhile," Lucinda continued. "Hopefully, he'll make some new friends."

"Julie's been talking about living in the house at 14th Street, once she graduates from high school this spring," Julio said. "We're all for it. She'll be safe there, and it's close enough that she can come home whenever she wants. It's perfect for a grad student." Julie, who had been accepted into university, had three more years of school ahead of her.

"We were thinking," Anna began hesitantly. "What do you think of letting Zach live there with her? It might be a good thing, let the relationship between the two of you cool down a little."

Manny looked questioningly at Marya. She didn't seem surprised; probably she and Anna had discussed it already.

"Maybe," Manny hedged. "On the one hand, it would make things easier around here. But he's young, and we can't ask Julie to keep an eye on him; he's not her responsibility. Maybe in another year or two."

"I'm so relieved to hear you say that!" Marya said. "I think it would be great if he were, say, fifteen or sixteen. But not yet."

The evening dragged on, hour after hour. Alone in his study, Manny went over his plans one last time. Finally, he went upstairs to his bedroom, where Marya was mostly asleep.

"Goodnight," he said softly, climbing into bed next to her and faking a yawn. He held very still, and she was soon asleep.

Wide awake, Manny dared not move for fear of disturbing Marya. He knew that deep sleep doesn't happen right away, and he didn't want any questions about where he was going.

He waited until 2:00 am. *At least I don't have to open the bedroom window and slide down the roof,* he thought with a chuckle. He'd been much more agile when he was sixteen.

He gently slid out of bed, picked up the knapsack from his closet, and tiptoed out of the bedroom. He changed clothes in the kitchen, slowly and silently. Dressed and ready, he was out the door by 2:15 am.

All was quiet and still outside. Manny didn't pass anyone on his way to the Johnson house. He walked right up to the house, making sure he was hidden behind the bushes in front of the window, and sat down to wait for the next police patrol to pass. While he waited, he removed the light gray teeshirt and stuffed it into his knapsack, and pulled on the black hat. Dressed completely in black, he was all but invisible behind the bushes.

The patrol was right on schedule. Manny didn't recognize the two officers, who strolled along talking amiably to each other. They seemed to be deeply in conversation about whether or not to stop for coffee. Manny waited until they passed, then waited another several minutes. Finally, he pulled his black hat down low over his forehead and turned to face the window.

Without Julio to give him a boost up, it was a lot harder to raise himself up to the level of the windowsill, but Manny was very strong from years of boxing and lifting weights. He managed to pull himself up, balancing on one hand while the other fumbled with the window. It raised easily; it wasn't even locked. He swung one leg over the windowsill, then the other, and dropped down inside.

Once inside, he breathed a sigh of relief. The two officers wouldn't be back for at least an hour, maybe longer, and there was no surveillance in the building. He flipped open his padlet and turned on the flashlight app. As he had instructed class after class of new cadets, he divided the room into equal sections, shining his flashlight on one section at a time, beginning with the far left corner of the room.

On the floor over by the window, there was something shiny. Excited, Manny pounced on it, but it turned out to be nothing, just a bit of glass. *Take your time,* he cautioned himself, *you only get one shot at this, so do it right.* He returned to systematically shining his light in short, sweeping motions.

There, over by the door! The rush of water streaming across the floor had swept debris into a little pile. There were several little points of light reflecting back from his flashlight. Any one of them could be a piece of jewelry.

He was about to move closer to the door, when he was stunned to hear voices. It sounded like the same two police officers who had passed by the house previously, coming from just a house or two away.

"Come on, Priscilla, how long does it take to tie a shoe?" complained one of them.

"They need to be even, so I have to retie both of them," replied the other voice. "Wait, Edna, did you see that?"

"What? I didn't see anything!" replied Edna. "Are we getting coffee or not?"

"No, I'm sure I saw something," Priscilla insisted. "It looked like a flashlight, like someone was inside looking around."

"I didn't see anything! Please, I thought we were going to get coffee," her partner pleaded. "I really need caffeine, come on, Priscilla! I've been up all day taking care of my little guy, barely got any sleep at all."

"Look, Edna, this is our job. If you want to go get coffee, then you go ahead," said Priscilla. Crouching down low beneath the windowsill, Manny was torn between admiring her work ethic while cringing at the thought of being caught by her. "I'm going inside to make sure everything is OK."

"I promise, we'll come right back! There's a Twenty-Four-Seven right up ahead," Edna wheedled, referring to the chain of convenience stores that were open 24/7.

"OK, we'll get coffee, but that's all," Priscilla conceded. "Then we're coming back here." The two continued talking, their voices fading as they moved away.

Manny quickly scanned the floor one last time. He dearly wanted to take a photo of the pile of debris to enlarge and examine later at home, but resisted the impulse. *That's a good way to get caught,* he advised himself. He stuffed his black

146

teeshirt and hat into his knapsack, putting on the other teeshirt. Then he walked to the front door, opened it, and sat down on the front steps to wait.

The two officers returned to the Johnson house in short order, both holding steaming cups of coffee. They were quite surprised to see the front door open, and Manny sitting on the front steps.

"Who are you? Identify yourself! What's your business here?" demanded Priscilla, her billyclub in her hands.

Edna shook her head urgently, leaning over to whisper in her ear, "Don't you know who that is?"

"No, I don't. Whoever he is, he's not supposed to be *here*, in the middle of the night," Priscilla replied, raising her voice. She turned to Manny. "What're you doing here?"

"I thought I saw a light flickering inside the house, Officer," Manny replied courteously, "so I went inside to investigate. The front door wasn't locked."

"Really. The door wasn't locked," Priscilla repeated, her skepticism obvious. She slowly tapped the billyclub into the palm of her hand, tap tap tap.

"Priscilla, no!" Her partner reached over and grabbed the billyclub. "That's the Commissioner! Don't you recognize the Police Commissioner?" she whispered urgently.

"He's – what?" Priscilla said in disbelief. "*Here?*"

Manny stood up, brushing off his pants, which were covered with dust from kneeling on the floor. "It's entirely understandable that you didn't recognize me, Officer. I'm not in uniform, and we're not at the office."

Both officers saluted. While it was obvious that they wanted to know what Manny was doing there, neither one dared to question him.

"I've been having trouble sleeping," Manny offered by way of a plausible explanation, "so I sometimes go for a walk when I can't sleep. When I walked by this house, that's when I thought I saw the light."

"I also thought I saw something," responded Priscilla. "We were about to investigate."

"But instead, you decided to get coffee!" Manny said sternly. "What if there had been a serious situation, drug dealers or worse? From inside, I could hear your voices clearly; anyone inside would have heard you, announcing that you'd be back in a few minutes. That's sloppy police work!" He looked pointedly at their name tags.

"Apologies, Sir!" they replied in unison. They were standing at attention, eyes forward, as taught in the Academy. Edna added, "Do you want us to go inside now to look around?"

"No, there's nothing inside, no sign of intruders, no damage," said Manny, turning to pull the front door shut behind him.

The two officers were still standing at attention. "Dismissed!" Manny said. "And remember what I said. Next time, don't announce that you're coming back soon."

Chapter 25.

A week had passed since Manny's unsuccessful attempt to recover the two rings. While there didn't seem to be any particular fallout from the "adventure," nothing had been gained by it, either. He guessed that the two female officers who had seen him at the Johnson house had added that information to their notes for the day, but there had been no evidence that Manny had done anything wrong. Hopefully, their supervisor would simply consider it to be odd, but not worth investigating further.

The only thing that had gone well this week was an unexpected reprieve from the workmen's schedule; the crew slated to complete the repairs on the Johnson house had been rescheduled again; it would be another two weeks before they would arrive. No reason was given, and Manny didn't want to attract attention by asking for an explanation. *At least this gives me more time to plan,* he thought.

Meanwhile, there was no shortage of other issues to deal with. For instance, there were problems with the emergency shelters. He'd met with Hasan earlier in the day; the two men walked outside to the spot where Hasan and his men had located a source for water.

"The well will go right here," Hasan had said. "It will have enough water for at least two shelters full of people, maybe three."

"And after that?" asked Manny.

"We sink another well," replied Hasan, "but first we need one shelter with one working well. Then we can move on to the second shelter."

It was noon, and the sun was high. The day was very warm and sunny; Manny was perspiring heavily. He sat down in the shade beneath an enormous tree. Hasan had gone off to speak to his men, who were having lunch. Manny noted with amusement that the workmen liked to eat lunch among the ruined hotels and apartment buildings that had once graced Central Park South and Central Park West. Any place close to the work site where there were broken walls to lean against, there were workmen spread out enjoying their lunch hour.

Manny listened to the far-off sounds of their conversation, as he sat beneath the tree. *I can't go back there again,* he thought, his thoughts circling back to the Johnson house. *I'm lucky I didn't get caught the first time. No, I've got to find another way to see if those rings are there.*

He toyed with the idea of enlisting the help of a couple of young officers, maybe telling them it was a clandestine operation that they had to keep quiet, something outside the boundaries of ordinary police work. The problem was, as Manny knew well, that the more people you tell, the greater the chance of being caught. No, he had to do this himself.

If only I was still a kid, he thought, *I'd slip in and out of there so fast that no one would catch me.* When he and Julio had done their burglaries, they were strong, athletic teenagers. If a homeowner happened to be at home when they broke in, which happened more than once, they took off running, often right out the front door, laughing all the way home. They never got caught.

It wasn't until Manny was older that he learned in a conversation with his predecessor that his father, the Commissioner and Deputy Commissioner had known all about the burglaries. There was an unspoken agreement that no one was to interfere with the Chief's son, or his best friend Julio.

It's too bad Zach isn't a burglar, Manny thought with an inward chuckle. *He's strong, fast, and judging from the police reports, not averse to breaking the law.*

Manny sat bolt upright. Zach.

If Zach got caught breaking and entering, nothing would happen to him because he was underage, and had no record. Electrified, Manny ran through the scenario in his mind, over and over. Zach could do it for him. Even if he got caught, Manny could see to it that there was no record of it, and that Zach wouldn't be punished.

But it's wrong, Manny argued with himself. *I can't ask my son to commit a crime for me. What kind of a father would do that? Even Patrick would have drawn the line on that one.*

No, it didn't feel right.

Tangled in his compelling internal argument, Manny hadn't noticed that the sky had turned gray, or that the breeze had picked up. He looked around for Hasan and his crew, but they seemed to have gone home and left him sitting underneath the tree. *They probably didn't realize I was still out here,* he thought.

Manny stood, brushing leaves and dirt from his pants. The wind streamed past him, remarkably powerful. He staggered back, leaning against the tree. He looked up at the sky again; it was growing dark, although it was only 4:00 pm. In the distance, a streak of yellowish light forked down silently from the sky to touch the ground.

Manny sheltered beneath the tree, watching the sky. *Why was it blue, and then all of a sudden it's gray?* he wondered. Then the first few raindrops landed on his arms and face. The rain was cold, splattering unpleasantly against his face and neck. It felt peculiar, and unnatural.

Time to go, he thought, turning towards home. It wasn't a long walk back to the subway entrance, but he was soaked by the time he reached it. Turning to look one last time, Manny saw that the sky was nearly black. Another streak of yellowish light touched down to the ground, this time followed by a loud cracking sound.

Transfixed, Manny stood motionless. Everyone knew the story of the great hurricane that had driven their ancestors underground; it was a violent storm, maybe even a storm like the one he was watching. The trees in the park were thrashing back and forth. Then a dark wall of rain swept towards him, blotting out the park, and Manny flew down the steps. He ducked behind the fire-and-waterproof door, slamming it shut behind him with a sigh of relief.

The week dragged on. He managed to keep up appearances at the office, holding meetings and doing paperwork. But at night, he had trouble falling asleep. When he did sleep, he dreamed of the Johnson house, and the pile of debris that had accumulated in the corner by the door. In his dream, the pile was filled with hundreds of glittering diamond rings, reaching all the way up to the ceiling. He was floundering unsteadily on the top of the pile, desperately trying to conceal them.

"Manny, Manny! Wake up," Marya said, shaking his shoulder. "You're having a bad dream."

"Huh? Oh, sorry," he mumbled.

"You're sweating, Manny. Are you feeling OK?" she asked, concerned.

"I'm fine, just a little warm, that's all," he replied. He gave her hand a quick squeeze. "Sorry I woke you."

It was 4:00 am, far too early to get up for work. Manny lay quietly, listening to Marya's gentle breathing, staring up at the ceiling until 6:00 am.

He was the first person to arrive at the office, so he went into the tiny kitchen himself to make his morning cup of tea.

"Good morning, Commissioner," said an unfamiliar voice behind him. Turning around, he saw the detective from IAD, the one who had been quietly investigating him for the past couple of weeks.

"Let me introduce myself," the man said courteously. "My name is Detective Andrew Jenkins."

"I know who you are," Manny said dismissively.

"I was hoping to catch you here early this morning, before the rest of the unit arrives," the man continued smoothly. "Can we go into your office?"

It was courteously phrased as a request, but there was no way to refuse. Manny nodded, leading the way into his office, closing the door behind the two of them.

"I'll get right to the point, Commissioner," Jenkins said. "We'll be doing a search of your home this morning. I know that you'll want to see the search warrant; if you'll kindly bop your padlet to mine, I'll transfer it to you now."

Manny held out his padlet to bop Jenkins's padlet, and the search warrant bloomed on his home screen. He glanced at the signature, but didn't recognize the judge's name.

"With respect, Sir," Jenkins said, "I'll take your gun and badge now. Please."

"You'll *what?*" asked Manny, caught off guard by the request.

"I'm sure that I don't have to explain to you how this works," Jenkins replied. "You'll be confined to desk duty while the search is being conducted. Your Deputy's house is also being searched this morning, so for the time being, the Acting Commissioner is Lieutenant Chandler."

"You're searching Dave's house, too?" Manny asked in surprise. "What on earth for?"

"Well," began Detective Jenkins, sitting down in the chair in front of Manny's desk, "do you recall a certain gift of land that you gave to Dave not too long ago?"

Manny realized too late that he should not have asked any questions. He should have kept the conversation to a bare minimum. Now here was Jenkins, comfortably seated in front of his desk, not just listening to his words, but judging his demeanor by watching his face, his body language, his eyes.

"Yes," Manny replied.

"What was that for, Commissioner?" Jenkins asked.

"For?" Manny replied. "It was a gift; it wasn't 'for' anything."

He was about to say that Dave was his friend, that the two of them had been partners back in the day, that they had worked together for decades, when he realized that his explanation could be interpreted to mean that Dave would do anything for him, including cover up a crime. *Shut up,* he warned himself; *guilty people talk too much.*

"Mmm?" prompted Jenkins, one eyebrow raised.

"I'm a busy man, Detective, and I've got a lot of work to do, so if you'll excuse me," Manny said, picking up some file folders from the corner of his desk.

Jenkins rose to leave. "I'll just take your gun and badge, if you don't mind," he repeated.

"I do mind, and no, you can't have my gun and badge," Manny replied. He dearly wanted to throw this impudent jerk out of his office.

"This isn't a debate, Commissioner," Jenkins replied sternly, holding out his hand.

"I'll give you my gun, but not the badge," Manny countered. "I won't be embarrassed here in the office in front of my people." He removed his gun from its holster and handed it to Jenkins. Immediately, he felt the absence of the gun under his arm. He felt almost naked in front of this man whose sole purpose was to derail his career.

Jenkins moved towards the doorway, putting Manny's gun in his jacket pocket. He stopped with one hand on the doorframe, turning back towards Manny as if something had just occurred to him. It was an old police trick.

"Oh, one last thing, Commissioner. You were seen by two patrol officers at the Johnson house in the middle of the night, sitting on the front steps in front of an unlocked and wide open front door. Apparently, your pants were covered with dust. Would you care to comment on that?"

"Get out of my office," Manny said sternly, using the voice that made his cadets cringe.

Manny sat quietly behind his desk, his hands visibly trembling. *It's enough to drive a person to drink,* he thought shakily. He took a deep breath to steady himself.

Not a moment later, his padlet lit up with an urgent hologram from home. *Now what?* he thought.

Marya's form appeared on his desktop. "Manny, there are police here! There must be two dozen of them! They said they want to *search the house!* Manny, what should I do? They're waiting outside in the yard while I talk to you."

Manny replied, "You need to *invite them* into the house, not just open the door for them, do you understand? Say, 'please come in, officers.' Can you do that for me, Marya?"

"But, Manny," she screeched, "what do they want? If they're searching for something, they're going to rip the house apart, and suppose they break things? I don't want a male officer going through my things, my underwear drawer, my closet! Manny, tell them they can't do this!"

"I need you to listen to me, Marya. I can't make them stop," he replied. "They're going to search the house with or without our cooperation. Let them in, and then go into the front parlor and stay there. Whoever is home with you should stay in the front parlor, too, all of you in one room."

"But, Manny! For how long? I've got things to do," she protested. "What if I don't want to spend the day sitting in the parlor! Why can't you just give them whatever it is they are looking for? I don't understand!"

"I'm on my way," he said, before he hung up.

Chapter 26.

Manny hologrammed Tyler Watkins, his lawyer, telling him to meet him at his house with half a dozen of his employees. Then he picked up his jacket and hat and headed for the stairs. He was met in the hallway by Dave, who was also on desk duty until the searches were completed.

"Manny," he said with surprise, "where are you going? You can't leave!"

"I'm going home to sit with Marya while the search is being conducted. She's really upset! Don't worry, I'm not going to interfere with the search in any way." He continued down the stairs, aware that Dave was watching him. *Careful,* he cautioned himself, *it's only going to make things worse if I make Dave suspicious.*

When Manny arrived at home, Marya, Anna, Julio and Zach were seated in the front parlor. "Where are Lucinda and Luis?" Manny asked.

"They went home," Julio said. "They have nothing to do with this, and technically, they don't live here, so they were allowed to leave. Julie's over at a friend's house, so we texted her to stay there."

"I don't understand," Marya said plaintively, twisting her hands together over and over in her lap. "What are they looking for?"

"The rings, Marya, same as last time, remember?" Manny said, impatiently. Turning to Julio, he asked, "Is Tyler here yet?"

"He's upstairs with a bunch of lawyers, talking to Naomi," Julio replied.

Manny went up the stairs, where he was met on the landing by Naomi. She knew Manny well; he had promoted her to her current position. She had been one of the police who escorted

Marya to City Hall on their wedding day. But today, things were formal.

"Commissioner," she said crisply, standing at the top of the staircase, an arm on either side of the railing, effectively blocking his way.

"Acting Commissioner," he greeted her politely, nodding. "Anything you can tell me?"

"We're doing this by the book," she said to her boss. "It's going to take awhile; this is a big house. You'll be more comfortable downstairs with your family, I'm sure."

"Of course," Manny responded. "Please let me know if I can help in any way."

"I appreciate you, Commissioner," she replied. "When it's time to copy the electronics in the house, we'll talk again." The two bowed politely to each other.

Behind Naomi, Manny could see Tyler in the hallway in front of the bedrooms, padlet in hand, a small army of attorneys crowded behind him. He barely acknowledged Manny as he continued dispatching his team.

"You four!" Tyler snapped, addressing four young attorneys standing by the staircase. "I want one of you in every bedroom, filming as they search, clear and complete videos!" He then sent another attorney to the study, one to the kitchen, and one to the living room. Then he turned his attention to Manny.

"You've seen a search warrant, I presume?" he said by way of greeting.

"Yeah, I've got it here," Manny replied, holding out his padlet. Tyler quickly bopped the search warrant to his own padlet, then skimmed through the document, checking to be sure all was in order. The two men returned downstairs to the front parlor, where the rest of the family was sitting.

"Where's that detective, Jenkins?" Manny asked. "Is he around here somewhere?"

"Jenkins? No, he's not here," Tyler responded. "He's gone to search the Johnson house."

"He's ... he's what?" Manny asked weakly, his knees suddenly turning to water. He grabbed the back of the sofa to steady himself.

"Manny! Are you OK?" asked Marya. "Your face is all white!"

"I'm fine, it's nothing, just my sciatica," he replied, putting on his unreadable face, the blank facial expression he had perfected as a child when living with Patrick.

Tyler, though, knew well what panic looked like on the face of a client. "Manny, shall we go outside and talk?" he asked.

Upstairs, there was an extremely loud bang. Marya shrieked and got up from the sofa. "Sit down," Manny said sternly. "You're not to leave this room."

From upstairs, they could hear Naomi's voice shouting: "Have you forgotten whose house this is?! We are searching one of our own, people! Pick that up off the floor and put it back!!"

Marya's face was white and strained. Anna put her arm around her. Even Zach, sitting on the sofa, looked scared and uncertain, forgoing his usual tough-guy persona.

Tyler prompted softly, "Outside, hmmm?" The two men went outside, closing the front door behind them. Marya appeared a moment later, hoping to join in their conversation.

"I thought I told you to stay in the front parlor," Manny said coldly, frowning at her. "Don't make this any harder than it has to be." Visibly annoyed, Marya returned to the house, closing the front door in a huff.

"Let's start at the beginning," Tyler prompted him. "The case against you was reopened, I see. Why was that?"

"The al-Sayed family found photographs of the old lady wearing her rings. Apparently, the photos are good enough to identify the rings," Manny explained softly. "Mrs. al-Sayed's daughter has decided, with a little prompting from my enemies, that she wants the rings back for their sentimental value. She says she'll return the insurance money, if the rings are found."

"OK, but where are the rings now?" Tyler asked, taking notes.

"That's the thing, Tyler," Manny said hesitantly. He glanced over his shoulder to make sure that they were not being overheard, motioning to Tyler to come with him as he moved further away from the house. When he continued, it was in a near whisper.

"For years, I've denied that I knew anything about their whereabouts, saying that my father told me he'd returned the rings to the old lady in exchange for her not pressing charges against me. And that was the truth, or at least it was what I believed," Manny said. "But then one night about ten years ago, I discovered my father's hiding place in the master bedroom for his bourbon. He had a handy little compartment in the floorboards underneath a chair. That's where I discovered the two rings."

"I see," Tyler murmured, continuing to take notes. He didn't ask why Manny had never told him about this, or why Manny was digging around in the floor beneath the chair in the first place. It was one of the reasons why Manny loved working with Tyler. He was all business, with no wasted words.

Lowering his voice to the barest of whispers, Tyler said, "What did you do, once you found the rings here in your house?"

"First, I never told anyone about finding them, not even Marya or Julio, to protect them in case they were ever questioned about the rings," Manny answered. Tyler nodded appreciatively.

Manny continued: "I hid them for a while in the kitchen, covered with marinade in a container of tofu."

Tyler looked up blankly from his notes. "You did what?" he asked.

"You heard me," Manny said grimly. "It was just until I could figure out what to do with them. Then, by some amazing stroke of luck, I learned that there was construction being done at the Johnson house. This was back when Marya and I were dating. One night after dinner, she and I took a stroll, and I showed her the house. She's an engineer, you know, so she's interested in what a foundation and wall look like on the inside."

"And what? You brought your marinated tofu with you?" asked Tyler. It was the closest thing to a joke that Manny had ever heard from Tyler.

"I retrieved the rings from the tofu, putting them in my pocket. Then when Marya and I were leaving the Johnson house, I told her I'd lost my hair ribbon while we were inside, and went back alone to get it. It only took a minute. I dropped the two rings into the foundation, covering them up with debris," Manny explained. "She never saw me with the rings, and never suspected a thing."

"OK, so I'm guessing that the rings were successfully hidden until recently, when the pipes in Ms. Johnson's wall burst again?" Tyler said.

Manny nodded miserably. "I watched the schedule to see when the repairs had been made. They film their work now, so I looked at the video. There was debris all over the floor, you know, bits of glass and metal scraps. Any one of those could have been the rings."

"Did you take any action after watching the video?" asked Tyler, all business as usual.

"I devised a plan to go in person to see what was lying on the floor," Manny replied. "It was in the middle of the night. No one at home knows anything about this. But I barely had any time to investigate," he added.

Manny explained how the two officers had walked by on patrol, nearly catching him when they unexpectedly came back. "There was no way to avoid being seen. So I opened the front door and sat down on the steps," he said. "I couldn't let them catch me inside, it would have been impossible to explain."

"What did you say to them? Try and remember exactly, please. The two officers have mentioned seeing you at the house, in their daily report. You're not accused of any wrongdoing, but they do note that it seemed unusual," Tyler said.

"I told them that when I can't sleep, I like to go out for a walk," Manny recalled. "I said that I was passing by the house and thought I saw a light inside, so I decided to investigate, that the front door was not locked."

"Not locked," repeated Tyler as he continued to take notes. "Good. That's important. Anything else?"

"No," Manny said miserably, "except that I hope to keep my job."

"If they don't find the rings, you'll be off the hook for good this time," Tyler replied, rolling up his padlet and snapping it shut.

"Jenkins and his team are over at the Johnson house right now, sifting through the debris that's spread out all over the floor, going through it with a fine-tooth comb. If he finds the rings, then I'm dead," Manny whispered, looking down at his shoes.

"Hold on there, maybe not, maybe not," Tyler said softly. "Nobody's found the rings yet. Let's not anticipate future pain. For now, you keep on as if you haven't a clue where they are."

Manny and Tyler went back inside. Tyler headed upstairs to supervise his team of lawyers, while Manny went into the parlor, where his family waited expectantly. All eyes were on him as he walked into the room.

"Well?" said Julio. "Any news?"

"Nothing yet," Manny said.

"How can they do this to you again, Manny?" asked Marya. "After that man shot you?"

"Raimone never actually searched the house," Manny explained. "There was a search warrant issued, but it was never executed after he was hauled off to jail for shooting me." Manny

159

explained about the new photos that had come to light, that now the police had a way to identify the rings, if they were found.

A sudden crash of breaking glass caused everyone to rush out into the foyer, where they could see into the kitchen. A shamefaced young officer was on his knees, sweeping up broken drinking glasses, while one of the lawyers stood directly in front of him, filming his every move.

"My apologies, Commissioner, Mrs. Stewart," he said. "I was searching the cabinets; it was an accident."

Manny turned around, holding his arms spread wide, corralling his family. "Back to the parlor, everyone," he said.

It was a very long morning, and an even longer afternoon. Finally, at 7:00 pm, Naomi came downstairs.

"Sir, if I could have all of the electronics in the house brought into the kitchen, so we can copy them," Naomi said, "then I think we'll be done here."

Manny turned to his family. "Padlets on the kitchen table, please," he said.

"They're not taking my padlet," Zach exclaimed stubbornly.

"Zach, they're not taking them, they're just copying the hard drive," Manny explained wearily.

"It won't hurt your files, Zach," Anna added gently. Anna, an IT specialist and supervisor at the computer institute, was trusted by all of them.

Everyone's padlets were delivered to the kitchen, where a young officer from the Tech Division sat at the end of the table with his police padlet open. Anna knew him; the two exchanged greetings. One by one, he took their padlets and copied the hard drives.

Naomi appeared in the kitchen to check on the progress. When the young officer was finished, she turned to Manny.

"Sir," she said formally. "We are finished with our search. We didn't find any rings matching the description of the ones we're looking for. We did our best to be respectful of personal property. Please make a list of anything damaged, and we will do our best to compensate your family."

"Thank you, Acting Commissioner," Manny said just as formally.

"The search at the Deputy Commissioner's house also has turned up nothing," Naomi continued. "You'll be hearing directly from Detective Jenkins about the results of his search at the Johnson property."

"Any idea when he'll be done?" Manny asked, trying to sound purely businesslike.

"No, I'm not sure how long that will take. Once that's finished, I believe we're done," she said, her formality slipping away, "and I'll be returning your command to you. Thanks for your cooperation today, Sir. I'm sure this wasn't easy for you or your family."

His lieutenant bowed formally to him, a respectful and personal gesture. He returned her bow, saying, "I'll see you at work in the morning."

Manny walked Naomi to the door, and watched as she and her crew left. The house was suddenly very quiet. Marya went into the kitchen, while Zach, Julio and Anna went upstairs. Manny was left alone for a moment, standing in the foyer.

I'll see you at work in the morning, he thought sadly, *unless I'm relieved of my command and sitting in one of the interrogation rooms.*

The night dragged on. Although the search had been conducted carefully, there were drawers and cabinets sagging open, contents rumpled and in disarray. Marya went from room to room, loudly proclaiming her displeasure each time she found something out of place. Zach was playing his music louder than ever, from behind his closed bedroom door.

Anna made sandwiches, but Manny wasn't hungry. He sat in his study, staring into space until it was quite late. One by one, everyone went to bed. The room had darkened before he finally roused himself and went upstairs.

Marya was already asleep, breathing softly into her pillow. Manny slipped into bed quietly so as not to wake her. Hour by hour, he stared up at the ceiling, waiting for his padlet to light up with a message saying that the search of the Johnson house was over. Morning light was beginning to stream through his curtains when he finally fell asleep.

Chapter 27.

The search had been conducted on Thursday. The next day threatened to be the longest day of Manny's life. He spent most of it in his office with the door shut. Dave was out of the office all day with the Mayor, attending a meeting in Manny's place. He hadn't seen Dave, but they had hologrammed earlier in the day:

Dave: *The search turned up nothing, of course. What a waste of time and resources! It took up most of the morning, and then it took the rest of the day to put things back together. Jenny was so upset with the mess they left behind. How'd your search go?*

Manny: *Pretty much the same, only the house has a lot of rooms, so it lasted well into the evening. Afterwards, Marya walked from room to room, yelling about what a mess they made. I'm just glad it's done.*

Dave: *Are you reinstated yet?*

Manny: *Not yet. I haven't seen Jenkins all day. Did you see him?*

Dave: *Yes, he was talking to the Mayor when I got here. I'm officially reinstated.*

Manny: *So you're the Acting Commissioner now! It's like musical chairs around here.*

Dave: *Don't worry, I'm sure Jenkins is just off somewhere investigating someone else, and will get back to you soon.*

But Detective Jenkins did not contact Manny all day Friday, nor on Saturday, nor on Sunday. By Sunday evening, Manny was completely exhausted from worry and lack of sleep. He went into his study and hologrammed Tyler Watkins.

Manny: *Tyler, I know it's Sunday, but are you free to come to the house?*

Tyler: *Now?*

Manny: *Now would be good.*

Tyler: *On my way.*

When Tyler arrived, Manny ushered him into his study and closed the door. *My Dad used to do this,* he thought uneasily, thinking back to the many times in his childhood that Patrick and Tyler had met in the study, behind closed doors, while Manny sat at the top of the stairs and tried his hardest to listen to their conversation.

"Tyler, I haven't heard a word from Jenkins since the search," Manny said. "He's talked to Dave and reinstated him, so now Dave's Acting Commissioner. Can you get in touch with Jenkins and find out what's going on?"

"Do you really want me to do that, Manny?" asked Tyler. "An innocent man would be unconcerned at this point, after the house search turned up nothing, and not pressing to see what's causing the delay. Let's not make him more suspicious."

"What do you think he's up to? I mean, if you had to guess," Manny asked.

Tyler took a moment to consider. "I'd guess he's found nothing, and now his only hope is to try and rattle you into confessing. That, or maybe he's trying to find a judge who will issue a search warrant allowing him to tear open all of the walls, but that's a long shot. You checked, of course, that there is no surveillance on the property?" Manny nodded.

"Whatever you do, Manny, stay away from the Johnson house," Tyler warned. "No casual stroll past it to see what's happening, nothing."

"I agree," Manny said wholeheartedly. He'd already returned to the scene of the crime once, and had nearly been caught.

"Right now, your job is to wait, and to say nothing to anyone," Tyler advised. "For now, we do nothing."

But doing nothing can be very hard to do. Manny forced himself to stay home all evening; then he tossed and turned through another sleepless night.

On Monday morning, Manny was up and dressed for work an hour earlier than usual. There were dark circles underneath his eyes and his face showed the strain of the past several days. After pulling on his uniform, he reached for his holster and gun, hanging on their hook in his closet, as he had done every morning for decades, but he'd surrendered his gun. The holster was empty.

Manny dearly missed his service weapon snugged safely beneath his arm in its leather holster, under his uniform jacket. Although Manny had rarely fired his gun, it belonged to him. He'd had the same gun for his entire career.

Manny had a sudden inspiration. He owned two other guns. He'd simply carry one of the others, until Jenkins returned his gun. He turned to the shelf, reaching far into the back, where the lockbox was kept.

The lockbox was not there.

The detectives probably misplaced it, after they finished searching the closet, he thought. Unconcerned, he went downstairs and sat in the kitchen, yawning, waiting for his coffee to finish dripping into the carafe.

Anna came into the kitchen, her bathrobe hanging open over a rumpled nightgown. "You're up early," she said.

"Couldn't sleep," he mumbled. "It was a bad night."

"Maybe you should see your doctor about that," Anna said, concerned. "You look exhausted."

"Thanks for that," he replied wryly, retrieving a cup of coffee for himself and one for Anna, sitting down at the table with her. "Actually, that's not a bad idea. Maybe I'll do that."

The two sat in quiet companionship, sipping their morning coffee.

"You haven't by any chance seen the lockbox where I keep my guns, have you?" Manny asked.

"No, why? Was it misplaced during the search?" Anna replied.

"Probably," he replied. "It's not where I usually keep it. I'll look around for it later."

"Try looking in the laundry room," Anna said, laughing. "That's where Marya found her hairbrush."

Manny walked slowly to the office, the empty holster beneath his arm feeling sad and limp, wondering if today would be his last day as Commissioner. He nodded to several people as he made his way to his office, as he always did, and then sat down heavily behind his desk. While waiting for Nigel to bring him his morning cup of tea, he began going through the day's email.

There were the usual memos and bulletins filled with mostly forgettable facts, and there was a report on Zach's activities for the past week.

Grateful for the distraction, Manny opened the report on Zach. On most days, Zach came straight home after school, although he had seen Raj and Eddie at least once. He had not been involved in any criminal activity, either with just the two of them or with the gang. Manny breathed a sigh of relief. Maybe things were settling down after all.

Nigel knocked on his door. "Do you have a moment, Sir?" he asked.

"Come on in, Nigel," Manny replied to his aide. "Have a seat."

Nigel sat down, looking distinctly uncomfortable.

"I've heard something that might interest you," Nigel said. "My sister-in-law has a cousin who lives next door to a judge. Their kids play together." He paused to clear his throat, while Manny's stomach dropped through the floor.

"It seems that this Detective Jenkins, you know, the Internal Affairs guy? Jenkins has been very busy over the weekend running down a list of judges, trying to find one who will issue a search warrant for a particular house, the Johnson house. Remember, the one that had a bad leak? The leak's been fixed, but Jenkins wants all of the walls torn open down to the foundation! This judge, he said he thought that Jenkins had lost his mind. He's spouting some outlandish nonsense about *you*, Sir, that you've been hiding things in the wall over there."

Manny laughed out loud. "That's how rumors get started, Nigel!" he replied. "I hope I can count on you not to repeat that to anyone."

"Of course not," Nigel replied loyally.

"Thanks for bringing this to my attention. I appreciate you," Manny said. Nigel bowed slightly and left.

Tyler was spot on, Manny mused. *Let's hope the bastard can't convince a judge to issue that warrant.*

Manny moved on to other work, reading through his reports and memos. He reached across his desk for a folder and was shocked to see Detective Jenkins standing silently in front of his desk, watching him.

"How long have you been standing there?" he spluttered, too late to hide his reaction.

"Long enough," Jenkins replied. "Your Aide was busy elsewhere, so I showed myself in." Uninvited, he seated himself comfortably in the visitor's chair, crossing his legs, taking his time.

"I have to say, Commissioner, that I was surprised when the search of your house didn't produce anything," Jenkins said conversationally. "Then I realized that the rings weren't at your house, probably hadn't been there for a long time. You've hidden them somewhere, haven't you?"

Jenkins stared at him, unblinking. He had light brown eyes; the whites showed all the way around. His cold stare was unnerving, as intended. Manny bit down hard on the urge to respond, and said nothing. The silence became uncomfortable.

Finally, Jenkins stood up. He sighed resignedly. "I'm returning your firearm, Commissioner," he said, taking Manny's gun out of his jacket pocket. Jenkins held the gun in the palm of his hand, running his thumb over the warm metal, balancing it on his palm, taunting Manny. "I'll be reinstating you officially as Commissioner later this morning. I just have one question."

Of course you do, Manny thought wearily. It was an old detective's trick, let the perp think he's about to be set free so he lets his guard down, and then get him talking.

"When I got to the Johnson house, there was nothing there," Jenkins said, sounding almost petulant. "The workmen had repaired and painted the back wall and swept the place clean. There wasn't a speck of dirt on the floor." He continued to look hard at Manny. "Do you know anything about that, Commissioner? The timing seemed a little odd."

"If you have any more questions for me, Detective, I'd suggest that you call my lawyer, Tyler Watkins," Manny replied. "Now if you'll excuse me, I've got a busy morning here." He stood and held out his hand for his gun, his face expressionless.

The two men stared at each other. Manny did not look away, his stance reminding Jenkins that he was, after all, dealing with the Commissioner of Police. Finally, Detective Jenkins handed Manny his gun, turned and left the office without another word.

Manny wiped his sweating forehead, and gratefully put his gun back in its holster, giving it a little pat. He got up and walked down the hall to Dave's office.

"He's done," Manny said, as he settled himself into Dave's extra chair. "He gave me back my gun. Jenkins has left the building."

"That's great, Manny!" Dave replied. "I hope he crawls back into his hole and stays there."

At 11:00 am, Manny left the office to pick up lunch. He was standing in line in a local coffee shop when a voice said in his ear, "Your house. 7:00 pm?"

Manny knew that voice. It was Loosey, behind him in line. He nodded once, while continuing to face the front. Behind him, he knew that Loosey was already gone, melting seamlessly into the noonday crowd.

Manny left the office at exactly 6:30 pm, walking home slowly. His leg was paining him, holding him back with each step he took. *Maybe Marya's right, I should leave a cane at the office,* he thought, then dismissed the thought. A cane made him look weak, less than strong and capable, not an image he wanted to project to the public.

As he walked up the path leading to his front door, he heard Loosey from behind the bushes: "Sssst!"

"Here, come on in," said Manny, waving his hand over the front door Scentsor, which identified his scent and unlocked the door.

Once inside, he ushered Loosey into the library. They sat down facing each other in armchairs separated by an antique end table, in front of a floor-to-ceiling glass-enclosed bookcase. Loosey picked up a priceless carved African ivory figurine from the table and admired it, tossing it lightly from one hand to the other. "Is this real?" he asked. "What's it made out of, bone?"

"You have my full attention," Manny said, reaching across and taking the ivory carving out of Loosey's hand. "What's going on?"

"It's something I found out, Manny, some information I think you'd want," he blurted excitedly, words spilling out in a rush.

"Take your time, Loosey," Manny replied encouragingly, overlooking the too-familiar use of his first name.

"I overheard him talking about it! My, uh, colleague, shall we say? He was bragging that a couple o' kids brung him two very pricey old-fashioned rings. These kids, they didn't realize what they had, how valuable the rings were. He said he bought them for practically nothing. So I asked if he'd show them to me."

Manny said nothing, feeling light-headed.

"I saw them yesterday, and right off the bat, I thought maybe they were the rings that, you know, the ones you'd lifted when you were a kid. I got him to sell them to me! The joke's on him," he finished proudly, "he didn't know what they were worth, either!"

Manny felt a sudden wave of horror. Had Loosey brought the rings back into his house? "You have them with you?" he croaked, hoping Loosey would not hear the panic in his voice.

"Nah, I wouldn't do that, now would I?" Loosey crowed. "First, I looked at the photo of the rings that the al-Sayed family's been showing around." Manny looked at him quizzically.

"Hey, I got connections," Loosey said. "The photos have been making the rounds for awhile now. There's a reward, you know. The two rings looked exactly like the ones in the photo, white gold and diamonds."

"Where are they now, Loosey?" Manny repeated, feeling nauseated. Sweat trickled down from his underarms, soaking into his shirt.

"I took them to my guy, you know, my jeweler. I asked him if I could watch while he melted them down," Loosey replied. "I saw him do the whole thing. When the gold was melted into a little puddle, he put the diamonds into this wooden box, along with all his other loose gemstones. The rings are gone, man, solid gone!!" Loosey grinned wolfishly at Manny, knowing he had done him a huge favor.

"Well done, Loosey, well done!" Manny exclaimed. "Thank you!" He laughed out loud with relief. The rings were melted down, vanished, never to return! He took a deep breath, feeling like it was the first time in days that he could really breathe.

"These kids, the ones who brought the rings to your ... let's call him your colleague. Do you know who they are?" Manny asked.

"No, I don't know their names. But they're not Skulls, if that's what you're asking," Loosey replied. Manny breathed a sigh of relief.

"I'd like to do something nice for you, Loosey, to show my appreciation. I wish I could repay you for what you spent on the rings, but you know I can't give you money," Manny said. "That would clearly show quid pro quo. There must be something else I can do for you?"

"Yeah, as a matter of fact, there is," replied Loosey. "I been thinking. I want out, Manny. I don't wanna be in this line of work anymore. I'm getting older, you know, time to start thinking about retirement. What I need is a real job, a steady paycheck so I can save. The problem is, I don't have any other skills."

Manny considered for a moment. "Would you like to work for Suarez & Sons?" he asked. "We always need porters and men to work in the warehouse, stacking boxes and keeping inventory straight."

"Yeah, that sounds great, thanks!" Loosey replied. "Would I be working for you?"

"Not me personally, no. I'm a silent partner," Manny replied. "You'd be working mostly with Julio." Loosey nodded; he had known Julio for years, having fenced for both Julio and Manny when they were teenagers. "It can't happen right away, though, we don't want to draw any attention to it. Maybe three or four months from now?"

If Loosey was disappointed by the long delay, he didn't show it. "I can't thank you enough, Commissioner," he said.

"Please, call me Manny," he replied.

Chapter 28.

Manny, you're looking much better this morning," Anna remarked, carrying her cup of coffee to the table and sitting down next to Zach.

"Thanks," Manny replied. "There's nothing like a good night's sleep." After his conversation with Loosey, Manny had skipped dinner and gone straight to bed, sleeping soundly through the night.

"I'm going to need some help later," Manny said. "I can't find my lockbox, ever since the house was searched. I'm sure it's here, just misplaced during the search. I'd be grateful if everybody could search their bedrooms to rule out the upstairs. That would give me fewer rooms to search."

"No problem," Anna replied. "I'll tell Julio and Julie."

"You, too, Zach," said Manny, turning to his son.

"Yeah, OK, after school," he mumbled. His eyes slid sideways in the direction of his backpack, lying on the floor in the foyer near the front door. "I gotta go, I'm late."

"Finish your breakfast," Anna admonished, but Zach was already in the foyer, pulling on his backpack, opening the door. "Bye," he said, without turning around.

"A man of few words," laughed Anna. "I should get going, too, Manny. Have a good day." Anna picked up her coffee cup and turned towards her in-home office.

Manny finished his breakfast and went into the study, where he searched systematically from one end of the room to the other. The lockbox was not there. He also searched the front parlor, the kitchen and the laundry room. The lockbox definitely wasn't on the ground floor.

I'll search the guestrooms after work tonight, he thought. *It's here somewhere.*

Manny headed upstairs to put on his uniform. He sat down on the newly reupholstered chair to put on his shoes and socks.

The designer had retrieved the original wooden frame for the chair, and covered it in velvet which was almost identical to the original.

Manny took a quiet moment to appreciate his service weapon, hanging in its holster, before he put it on. It felt snug and reliable beneath his arm, like it belonged there.

He was half-way down the stairs when he suddenly changed his mind and turned around. *Maybe I'll just have a look in Zach's room, now that he's not home,* he thought.

Zach's room was a mess, clothes on the floor, posters on the walls, unmade bed. Manny started with the bed, systematically looking underneath it, under the mattress, under the covers. He moved on to the dresser, and then the twin closets. The lockbox was not small; Manny knew that most likely, it would be sitting on a shelf or on the floor. Being very careful not to change the position of any of Zach's things, he felt through the pile of clothes on the floor. There was no lockbox.

Manny sat down for a moment on Zach's bed, thinking. The hair on the back of his neck was standing up, and Manny knew from experience that this sixth sense should never be ignored. Something about Zach this morning had made Manny suddenly decide to change course and search Zach's room himself. But what was it?

Stunned by a sudden realization, Manny stood up so fast that his sciatica rebelled. He gasped, standing motionless, while the sharp stabbing pain streaking down the back of his leg held him prisoner, waiting for it to subside. *Not now!* he told himself sternly, *I need to stop him!* But there was nothing he could do but wait until the pain subsided.

The door to the master bedroom opened, and Marya came out into the hall. "Good morning, Manny," she said, yawning, coming to stand in Zach's doorway. She looked at him. "Are you OK?"

"I'm fine, actually in a hurry to get to work, but then my leg started up again," he said, "so I'm hurrying very slowly."

"Maybe you should see Dr. Patel about the sciatica," Marya said worriedly. "It seems like it's better, but then it always comes back."

"I'll do that, Marya," Manny agreed in a rush. The last thing he needed right now was a conversation about his sciatica.

"Do you want me to get your cane, Manny?" Marya asked solicitously, hovering near him.

"No! No, thank you. Right now I just want to get down these stairs," Manny said, beginning to perspire. He stepped downward gingerly on the first step. "I've got to get to work." He took another step down, being very careful.

He took another step down, and another. Finally, he reached the bottom of the staircase. He turned to look up at Marya. "See you tonight," he called, and determinedly made his way to the front door.

The walk to Zach's school took a lifetime. Manny couldn't hurry because of his leg. He tried to stroll along as if he were out for a pleasant walk, while inside, his mind was racing.

It was well known that a thief would often look in the direction of his hidden loot, if confronted and questioned by the police. Why had Zach looked in the direction of his backpack, when Manny asked if he would help find the lockbox?

What if Zach had taken the gun to school? It seemed outrageously implausible, but that didn't mean it hadn't happened. Manny knew from the reports he received that Zach had been seen occasionally with Raj and Eddie, but he was no longer involved in their illegal activities. Had he decided to steal his father's gun to impress them?

In the Colony, shootings were rare. Only police officers and security guards were permitted to carry guns. All of the Colony's guns were stored at the Armory, where a staff of dedicated technicians maintained the guns in good working order, oiling and cleaning them regularly.

The guns had all been brought into the subway by the original founders of the Colony after the great hurricane in 2085 AD; every single one of them had been smuggled in illegally in backpacks, duffel bags and handbags, as guns were not permitted to be carried in the subway. Even with attrition over the hundreds of years since then, the Colony still had more guns than people.

There were strict penalties for losing control of a properly owned and licensed gun. There was a hefty fine, plus the humiliation of having to take a gun ownership and safety class at the Police Academy, along with the cadets.

If an adult owned a gun and a child in the household gained access to the gun, the penalties for the owner were even more strict, with mandatory public service for twelve months, and a stiff fine for each of three years. If the gun was used by a child to accidentally or intentionally shoot someone, the child would serve time in a juvenile facility, but the parent would be sentenced to a mandatory two years in prison. It would effectively end Manny's career.

Manny walked along, taking careful steps, while his heart raced and pounded. Finally, at 9:00 am, he arrived at the middle school. He took a moment to mop his perspiring forehead with his handkerchief and straighten his uniform jacket. Then he rang the bell, announcing himself and asking to see the principal.

"Principal Pham, I am Commissioner Stewart, Zach's father," he introduced himself. "We've met before."

"Yes, Commissioner, I know who you are," the Principal responded warily.

"I would like to see my son, please," Manny requested.

"Let's wait until classes change, Commissioner," Principal Pham replied. "That way we can avoid interrupting the lessons."

"I'm sorry, this can't wait," Manny said, sitting down uninvited in front of the Principal's desk. His leg was paining him, but he forced himself to smile, to be casual and polite. "I'd like to see him now, please."

"Commissioner," replied Principal Pham, "it's disruptive to the other students to have a student pulled out of class before instruction is over. You will have to wait until classes change. That will be in exactly forty-one minutes."

"That is unacceptable," replied Manny abruptly. "I need to see him now. The matter is urgent. There's no reason why you shouldn't allow this reasonable request."

The Principal folded his arms across his chest. "Pulling him out of class would only distract the other children from their lessons," he said smugly. "I'm sorry, I simply won't allow it."

Manny stood up, putting the palms of his hands down flat on the desk and leaning far over it. "Do you like your job, Principal Pham?" he asked, his face darkening dangerously, his eyes riveted on the Principal.

Principal Pham cleared his throat, then stood up, and keeping a careful distance from Manny, made his way to the office door and opened it. "I'll be right back," he said with as much dignity as he could muster.

When the Principal reappeared with Zach, Manny gripped him by the elbow and steered him out into the hall.

"What have you done?" he asked his son quietly.

"What do you mean?" Zach asked innocently.

"Let me see your backpack, young man," Manny ordered, keeping his grip on Zach's arm. "Now."

"It's in my locker," Zach protested. "It's mine, it's private! You can't have it!"

"Get it!" Manny ordered sternly. Zach reluctantly went over to his locker, with his father watching over his shoulder, and unlocked it. He reached into the locker and slowly pulled out the backpack.

"Open it," Manny growled.

Zach mumbled something about his rights, but Manny gripped the nape of Zach's neck, squeezing it angrily. "Now!" he commanded. Unhappily, Zach unzipped the backpack and handed it to Manny, averting his gaze.

Manny looked inside the backpack. He saw books, a notepad, a moldy teeshirt, and there, at the bottom, wrapped in a dirty towel, was his gun. Automatically, he checked to make sure the safety was on. Then he removed the ammunition, putting the precious bullets in his pocket, along with the gun.

Manny turned to Zach, who looked as though he wished the floor would open up and swallow him. "You're coming home with me," he said determinedly. Backpack slung over one shoulder, Manny gripped Zach tightly by the wrist, steering him towards the exit.

"I have to go back to class!" Zach protested.

"You're going to come home with me, and you and I are going to have a private conversation about what it means to break the law," Manny retorted, his mouth a grim line as he struggled to control his rage.

As the two turned towards the exit, Principal Pham walked towards them from the other end of the hall. "Everything OK here?" he asked worriedly, looking from Manny to Zach.

"Fine," replied Manny, steering Zach past the Principal.

"Zach will be returning to class now, I hope?" Principal Pham continued.

"Zach is coming home with me," snapped Manny. Wordlessly, Principal Pham flattened himself against the lockers as Manny and Zach rushed past him.

It was an awkward and quiet walk home. Zach, sulky and stone-faced, said nothing the entire way home, while Manny alternated between walking carefully to favor his bad leg and fuming over his son's utter recklessness.

When they arrived at the house, Marya was in the kitchen. She came out into the foyer, saying, "Now what? Zach? What have you done?"

Zach tried to dash up the stairs to his room, but Manny was faster, grabbing his jacket as he made a run for it. "Not so fast, my friend," he said, turning him around to face them. "You're going to stay right here and tell your mother what you did today."

"Zach? What?" Marya asked fearfully.

"I took Dad's gun to school," Zach said defiantly. "I'm supposed to meet up with Raj and Eddie at lunchtime, to show them that I'm not afraid, that I can follow orders. Raj says maybe he can get Kiaan to put in a good word for me, so I can join the gang."

"That you're not afraid of what?" Manny questioned him. "Afraid of handling a gun? Afraid of stealing it from me?"

Zach struggled to free his arm from his father's grip. "At least when I'm with them, I feel like I belong!" he exclaimed. "They treat me like family."

"Zach, you have a mother and father!" Marya protested. "You belong here, with your own family. We love you."

"You love me, but you're not really my mother, are you?" Zach retorted. Marya winced visibly at this jarring reminder that technically, she was Zach's stepmother and aunt.

"And what about Dad, you don't seriously think *he* loves me, do you?" Zach asked rhetorically, pointing to Manny with derisive nod of his head.

Manny blinked. One moment, they had been talking about Zach stealing a gun, and the next, they were talking about whether Manny loved his son. He was so surprised that he let go of Zach's jacket.

Zach took the opportunity to dart up the stairs, slamming his bedroom door behind him.

Marya and Manny looked at each other, momentarily speechless.

"Why does it always come down to this?" Marya demanded angrily. "Can't you have a conversation with him without shouting?"

"He stole my gun, Marya!" Manny exploded. "Don't try and tell me how to deal with him. You don't know what to say to him any better than I do!" He turned and stomped up the stairs, flinging Zach's door open so hard that doorknob smashed into the wall.

Chapter 29.

W e are not finished, young man!" he said sternly. "I want to know what you had planned with the gun. Why was it loaded? Were you going to shoot at something, to show off for your friends?"

"Yeah, it was loaded! A gun that's not loaded is just a prop," replied Zach scornfully. Manny wondered where he had heard that. "I just needed to show it to Raj and Eddie, to prove that I'm not afraid to handle a gun."

"And then what?" Manny demanded. "Will you have to stab someone to prove that you've got nerves of steel?" Manny referred to an incident that had happened recently, allegedly involving gang members during an initiation. The innocent victim had died.

"Why do you always have to ruin everything?" Zach demanded. "You don't let me do anything!"

"You want to join this gang, Zach? And do what? Become a thief, a criminal?" Manny demanded. "Where will you be in ten years? No career, no college degree, what's going to become of you?"

"Why can't you just leave me alone!" Zach exclaimed, his face contorted with rage.

Deliberately trying to shock his son, Manny added, "And if you try to leave the Skulls, they will slit your throat and leave you bleeding on the ground as a warning to others, rather than let you quit. Is that what you want?"

Zach was trembling all over. "Like you care!" he shouted. "You don't care about me, all you do is yell at me and hit me! Why can't you be like the other fathers? They actually like their kids." Zach picked up his jacket from the floor, pulling it on.

"Where do you think you're going?" Manny demanded.

"Anywhere you're not!" Zach replied defiantly, his eyes cold and hard.

Headed for the doorway, Zach stepped past Manny, bumping his father's shoulder hard enough to push Manny a step backwards. It was no accident.

Manny grabbed Zach's shoulder and spun him around, slapping him hard across the face with the back of his hand. "Don't you *ever* disrespect me like that!" he warned.

Zach pulled himself free from his father's grip, and then put both hands on Manny's shoulders and shoved backwards, hard. Manny took a half-step back, surprised.

Zach moved away from Manny, circling him in a classic boxer's stance. There were dark red welts on his face where Manny had hit him and tears of anger in his eyes.

Manny kept far away from Zach, continuing to stay well out of his range. The boy was stronger than he'd realized. And his reflexes were quick, faster than Manny's. But Manny had one advantage: Zach was furious, and as every fighter knows, if you're fighting angry, you're not in control.

"You don't want to do this, Zach," he warned his son. "It's not going to end well."

"Didn't think I'd fight back, did you?" Zach said bitterly, crying openly now. "I'm not some little kid you can bitch-slap whenever you feel like it." He charged straight at Manny, fists flailing.

A floodgate of memories spilled over into Manny's mind as he remembered himself as a child, desperate to stay away from his father's fists. How he had wanted to fight back! But he truly was afraid that his father might really hurt him.

Distracted by his thoughts, he wasn't watching Zach, who took advantage to hit him with a strong uppercut landing squarely on his chin. With quicksilver reflexes, Zach danced backwards on his toes, both fists clenched. The two circled each other warily, Manny's arms loose down his sides, waiting.

Finally, Zach charged straight at Manny. Veteran of many street fights, Manny leaned out of the way, hooking his foot around Zach's ankle, knocking him off balance. Then he grabbed Zach by the jacket, holding him up while he used his fist to punch him with all of his strength in the solar plexus, twice. Zach folded over and vomited on the floor.

Manny stood over his son. "Breathe in a little at a time, it's just the wind knocked out of you. It'll go away in a minute," he said. He reached down to help Zach stand up.

Zach angrily pushed Manny's hand away. His breath came in short gasps as he sat up, wiping his mouth, facing his father.

"Don't pretend you care about me. I know you can't stand me!" Zach spluttered.

"Zach! What are you talking about? Of course I care about you," Manny replied.

"Liar!! Remember when I was five and you gave me away? Well, I do! You didn't visit me that whole summer," Zach shouted.

Dumbfounded, Manny sat down on Zach's bed. "Zach! I was … I became an alcoholic after your mother died," Manny protested. "I spent that whole summer getting sober."

"Maybe. Maybe you needed to be alone to get sober. But you lived across the street, didn't you?" Zach accused. "You hardly ever came to see me. I used to think it was my fault, but now I know better."

"What's going on in here?" demanded Marya, standing in the doorway.

"We're talking, that's what you wanted, isn't it?" demanded Manny sullenlly.

"I heard shouting," she said worriedly, coming into the room. "You didn't hit him again, did you?" she asked, looking anxiously at Zach's face, covered with red splotches, and at the patch of vomit on the floor. "Manny, what have you done?"

"I warned you, Marya, stay out of it! Don't tell me how to discipline my own son!" Manny retorted, standing up to face her.

"He's *our* son, Manny!" Marya replied. She stepped between Manny and Zach, turning to face Manny. "Enough!! I will not stand for this any longer!"

Like a charging bull that is suddenly presented with a better target, Manny's rage reoriented itself to Marya. Before he realized that he'd moved, his arm lashed out. At the last instant his clenched fist opened to slap her hard across the face. She spun around and collapsed, hitting her head with a sickening thud squarely on the corner of Zach's dresser. For a moment, no one moved.

"Marya, Marya!" Manny exclaimed, dropping to his knees next to her. He took her hand, but she didn't respond. Finally, she turned her head and opened her eyes, moaning. Dazed, Marya tried feebly to push Manny's hand away. Zach reached down and helped her sit up. Then he scooped her up and placed her gently on his bed.

"You keep away from her," Zach hissed, turning to look over his shoulder at Manny. "This isn't her fault."

"What's going on in here?" demanded Lucinda, walking into the room. "We can hear you downstairs!" She looked from one to the other. "Marya, are you alright?" Marya, lying on Zach's bed, nodded once, her wary eyes on Manny.

"Well?" Lucinda demanded. "Someone had better start talking!"

"Zach stole my gun and took it to school. He was planning on showing it to his friends Raj and Eddie at lunchtime, to impress them," Manny explained. "Fortunately, I went to the school and caught him before anyone saw the gun."

"Zach! How could you do such a thing? This is a huge mistake," Lucinda said, turning to Zach. "There are serious consequences for stealing a gun. You could wind up in a juvenile detention center."

"Juvie's no big deal," Zach said scornfully. "It's like boarding school."

"I don't know what your friend Kiaan has been telling you, Zach, but don't kid yourself, it's no boarding school," Manny said.

"Besides, I'm a first-time offender, so I'd probably just get probation," Zach continued coolly. "Or not even that, since I'm your son."

"I'm done protecting you, Zach," Manny warned. "The next time the police catch you, you're going into the system. From now on, I won't lift a finger to keep your record clean. Think about that, the next time you and your friends decide to do a little breaking and entering."

"Zach, did you know that your father could be put in prison for two years, if you take his gun and shoot someone?" Lucinda asked.

"Nobody's shooting anybody," Zach replied confidently. "They just asked me to bring it in to show them I'd do it."

"They asked you to bring them a loaded gun?" Manny repeated sardonically. "What if they said they'd just keep it overnight? If they took it from you and used it to commit a crime, we'd both be held responsible, you and I."

Zach blinked. Clearly, he hadn't thought of that. "They're my friends, they wouldn't do that," he said, sounding slightly less confident.

"They're using you, Zach," Manny said bluntly. "Open your eyes."

"Let's give Zach a little time to digest this," Lucinda said smoothly. "Marya, are you alright now?"

Marya nodded. Along the side of her face, there was a wide dark red bruise forming, the size of Manny's palm. "Why not go lie down? I'll ask Julio to bring up some ice for your face," Lucinda suggested.

Lucinda turned to Manny, her eyes steely with anger. "Let's you and I go downstairs."

Manny sheepishly followed Lucinda down the stairs, where she stopped briefly to ask Julio to bring some ice to Marya. Then she and Manny went into the study, closing the door.

"What's gotten into you?" she demanded. "We could hear you all the way downstairs, shouting at Zach. You hit him again?"

He nodded, his anger replaced by guilt, shame and remorse, the trifecta after-party of bad behavior.

"Zach's found a way to get your attention," Lucinda said. "If the two of you continue like this, I'm afraid that someone is going to get seriously hurt."

"But, Lucinda!" Manny protested. "If he joins the Skulls, he'll regret it for the rest of his life. I can't make him understand!"

"I see that you care about what might happen to him," Lucinda pointed out. "That's good. You should tell him that," she said.

"I try reasoning with him," Manny replied. "He refuses to listen!"

"What's your solution? You'll hit him harder?" she asked rhetorically. "You're escalating, Manny, you hit your son *and* your wife today. Are you proud of how you're acting?"

Manny, deflated, looked down at his hands. "No," he admitted.

"I understand that you had a terrible role model in your father," she said sympathetically. "When you get angry, your first impulse is to act the way your father did when he was angry."

"I know, I see that," Manny replied miserably. "I just don't know how to change it."

"I'm curious," Lucinda said, "do you know if Patrick was abused by his father? Abused children very often grow up to be abusive parents."

"The only thing I know is what he said to me right before he was euthanized, that his old man used to beat him with a belt. To tell you the truth, it wouldn't have mattered to me if I'd known it earlier," Manny said. "I just wanted him to stop hitting me."

180

"That's how Zach feels about you," she pointed out. "He just wants you to stop."

Manny blinked. He hadn't thought about it from Zach's point of view.

"You can't help the way you feel," Lucinda said. "But you are responsible for your actions, as we all are. It takes a strong, motivated person to break the cycle of abuse, Manny, but I've seen how strong you are! I watched you go through the alcohol withdrawal, all alone in this big house. I know that was very hard, but you did it. You should be proud of that."

Manny raised his head and looked at her. She was right; he had struggled mightily with the alcohol addiction, but his will was strong. He had prevailed.

"How do I even begin?" he asked. "Zach hates me."

"Start by being kind to him. Show an interest in his day, ask him about school," she suggested. "Maybe the two of you could go running more often."

Manny smiled ruefully at the idea. "He runs circles around me, Lucinda."

"Then let him do that," she said. "You can laugh about it afterwards. Lighten up, Manny! Be his friend as well as his parent. Be patient with him. Show him that you care about him."

Lucinda rose from her chair. She took both of his hands in hers and said, "Every time you make a fist, you make a choice, Manny. No one is making you hit him. Choose a different path."

He nodded, tears of shame and frustration in his eyes.

"Let's be clear about one thing," Lucinda said, her eyes holding his. "I love you both. I won't stand by and watch you abuse my grandson. Understood?"

"Yes," he said simply.

"Now go find your wife and tell her that you love her," Lucinda said.

~ ~ ~ ~ ~ ~

The bedroom was dark despite the early hour, curtains drawn, filled with shadows. Marya was lying down on the bed with an ice-filled cloth held to the growing lump on the side of her face. When Manny walked over to the bed, she didn't move.

"Marya?" he whispered. "Are you sleeping?"

"No," she said. "What do you want?"

"I came to apologize," he said, dropping to his knees next to the bed. "I'm so sorry, Marya. I don't know what came over me. I promise it will never happen again."

"I don't believe you, Manny," she said, sitting up and looking at him. Her face was swollen on the side where he'd hit her, the bruises already beginning to turn blue. Remembering Lila Rose, who had sat on this same bed with bruises all over her beautiful face, Manny found that he couldn't quite look at his wife.

"Marya, you are my life," he said, using Dave's best-ever apology. "I can't live without you."

"You certainly don't act like it, Manny," she said coolly.

"What can I do, Marya? To show you that I mean it?" Manny asked, beginning to flounder. Wasn't this the part where she was supposed to gracefully accept his apology, so they could move on? Was there something else he was supposed to say?

"There's nothing you can do. I'm leaving you, Manny," she replied. "I won't live with a child abuser, a wife beater! I am taking our son and moving out. We'll live at the house on Fourteenth Street until Zach is seventeen. I think it's best for all of us."

"But I'm not a child abuser or a wife beater, Marya!" he exclaimed, dumbfounded. "I just made a mistake, that's all. Maybe I got a little carried away. And I said I'm sorry," he pointed out. It had never occurred to him that this might be the result of his actions.

Marya shrugged indifferently. "You can come and visit our son whenever you want, Manny."

Chapter 30.

About a week after Marya and Zach had gone to live in the old house, Manny stopped by the Stewart mansion in mid-morning to pick up something he needed for work, and there was Marya, sitting in the kitchen talking to Anna.

"Marya!" he exclaimed, surprised. Since she had moved out, she had not tried to contact Manny, and he had stubbornly refrained from contacting her.

Marya, who had chosen to visit her sister during the day because Manny would not be there, stood up, then sat back down, her consternation obvious.

"I'll just leave you two alone," remarked Anna, slipping out of the room and down the hall, closing the door to her office.

Manny took off his hat and sat down. "How are you?" he asked, as if nothing had changed.

"OK, Manny," she said coolly, looking down into her coffee cup. A moment passed, then another.

"How's Zach?" Manny asked finally. He knew from the school's attendance logs, which he checked each morning, that Zach had been going to school. He continued to see Raj and Eddie, but they had been staying out of trouble.

"He's OK," she replied. "He was pretty quiet for a day or two, but he seems to have adjusted just fine. I think he likes being there with just me."

"That's good, I guess," Manny replied. "And you?"

"It's a little dull there, during the day," she admitted. "Once Zach gets home from school, we make dinner and we talk, but there's not much happening during the day. I miss Anna and Julio." *But not me,* he thought.

"You know, you don't have to sit there all alone during the day," Manny suggested. "You can come here any time you want."

"I know that," she said, looking down at the table.

"I meant what I said, Marya," he said softly. "I promise you, I'll never hit you again. I'll never hit Zach again, either." He reached out and took her hand in his.

She looked down at their two hands, sighing. It was a wistful sigh, filled with regret.

"I mean it, Marya," Manny insisted.

"I know you do, Manny. And I appreciate your sincerity. But I also know how hard it will be for you to keep that promise," she replied.

He was about to protest, when he thought of his conversation with Lucinda. "You're right, it will be hard for me," he admitted. Her eyes widened in surprise.

"It's kind of like the drinking, you know," Manny explained. "It was hard for me to stop, but I did it. I see now that I've only made things worse with Zach. And with you. I'll stop, Marya. I've stopped."

She looked at him, searching his eyes for sincerity. "Do you really mean that?" she asked.

"Yes," he replied simply, still holding her hand. He waited for her to relent, to say that everything was OK now, that she would be coming home.

"You should talk to Zach, Manny. Maybe take him out for lunch or something," she said, getting up from the table. "Here, I'll walk out with you."

There was a large duffel bag near the door, its contents bulging against the seams. Marya picked up the bag, putting it over her shoulder. *Her clothes,* Manny realized, *she came home to get more of her things.* "It was good to see you, Manny," she said. Then she was gone.

Manny, disappointed, stood in the doorway, watching her walk away. *She must have half her wardrobe in that bag,* he thought.

He shook his head to clear it. He needed to get going; he was almost late for his appointment with Hasan, outside by the site of the excavation.

Manny spent some time with Hasan, walking around the site of the first shelter. The foundation had been outlined with four posts and a rope, but the digging had not yet begun. They would be using cinder blocks and large broken pieces of cement, taken from the plethora of broken buildings surrounding the park, to create a stable foundation.

"How long before the foundation is dug?" Manny asked, gesturing at the area outlined by the rope.

"If the weather cooperates, about a month, I'd guess," Hasan replied. "Then we'll add the walls and roof. Once it's enclosed, it doesn't matter what the weather is like."

"Let's make sure each shelter has at least one of those solar things, you know, the lights," Manny remarked.

"You mean QWNN, the little lights that charge in the sun? The Parts Department found a few dozen of them still in their boxes, but nobody's tried to charge one yet," Hasan replied. The solar charging lights were invented by Alice Chun centuries earlier, but there was no use for them in the subway; they did not work with the Colony's underground Zolar lights.

"We might be better off with candles," Hasan added, glancing sideways at Manny. Everyone knew that candles were illegal, just as everyone knew that they were widely available on the black market.

Manny nodded absent mindedly, making a mental note to stock candles, matches and holders in each of the shelters as they were built.

After Hasan left, Manny sat down on the ground, on what would become the foundation of the first shelter. He leaned back and looked up at the sky. Somehow, the blank pale blueness calmed him, helping him think. Or maybe it was the breeze blowing gently past him, ruffling his hair. He breathed deeply.

Things were not going well. His son hated him, and his wife had left him. The shelters were a joke to most people, an eccentric indulgence by one of the wealthiest men in the Colony. The project had been dubbed "Stewart's Folly."

Manny sighed disconsolately. *One problem at a time,* he thought. Work on the foundation had stopped for the noon hour, and the workmen had taken off to find comfortable places to eat their lunch.

All up and down what had once been Central Park West, there were ruined apartment buildings, falling down or worse. Most of the buildings had at least part of one wall from the first floor still standing, and that was good enough to lean against for an hour while eating lunch.

It's going to take a year, give or take, before the first building is finished, he thought, *and that's way too slow.* One building would hold about two hundred people. They couldn't build more than two stories high; they didn't have the technology or skills to build any higher. *And if one building holds two hundred people,* Manny mused, *how many buildings would we need to house the entire population of*

185

about 6,500 people? At least 32 shelters. And right now, we can't even shelter 200 people.

And what about the people who live far from midtown? Manny thought. *What will I say to them, when I announce that the first few shelters are ready here in midtown, in case we need to evacuate?*

Manny sighed heavily. *Maybe I was wrong to do this,* he thought. *Maybe it's all just a wild goose chase, pouring money into a project that in the end will be a colossal failure. That's not the kind of legacy I want to leave.*

His thoughts turned to other things, but there was no comfort there, either. *Zach hates me,* he thought. *I need to try and explain myself to him, if he'll listen.* Manny thought again of their fight, how he'd slapped Zach, who had responded by coming out swinging.

He wanted to fight me like a man, not like a little boy, Manny thought. *Maybe I hit him too hard in the stomach, but that fight had to end quickly, or he might have won.* Manny chuckled ruefully to himself. His son had won his grudging respect for his quick reflexes and hard-hitting fists. *Besides, it would have humiliated him if I didn't fight him like a man.*

Manny clumsily pushed himself up off the ground, struggling to stand up. He brushed off his clothes and headed for home.

~ ~ ~ ~ ~ ~

Several days went by. Manny had heard nothing from Marya or Zach, although he continued to keep tabs on Zach's whereabouts through his surveillance reports. *Not acceptable,* he thought, *a man should be in touch with his wife and child.* After lunch, he decided to take a break and walk over to the old house on 14th Street.

When he arrived at the house, he paused at the door. *Should I knock?* he thought. *Or should I just open the door and walk in?* He decided to do both; he knocked on the door once and then unlocked it.

"Marya?" he called. "It's me."

Marya didn't answer, but Manny could hear her upstairs in the shower, singing. With a guilty pang, he realized that he hadn't heard her sing in a long, long time. He sat down on the sofa in the tiny living room to wait.

Several minutes later, Marya came down the stairs in her bathrobe, her long russet hair hanging shiny and wet down her back. When she saw Manny sitting on the sofa, she screamed.

"Marya! It's just me," he said calmly. "I didn't mean to startle you."

"Startle me!" she exclaimed. "Manny, you can't just walk in here! I wasn't expecting you!"

"I knocked," he said truthfully, "but there was no answer."

"Then you should have waited!" she scolded him. "I live here now. This is my space."

"Marya, I lived here for years when Julio and I were kids," he replied. "It just seemed natural to let myself in. Besides, I own this house. I bought it years ago, and paid off Luis and Lucinda's mortgage. If I want to walk right in, I'm entitled."

"That's your problem, Manny, you always feel entitled! You just do whatever you want," she replied.

Great, he thought, *I just got here and we're already fighting.* He was saved from making an angry reply when the door opened, and Zach walked in.

"Dad!" he exclaimed, putting down his backpack. He came to stand close to his mother, the two of them peering down at Manny sitting on the sofa. "What are you doing here?"

"Just visiting," he replied. "How are you home from school so early?"

"I had study hall, so I left," Zach replied. He pulled off his jacket. "Don't worry, nobody cares. They don't even notice." Turning, Zach put his jacket down on the armchair.

"What's that?" asked Manny, pointing to Zach's arm.

"Oh, this?" Zach replied, pulling up his short sleeve so his father could get a better look. "It's a tatoo. I got it yesterday."

"You got a tatoo?" Marya asked, surprised. "But you need a parent's permission for that!"

"You do, if you go to a tatoo parlor," he replied. "This was done privately." He proudly showed his colorful tatoo to his parents. "Raj's sister knows someone who does tatoos. She did it for me."

Manny leaned over and took a closer look at the tatoo. It was a filled bright red arm band about three inches wide, containing a solid white circle on which was a bold, black swastika.

"Do you know what that is, Zach?" asked Manny.

"Yeah, it means power and strength," Zach replied.

"It's a swastika, Zach," explained Manny. "Didn't you learn about Nazis in school?"

"Not-Sees?" he replied. "Like, what? A society for the blind?"

187

"I'm surprised you don't know this," Manny replied. "Nazis were a political party in Germany, centuries ago. They built death camps and killed millions of people. And that, young man, was their symbol."

Zach, rather than being dismayed, seemed rather pleased with his unwitting choice.

"It's not a joke, Zach," replied Manny. "Nazis were cruel, horrible people who rounded up their citizens and murdered them."

Marya was looking at Manny, beseeching him with her eyes, pleading with him to let it go, not make a big deal out of it.

Manny sighed. The tatoo was permanent, and nothing Manny might say about it could change that. He thought of his conversation with Lucinda, willing himself to stay calm.

"Don't get any more tatoos without our permission, OK?" he said. Zach nodded.

"I have to get back to the office now," Manny said. "I just stopped by to see how things are going. Marya, would you walk out with me?"

Outside the house, Manny said, "How could you let him get that tatoo, Marya? That's permanent! He'll have it the rest of his life."

"I didn't know he was going to do it, Manny!" she replied. "He doesn't tell me every little thing he's going to do."

"This never would have happened if you and Zach were still living at home," Manny replied sternly. "If he had had proper supervision, this could have been avoided."

"And what about the day he took the gun to school?" she countered angrily. "Didn't he have proper supervision then? That didn't stop him! We can't control everything he does, Manny."

They glared at each other.

"I didn't come here to fight with you, Marya!" Manny replied. "I came here because I miss you."

"You have a funny way of showing it, Manny, letting yourself into my house without any warning, and then arguing the whole time you're here," she retorted. "It's a lot more peaceful here without you."

She turned and went into the house, slamming the door behind her.

Chapter 31.

One day a few weeks later, Manny was on his way home from work, when he turned into his yard and found Zach, sitting on the front steps.

"Zach! What are you doing here?" he asked, surprised. He hadn't seen Zach since he visited the house on 14ᵗʰ Street.

"Mom said you should see me," he said sullenly. He dug his toe into the yard, working it back and forth. "She said I had to come."

"Well. Ok, then," Manny replied. "Come on in the house and you can get something to drink, while I change from my uniform."

"Zach!" exclaimed Lucinda, coming into the foyer. "How are you, my friend?" She wrapped her arms around him, giving him a big hug and kiss.

"I'm good, Abuela," he said, his face pink as he tried to wiggle out of her embrace. "Mom said I had to come home and see Dad."

"Sit down, sit down! Tell me, what's it been like, living in the old house?" Lucinda said, leading him into the kitchen.

Upstairs, Manny quickly changed his clothes. Zach's visit had caught him by surprise; he was at a loss as to what he should say to him.

"Let's go outside," he suggested to Zach as he came downstairs. "We can go for a walk while we're talking."

Once outside, an awkward silence settled over them. They turned towards the nearest rest-up, where they could sit and talk. Neither one spoke until they got there.

"I want to tell you a few things about myself," Manny began.

Zach groaned dramatically, rolling his eyes up at the ceiling. Manny determinedly plowed ahead.

"I want to tell you what it was like for me, when I was a kid. My old man was a monster," he said simply. Surprised, Zach turned towards him, listening.

"He was one of the meanest men I've ever met, and he really hated me. He used to find excuses to hit me, you know, bait me into disagreeing with him so he could justify pounding on me," Manny explained. "Every night, he'd come home from work and open a bottle of bourbon, and make me sit there with him at the kitchen table. Then he'd talk to me about his day, while he got sloppy drunk. Half the time, he'd pass out and I had to drag him up the stairs and put him to bed."

"I never heard you talk this way about Grandpa before," Zach said. "I mean, I know he was an alcoholic and all. He was Chief of Police, though, right?"

"Yeah, he was the Chief alright," Manny replied. "He ran that department with an iron fist. Nobody dared cross him. You know, this family is rich because of him. He was ruthless. The whole black market was his idea, back in the day."

"I didn't know that, either," Zach said. "But about the alcoholism. Is that why you were an alcoholic, too?"

"Actually, no," Manny admitted. "First of all, once an alcoholic, always an alcoholic. But the problem was, Patrick wasn't my biological father. I found out when I was about your age. My Mom had an affair with a friend of hers, but afterwards, she reconciled with Patrick. Then later, when she found out she was pregnant with me, she and the old man decided to make a go of it, because they loved each other. They didn't know if the child was Patrick's or not."

"Wait. I have another grandfather?" Zach asked, eyebrows raised. "Who was he?"

"His name was James Mayts, and he was a teacher at the elementary school. He died of a heart attack when you were a few years old," Manny said. "He had children, a boy and a girl. I met them once. But his wife didn't know about me before they got married, and she wasn't happy to find out that her husband had a son by another woman. I don't have any relationship with her or my half-siblings."

"Why are you telling me this?" Zach asked.

"Because you need to know who I am, Zach," Manny said simply.

Zach looked at him, not understanding.

"I spent most of my childhood trying to stay out of range of my father's fists. He was my role model," Manny explained.

"Now, as an adult, when I get angry, the first thing I think of is to use violence, because that's what I saw, day after day."

Zach turned away, his mouth pressed into a grim line to keep it from trembling.

"I don't like what I've done," Manny confessed. "I've alienated your mother. And I've made a mess of my relationship with you, Zach. I never meant for us to be enemies. I promised your mother I'll never hit her again, and I also make that promise to you. Never again, Zach. I'm so sorry that it's gotten to this point, but I'm going to make it up to you, I swear."

Zach turned to him, his face dark with anger. "Great," he said resentfully. "I'm supposed to forgive you? Why should I believe you?" Zach demanded. "The next time you get mad, you'll just hit me again."

"No, Zach, I won't," Manny insisted, surprised by his son's reaction. He'd already apologized; why was Zach still angry? "A promise is a promise. If I forget, I expect you to remind me, loud and clear. OK?"

Zach got up from the bench. He took his time, pulling up his socks and retying his shoelaces. "Can we go home now?" he asked.

"Sure," Manny replied. The two walked home side by side, in silence.

As the house came into sight, Zach turned to Manny and said, "How do you know you're not Grandpa's son? You know, that this other guy was your father?"

"Apparently, as I grew up, I started to look more and more like James. Grandpa had flaming red hair, sort of like yours, and a slender, wiry build," Manny explained. Manny, with broad shoulders and chest, dark hair and complexion, was the image of his father – but that father wasn't Patrick.

"We can talk again, you know," Manny said hopefully. "If you have questions or something."

Zach turned his head away, making an unintelligible snorting sound.

Manny, disappointed that opening his heart to Zach had not changed Zach's attitude towards him, wracked his brain for something the two of them could do together, something enjoyable that would get Zach excited. On impulse he said, "How would you like for the two of us to go outside? You know, out there?"

"You mean, like, *outside*?" Zach replied, astonished. He stopped walking. Nobody his age had ever gone outside, not that he knew of, anyway. "Are you kidding me?"

"Definitely not kidding you," Manny replied. "When do you want to go?"

"Can we go tomorrow?" Zach responded. "I have to ask Mom, right?"

"Sure, ask your mother," Manny replied. "She wants us to spend some time together. This'll be good, Zach," he added. "Tomorrow's Saturday. How about we bring lunch with us?"

Zach nodded. They had reached the front door of the house. "I'm starving. Can I stay for dinner?" he asked, opening the front door. Not waiting for an answer, he walked in before Manny.

~ ~ ~ ~ ~ ~

"You're taking him *where?*" spluttered an astonished Marya. Her ghostly white hologrammed figure fairly danced with indignation.

"You want us to spend time together, right?" responded Manny. "He wants to go, Marya, he's really excited!"

"Yes, but I thought maybe you'd go out for tacos or something! Not take him wandering around in the wilderness! I'm glad that he's excited, but Manny, is it safe for children?" Marya asked worriedly.

"Marya, Julio and I have been going outside since I was a few years older than Zach. Nothing's happened to us yet," Manny protested.

"With the exception of you two, there haven't been any children outside in eons, Manny," she replied. "Does anyone even know how the air affects a child?"

"Why don't you come with us, Marya?" Manny asked. "You can keep an eye on Zach, and see for yourself that it's perfectly safe."

"*Me?* Go outside?" she exclaimed. "Manny, you've completely lost your mind."

"Marya, be serious," he responded. "You know that Hasan and his crew are outside all day long, five days a week. They're fine. Not one of them has reported any problems."

Marya wavered, her reluctance obvious. "Well, I don't want to go. But Zach ... I guess if you don't stay outside too long, and you make sure that you know where he is, then OK."

"He'll be fine. I promise, I won't let him out of my sight," said Manny reassuringly. "We'll be outside for an hour, maybe two hours tops. Then I'll return him to you safe and sound."

~ ~ ~ ~ ~ ~

At precisely noon, Zach appeared in the foyer of the Stewart mansion, backpack dangling from one hand. He was wearing hiking boots, heavy pants and his favorite Scuba.

Manny was in the kitchen, surveying the spread that Anna had prepared for the expedition. "We're going for a couple of hours, not a weekend," Manny protested, laughing, as Anna handed him sandwiches, cookies, juice and two apples to put in his backpack.

"Just in case the two of you get extra hungry," she explained. "Where is Zach?"

"Here I am," said Zach, coming into the kitchen. Anna gave him a big hug, kissing him on the forehead as he tried to escape.

"We've missed you! It's good to have you around again, Zach," she said.

Well-fortified with supplies, Manny and Zach walked from the Rockefeller Plaza stop to the 59th Street Columbus Circle stop in companionable silence. Zach seemed excited and eager to get there. The previous night, Manny had carefully planned how he would give Zach plenty of time to adjust to the sights and sounds of the outside world.

We'll stay close to the subway entrance until Zach is able to walk around without feeling too wobbly, Manny decided. Then he could show Zach where the first shelter would be built, and where the well had been dug.

When Manny and Zach came up out of the subway stairs, Zach stopped dead in his tracks. "No way!" he exclaimed, taking a few tentative steps out onto the grass, spreading his arms wide and turning around in a complete circle. Then he looked up at the sky, and staggered backwards.

Manny was right there, his hand on Zach's elbow, guiding him back to lean against the solid façade of what had once been a grand hotel. "It takes some getting used to," he said reassuringly, prepared to give Zach as much time as he needed.

Zach responded by impatiently shaking off his father's hand. He took a deep breath and pushed away from the wall, moving forward, boldly walking towards the park.

"You coming or what?" he called over his shoulder.

Manny struggled to catch up to Zach, who apparently had worked through his trepidation, as he was now taking long, quick strides across the grass.

"Zach! Wait up!" he called. "I want to show you where the shelters will be built."

"Cool. Is that the first one, the one that was a dud?" asked Zach, pointing to the foundation of the first shelter, which had been abandoned.

"Yeah, that's the reject," Manny replied. "It's too far from the well. They've taken all of the building stones out and moved them over to the site of the new foundation, over there." He pointed to the new site, which was delineated by four poles and a rope, next to a pile of rocks.

"That's it?" asked Zach, scrutinizing the area which had been cordoned off.

"Yeah, that's where the new foundation will be dug. We hope to have the building up and running in a year's time," Manny replied proudly.

"A year?" exclaimed Zach. "For just the first building? How long before there are enough shelters for everybody?"

"It's going to be awhile," Manny admitted. "But we've got to start somewhere. We don't have huge machines to dig the foundation, or move the bricks and cinderblocks. Look around at the buildings," he continued, pointing to the fallen down skyscrapers, hotels and apartments. "There's such a mountain of building material for us to use, but it's hard to move it. It takes time."

Zach looked again at the building site, four poles and a rope. "Can't they work faster? You know, hire more men or something?"

"Let's see how the first building goes, before we start streamlining the way they work. Also, there's weather to deal with. When it gets cold, the ground gets rock hard, so we have to wait until it warms up again," Manny explained.

Zach nodded. Manny felt heartened by his interest. *So far, so good,* he thought.

They walked further into the park, looking all around at the trees and bushes. It was peaceful, a warm and sunny afternoon. Insects buzzed drowsily all around them, invisible in the undergrowth. Sunlight filtered through the trees, dappling the thick carpet of pine needles and dead leaves on the ground. The sound of birds chirping in the trees caught Zach's attention.

"Where do the birds come from?" he asked. "I mean, who takes care of them?"

"Nobody takes care of them," Manny explained. "They're wild. They take care of themselves."

"It's weird, isn't it?" asked Zach, looking around. "I've never been someplace where there weren't any other people. It's so quiet." Manny breathed deeply, something he often did when outside. The silence was a welcome respite from the constant noise and clatter of life in the subway, where privacy was a luxury and where true silence was truly impossible.

The two walked companionably side by side, admiring the enormously tall trees and fallen-down, ruined buildings that surrounded the Central Park. Three centuries had not been kind to the skyscrapers that had once towered over the park; most of them had broken into pieces long ago, jutting their cracked, jagged faces towards the open sky.

"What's that, over there?" Zach asked, pointing to an enormous outcropping of gray rock jutting up from the ground. He strode boldly over to the rock, and grabbing hold of its uneven surface, began to climb upwards.

Chapter 32.

Zach, get down from there!" Manny shouted, rushing to reach his youngster as quickly as he could. "You could fall and get hurt!"

Zach laughed, climbing higher. Manny watched helplessly with his heart in his throat. Finally, Zach stood tall on the top of the rock, arms spread wide, whooping and hollering, "I'm King of the World!"

"Zach! Come down from there!" Manny demanded. Instead, Zach sat down on top of the rock, kicking it with the back of his heels.

"You should come up here, the view is mad cool," Zach said playfully. "Can you climb up?"

"No, I can't climb up there," Manny replied, keeping a firm hold on his impatience. "It's not good for my leg, Zach. Now, please. Come down. If anything happens to you, your mother will never forgive me."

Neither Manny nor Zach knew that the outcropping of rock had been named Umpire Rock, a very large, scarred and grooved rock formation that had been created some 500 million years earlier, and had once been covered by a glacier, right where Zach was seated.

"Come on then, let's see what else is out here," Zach said, sliding down and landing next to Manny with a thump. "Where's my acre? You said we each had an acre of land out here. Where's mine?"

"I don't know exactly," Manny replied. "We'll have to get an engineer out here to do a proper survey and show us where each one is."

"It's mine, right? I can do whatever I want with my acre of land, after I'm seventeen?" Zach asked.

"Yeah, it's yours, but remember, we're building shelters out here. Your land will have shelters on it just like the rest of us," Manny replied.

"What if I don't want a shelter on my land?" Zach challenged.

"What else would you do with it, Zach?" Manny responded. "As you can see, there's nothing out here, no people, nothing to do."

"Maybe I want to put up a yurt and have parties with my friends on weekends," Zach replied. "Can I do that?"

Manny blinked. In his mind, the land had been purchased for the shelters; he had not considered that Zach would want to do anything else with his land.

Yurts were temporary, portable structures used centuries ago by nomadic tribes. Some of them were quite large, able to hold up to eighty people. Manny had considered using yurts as shelters before deciding that the more permanent buildings, more weather-resistant and with larger capacity, would be better suited to their needs.

"No, I don't think that's a good idea," Manny began. "There's no water, no way to store food, and no services all the way out here to handle an emergency, if there was one. It's too far from home."

"Maybe I don't want a shelter on my acre of land," Zach repeated stubbornly. "Maybe I want to do something different. You know, be my own man."

"We can see about that, Zach," Manny agreed evasively. "Maybe when you're older, we'll revisit this conversation." *There,* he thought, *that was good. I deflected his questions, and we're not fighting.*

Zach and Manny walked silently for several minutes. Manny's leg was beginning to hurt. The sky had gone from blue to cloudy and overcast, with a humid breeze beginning to pick up. "Zach, let's stop and rest for a bit. Want lunch?" he asked.

The two sat down on the ground, opening up the food packed earlier by Anna. "Cool," Zach said, looking around. "We've got the whole world to ourselves out here."

As it turned out, the two of them were famished from their expedition, and finished every morsel that Anna had packed for them. Biting into his apple, Manny glanced up at the sky.

"Look over there, Zach, look at that bird!" Manny said. "I've never seen a bird that big before. Look how he circles around and around!"

"Wow! That thing is huge!" Zach exclaimed. "What kind of bird is that?"

"I don't know," Manny replied, as the two of them watched the magnificent bird, black with a pure white head and golden yellow beak, circling and gliding high above them. Suddenly, it folded its wings and dove towards the ground. At the last minute, the bird stretched out its legs towards the ground, its claws grabbing at a small creature with a long furry tail, carrying it struggling high up into the sky.

"What happened to the blue sky?" Zach asked. "Why is it all gray-like now?"

"I don't know," Manny replied. "It just is, I guess."

Manny and Zach continued to wander northward through the park, until they came to what had been a road, crossing the park from east to west. They could tell where the road had been from the concrete barriers still lining the sides of it.

"Let's go this way," Manny suggested, steering them towards the western side of the park.

"Seventy-ninth Street," Zach read out loud from a street sign. It looked odd, a street sign on a metal pole standing up straight among the trees, as if it had grown there.

"We should think about turning back soon," Manny cautioned, as the two of them wandered westward. "I promised your mother that I'd have you home in an hour or two, and we're already late."

"What's that up there?" asked Zach, pointing to an enormously high pile of rubble. A huge building had collapsed, pancaking one floor on top of another, leaving a mountain of crushed concrete.

"That? Just another crumbled building," replied Manny dismissively, but Zach was already sprinting towards it.

"Zach! Please! We need to stay together!" Manny pleaded, but Zach was already climbing up the side of the pile of rubble.

"Stop!" Manny shouted. "It could shift and fall on you!" Manny hurried as fast as he could, but his leg was twinging at him now, giving him little warnings to slow down.

Zach was climbing higher and higher. *How does he know how to climb?* Manny thought, exasperated. Suddenly Zach stopped, exclaiming, "Whoa!! Dad! You've got to see this!"

"Zach, come down from there this instant!" Manny insisted. "It's not safe!"

"There's this thing! I've never seen anything like it before! You have to see this! Come on, I'll help you!" Zach slid down most of the way and stopped, his hand extended. "I'll climb with you, we'll go really slow."

Manny certainly did not want to climb a huge pile of rubble in the middle of nowhere. He also desperately didn't want to aggravate his leg, since they were at least a mile from home. But his son was interested, engaged and calling to him. Reluctantly, he gave in.

"OK, but really slow. I mean *really slow*," Manny emphasized, taking a tentative step onto the pile. Using his hands to help climb, it wasn't too hard, once he got going. To his credit, Zach did stay close to Manny for the first several steps upward.

"I'm good," Manny said to his son, waving him away. Zach immediately clambered back up to the top.

Half-way up, Manny was breathing heavily and soaked in perspiration. He stopped to rest for a moment.

"Come on, *Malcolm!* If I can do it, you can do it, *Malcolm!*" Zach taunted him airily from the top, where he sat resting, watching his father's slow progress.

Why is he calling me Malcolm? Manny wondered. He resolutely pretended he hadn't noticed.

Out of breath and perspiring heavily, Manny arrived at the top of the pile. He mopped his face with a handkerchief. "OK, here I am. What was it that was so important?"

In response, Zach pointed wordlessly behind Manny, who turned around and almost lost his footing as he cried out, "What on earth is that?!" He sat down abruptly.

In front of them were six identical long, narrow objects, three on each side, set deeply into the mound, standing up vertically and facing each other as if they had been planted there. Each one was thicker than a man's arm as it came out of the rubble, tapering to a narrow point at the other end. The pieces were curved towards each other, forming a sort of archway, but stopped short of coming together at the top.

Zach walked easily through the arch-like space created by these strange objects, stopping to put his hand on one of them. He looked upwards.

"What do you think this is?" Zach asked wonderingly. "Look, there's more of them over there." He pointed to the far side of the pile, where several more of the long, curved pieces had broken off and slid down.

"I don't know," responded Manny. Moving closer, he leaned against one of the objects, which did not budge. Grabbing it with both hands, Manny tried to move it, but it was deeply imbedded into the rubble.

"It feels like some kind of stone," Manny said, looking closely at its grayish-brown surface. "I've never seen anything like it."

"Maybe this was used in their religious services," Zach suggested. "Maybe they had weddings up here or something."

Manny tried to envision a bride and groom standing beneath the arch. He shook his head. "No, it's too narrow for two people side by side. Besides, why all the way up here?" He leaned back against one of the objects and put both feet up on the one closest to it, pushing with his legs as hard as he could. Nothing moved, not even a little.

"Let's see what else is here," Zach said, beginning to search the area around them. A moment later, he cried out, "Dad! Over here!"

An object made from the same stone-like material was sticking up out of the ground. Reaching down with both hands, Zach tried to lift it, but it was deeply buried. Manny and Zach sank to their knees, using their bare hands to brush away the dirt and loose stones. It was hard work for a warm, humid afternoon. Finally, they were able to uncover an object about four feet long. Together, they tried to lift it, but it was too heavy.

Manny crouched down to get a better look. He ran his hand over the length of it. Surprisingly, the hairs on the back of Manny's neck suddenly stood straight up. *What the hell?* he thought uneasily.

"Look, here's a smaller piece of it," Zach said, turning to another fragment on the ground.

Made from the same material, this was a section about two feet long. There were long, pointy projections curving straight up from the piece, each one about six inches long.

Manny looked at it with a mixture of curiosity and dread. A grim realization crystallized slowly in his mind. As a policeman, he'd seen enough grisly crime scenes to recognize a fragment of jaw with teeth still embedded in it.

Manny shivered. *Is that possible, they're teeth? And if the teeth are that long,* he wondered, *how big was the whole creature?* It seemed wildly unlikely that anything alive could have been that big, but there was no denying what he was seeing. He looked back at the curved arch. Had he and Zach been standing inside the ribcage of some huge creature? Had it somehow died up here?

There's no such thing as just one of a species, Manny reminded himself. *Are there more of them nearby?* He listened intently to the sounds of the park, the birds calling to each other, bees humming gently as they searched for flowers, small creatures rustling the dead leaves on the ground as they foraged for food. The quiet peace of their afternoon suddenly seemed sinister, as if it were hiding something.

Manny decided not to share these thoughts with Zach. Instead, he looked up at the sky, where the hazy sun had passed its zenith. They should have been home already; Marya must be growing concerned.

"Time to go, Zach," he said.

"Wait, I want a souvenir," said Zach. Using both hands, Zach snapped off two of the six-inch-long pointy, curved projections, leaving the rest of it on the ground. "To remember our expedition," he said, grinning. "Here, I got you one, too."

"Thank you," Manny replied. "I can always use another paperweight." He put the six-inch-long serrated, fossilized tooth of the Tyrannosaurus Rex into his backpack.

"Let's head home," Manny said. "It's late, and you know your mother, she's going to be worried."

Zach unceremoniously slid down the pile of rubble, which three hundred years earlier had been the state-of-the-art American Museum of Natural History, complete with dinosaur exhibits on the top floor.

"Come on, Dad!" he called. "Slide down! You don't want to be late for dinner."

Manny carefully climbed down, taking his time, much to the amusement of Zach, who had arrived at the bottom and was comfortably seated on the ground, ankles crossed and leaning back on his elbows, watching his father's slow progress. Manny, for his part, was trying hard to favor his bad leg. *I have a long way to walk,* he thought, *I'd best be careful.*

Finally, Manny reached the bottom of the pile. Zach jumped up, pulling on his backpack, refreshed and eager to get going.

Instead, Manny sat down, sliding his backpack off his back. "I need to rest for a bit, Zach," he said. He took the stone jug of water out of his backpack, taking a long drink. "Want some?" he asked.

"Thanks," Zach said, drinking. He reached over and briefly touched Manny's shoulder. "How's your leg, are you OK?"

This simple question brought tears to Manny's eyes. He couldn't remember another time when his son had shown any concern for him. When they weren't arguing, Zach was in his room, Manny was at work. It was too easy to avoid each other.

"I'm good, thanks," he replied.

Chapter 33.

The two explorers headed home, walking down the middle of what had once been Central Park West, but which was now a grass-covered extension of the park. Zach was in fine form, running off ahead and doubling back, keeping himself amused as he and Manny made their way south back to the 59th Street subway entrance. Finally, he tired himself out and resumed walking next to Manny, who was walking slowly and carefully.

"I've been thinking," Zach began tentatively.

"Yeah?" Manny asked encouragingly.

"About the black market. It's not legal, right?" Zach asked.

"That's right, it's not legal to import goods from anywhere into the Colony," Manny confirmed. "We're a closed society."

"You own it, though, right? You and Julio and Abuelo?" Zach asked. Manny wondered fleetingly why Zach thought it was OK to call his uncle by his first name, but not his grandfather.

"Well, no, not exactly," Manny replied. "We own the company, Suarez & Sons, and we have investors in that company. They own shares of it, too."

"But you're the Police Commissioner," Zach said. "Aren't you supposed to make sure nobody breaks the law?"

"Zach, the world is a complicated place," Manny replied. "The black market fills a need, and people are glad to have things they couldn't get otherwise. Besides, most of the investors are from within the police community and the Mayor's office. Everyone turns a blind eye because there is so much money to be made."

"But it's wrong, isn't it?" Zach asked.

"Technically, yes," replied Manny. "But it's a victimless crime. The laws which make us a closed society were written three hundred years ago. Some people think they are still on the books because merchants like it this way. They don't want a lot of new competition flooding their markets."

Zach shook his head in bewilderment. Truly, the adult world was complicated and surprising in so many ways.

"My father set it up and ran it for years, and no one ever challenged him or made him stop," Manny said. He shrugged. "No one gets hurt, everybody gets what they want, and it … it's just always been this way."

Zach was silent for several minutes, while Manny limped along. Finally, Zach blurted out, "Where do the things come from? You know, the stuff that's sold on the black market?"

Manny sighed. He had always known they would have this conversation; he just hadn't been prepared to have it today. "Philadelphia," he replied.

"Very funny," responded Zach. "Seriously. Where do you get the things you sell on the black market?"

"Like I said, Philadelphia," Manny replied, and spent the rest of the walk home explaining how a high school student, trying to help her father by creating a better battery for the mixer in her father's bakery, had invented a Zolar battery that could recharge from artificial light. Patrick, realizing the potential for Zolar batteries, had experimented tirelessly on the ancient, rusted-out trains abandoned outside of the Colony, still sitting on broken and overgrown railroad tracks. Finally, he had found one train that would move, albeit extremely slowly, when hooked up to the Zolar battery.

Patrick boldly had taken the train as far as it could go, not knowing where the tracks would lead. Eventually, he could see a city off in the distance. Although the tracks stopped short of the actual city gates, he could easily walk the rest of the way, and he did. The first person he encountered was Joshua Spellman, and the rest was history. Manny and Julio were still dealing with Joshua as their front man, just as Patrick had.

"But, about Grandpa," Zach persisted. "Was he a thief?"

"No, definitely not," Manny replied. "He bought things in Philadelphia and sold them to people at home, and made a tidy profit doing it."

"But he was a criminal, right?" Zach persisted. "A person who breaks the law is a criminal?"

"That's right, I guess," Manny conceded, wondering where this conversation was going. Zach was silent for several minutes.

"Weren't you caught breaking and entering with Julio, when you were kids?" Zach asked finally, looking at Manny from the corner of his eye and then down at the ground.

"Who told you that?!" asked Manny, surprised.

"Julie. Julio told her all about the two of you, when you were kids living in the 14th Street house," Zach replied.

Manny laughed self-consciously. "We were just kids, out to have a little fun. But once, I got caught red-handed stealing jewelry from an old lady's house," Manny admitted. "My dad was so enraged that he locked me in a cell overnight at the precinct, no food or water, no padlet, nobody else on the entire floor, just me."

"Wow, the old man really meant business, didn't he?" said Zach, with something suspiciously akin to admiration.

"Like I told you, Zach, he was a mean bastard, and I hated him," Manny stated flatly. The last thing he wanted was for his son to admire Patrick Stewart.

"Life is funny, you know," Manny mused. "The burglaries taught me how to think like a thief, something that is very useful now, in my line of work."

The two continued walking until they reached what had once been Central Park South, coming finally to the 59th Street subway stop. They paused close to the entrance to the park. A statue had fallen to the ground many years earlier, crashing into pieces. Strangely, the head was nearly intact, lying near the pedestal, overseeing the park with sightless eyes.

It had gotten cooler, and a light breeze had sprung up, clearing away the earlier haziness. The sky had turned a deep shade of cornflower blue, with a few puffy white clouds. Manny turned to Zach and asked, "Do you want to stay out here a little longer? We could watch the sun go down, if you'd like."

"Yeah, OK," Zach replied. "We should let Mom know, though, right?"

"I'm surprised she hasn't texted us," Manny said, sitting down on the ground and taking out his padlet. "She must be wondering where we are." He opened his padlet, and a long string of texts downloaded all at once.

"Yikes," Manny muttered guiltily, reading through the texts, which mostly asked where they were, each message more aggressively worded than the one before.

He hologrammed Marya so she could see that he and Zach were in one piece. "Before you say anything," he interjected quickly, as her figure materialized on the ground next to them,

"I just got all of your messages, all at once. We're fine. Look, here's Zach."

Zach waved, grinning. Marya drew herself up to her full height. "You must have known I'd be worried, even if you didn't get my texts," she exclaimed, annoyed. "Would it have been too much to take a moment and let me know you're OK?"

"Wait until you hear about our expedition, Marya!" Manny replied, neatly sidestepping her question. "We've had quite a day!"

Zach took his souvenir out of his backpack and waved it at his mother. "Look at this, Mom!" he said. "Dad's got one, too!"

"We're going to stay outside a little longer," Manny said casually. "Don't worry, we're at the southern edge of the park, so close to the subway entrance that we could almost reach out and touch it. I just want to show Zach what a real sunset looks like."

"Not too long, Manny, you know how I feel about the night air! Anyway, I'm glad to see that the two of you are having such a good time," she conceded. "Zach, I'll see you when you get home."

"He's coming to our house, Marya, not to the house on 14th Street," Manny said smoothly. "It's closer, and he's had enough walking for one day! Why don't you join us? We can all have dinner together at the house." He held his breath.

"OK," Marya said. "Then we'll walk back afterwards."

Manny rolled up his padlet, glad that she had agreed. It would be the first time since they moved out that she and Zach would join them for dinner at the mansion.

Manny put his backpack on the ground behind him and sat down, settling back against it. "Tell me what you did in school this week, Zach," he suggested. "Was it interesting?"

"Nah, mostly it's pretty boring," Zach replied, sitting cross-legged next to Manny. "But there was this one thing. I got an 'A' on my earth science paper."

"An 'A'! That's wonderful, Zach," Manny said, and meant it. "What was the paper about?"

"It was about Tuvalu, you know, the group of little islands in the Pacific Ocean that disappeared under water during the 2100's. As far back as the 2030's, they knew that the sea levels were rising about a quarter inch each year. Because it was a steady increase each year for several years, they thought that it would continue that trend," Zach explained.

"I've never heard of Tuvalu," replied Manny. "What happened?"

"One morning, they woke up to find themselves ankle deep in water," Zach said. "The whole place was washing away. Because they lived near the water, every family had at least one boat. They loaded up the boats and set off for Australia, their nearest neighbor. But Australia didn't want them, too many new people all at once. They wouldn't let them land."

"And?" asked Manny, sincerely curious.

Zach shrugged. "They all drowned," he said. "The Aussies fired on the boats, making holes in them so they would sink."

"Wow," Manny said. "No survivors?"

Zach shook his head. "Our teacher said that for years, none of the Tuvaluans wanted to accept what was happening, they just wanted to keep on living their lives like they always had. Even the people who believed what the scientists were saying didn't prepare to evacuate in time."

"Humans have made that same mistake over and over again, Zach," Manny said. "In the 2000's, they thought they could predict how fast the earth was changing based on prior years, but they were way off. Did you know that Manhattan used to have another borough called Staten Island?"

"Staten what?" asked Zach.

"Staten Island," Manny repeated.

"Never heard of it. Who was Staten?" asked Zach.

"That's a good question, Zach, I don't know," replied Manny, as Zach settled down next to him, using his backpack for a pillow.

The bright blue sky was beginning to darken, and the two of them lay silently, watching. The sun slowly dipped down towards the horizon, turning a fiery shade of pinkish-red before slipping down out of sight. The clouds were painted across their underbellies with streaks of pink and red. The sky turned darker blue, then midnight blue, and finally, a velvety shade of black. A tiny star appeared, then another and another. A crescent moon rose, the barest sliver of silver.

"It's mad cool," Zach breathed. "Kind of magical, you know?"

"I know," Manny replied, gratified that his son was impressed. "I remember my first sunset. It took my breath away."

They lay quietly, gazing up at the stars, each with his separate thoughts. Finally, Manny said, "Time to go, or your mother is going to be on the warpath."

They walked the short distance to the subway stairs, turning for one last look at the park before returning home. "Someday, there will be a row of shelters here, one after another," Manny said, gesturing expansively at the empty vista in front of them. "This will be my legacy, Zach. There will be enough shelters so that everyone in the Colony will be safe."

"Why just shelters?" Zack asked. "Maybe there could be a whole row of yurts out here, each one different. There could be restaurants, and a nightclub. We could clear away some of these trees and make a place to play sports."

"Now you're just talking crazy," Manny laughed. "Nobody's coming out here to play sports, or to eat dinner and take in a show."

"Why not?" replied Zach. "People are always looking for something new to do, right?" The two clambered down the stairs into the subway, heading for home.

At the bottom of the stairs, two women were sitting together, chatting. At the sound of footsteps, they rose together and looked directly at Manny, who recognized them as the women who had worked with Madame Elayna. Before he could speak, they turned and walked rapidly away. *Are they following me?* Manny wondered.

His thoughts returned to Zach.

"Those are interesting ideas, Zach. It's a rare person who looks at something and sees not just what is, but what might be," Manny remarked thoughtfully. "Some people are natural planners. It's a good quality to have. Maybe someday you could put that to good use."

As Manny walked alongside Zach, he reflected on the conversations he had had with his predecessors, Daniel Malone and James O'Brian, the Commissioner and Deputy Commissioner, before he had been promoted. Both men, now long deceased, had commented on Manny's ability to envision the future. *It seems I passed that down to my boy,* thought Manny. The idea made him feel quite proud.

Chapter 34.

D inner was a lively affair. Manny, worn out from the day, was happy to let Zach do most of the talking, as he described in vibrant detail how they had climbed up the mound of rubble and discovered the Thing. Zach removed his souvenir from his backpack and showed it to everyone at the table.

"Zach, that's dirty," Marya admonished, frowning. "Maybe this isn't the right place, showing it at the dinner table."

"No, wait, let me see," said Luis, holding out his hand. "What on earth do you think this is?"

"We're not sure," replied Manny carefully. "Maybe a very big model of a tooth, you know, like for showing students during a lecture."

"I've never seen a tooth curved like that at the end, though," Luis said thoughtfully, rolling it back and forth between his hands.

Don't snakes have teeth like that? Manny thought uneasily. *They're curved to prevent their prey from backing out of their mouths.* There were snakes occasionally in the subway, mostly harmless little garden types near the greenhouse complex. He shivered, once again picturing the silent, empty park in his mind. Was it truly empty, or had something been watching them?

After dinner, Marya and Manny took steaming cups of butterfly pea shoot tea into the library to talk. Zach, tired from the day, was fast asleep on the sofa in the front parlor.

"Marya, why don't you stay here tonight?" Manny said. "You can sleep in one of the guest bedrooms, if you don't want to sleep in our room. Zach would be closer to school in the morning. He could get another hour of sleep if he stayed here."

"No, I don't think so, Manny," she said, shaking her head.

"I meant what I said, Marya," Manny replied softly. "I'll never hit you again. You have my word on that."

"It's not just that," she said hesitantly. "I've never had my own place before! It's just me and Zach, and he's gone from early morning until dinner time. It's the first time I've had any real privacy! My childhood home was always so crowded and noisy. Our house is big, but it can get pretty noisy, too. I like having a place where I can close the door and be alone."

"I thought you were bored there, all alone," Manny protested.

"Sometimes," she admitted. "But mostly, I like it. I've started painting! Maybe I'll even take some classes. It's good to have room to spread out."

"But what about Zach?" Manny pointed out. "We got along really well today, no fighting at all. And now you're going to take him away from me, just when things are beginning to turn around."

Marya sipped her tea, considering. "Zach can stay here tonight, if he wants to," she conceded. "I don't want to keep you two apart, especially since things are going so well. But Manny, I'm not ready to spend the night here."

"OK," he said, not trying to hide his disappointment. "Here, I'll walk you home."

"No, thank you!" she replied. "I'll be fine walking home alone. Besides, you've already had such a day."

"Then at least let me get you a police escort, a couple of female officers to walk you home," Manny said, pulling out his padlet.

"No, Manny, I don't want an escort," she replied. "I don't need your protection! I'll be fine."

"Marya, I don't understand," he said dejectedly. "What do you want me to do? How can I convince you that I meant what I said?"

"You can't convince me, Manny. It takes time to rebuild trust. You don't just snap your fingers and that's it," she replied, getting up from her chair. "I'll go say goodbye to Zach, and then I'll be on my way."

Manny watched helplessly as Marya woke up Zach and asked him where he wanted to sleep. Rubbing his eyes as he sat up, Zach said, "I'd like to stay here, if that's OK with you. It's closer to school."

"That's fine, Zach, I'll see you tomorrow, after school," Marya said, kissing him on the cheek. Then she was gone.

"After school, can I come back here?" Zach asked Manny, once Marya was gone.

"Sure, just let your Mom know," Manny replied, gratified that Zach wanted to stay.

"Thanks. It's too confusing, you know, remembering which house to go to," Zach replied. "All my stuff is here."

Manny went into his study to do some work, even though it was the weekend. Baggers had been targeted by roving groups of kids "funning," as they called it, brazenly breaking into their homes, stealing their belongings, scattering them all over their neighborhood as they ran away laughing.

The Council had requested an engineers' report on the status of the pumps which kept their underground home dry. Only about half of the pumps were still operational, the report stated. They could handle occasional leaks and water coming in through groundwater seepage, vent gratings and manholes, but a significant storm could flood whole sections of the system right up to the ceilings within a few days. *Not likely,* Manny thought, snorting derisively. *All of the pumps would have to fail at the same time.*

There was a request from the Mayor's office for Manny to sign off on the latest release of prisoners due to overcrowding, something which happened from time to time.

And lastly, there was the official rollout of new padlets. The replacements for the traditional padlets were to be "padlet rings." Similar in design to the earlier "padlet cuff," this was even smaller, and fit on the wearer's finger.

It had the same five color-coded buttons as the earlier prototype. There was a button for projecting a virtual screen onto the wall; a button to place a keyboard onto a desk or table; a button to send a text; another to send a hologram; and a button to connect to Millicent, the Colony's AI assistant.

Manny made a note to speak to Nigel in the morning about the new padlet rings. He had no interest in being a tester for their new invention, as he had specifically told Nigel when the padlet cuff was presented.

A knock on the door interrupted his thoughts. "Come in," he responded, rolling up his padlet.

Zach opened the door. "Manny, can we talk?" he asked. He looked so grown up, a glass of rainbow spritz in his hand, standing in the doorway. Manny noticed that he was still calling him by his first name. He decided to ignore it.

"Sure, Zach, what's on your mind?" he replied, sitting back and folding his hands across his middle.

"I've been thinking," Zach said, settling himself in one of the leather armchairs as he had seen his elders do so many times. "Do you think I could spend the night outside? I could invite Raj and Eddie to come with me."

"I'm not so sure it's safe to do that," Manny hedged.

"The three of us could make a cool video, post it on SoshMedia, all the kids would see it," Zach added persuasively. Manny could hear the excitement in his voice.

"Zach, the three of you can't go out there alone," Manny replied. "Nobody has been outside for an entire night for hundreds of years!"

"But what about if there's an emergency? Won't the people have to go outside at night to get to the shelters?" asked Zach. "You're telling them that it's safe to do, right?"

"Yes, but that's only if there's a life-threatening reason to do it," replied Manny. "It's not something to take lightly."

He considered for a moment; maybe Zach had the right idea. The Colony's citizens had been successfully indoctrinated, generation after generation, to stay underground, to believe that the surface of the planet was hostile to human life.

Obviously, it's safe enough during the day, Manny thought. But at night? No one knew for sure if it was safe out there at night. *There's really only one way to find out.*

"Why don't you and I go?" Manny said. "We could stay close to the exit, in case there are any problems. We could spend the night out underneath the stars, and you can record the whole thing."

"And Raj and Eddie?" asked Zach hopefully.

"Zach, you know I don't like them," Manny replied. "I hope when you start high school in the fall, you'll find better friends."

"Nah, I don't want any other friends," Zach replied easily. "They're like family to me."

Manny carefully steered the conversation away from Raj and Eddie. "We'll have a good time, just the two of us. You can document the whole thing. Your video will be picked up and shared all over the Colony! Just think, Zach, you'll be a famous videographer."

"Yeah, OK," Zach said. "It'll be fun. I have to ask Mom first though, right?"

"No, let me. I'll handle your mother," Manny replied, and they both laughed.

~ ~ ~ ~ ~ ~

"Have you lost your mind?" Marya demanded, sitting down next to Manny on the sofa in the tiny living room of the house on 14th Street.

"No," Manny replied patiently. "I think this could be a good thing. Hear me out, please!" he added, as she tried to interrupt him.

"First of all, it will be good for Zach and me, to share such a unique adventure. He is so excited, Marya, he wants to make a video and share it online afterwards on SoshMedia. He'll be a hero! But more than that, Marya, it just might be the way to convince people that the surface is no longer deadly to us. If we can spend the night outside and be perfectly fine and healthy, then we can show everyone it's safe."

"You're not experimenting on our son!" she said, crossing her arms over her chest.

"Marya, we'll be fine! We won't go any farther than a few steps away from the entrance to the subway, I promise. And I'll bring my two guns for protection," he added.

"Protection from what?" she asked, frowning. He did not reply. "And the night air? How are you going to protect him against that?" she demanded.

"Honestly, I don't think there is anything to worry about. Dr. Patel said that the air doesn't suddenly become dangerous just because the sun goes down, and I believe her," Manny replied.

"Is Dr. Patel going with you?" Marya asked rhetorically. "What if you go to sleep and never wake up?"

"Do you hear yourself, Marya?" Manny asked.

"You don't know what's out there, Manny," she insisted. "There could be animals, we don't know. Maybe not all of them are extinct."

Manny thought briefly of the huge white-headed bird, swooping down out of the sky, claws stretching out to impale a wriggling little creature. "That's why I'll be bringing guns," he replied. "How about if I invite Dave to come with us, Marya? He could bring his guns, too. Zach will be the best protected child in the Colony."

"You'd invite Dave, too?" Marya said, softening a bit.

"Yes, Zach will have a police escort," Manny replied, reaching across the table to take her hand. For a moment, she did not move. Then she slowly turned her hand over, entwining her fingers with his.

"OK, yes. If Dave goes, too," she said. "And I'm sorry that we fight all the time. I feel like whenever we see each other, all we do is fight."

213

"We fight over Zach," Manny replied. "Everything else is fine."

"Fine?" countered Marya. "We live apart. How is that fine?"

"I wish you would come home, Marya," Manny said softly. He clasped her hand in both of his hands. "I miss you. I can't sleep at night without dreaming of you. You are my life, Marya. Please come home."

Manny had said similar things in the past, but there was something different this time. She heard it in his voice. He meant it.

"Manny," she began, "I still love you, you know that. But when you hit me, something in me died. I feel like I can't trust you completely, not after that. If you really love me, you wouldn't be able to hurt me. It would be unthinkable to you."

"I'm a flawed man, Marya," Manny admitted. "There are things about myself that need work, that's for sure. But I swear I'll never hurt you again. I see now what would happen if I did. I can't risk losing you."

The two sat looking at each other for a long moment. A single solitary tear slid down Manny's cheek. Embarrassed, he brushed it away.

Still holding his hand, Marya rose and walked towards the spiral staircase in the corner of the living room. "These triangular shaped steps can be a little tricky," she warned him, looking back over her shoulder.

"That's OK," he replied, "I remember them well."

They sat down next to each other on the bed in the tiny upstairs bedroom. "This was my bedroom, my senior year in high school," Manny said to her. "After Julio got married and moved in with Anna's family, it was just me here, with Luis and Lucinda."

"I didn't realize that, a whole year here with just the three of you," Marya replied. "Was it strange being here without Julio?"

"It was a little weird at first," replied Manny, "but it worked out fine." He was gratified that she was interested, but he was more interested in removing her blouse. Did it go over her head? Were there buttons on the back or something?

She lay back and smiled at him, and suddenly, he remembered their wedding night. Her smile as she gazed up at him had lit up their bedroom. Lying down beside her, he pulled her close and kissed her. "Marya, I'll be sorry every day for the rest of my life for driving you away," he murmured. "Please forgive me."

She sighed, fingers tracing his chest and shoulders. "I forgive you, Manny," she breathed. "But I don't think I'll ever forget it."

"That's a start," he replied. "I'll make it up to you, Marya, I promise." Placing one hand on either side of her face, he kissed her softly, holding her as if she were a precious vessel that might break.

Manny Stewart made love to his wife with tenderness and passion. They'd had many nights together over the years, but this was different, meaningful and joyous.

Afterwards, he looked around at the tiny bedroom. Except for their clothes strewn all over the floor, the room looked much the same as it had when he was sixteen years old.

"This was my bed," he mused. "I never thought that I'd be lying in this bed with my very naked wife."

She sat up, brushing her hair from her face. "My goodness, look at the time! Aren't you supposed to be at work, Commissioner?"

"Yeah, I am," he said reluctantly. "You're kicking me out?"

"Zach will be home soon," she replied.

"Yeah, OK. Let me know when you're packed, and I'll have some people come and help you move," he said matter-of-factly.

"Not yet, Manny, not just yet," she replied.

"But, Marya!" he exclaimed, surprised. "You forgive me! You said so!"

"Listen," she replied. "Do you hear that?"

He listened, then shook his head. "I don't hear anything."

"It's the sound of nothing, Manny. It's solitude. I've never had a place of my own before, and once I move back to the house, I never will again," she replied.

Chapter 35.

Yeah, I can do that," Hasan agreed. "But what made you ask me?" He and Manny were outside enjoying the late afternoon mid-summer sunshine, sitting on the edge of the newly dug foundation of the first shelter. The foundation, about three feet deep, was lined with cinderblocks and bricks that had been gleaned from buildings around the edges of the park. It seemed solid and permanent to Manny, who sat admiring the work.

"I need to have someone I can rely on," Manny replied, "someone who has been outside and knows his way around. We're trying to show the public that there's nothing to be afraid of out here, that they would be safe if they had to evacuate to the outside. Zach is going to make a video of most of the time we spend outside, like a documentary, and I want to be sure everything goes smoothly."

"Why not Dave, or one of the other officers?" Hasan asked. "At least they would have guns."

"I'll have my gun, although I doubt I'll need it," Manny replied. "The main thing is that we're trying to reach the young people, the ones who are Zach's age. If we can show them that it's safe out here, they won't be afraid to go outside. You should have seen Zach, the day the two of us were out here exploring. He was so excited! He still talks about it."

"What would I need to bring?" Hasan asked.

"All you need to bring is the food you'll want to eat from Saturday dinner to Sunday lunch," Manny replied. "I'll take care of the rest, sleeping bags, tents, everything."

"Do you have a date for this expedition?" asked Hasan.

"In a couple of weeks, I think," Manny replied. "We still have some details to take care of."

After Hasan left, heading back to his office, Manny sat alone on the edge of the new foundation. He'd learned that the foundation takes the longest to build, so there was hope that the walls and roof would go up quickly, before the winter. *One down, thirty-one more to go,* he thought wryly.

It had been a rough week. First, Manny had asked Dave to go camping with himself and Zach, but Dave wisely pointed out that the Commissioner and his Deputy Commissioner should never go out on a dangerous mission together, regardless of whether it was official police business or not. The Deputy Commissioner belonged inside the Colony, poised at the helm in case anything happened to the Commissioner.

Second, Manny had requisitioned a tent and sleeping bags from the Parts Department, but hadn't yet heard back from them. Most of the items like camping equipment had deteriorated long ago and had been repurposed into other, smaller objects. *But there has to be some camping equipment that's still usable,* he thought.

Lastly, Marya still stubbornly refused to come home. Manny visited her every few days, and she had come to the house for dinner several times, but she would not move back home. She had immersed herself in her painting, an eccentric rarity in the Colony. Few people had the space, free time or money to pursue such a hobby. The tiny house on 14th Street looked like an artist's exhibition; her canvases were lined up against every wall as well as strewn all over the sofa and tables.

"It requires solitude, Manny," she explained. "Lots of space, and quiet. I am really enjoying it."

When Manny pointed out that she could have one of the mansion's spare bedrooms as an art studio, or even could keep the house on 14th Street as her private space for painting, she murmured vague platitudes, like "we'll see," or "maybe soon."

Although she insisted that she only stayed at the 14th Street house because she didn't want to give up her privacy, Manny was beginning to have his doubts. It wasn't right. *A man's wife belongs at home,* he thought, *not off somewhere finger-painting, or whatever the hell she was doing.*

Meanwhile, Zach had been spending more and more time at the house with Manny and the rest of the family. His hair was growing back in time for school to begin again; his bright red inch-long head of hair bore a comical resemblance to a puffball for now, but as Zach said, "I'm a patient man."

Zach was enthusiastically planning his documentary, and had bought two antique cameras with his own money. Anna had arranged for Zach to take lessons from a photographer who was the brother-in-law of one of her employees. In this age of digital photos, only professional photographers knew how to handle the antique cameras.

Manny leaned back, then lay back flat on the grass with his eyes closed, allowing the summer sunshine to warm him. He breathed deeply, enjoying the quiet and the intoxicating fresh air. Somehow, it was always easier to think outside.

To his surprise, Manny felt the ground beneath him move. It shimmied for a few seconds, then stopped. Had he imagined it? He held his breath, waiting, but there was nothing else. These little tremors were annoying, and frightening. But nothing else seemed different; even the birds, who had stopped singing, resumed their usual chatter. Manny closed his eyes again and relaxed.

Returning to the office, Manny sifted through the memos and reports that had come in while he was gone. Then he hologrammed Tyler Watkins, his attorney, and asked him to come to the house.

"How's tonight around 7:00 pm, Manny?" Tyler responded. "I can stop by on my way home from work."

"Thanks, Tyler, I'll see you later," Manny replied.

Tyler was punctual as always. The two men went into Manny's study, closing the door as Manny's father had always done, whenever Tyler came to see him at home.

"I want you to draw up a deed for me," Manny said. He explained what he had in mind.

"Yes, I can do that," Tyler replied. "I'll see to it personally. I'll have the papers for you by tomorrow afternoon, for your review." True to form, he didn't ask any questions, and Manny didn't offer any explanation.

The next day, Tyler stopped by Manny's office to deliver the papers in person. "I think you'll find everything in order," Tyler said, standing in front of Manny's desk, "but if there are any changes, let me know."

"Thanks, Tyler," Manny replied, getting up to walk him to the door. "I appreciate you."

The two men bowed. As soon as Tyler left, Manny sat back in his desk chair to read through the papers.

A few days later, Manny arrived at the house on 14th Street in the late afternoon. This time he remembered to knock, rather than just walking in. Marya answered the door, paint streaked in her hair and smudged on her shirt.

"Manny!" she exclaimed, "I thought you weren't going to just drop by any more without letting me know you're coming."

"I'm sorry, I was so excited that I forgot to text you. I have a surprise for you," he said, pulling the papers out of his pocket. "May I come in?"

Sitting on the sofa in the tiny living room, Manny handed the papers to Marya.

"What's this?" she asked, reading through the first paragraphs. "It says 'Deed' across the top, and my name."

"It's the deed to one of the new townhouses," Manny explained. "It's far enough from the mansion and from Luis and Lucinda's townhouse that you'll have as much privacy as you want."

"For me?" she marveled. "You're giving this to me?"

"Yes," Manny replied. "It's yours, and only yours. You can do whatever you want with it, Marya. You can live there during the week and come home on weekends, or you can go there whenever the mood strikes you. You can have Zach live there or not, although Zach's been doing well at home. You could even rent it, if you want to."

"I've never owned anything in my life," Marya replied. "I came to you straight out of my parents' home, and never had a chance to see what it's like to be on my own." There were tears of gratitude in her eyes. "And you won't care how much time I spend there?"

"Of course I care," Manny replied. "I miss you, you know that! But I think this will be a good compromise. You'll have as much privacy as you want. It's so much closer to home, Marya, just think: Zach won't have to walk so far to school every day." Manny didn't mention the obvious advantage to himself. With his bad leg, he sometimes couldn't comfortably walk that far either.

"Thank you!" she replied.

"You can move in whenever you want. I've ordered a few things, just basics, you know, like beds and dishes. I know you'll enjoy decorating the house, so I'll leave the rest of that up to you," Manny explained, glad to see that his gift was well received.

"I can't wait to see it!" she exclaimed excitedly. "When can we go?"

"How about after dinner?" Manny replied. "Would you like to come to the house tonight and have dinner with everybody? You can show us all your new house after dinner."

Marya and Manny walked back to the house together, holding hands like two newlyweds. More than a few passersby smiled at them, the Commissioner and his wife out for a walk in the afternoon.

At the house, Zach was sitting on the floor in the foyer putting on his running shoes. "Manny! Wanna go for a run?" he asked.

Manny turned to Marya. "Would you mind?" he asked. "I won't be more than an hour."

"Of course not," she replied. "Go, both of you! I'll give Anna and Lucinda a hand with dinner." She walked into the kitchen.

Manny went upstairs to change into shorts and a teeshirt, smiling to himself. *She's acting like part of the family, not like a visitor,* he thought, pleased. *Besides, Lucinda can use the extra help. She's not getting any younger.* The other day, he had had to help Lucinda lift a heavy pot off the stove and carry it towards the sink. Her shoulders were bent with age; her hair was completely white now, arranged in a little pouffie thing on top of her head. She was shorter, more stout, and walked with a halting, careful gait.

Anna, too, was aging. She had grown thicker around the middle. Her hair, once light brown, was now nearly completely silver, and she'd taken to wearing it up on top of her head like Lucinda.

Manny also was showing his age. He was in his late thirties, fast approaching the age of forty, when a person's life should be well settled, with a family and career firmly in place. He'd put on weight around his middle because of his bad leg, something that bothered him. Still very strong from lifting weights and boxing, Manny hoped that his sciatica would just disappear.

Marya alone continued to be as beautiful, if not more so, than she had been several years ago, despite the long strands of silver hairs mixed in with her beautiful auburn hair. She was twenty-nine years old this year, an age when most women were entering menopause.

"Come on!" urged Zach from the foyer, and Manny hurried down the stairs.

Zach and Manny ran their usual route, to the rest-up and back. Zach ran more slowly when he was with Manny, keeping pace with him side by side. They talked while they ran, exchanging bits of news about their day. Zach talked easily while running, but it was more of a challenge for Manny. They didn't pause at the rest-up, running straight back to the house.

"Your mom has a surprise for you after dinner," Manny panted as he swiped his hand over the Scentsor at the door. "Actually, a surprise for everybody."

"Intriguing," Zach said, his hand thoughtfully stroking his chin, where the barest whisper of a red beard had begun to appear. Manny seriously doubted whether such a tiny patch of fuzz needed to be stroked, but he resisted the impulse to tease him.

Once everyone was seated at the kitchen table, Marya cleared her throat and said, "I have an announcement to make! After dinner, you are all invited to my new house."

"Your ... what?" asked Anna. "Isn't this your house?"

"Yes, but now I have another house, too! It's mine, to do whatever I want with," explained Marya.

Questions abounded all through dinner, as everyone offered suggestions for different ways to use Marya's new house. Afterwards, as Manny and Julie were doing the dishes, Julio came to stand next to Manny by the kitchen sink.

"Thanks a lot, bro," he said playfully, punching Manny in the shoulder. "Now Anna's going to want her own house, too!"

"Everybody!" called Lucinda from the foyer. "Let's go!"

Chapter 36.

Once everyone was assembled, it was a short walk to Marya's new townhouse. Manny unlocked the door, and the family walked into the foyer, looking all around and up to the second floor. This townhouse had a similar layout to Luis and Lucinda's townhouse, with a graceful, curved staircase and a beautiful, high cathedral ceiling in the foyer.

"Look, there's a kitchen, living room, a little den, a study and a bathroom on this floor," Manny said, "and two smaller bedrooms upstairs, an airing closet for clothes, a master bedroom with a private bathroom, and plenty of room for a studio for your painting," Manny said, showing them around.

"Which room is mine?" asked Zach.

"You'll have to ask your mother," Manny replied. "It's her house."

The kitchen had been stocked with basics. There were a few dishes in the cabinets, but mostly, the house was empty. Upstairs, the bedrooms had bed frames in place, but no mattresses.

"Where are the beds, Manny?" asked Marya.

"I don't know, they were supposed to have bed frames and mattresses here by the end of the day," Manny said, pulling out his padlet. "Maybe they're running late."

He made a pretense of checking his email. "I see. There was a mix-up at the store. The mattresses will be delivered first thing in the morning," he explained.

The mattress store owner had been puzzled when Manny instructed that he wanted the bed frames delivered immediately and the mattresses delivered the following day, but he was eager to please his wealthy new patron, and had carefully followed Manny's instructions.

Marya's disappointment was plain to see. "I guess I'll be going back to the old house tonight after all," she said.

"Why don't you stay at our house?" Manny asked her. "Now that you're sure you have a place of your own, what difference is one more night? You can sleep here tomorrow night." For a heartbeat, Manny held his breath.

"OK," Marya said, "that works."

Later that evening, upstairs together in the sanctity of their bedroom, Manny settled back against the pillows with his arm around Marya, pulling her close. It felt good to have her home, back in their house, back in his bed. "I've missed you," he whispered, kissing her forehead.

She sighed. "I've missed you, too," she replied softly. The house was quiet, everyone in their bedrooms. "I've missed my loud, noisy family! It's good to be home." She settled herself more comfortably against Manny, one hand playing with the little hairs on his chest. Manny smiled to himself, waiting.

"Manny," she began.

"Yes?" he said.

"Did you have anything to do with the delay in delivering the mattresses?" she asked, drawing back and looking up at him.

"Maybe," he said. "Let me see, now." He stroked his chin in a perfect parody of Zach, making her giggle like a teenage girl. "I may have told him to take his time, or something like that."

"You are so bad!" she exclaimed, pretending to be displeased.

"I am," he agreed, pulling her close again. "Tired?" he murmured in her ear.

"No, not really," she replied. "You?"

"No, not really," he answered.

~ ~ ~ ~ ~ ~

At work the next morning, Manny was sitting at his desk when Nigel came in, holding one of the new padlet rings. "Get that thing out of here," Manny ordered. "And tell them I don't want any part of this! Let them try it out on somebody else."

"They've already done that," Nigel pointed out. "This is part of their soft rollout. Rather than have the entire Colony switch over to the new system all at once, they are targeting specific segments of the population to see how it functions. It's our turn."

"No," said Manny. "I won't put my people at risk. The police need rock-solid reliability. Our department should go last."

"I'm so sorry, Sir," Nigel said tactfully. "The memo is from the Mayor's office. They will be collecting our old padlets in a week. Maybe you might want to use the ring and see how you like it, while we still have our old padlets."

"We can still use both?" asked Manny.

"For this week, yes, both will work," Nigel replied.

Manny tried the ring on. It was bulky and uncomfortable. Tempted to throw it across the room, Manny instead took it off and put it in his pocket to try out later.

After lunch, a text came in. *OK, let's see if your little toy works,* he thought, looking at the ring. One of the buttons was blinking cobalt blue, a personal text of no particular urgency. He pushed the button. Nothing happened.

Snorting with disgust, he put the ring back in his pocket and answered the text with his old padlet.

Marya: *Dinner at my house tonight! The whole family is invited. Please come. 6:30 pm.*

Manny: *You bet! Can I bring anything?*

Marya: *No, I'm ordering in Italian food from Carmine's. I bought dishes, silverware and glasses today, and a table and chairs, but I am definitely not cooking!*

Manny: *Sounds like things are shaping up! Did the mattresses arrive?*

Marya: *Hahaha, yes, they're here!*

Manny: *See you tonight!*

Not long afterwards, Nigel appeared in the doorway. "Someone to see you, Commissioner. He says he works in your warehouse." Standing in the doorway behind Nigel was Loosey.

"Come in, come in!" he said, motioning for Loosey to come in. "What can I do for you, Loosey?"

"I don't want to take up a lot of your time, Manny, but I brung you something I think you'll want to see," he said. From his bag, he pulled out a small object wrapped in burlap, setting it down on Manny's desk. "I think this is yours."

Manny carefully unwrapped the object, surprised to see that it was the antique ivory figurine from his house. He hadn't realized it was missing.

"How did you come to have this?" he asked Loosey.

"One of the guys at work was shopping it around, trying to sell it," Loosey replied. "I recognized it from your house, remember I was holding it? So I said, 'Where did you get this?' and he said, 'You wouldn't believe me if I told you,' and I said,

'Is this from the Commissioner's house?' and he said, 'Yeah, can you believe it?' So I bought it from him."

"Thank you for returning this, Loosey," Manny said. "It's been in my family for generations. It would be a shame to lose it."

Loosey nodded, his eyes focused on his hands. Manny, who had known Loosey for decades, understood that he was trying to decide whether or not to tell him something. He waited.

"You know you got guys working for you who are very cozy with the Skulls, right?" Loosey said finally.

"No, I didn't know that," Manny replied, surprised. "Who are they?"

"Well, Dwite Parker for one, he's the brother-in-law of one of the Skulls; it was him who come to me with the statue. And Carlson Weeblie, his wife's step-uncle is one of the Skulls. And your receptionist? She's engaged to one of 'em."

Loosey grinned at Manny. "At first, they all thought I was still in the business, you know, so a couple of them brung me stuff to see if I would buy it from them. Word got around pretty fast, though."

Manny held the miniature ivory figurine in his hands. "I'm grateful to you for telling me." He sat back in his chair, thinking.

"Loosey," he said, "how'd you like to work for us in security? There's an ongoing problem with attrition, a few things missing from every shipment. We've always had 3-4% attrition, nothing major. Maybe you could catch someone in the act and put a stop to it."

Loosey nodded. "That sounds right up my alley, Boss," he replied. "May I ask what it pays?"

Manny laughed. "I'll have to talk to my partners about that, but more than you're making now."

After Loosey left, Manny considered carefully how the ivory figurine could have been removed from his house. Zach's friends Raj and Eddie had not been to the house in months. No one in his family except Zach would likely have taken the statute. But why would Zach take it? He had a generous allowance, he didn't need money. He and Zach had been getting along so well, everyone had noticed.

Fuming, Manny opened up his padlet and did something he very rarely did. He carefully reviewed the CCTV security footage from inside his own house, one day at a time for the past several weeks. Carefully ignoring the footage from inside the bedrooms, he focused primarily on the grounds outside of the house, the ground floor and Zach's bedroom.

Finally, there it was: a figure dressed all in black from head to toe climbing up the trellis onto the roof outside of Zach's room, lifting the window and entering the house. A half hour later, the figure came out the same way, onto the roof and down the trellis onto the front lawn, walking away very quickly, disappearing into the night.

Strangely, the person was not Zach; Manny was sure of it. His height, his gait, all were different. It was not his son; in fact, it seemed like it was a woman.

His anger multiplying like storm clouds on the horizon, Manny grimly rewrapped the figurine and headed to Marya's house for dinner.

When Manny walked in, the family was assembled in the kitchen, nibbling toasted corn crackers and purple hummus while Lucinda carried dishes to the table. Zach was sitting next to Julio, animatedly describing his photography lesson earlier that afternoon. Manny walked over to the table and set down the burlap-wrapped figurine.

"Zach, do you know anything about this?" he asked in a conversational tone of voice.

"What is it?" Zach asked. He reached over and unwrapped the figurine, then sat quite still for a moment with it in his hand. His eyes looked out warily at his father.

"What's that doing here?" asked Julio. "Isn't that from the house, in the library?"

"That's right, from the table next to the sofa in the library," confirmed Manny, without taking his eyes off his son. "What I want to know is how it wound up in our warehouse, in the hands of one of the workers. He was trying to sell it. Lucky for us, Loosey recognized it and bought it from him. Then he brought it to me at work today."

"Zach, did you take this and try to sell it?" Manny asked.

"No," he replied shortly.

"Do you know anything about how it came to be in the warehouse?" Manny asked patiently.

"No," he repeated.

"Do you know who took it from the house?" Manny persisted.

Zach's face closed up, his expression blank and unreadable. He shifted uneasily in his seat. "I might," he replied.

Chapter 37.

"Would you care to share with us?" Manny asked, as his son sat silently, staring uneasily at the figurine in his hands.

"It's valuable, isn't it, Manny?" asked Lucinda. "I didn't realize it was missing."

"Valuable? It certainly is. It's antique, carved from real ivory from an actual elephant. It's centuries old," Manny replied, impatient with her interruption. Probably she sensed his anger, and was trying to break his momentum, he thought.

"Geez, I didn't know that," Zach muttered, his face beginning to redden.

"Why don't you tell us what you know about this," invited Manny. While his words were non-accusatory, the whipcord tone of his voice told everyone in the room that he was furious.

"It was a test, you know, like a dare," Zach said. "Jaynee Adhveeka is Raj's older sister. She's always wanted to be in the Skulls. She thought when Kiaan came home, maybe then he'd let her in. But Kiaan, he's very strict with her."

"Wait. Kiaan's out of jail?" Manny asked, surprised. Then he recalled signing the Mayor's order to release prisoners due to overcrowding. Kiaan must have been in that batch of prisoners.

"Yeah, he's been out for a few days now. Jaynee was going on and on about how it's not fair to keep her out when Raj and Eddie are in, and Kiaan said, 'OK, then prove to me you're Skulls material. Break into the Commissioner's house and take something. Then we'll know you've got what it takes.'"

"How did Jaynee get into the house, Zach?" asked Manny. "We've got a robust security system. I turn it on every night before I go to bed." All eyes were on Zach, as he shifted uncomfortably in his seat.

Finally, he said, "I told her how. I gave her the guest passcode, OK? I didn't know anybody would even miss that little thing. It didn't seem like such a big deal." He shrugged dismissively.

"You gave her the passcode to override the security system?!" thundered Manny. "Why on earth would you do that?"

Zach looked up at his father. "You wouldn't understand," he said defiantly, his eyes cold and hard. Manny had the unnerving feeling that he was talking to a version of himself as a teenager.

"Tell me, Zach. What wouldn't I understand?" retorted Manny.

"She's my friend!" Zach said. "And when a friend asks you for help, you come through for her!" He folded his arms across his chest, glaring back at his father. "It's what families do for each other. They help each other."

"This is your family, Zach! You belong here, with us," Manny retorted. "Tell me, is she more than your friend, Zach? Is she your girlfriend?"

"What if she is?" replied Zach. Lucinda had stopped carrying dishes to the table and was listening intently, standing next to Luis, by the kitchen counter.

"Zach, you little idiot," Manny exclaimed scathingly, slamming his hand down on the table, making the glasses jump. "What does an eighteen-year-old *woman* want with a *fourteen-year-old boy*?" Zach did not reply.

"They're manipulating you, Zach. She sweet-talks you a little and you do whatever she says! Come on, Zach, you're not stupid," Manny said. "First the gun, and now this? She must have had a nice look-around after she broke in. Who knows what they might be planning?"

"They're not planning anything! Besides, Jaynee cares about me. She promised me that she wouldn't tell anyone what the passcode is," he finished lamely. For the first time, he sounded uncertain.

"Zach, you watch yourself. Don't be naïve, now. If you touch her, if you put your hands on her, you're going to find yourself married into that family before you know what hit you," Manny warned. "Is that what you want, for Mr. Gopalaswami to be your father-in-law?"

"You think just because they're poor and uneducated, that makes them bad people," Zach exclaimed. "They're actually a nice family."

"They're criminals, Zach, a den of thieves!" Manny retorted. "How can you want to be part of that?"

"What about you? Aren't you all criminals, too? You and your brother? And Abuelo, too?" Zach demanded accusingly. He stood up. "You said so yourself, it's against the law to import stuff into the Colony, but you do it anyway because it makes you rich!"

Manny opened his mouth to reply. He looked at Luis and Julio, who were looking back at him with eyes round in surprise, and suddenly, he had nothing to say.

"You know what you are, *Malcolm?*" Zach sneered. "You're a big fat hypocrite!" His chair screeched as he pushed it back out of his way, eyes darting briefly towards the front door.

A slight, furtive motion of Zach's right hand caught Manny's eye. He glanced at the table in front of Zach. Every place setting at the table had a sharp, serrated knife, except Zach's, whose right hand was curled closed, the long sleeve held tightly against his body.

"Put it down, Zach," Manny said softly. "What are you going to do with it, except get into trouble? Put it down."

"Put what down?" Zach asked brazenly, but he did not move.

"Manny, what are you talking about?" demanded Marya, dismayed.

"Put it down, Zach," Manny repeated softly, ignoring his wife, never taking his eyes from his son's face. "Do it now, and we'll consider this merely a moment of poor judgment. But hurt someone with it, and you'll sleep in Juvie tonight. I won't lift a finger to help you."

Zach didn't move. His wariness reminded Manny of a mouse that's just realized he can't get past the cat.

"Are you planning on stabbing someone?" Manny asked conversationally. "If not, then you don't have any need for a knife."

"Whenever a man leaves the house, he should be armed," Zach explained. "I can't be the only one without protection! They'll think I'm a little kid."

"Who told you that, Kiaan? The man is an ex-con, Zach. He's not the person you should be listening to," Manny replied.

"Zach, give the knife to your father," Lucinda implored softly. "It's nothing but trouble from here on, if you don't."

Instead, Zach bolted for the door. Manny, who had been anticipating such a move, reached him first, tripping him and then pushing him face down onto the floor. Sitting with all of his weight on Zach's back, Manny twisted his arm back and

229

pulled the knife out of his sleeve, sliding it across the floor, where it came to a stop far out of reach.

"Manny! Manny! Stop it, you're hurting him! What are you doing?" screamed Marya.

"I'm disarming him! What does it look like I'm doing!" he retorted angrily.

"You promised me you wouldn't hurt him," she said, her voice pleading with him.

"What would you have me do, Marya," Manny said, "let him run out the door, armed like that?"

Manny stood up, letting Zach get up off the floor. He held out his hand to help him, but Zach ignored him.

"You know what? Take your damned documentary and shove it," Zach said, "or make it yourself, for all I care! I hate you!" He grabbed his backpack and padlet on his way to the front door, slamming it with a bang as he closed it behind him.

"You see? You see what you've done?" Marya cried.

"What *I've* done?" Manny replied incredulously. "How is this my fault, Marya?" Manny demanded.

Luis spoke up, his voice deep and strong. "This was not Manny's fault, Marya, not this time."

Marya looked at the disapproving faces turned towards her. Deflated, she abruptly sat down. Anna sat down next to her, speaking softly to her, her arm around Marya's shoulders.

"I'm sorry, Manny," Marya said a few moments later. "I lost my temper, and I apologize."

Manny sat down on the other side of her, taking her hand. "It's OK," he said simply. "Please, let's not ruin this first dinner in your new house. Zach will come home when he's ready. Why don't we all sit down and eat?"

Dinner was nothing like the celebratory event that had been planned, but at least there were no further disruptions. Afterwards, as they were leaving, Manny said to Marya, "Come back to the house with me and spend the night there. You can leave in the morning and spend the entire day here."

"I don't know, Manny, maybe not tonight," she replied uncertainly. "If Zach comes back here, he can't get in. I never had the chance to give him the security code."

"He'll text you, if that happens," Manny said persuasively. He reached for her hand. "Come on, I feel like we should be together tonight."

Still, she hesitated. He tried again. "Fighting about Zach has ruined too many of our evenings, Marya. Please. Come home with me tonight."

She considered for a moment. "You're right, Manny. I'll come back to the house with you."

Zach didn't return to Marya's house that night, nor did he return to the Stewart mansion. No one heard from him.

"Zach will come home when he's ready," Manny reassured Marya in the morning. "He's probably over at Raj's house."

~ ~ ~ ~ ~ ~

After Manny left for work, Anna and Marya lingered over their breakfast. "I'm going to have some coffee. Do you want some?" Anna asked Marya, getting up and going over to the counter.

Marya nodded. Anna returned to the table with two steaming mugs, handing one to Marya. Anna took a long drink from her cup, settling back in her chair.

Marya lifted the cup to her mouth, sniffing appreciatively, and then abruptly put it back down, her face turning greenish-gray. Clapping her hand over her mouth, she ran down the short hall to the bathroom. From behind the closed door, Anna could hear her vomiting.

A few minutes later, Marya returned to the kitchen. "Are you OK, Marya?" asked Anna, concerned. "Should I make you some basil and ginger tea?"

"No, thanks, I'm fine," Marya replied, leaning against the door frame. Her smile lit up the room. After a moment, Anna put her arms around her sister and hugged her.

"Have you told him yet?" Anna asked.

"No, not yet," Marya replied. "I sort of wanted to keep it to myself for a little while, you know? Please don't tell anyone."

"No, of course not," Anna replied. "It's yours to tell."

~ ~ ~ ~ ~ ~

"Have you heard about what's going on uptown?" asked Dave, coming into Manny's office, sitting down in the visitor's chair.

"No, tell me," replied Manny, pausing in reading the endless waterfall of memos and reports on his desk.

"Some kids were roughing up the Baggers, you know, taking their belongings and scattering them on the ground as they ran away, and apparently, this time the Baggers fought back," Dave said. "They came at the kids with baseball bats and crow bars."

Manny smirked. "Maybe they can knock some sense into them," he said.

"The Baggers? Or the kids?" joked Dave, and the two friends laughed.

It was a thorny problem. On the one hand, Baggers were homeless, mostly jobless, often drug-using squatters who owned nothing and paid nothing in taxes, living on handouts and charitable donations. On the other hand, they were entitled to protection like any other citizens.

"What's your schedule like this afternoon?" Manny asked. "I thought maybe the two of us could go over the stats from the Task Force."

"I've got a meeting after lunch over at the Mayor's office," Dave replied. "Maybe we could do that tomorrow?"

Nigel knocked discreetly on the door, then ushered Naomi into the room.

Naomi bowed politely to the two men, and then said to Dave, her immediate superior, "They need backup, uptown. Which unit shall I send?"

"What's going on?" asked Manny.

"Apparently, there's a small riot. The Baggers chased away all of the kids who were harassing them except for one. He's got his leg stuck inside the subway car and couldn't escape along with his buddies," explained Naomi. "We need officers on scene to protect him from the crowd, until the EMTs arrive to cut him out of there."

"Send one of the units downstairs, Dave," advised Manny. "Not the task force."

"Nigel!" Dave called. When Nigel appeared in the doorway, Dave issued a few terse commands.

"On it, Dave," Nigel replied, disappearing. Naomi, promising to provide updates when she had them, nodded to Dave and Manny and left.

"Anything else on your schedule today?" Manny asked, when the two of them were alone once more.

"No, you never can tell how long those meetings are going to run," Dave replied. "I've been stuck over there for hours over an issue that could have been resolved with a couple of emails."

"I know, it's wildly inefficient," Manny agreed. "Still, she's the Mayor."

Dave shifted in his chair, his hand reaching into his jacket pocket. "Do you have a moment?" he asked, suddenly shy. Manny nodded, folding his hands across his lap.

Dave retrieved a small object from his jacket and handed it to Manny. "This is from Jenny and me. We just wanted to say thank you for the gift of an acre of land out there in the park. It was very generous of you and Marya."

Manny took from Dave's hand the small black leather pouch tied at the opening with a leather thong. Inside was a sterling silver ring, polished to a beautiful mirror-like shine. It had five different gemstones, little round beauties so glossy and smooth, blue sapphire, red ruby, green emerald, black onyx and bluish-green opal, evenly spaced around the band.

"It's a padlet ring," Dave said, as Manny admired it from all angles. "I know you don't really like the new padlets. But since they're coming on Monday to gather up our old padlets, we really don't have a choice. Anyway, I hope you like it."

Manny slid the ring on his finger. It was a little loose; he would take it to one of Marya's jewelers to have it sized.

"Thank you, Dave!" Manny said. "And please, thank Jenny, too. This is very thoughtful of you. And beautiful custom work."

A knock on the door interrupted them. Naomi walked in, padlet in hand. "We've just gotten an update from the commanding officer at the scene," she began. "There is a teenage boy badly injured inside one of the cars, unable to get himself out of there without assistance. The Baggers have finished chasing the rest of the kids out of the neighborhood, and now they are menacing the injured boy with bats and crowbars. So far the officers are keeping them away, but the crowd is growing and getting louder. The officers are calling for additional backup."

"Send the task force," replied Manny. Naomi saluted and returned to her unit. As one, the unit rose and exited the building, running swiftly and silently to the scene.

"I should go, too," offered Dave, getting up. "I'll text you with an update when I get there."

"Good," Manny agreed. "And thanks again for the ring. It's really nice."

Dave nodded, turning to leave, when Nigel appeared in the doorway. His face was drawn and white.

"Commissioner," he said formally, clearing his throat, and Manny knew immediately that something was very wrong. "You need to go to the scene, too. Right away."

"Tell me," Manny urged, as Nigel was searching for words, swallowing hard.

"The boy, the one who's stuck in the subway car. It's Zach."

233

Chapter 38.

D on't wait for me, Dave, just go," Manny said, as they left the building. "I'm slower than I used to be." Dave nodded, taking off at a fast pace. Manny ran a steady, slower pace, careful not to aggravate his bad leg, and was the last one to arrive at the scene.

The place was a madhouse. Men armed with crowbars, baseball bats and other miscellaneous make-shift weapons stood around in groups of twos and threes, talking in low voices, glancing over their shoulders at the police. Baggers had an uneasy relationship with law enforcement; there was deep distrust on both sides.

There was no need to ask where Zach was. Manny could hear him screaming as he got closer. There was a ring of police officers concentrated around the entrance to the last subway car, keeping everyone away from Zach.

"Dave, Dave!" Manny called to his Deputy Commissioner. "How far out are the EMTs?"

"On their way, five more minutes," Dave replied. "Also, someone called your family physician. She's on her way, too."

"I'm going to see Zach," Manny said. He walked resolutely towards the end of the platform, trusting that the Baggers would move out of his way. Sullenly, the crowd parted to let him through, muttering as he passed, hands clenched around their weapons. The police officers surrounding Zach parted respectfully to let Manny pass. Zach, hearing his father's voice, raised his face to look for him.

"Dad! DAD!! Help, I have to get out of here," he babbled, his eyes showing white all the way around as he stretched out his hands to his father.

Zach's legs had broken through the subway car's wooden floor, the rotted material giving way as he and his friends had run gleefully through the car on their way out. One of Zach's legs seemed able to move freely, while the other leg was trapped.

Manny sat down on the floor next to Zach. Taking his hand in his, he said simply, "It's OK, Buddy, I've got you."

Whether it was the use of his childhood nickname, or his utter relief that the most powerful man he knew, his father, was taking charge of the situation, Zach started to cry. Embarrassed, he wiped his face with his hands, hoping no one had noticed.

Sitting on the floor next to Zach, Manny had an unobstructed view of Zach's injuries. He looked closely, then had to turn his head away, breathing deeply. He understood now why Zach was unable to get up. The problem was not the wooden floor, which was actually a replacement floor added years earlier when the original floor had fallen apart. Beneath the wooden floor there was a metal floor, thinned and badly rusted with age.

One of Zach's legs had broken through both the wooden and metal floors, and was impaled on a long, jagged piece of metal. His friends' frantic attempts at pulling him up and out had simply driven the jagged edges of metal more deeply into his leg. The leg itself was hanging at a strange angle, the foot nearly facing backwards.

"What exactly are you doing up here?" asked Manny. "Did you come up here with your friends to razz up the Baggers?"

"You wouldn't understand," Zach replied, his defiance returning. He and his friends Raj and Eddie hated the Baggers, whom they regarded as leeches on society.

"Why don't you explain it to me," Manny replied mildly, hoping to distract Zach from his injuries.

"We were just funnin' with them," Zach said. "They deserve it, living up here rent free, while the working man can't afford decent housing."

"Funnin' with them? You mean stealing their things and scattering them all around outside?" Manny replied. Zach looked away, stonily silent.

"You know, it's true, the Baggers are living up here illegally, but that's not a problem for a bunch of teenagers to solve," Manny continued. "They have rights just like anybody else. Let the City Council deal with them."

Zach bent over his knee and peered down at his injuries, avoiding meeting Manny's gaze.

Now isn't the time to be arguing with him, Manny reminded himself.

"It could be a few minutes before the EMTs get here," Manny said to Zach. "Why don't tell me about your girlfriend – what's her name again?"

"Jaynee Adhveeka," he replied. "She broke up with me yesterday. Kiaan wants her to marry this older guy, he's a businessman. He's twenty-six! His wife died, so now he's stuck with two little brats. Mr. Gopalaswami says I should keep away from the house until they're engaged."

Thank goodness somebody's got some sense over there, Manny thought.

To keep Zach talking, Manny said, "Does your friend Kiaan ever talk about his grandfather?"

"Huh?" replied Zach, looking up. His eyes were glassy and there were beads of sweat on his forehead.

"The grandfather's name was Amir Gopalaswami," Manny added.

"Funny you should ask. Yeah, they do talk about him. It's like they really want me to know who he was," Zach replied. "He was some kind of hero or something."

"Did they mention that my dad put him away behind bars for years?" asked Manny.

"What? No," replied Zach, giving his father his full attention. "The old man arrested him? What happened?"

"Zach, listen carefully to me. Amir took over his father-in-law's gang, and changed the name to the Skulls. Eventually, Amir had a run-in with my father, who arrested him and put in jail for many years," Manny said. "That was how my dad got his first big promotion."

"OK," Zach said weakly.

"The thing is, Amir's wife was Venezuelan. And they're big on vendettas," Manny explained.

"So what?" Zach asked, shifting uncomfortably as he tried to ease his leg. Manny could see blood seeping through his pants leg.

"The girl who kissed you last year, the one who was at Raj's house when I came to get you, she's related to the grandmother, distant cousins or something like that," Manny replied.

Zach frowned. "And?" he asked. "What's that mean?"

"It might mean nothing," Manny replied. "Or, it might mean something. That's how police work is, Zach. Some things look like clues, but they're not; other times a clue isn't obvious at all. It may give us some insight as to why these people chose you, Patrick Stewart's grandson, to toy with."

"They're not toying with me! I keep telling you! They like me for myself," Zach protested.

"You need some new friends, Zach," Manny said. "These people are nothing but trouble."

"You don't even know them!" Zach said angrily.

"I know that they deserted you. They left you here, alone with a mob of angry Baggers, to fend for yourself," Manny pointed out. "These people are armed with bats and crowbars. They're angry, and looking for someone to punish. What do you think would have happened to you, if the police had taken a few minutes longer to arrive?"

Zach said nothing, but his face was a roadmap of both his loyalty to his friends and his anger at their betrayal.

"The police, now there's a family," Manny continued conversationally. "They take care of their own. They never leave a man behind. Or woman. They care about each other, and their families. Do you think this many police would be here, if you weren't the son of a police officer?" Manny waved his arm expansively at the dozens of police officers guarding Zach, keeping the angry crowd at bay.

Zach had been focused only on his injury. For the first time, he looked at the mob of people gathered on the platform, the uniformed officers and the Baggers. "You can't tell how many police are here just by looking, you know. Some of them aren't in uniform," Manny pointed out. "They were home with their families when the news broke that one of our own needed help. They came running."

Zach was indeed paying attention. "Kiaan says that the police are just another gang, only with guns," he said scornfully. "He says that they keep the working man from rising to his rightful place."

"What's this 'working man' stuff?" Manny asked. "Has Kiaan been talking to you about the working class?"

"He read a lot about society while he was locked up," Zach replied, shifting uneasily. He reached down towards his leg to rub it, then stopped as his hand came away covered in blood.

"Kiaan's not the perfect role model, Zach," Manny continued smoothly, hoping to keep Zach calm. "He's a convicted felon, for one thing. He still lives at home with his father and siblings, no job, no career, no wife or kids. Is that what you want, when you're his age?"

Zach sighed, but didn't answer. His face looked exhausted, drawn and gray.

"I'll tell you what, Zach, if you'll promise me here and now that you're done with the Gopalaswamis, then I promise you that when you graduate from high school, I'll get you into the Police Academy. What do you say?" Manny said.

"I thought you said I wasn't police material!" Zach scoffed. "How do I know you won't change your mind?"

"Maybe I was wrong, when I said that," Manny replied easily. "Let me do this for you, Zach. It will be such a good thing. You're a natural for undercover work. You could be a great detective, catch bad guys and put them behind bars. Remember the day you stopped that woman from leaving the restaurant? If not for you, she'd have gotten away, and her boyfriend would have gotten off scot-free. That was good police work. In a few years, the Police Department will be glad to have you on board."

"You're being serious now? You promise you'll get me into the Academy?" Zach asked.

"Absolutely, if you stop hanging around with Raj and Eddie," Manny reassured him. He looked up to see Dave standing next to him.

"What do you think, Dave? Do you think Zach would make a good police officer?" Manny asked him.

"Yeah, I think he'd be good at it," Dave confirmed. "You've got just the right temperament for it, Zach." Turning to Manny, he added, "The EMTs are here, just arrived."

"Zach, I'm going to go with Dave to talk to the EMTs. You stay here, OK?" he added, hoping the bit of humor would amuse Zach. It did not.

Dave pulled Manny out of earshot and said quietly, "The EMTs are saying that they don't think they have the equipment to handle this kind of accident."

"And?" Manny asked. "What's their plan?"

"They're trying to come up with a plan," Dave said.

"Reach out to Hasan, would you?" Manny asked Dave. "Tell him to bring six strong workmen with saws. And a welder, with metal cutters. And an extra piece of plywood, if he has one." In response to Dave's quizzical look, he explained, "To cover the floor afterwards, so no one else falls through."

Dr. Patel's voice could be heard as she pushed her way through the crowd. "Let me through! I'm the Commissioner's personal physician!" she said loudly to the officers blocking her path. Manny motioned to the officers to let her through.

"Manny, I came as quickly as I could!" she exclaimed. In one hand, she was carrying her usual black medical bag. In the

238

other hand, she had a larger black bag, almost as big as a duffel bag. He flinched at the sight of it, knowing that it contained, among other things, a bone saw.

"It's for field amputations," she said in an undertone. "Just in case."

Manny nodded, motioning her into the subway car where Zach was sitting very still, his eyes glassy. He looked up as Dr. Patel felt his pulse, looked into his eyes with her flashlight, and then stood for a moment with her hand on his neck.

"His pulse is strong, Manny, but he's losing blood. I can't tell how much because I can't see his whole leg," she said quietly. "We've got to get him out of here quickly."

The two rose and joined Dave, standing in the doorway of the car with their backs to Zach. "The EMTs say that they don't know if they can extricate Zach without further damage to his leg," Dr. Patel said softly. "My first concern is saving the life of my patient. If they remove the metal and the wound starts bleeding heavily, then we're really going to have a problem. It would be better to amputate his leg first and then remove him afterwards."

"Amputate his leg! But he's just a kid," Manny protested. "You can't be serious!"

"Manny!" she said sharply. "You're thinking like his father. Right now, he needs you to think like a professional! Let's get him out of here safely, not bleeding out all across the platform."

"If only there was a way to get up underneath the metal floor and see if his leg could be reached from there," Manny said. "Maybe that would free it up just enough so he could be pulled out."

"That's just wishful thinking. There's no way to get underneath a subway car," Dr. Patel replied.

"Maybe there is," replied Dave. "Did you see over here?" he asked, pointing to the end of the train. "Someone dug out a portion of the landfill and made themselves a nice little storage area. Come and see."

This practice was illegal. Landfill, gleaned from the ruined buildings above ground, was crushed and packed in as tightly as possible. The weight of whatever was built upon it compressed it even more tightly. While it might seem tempting to carve out a little extra storage space, every scoop of landfill removed contributed to weakening the structures above it.

Dave led the way, with Manny and Dr. Patel following behind him to the end of the subway car. The car should have been flush up against a solid wall of landfill, packed in tightly so it could not move. Instead, there was a gap about thirty inches wide. It reached from the edge of the platform all the way back to the wall and was large enough for a person to stand in.

"Has anyone ever gone down there to look up underneath a car?" asked Manny.

"Not that I know of. Can you even do that?" Dave asked, worried. "Suppose you got hurt?"

"If you're going to do it, then do it now," Dr. Patel warned. "We're running out of time."

Manny looked down at the opening. It seemed fairly straight-forward. If there was nothing that could be done from underneath the car, he'd come back up.

"I'm going down there," he decided. "Dave, send one of those cadets over here to spot me," he added, motioning towards the group of first-year cadets who were milling about under the careful eye of their unit leader, adding their uniformed presence to the scene. "You and Dr. Patel go supervise what's going on with Zach. I'll be fine," Manny insisted, as Dave started to protest.

Chapter 39.

Manny sat down on the edge of the platform and then gingerly dropped down onto the tracks. When he turned around, looking out at the crowded platform, he was on eye level with the crowd's feet; only his head was visible above the edge of the platform.

Someone had been busy down there, scooping out a tidy, organized storage area. Boxes lined the floor along one side. A row of jars gleamed back at him from a little shelf carved out of the landfill, while bundles were stacked up high along the back wall. The wall was lined with pegs hammered deeply between the subway tiles, holding up baskets and bags. Some of the subway tiles had cracked and fallen off.

Manny looked all around, and down at his feet. *Look at that, there really are tracks down here,* he mused. Ancient metal rails were visible at the bottom. *So much for the people who don't believe there ever were commuter trains.*

Manny pulled out his shiny new padlet ring, slipping it on his finger. *Where's the flashlight app on this thing?* he wondered. He pushed one of the buttons, but it opened up the texting app. Another button started the hologram app. Exasperated, he motioned to the cadet who was spotting him.

"Do you have your old padlet with you?" he asked. "Can I use it, please?"

A commotion from down the platform caught his attention. A woman was shouting something, struggling to get through the crowd. "Let me go! I'm his mother!" she exclaimed. A moment later, Marya came into view. When she glanced down and saw Manny in his foxhole, she stopped, dumbfounded.

"What are you doing down there? Are you out of your mind?" she demanded. "Who's with Zach?"

"I want to see if there's any way to reach Zach from underneath the train," Manny explained. There was no need to tell her where Zach was; he was complaining loudly about his pain to the team working on freeing him. Marya turned away, hurrying towards the sound of his voice.

Marya pushed her way towards the entrance to the subway car. Barred by the line of officers blocking the entrance, she leaned as far forward as she could and shouted, "Zach! I'm here!" Two of the officers recognized her and moved out of her way. Marya stepped into the car. As she did so, she got a good look at Zach's injuries.

Marya screamed, reeling from the sight of his leg impaled on shards of wood and metal. Her knees buckled, as she sank limply towards the ground. Two arms reached out from behind her and caught her, supporting her. It was Madame Elayna's apprentice, the tall blond one.

The other apprentice was there in an instant, reaching out to help support Marya. As Manny watched, Madame Elayna, dressed in swirling skirts and jingling bracelets, aggressively shoved and pushed her way through the crowd. She quietly said something to the two young women, snapping her fingers and pointing to the back of the crowd.

The two apprentices carefully half-walked and half-carried Marya, still reeling, through the gathering. They laid her down gently on the platform, kneeling on either side of her, protecting her from the milling crowd, each of them taking one of Marya's hands in her own. A moment later, Manny was relieved to see Marya sit up.

Madame Elayna was kneeling next to Marya, talking urgently with her. Marya tried to get up, but Madame placed her hand gently on Marya's belly, shaking her head. She motioned to her two apprentices to keep Marya where she was.

What are they doing? Is she hurt? Manny wondered. She seemed uninjured. He was grateful that Marya was not alone, but he didn't like the way they were so familiar, touching his wife like that. He'd have to speak to Marya about it later, when they had Zach safely back home.

Turning on the Strobe app, the police version of the ubiquitous flashlight app, Manny peered underneath the train. Although he could see clearly, he was not sure what he was looking at. *Hasan would know what this stuff is,* he thought, puzzled by the various metal plates, handles and rings. *I don't know anything about engines.*

There was a little space underneath the main carriage of the train, big enough for a person to lie down on the tracks and wriggle forward. Manny inched forward on his stomach, holding tightly to the padlet in his left hand. Surprisingly, the ground was wet. *I'll have to remember to tell Hasan about that,* he thought. *Why would there be water down here?* He shone the light on every bit of the undercarriage of the train, methodically moving the light from left to right.

"Manny, Manny!" came Hasan's urgent voice from above him. "Everything OK down there?!"

Manny snapped off the light and wriggled carefully backwards until he could stand up. "You should see underneath here, Hasan! It's like something out of a science fiction novel! I don't see any way to reach Zach, though. His feet aren't dangling down or anything."

"That's what I came to tell you!" Hasan said excitedly. "They've finished cutting through the wood floor. The welders want to know if you want them to start cutting through the metal."

"Yes! Tell them to go ahead. Tell Dr. Patel to make sure the welders pour cold water on the metal so it doesn't get too hot," Manny instructed. "I'll be right up. Thanks, Hasan."

Manny put both hands up on the ledge and was about to lift himself up onto the platform, when he glanced at his left hand. The ring was missing, his new padlet ring that Dave had given him earlier. *Damn,* he thought, *it must have slipped off my finger somewhere down here.*

Manny looked carefully at the ground all around him, in between the rotted wooden railway ties and along the sides of the metal rails. He did not see the ring anywhere. Up above him, he could hear Zach's shrill protests as the welders began working, and Dr. Patel's voice, urging them to go slowly and pour cold water on the metal.

Worried about Marya, and even more worried about Zach, Manny was sorely tempted to leave the ring where it was, but reluctantly decided against it. *It must have cost Dave two weeks' salary to pay for that ring,* he thought. *I can't just leave it here.*

Reluctantly, Manny dropped down onto his stomach and with the Strobe app, peered underneath the train. At first, he didn't see anything other than the undercarriage of the train, but a careful examination of the side of the tracks showed something reflecting back at him in the light of the Strobe app. *There it is,* he thought. Crawling forward, he found the ring, slipped it onto his finger and began to move backwards, out from beneath the train.

His hand on one of the metal rails, Manny stopped, surprised. *It's not exactly trembling,* he thought, *more like it's vibrating or something.* Was that normal? Manny didn't know.

Time to get out of here, he advised himself. Crawling backwards quickly, he emerged out from beneath the train. Standing up, he had both hands on the edge of the platform and was ready to climb up, when he heard a loud rumbling sound, coming from all around him, echoing off the walls and ceiling.

The ground shook, swaying this way and that. Manny was thrown backwards, and landed hard, sitting down on the tracks. A shower of dust hung in the air, drifting down from the ceiling. Then nothing. It had only lasted a few seconds.

There was a moment of absolute silence, before people began calling to one another, moving to help those around them. He could hear Dave nearby, organizing the officers to see if anyone needed medical assistance. Inside the subway car, the sound of the welders began once again.

"Sir! Do you need a hand up?" It was the cadet, hovering anxiously nearby.

"No, thanks, I'm fine. But you could check on how my wife is doing," he said, motioning in the direction towards where Marya had been with Madame Elayna and her two assistants.

"Yes, Sir!" replied the cadet, saluting. He hurried away importantly, on an errand for the Commissioner.

Manny didn't trust Madame Elayna, and while he was grateful that Marya was not alone, he didn't like the way they were hovering around her. What were they up to?

What was it the old witch had said to her, when they went for their "reading?" Manny couldn't recall. Instead, he recalled what she had said to him: *A single candle lights a thousand flames, Commissioner, and yet you will not live to see it.*

On the platform, a cheer went up as the welders finished their work. Zach was extricated from the floor and placed on a stretcher, where he sat clutching his knee and moaning. Dr. Patel carefully examined his mangled, bloody lower leg and foot. A good portion of metal remained embedded in his leg.

"You're going to be fine, Zach," Dr. Patel said. "Your leg is broken, and this is a deep, nasty gash, but it will all heal." Zach said something to her that Manny couldn't hear, and then she motioned to the EMTs. They picked up the stretcher and started the long walk to the infirmary, where the doctors could remove the metal embedded in Zach's leg.

Manny stood up, brushing himself off. His left foot was submerged in a murky puddle. It had broken through one of the ancient wooden railway ties when he fell backwards, and had gotten buried beneath the crushed stones that made up the rail bed. He tried to pull his foot out, but it was lodged firmly beneath a rotted section of the railway tie.

He looked up, hoping to see the cadet who had been spotting him. He was beginning to regret sending the lad away. Manny tried again to free his foot, but it would not budge. He bent over, digging around it with his bare hands. *Better take the shoe off,* he decided. But the shoelaces were soaked through, and impossible to untie. His fingers fumbled with the wet laces, somehow succeeding only in making a knot.

Out of the corner of Manny's eye, he saw the tiniest movement. Straightening up, he looked all around the space where he was standing. The train seemed closer, somehow. Had it ... had it *moved??*

What the hell!? he thought incredulously, unwilling to believe what he was seeing. He looked at it for a long moment, eyes round with surprise.

As Manny watched, he could see that indeed, the train was still moving, although almost imperceptibly. The train was supposed to be chained in place, padlocked and secure, as well as flush up against a solid wall of landfill, but this particular car was not flush up against anything. The chains, rusted through long ago, were lying in pieces on the tracks.

Manny redoubled his efforts to free his foot. He grabbed it with both hands and pulled, then tried moving it to the right and the left; then he pulled again. Sweat trickled down from beneath his underarms. It occurred to him for the first time that he might actually be in some danger.

He heard Dave's voice. "Manny, what are you doing down there? Come on up!" Dave's face appeared, peering over the edge. "Are you OK?"

"My foot is stuck!" he cried, glancing fearfully at the train. "Do you have a rope?"

"A rope? No," Dave replied. "Hold on, I'm coming down!"

"No, wait! Not by yourself!" Manny exclaimed. "We could both wind up trapped!"

Dave hurried off, urgently in search of help. Manny could hear him calling loudly. "You there! And you! Come with me! The Commissioner is in danger!" They raced towards where Manny was trapped.

"You! Take as many people as you can gather and fill up the subway car. Move people to the far end," Dave instructed, motioning towards the car. "You! Ask if anyone has a ladder. And you! Stay and spot me. I'm going down there."

Before Dave could drop down onto the tracks, the ground trembled for a few seconds and then stopped. It was not much of an aftershock, but it was enough to cause the train to shimmy forward. This time, Manny and Dave both saw it happen. They were running out of time.

Dave pulled his police whistle from his pocket and blew on it, hard. Every police officer on the platform turned as one, towards the sound.

"Human chain! Now!" he cried. A group of officers rushed to the edge of the platform. They linked arms tightly, stretching far back across the platform, with Dave closest to Manny. He lay down flat on the platform and stretched out his arm. "Come on, Manny! Reach!"

Manny stretched out his hand, but it didn't even come close to touching his friend. Dave turned his head and barked, "Give me your belt!" to the officer standing near him. He maneuvered himself closer to the edge, dangling precariously, held in place only by the officer gripping his ankles. He flung the belt outward as far as he could. "Reach, dammit! Come on, Manny, try!"

Manny stood up and tried his best to reach the free end of the belt, but it fell far short. He grabbed frantically at his foot with both hands and tried desperately to wrench it free. Unfortunately, the rotting railroad tie pinning it down was deeply buried in the loose gravel and stones of the railway bed.

When he looked up, his entire field of vision was filled by 67,000 pounds of cold gray steel looming high up over him, inches away from his face. His heart sank within him.

Time seemed to slow down; the sounds from the platform grew muffled and indistinct. A woman was screaming. He recognized Madame Elayna's voice, loud and commanding. Dave was barking orders, something about making a ladder. It all felt so pointless to Manny.

One memory after another raced through his mind, visions of Naztazya on the day they first met, Lucinda in the kitchen on 14th Street, Lila Rose reading a bedtime story to him, Julio as his best man twice, Luis taking him on the train for the first time, Marya naked in his bed on their wedding night – all of this flashed in front of his eyes, and then finally, Zach, on the day they had explored the Central Park, the two of them discovering the Thing.

Zach! He'd promised Zach about the Academy. His heart filled with sharp regret. But Dave had been there, he'd heard. "Dave!" he beseeched frantically, turning his head towards his friend. He blurted out, "Zach!!"

"I got you, man, I got you!" shouted Dave, tears streaming down his face. Behind him, all up and down the platform, the cadets and other officers were beginning to line up, standing at full attention, saluting to honor their Commissioner.

The car slid forward, unstoppable.

Epilogue: Thirty Years Later

W here is your brother, Ella?" Marya asked her daughter Emmanuella Rose, as the two sat outside together on the bleachers watching the children play soccer. Situated behind the row of yurts which now housed six restaurants, a theatre and a catering hall for parties, the athletic field was new; the schools were using it regularly now for their sports teams. Noah, Zach's ten-year-old son, was competing this afternoon, and as usual, his father was late getting to the game.

"He's always late," Ella replied. She eyed the dark clouds gathering on the horizon. "I think it's going to rain. I hope the game's not called before he gets here."

Zachary Stewart was on his way home to change out of his uniform. Now in his mid-forties, Zach had risen steadily in his career after graduating from the Police Academy. His undercover work on gang violence had been extremely successful. After five years, he had been promoted to detective, then first lieutenant, then captain in charge of his unit, and finally to the position of Chief of Police for the Colony, the position once held by his grandfather Patrick Stewart.

Emmanuella Rose Stewart, thirty years old, had been born seven months after Manny's heroic and untimely death. Ella's daughter Sarah, three months old, was nestled comfortably in Marya's lap while she and Ella watched the game.

The bleachers trembled ever so slightly, then stopped. Ella looked around, but no one had noticed. A moment later, it happened again, just a brief quiver, then nothing. Ella ignored it, rising with everyone else on the bleachers to cheer as Noah's team scored a goal.

Two years earlier, there had been a bad stretch of little tremors. Ella had seized the opportunity to run for Mayor on a platform of keeping the Colony safe. "Emergency shelters are already being built," she had pointed out, paid for entirely by her family's foundation, the Malcolm "Manny" Stewart Foundation. Ten shelters had been completed, with more to come. Ella had easily won the election.

The tremors had continued for weeks after her election. "Nothing to worry about," said the scientist who came to brief her. "New York has earthquakes, but they are always very mild." He hesitated, then added, "Although sometimes, a series of mild tremors can be the precursor to a larger event."

"Don't worry," the Commissioner had reassured her after the scientist left the meeting. "It might never happen." Commissioner David Wu had known Ella all her life; he was a trusted friend of the family. He was also her father-in-law; his son Jonathan Henry had married Ella ten years earlier. At sixty-seven, Dave's retirement was long overdue.

Hurrying past his mother's house, which had been a gift to Marya not long before the deadly accident, Zach returned to the Stewart mansion. Zach moved deftly up the staircase towards the master bedroom, despite leaning heavily on his cane, and changed quickly out of his uniform. Ella had said it looked like rain outside; he'd need a jacket. He rummaged through his closet, finally finding his jacket on the floor in his son's bedroom.

Zach was turning to leave, when he felt the same slight trembling beneath his feet that Ella had felt, sitting on the bleachers. *Not now,* he thought impatiently. The tremors were annoying and intrusive. As Chief of Police, he didn't want any emergencies on his hands.

Zach was half-way down the staircase when the shaking began in earnest. The staircase began to move like a live thing, bucking and tilting sideways to the left. Then it cracked in half, splintering down the middle like a child's toy, with the sickening sound of centuries-old oak wrenching apart. He half-walked, half-slid to the bottom. In the kitchen, glasses began to rattle in their cabinets, dishes sliding off the table and counters, crashing onto the floor.

Zach stood in the foyer, willing the shaking to stop. Usually, these tremors faded away after a few seconds, not longer. This one seemed to be growing stronger by the moment. A long, black crack appeared in the white marble floor of the foyer, moving towards the kitchen like a hungry snake.

Just in time, Zach moved to the safety of the front parlor doorway. The crystal chandelier, a family heirloom from Patrick's early days, swung crazily back and forth, then crashed down from the cathedral ceiling onto the spot where he had been standing, shattering glass all over the floor.

Like every New Yorker, Zach knew exactly what to do. After her election, Mayor Stewart insisted on monthly evacuation drills for the Colony. Zach found a duffle bag in the foyer, quickly gathered from the kitchen anything non-perishable like bread, cookies and fruit, sweeping it into the bag. He ran into the study and pulled the afghan off the couch. On impulse, he retrieved an ancient bullhorn from a shelf in the study closet.

When Zach opened the front door, he was shocked to see that there was water pouring down like a little waterfall from the ceiling far down the walkway. The water rippled like a live thing, spreading quickly. It pooled in a little eddy by the front walk, then hopped up onto the tiny yard, where it raced with astonishing speed towards the house. He slammed the front door shut behind him, as the water rose to his ankles.

Zach pushed the button on his padlet ring for the Colony's AI assistant. "Chief Stewart," Millicent responded instantly. "How can I help?"

"Emergency damage report," he said, walking quickly.

"Emergency damage report," she repeated. "Sector by sector or overview?"

"Overview," the Chief snapped. "Send to me. And the Mayor and Commissioner." He clicked shut the padlet and ran for the exit. All around him, people were coming out of their homes, exclaiming in dismay at the rising water, struggling to move quickly with bundles and children.

Slinging the heavy bag over his shoulder, Zach moved towards the 50th Street exit at Columbus Circle, slogging through water which was swirling deeper by the moment.

When Zach reached the stairs leading up to the exit, there was a long line of people ahead of him. Standing in water up to his waist, Zach hologrammed his sister.

"Ella, it's Zach," he shouted, trying to make himself heard over the din of the crowd. "Have you seen the damage report?"

"Yes, I have. I've initiated the emergency protocol. Where are you?" she asked. "Are you near an exit?"

"I'm on the stairs, waiting to exit into the park. The water's up to my waist. You should have seen the water rising in our front yard! I'm sure the house is flooded by now. We'll be lucky if any of it is salvageable. Ella, I'll be with you in a moment," Zach said, hanging up.

Zach turned to address the crowd. "No pushing, no shoving," he called out sternly. "Just like we've practiced it in our drills. Everyone gets out safely." His presence seemed to calm people, as they realized that the Chief of Police was there with them.

A moment later, the lights flickered and went out. Behind him, there was utter blackness, the blackness of a tomb. Simultaneously, hundreds of padlet flashlight apps clicked on. Zach raised his grandfather's bullhorn to his lips.

"No pushing, move quickly and quietly!" Zach shouted into the bullhorn. "Stay together! Once you are outside, move away from the building so everyone can exit safely!"

Outside, the soccer players and spectators were sitting on the ground, out in the open as they had been taught. A steady rain had started to fall. Ella and Marya looked around anxiously for Zach.

Marya's padlet lit up with a hologram. It was Anna; she and Julio had been visiting Anna's cousins uptown.

"There isn't much damage up here at all," Anna said. "Should we come join you? I could stop by the house first and pick up some clothes and food."

Marya did not have the heart to tell her sister that their house was flooded and might be uninhabitable. "No, stay where you are for now," she told Anna.

The ground trembled, a mild tremor that persisted, growing stronger by the moment. Then a ferocious sound came from deep within the earth, a rumbling, thundering, grinding cacophony that was like nothing anyone had ever heard before. The earth shook hard, forward and backward. A long black crack appeared along the ground, splitting and racing northwards up what had once been Central Park West.

As they watched in horror, the earth on one side of the crack rose up and up, widening the divide. Crushed cement, broken cinderblocks, shards of glass rained down as the ruined buildings surrounding the park tumbled to the ground. Parents clutched their children, holding them close. Rain poured down on them all.

People continued to stream out of the subway. Soaked to mid-chest from the rising water, they held their children on their shoulders or in their arms. Some of the older people had never been outside before; most of them had never experienced rain. They huddled near the exit, unable to go back, but too terrified to move forward.

Finally, Zach made his way up the stairs and into the park. He quickly found Ella among the crowd. She hugged him tightly. "The house?" she asked. "Is it OK?"

"No," he answered shortly. "But let's not focus on that right now. We need to get these people away from the exit." Looking around, he saw two sawhorses and a discarded piece of plywood lying on the ground near where Hasan stored his equipment.

"Here, Manny, let's raise you up so people can see you," he said, using his nickname for Emmanuella Rose. He was the only one in the family to call her Manny; he said that every time he used her nickname, he was reminded of his father, who had given his life to try and save him. Zach easily lifted his petite sister up onto the makeshift platform and handed her the bullhorn.

"People of New York!" Ella shouted through the bullhorn that had belonged to her grandfather, Patrick Stewart. Thunder rumbled far off in the distance. "Move away from the exit! Move into the park, to shelter number one," she said, pointing in the direction of the first building. "Your shelter captains will assist you."

Volunteer police and firefighters, serving as shelter captains, were stationed at the door to each shelter. As each group entered, they wrote down their names, gave out blankets, and assigned beds.

The sky opened up, rain pelting people as they exited the subway. Several ran screaming into the park, terrified by the strangeness of water falling from the sky.

Ella stood on her makeshift platform, one arm pointing towards the shelters, the other holding the megaphone to her mouth. Lightning split the velvet darkness, silhouetting her against the night sky. Waist-length copper hair streaming out behind her in the wind, she called out to her panicked citizens, "Listen to the sound of my voice! Keep moving into the park. You will be safe in the shelters!"

Sobbing with terror, people fled into the park, stampeding wildly from the exit into the pitch-black. Each clap of thunder, each fork of lightning frightened them even more. It was only the sound of their Mayor's voice, strong and calm, that saved them from devolving into utter chaos.

Marya watched in awe as her daughter directed the evacuation with efficiency and calm. *Look at her, Manny!* she thought. *You would have been so proud of her today.*

Standing in the doorway of shelter number one, Marya gratefully took a blanket from the shelter captain, a young volunteer firefighter. "Your name, ma'am?" he asked politely.

"Marya Stewart," she replied.

He looked up from his clipboard. "Any relation to the Mayor?" he asked.

"Yes," Marya replied, "I'm her mother."

"Thank you, ma'am," he said. "Your family has done so much for this Colony." He entered her name into his database. "The sixth cubby on the top floor," he instructed, holding out a box of candles. "Please take one, and light it here, before you go up." He gestured towards his table, where an antique hurricane lamp contained a single candle burning brightly in the night.

Marya took a candle, one of the many that her late husband had insisted on stocking in the shelters so many years ago. She tipped it towards the flame, sharing its warmth, its light, its hope.

~ ~ ~ ~ ~ ~

"Ella, come down from there," said Dave. It was nearly midnight, and the stream of survivors fleeing from the subway had slowed and stopped. "There's nobody else coming."

"No!" Ella protested. "We've only seen about six hundred evacuees. There are nearly two thousand people who live in midtown!"

Dave said gently, "There's nobody else coming, Ella. There's nobody else alive."

Ella, Zach and Dave gathered inside the Colony's new theater yurt, commandeering a corner of the theater as a make-shift office. Ella sent out texts to all police and other administration employees to join them in the yurt.

"Thank goodness we put servers in different spots around the Colony," Ella observed. "I don't know what we would do without the intranet."

"When these people wake up in the morning," Dave said, "they're going to be hungry. They're going to want to feed their children."

"The restaurant yurts have enough food for a few days," Zach said. "We need to resettle everyone before the food runs out. Society breaks down pretty fast when people can't feed their kids. We don't want any violence."

"Most people have relatives or friends uptown. I'll address the Colony in the morning," she said. "What's left of it," she added sadly.

"Once people are resettled with relatives, we can see about repairing the broken pipes and rebuilding midtown," Zach added.

Ella shook her head. "No. Zach, we need to focus our energy on building here, outside. Repairing midtown may be impossible. Water flows to New York from reservoirs north of here, miles away from us. It will continue flowing indefinitely, like a broken faucet, until we shut it off. Right now, while we're sitting here, the walkways and houses are filling up with water. How can anyone begin to work on the pipes, with water up to the ceilings inside the tunnels?"

"Then we'll cordon off and regroup uptown," Zach growled, clearly impatient with his sister's views. "The Colony will be smaller, that's all. It's still New York."

Dave listened with concern. He'd heard a version of this argument many times before. Ella, who was a visionary planner like her father, wanted to begin transitioning to living outside. Zach was less interested in planning for the next generation. A keen judge of criminal activity, Zach was more concerned with outsmarting criminals.

The problem was that Zach, fifteen years Ella's senior, had been a father figure to her as she grew up. Even now, it was hard for her to disagree with him. It was the reason that Dave had put off retirement, year after year.

Ella stood up, a tiny powerhouse of a woman. "Chief," she said formally to her brother, "your job is to protect and serve. The Mayor's job, and the Commissioner's job, is to plan for the future. No, you're going to have to trust your elected officials on this. Now, go! Collect your officers and keep the peace." Imperious, she pointed to the doorway.

Zach sneered at her. "*You're* giving *me* orders?!" he exclaimed. He glanced at Dave, who was his boss.

Dave nodded. "Do what she says, Zach. Set up your patrols and then get some sleep. When people wake up in the morning, we're going to need every man." Outranked and outvoted, Zach stormed out of the yurt.

Inwardly, Dave sighed with relief. *She's stronger than I give her credit for,* he mused.

"Dave, I'd like to build townhouses, a row of them on the other side of the playing field, to form a sort of square with the shelters and the yurts," Ella said. "People can live in them year-round, or as much of the year as they want. The family foundation will pay for the construction," Ella continued. "We can be landlords above ground, as well as underground." She paused to consider. "If we have any properties left underground."

Dave nodded grimly. "If we can't find a way to shut off the water, none of us will have anything left underground."

"Right," Ella replied. They both knew that if the water continued rising unchecked, it would destabilize the pillars in the subway that hold up the ceiling, which in turn supports the streets and heavy buildings above ground. With nothing holding up these structures, they were likely to collapse into the subway.

Ella was momentarily distracted by the nearby sound of her baby crying. A moment later, her husband Jonathan entered, carrying the baby, who stretched out her arms to her mother.

Baby Sarah was hungry. Ella held her close and stepped outside behind the yurt, to nurse her in privacy. The rain had stopped; the sky was just beginning to lighten, changing from black to wolf gray, the darkness soft and indistinct, muting the sharp, angular shadows of the forest in the park behind them. Ella sat down on a folded blanket, leaning back against the yurt, settling herself to nurse her baby.

Ella was exhausted. She closed her eyes, but only for a moment. *Sleep later,* she told herself firmly, *there's no time for that now.* To keep herself awake, she began to sing her favorite nursery rhyme, one that Marya had sung to her so often, when she was small.

> Winter's cold and summer's hot,
> Close your eyes and tell me not.
> Autumn's leaves are falling down,
> Listen, they make not a sound.
> Springtime sunshine comes at last,
> Dancing barefoot in the grass.
> When the flowers bloom in spring,
> We sing the song the flowers sing.

"All of this is yours," she said to little Sarah, motioning expansively to the lightening sky above them and the park filled with trees behind them. "This is your birthright, clean air and sunshine, yours to enjoy before you pass it on to the next generation."

A tiny silver star winked at Emmanuella Rose from the horizon. "We knew you'd be back," it seemed to say. "Welcome home."

www.ingramcontent.com/pod-product-compliance
Lightning Source LLC
Chambersburg PA
CBHW070908180626
46817CB00003B/961